HERSTORIES

AN ANTHOLOGY OF NEW UKRAINIAN
WOMEN PROSE WRITERS

GLAGOSLAV PUBLICATIONS

HERSTORIES

AN ANTHOLOGY OF NEW UKRAINIAN
WOMEN PROSE WRITERS

Edited by Michael M. Naydan

HERSTORIES
AN ANTHOLOGY OF NEW UKRAINIAN
WOMEN PROSE WRITERS

Edited by Michael M. Naydan

Introduction by Michael M. Naydan

Translations by *Mark Andryczyk, Svitlana Bednazh, Nataliya Bilyuk, Vitaly Chernetsky, Jennifer Croft, Natalia Ferens, Halyna Hryn, Roman Ivashkiv, Askold Melnyczuk, Michael M. Naydan, Uliana Pasicznyk, Alla Perminova, Svitlana Pyrkalo, Olha Tytarenko, Yuri Tkacz, Liliya Valihun* and *Olesia Wallo.*

Image courtesy of Oksana Zhelisko, *April.*

© 2014, Glagoslav Publications, United Kingdom

Glagoslav Publications Ltd
88-90 Hatton Garden
EC1N 8PN London
United Kingdom

www.glagoslav.com

ISBN: 978-1-909156-01-2

Contents

ACKNOWLEDGEMENTS

Emma Andijewska's "Tale about the Vampireling Who Fed on Human Will" and the "Tale about the Man Who Knew Doubt" first appeared in the journal *Ukrainian Literature*. An excerpt of Maria Matios's *Sweet Darusya* was initially published in *Metamorphoses*, the journal of literary translation. Eugenia Kononenko's "Three Worlds" was previously published in the journal *Glas* as well as in the Zephyr Press anthology *From Three Worlds: New Ukrainian Writing*. The excerpt from Oksana Zabuzhko's novel *Field Work in Ukrainian Sex* first appeared in the literary journal *AGNI* before it appeared in the edition published by Amazon Crossings. The story "Girls" by Zabuzhko was published first in the Internet journal *Words without Borders*. A portion of the excerpt from Iren Rozdobudko's *The Lost Button* was published previously in *World Literature Today* as *The Button* along with material that comprises the introduction to this volume. Tanya Malyarchuk's "A Village and its Witches" first was published in *Hayden's Ferry Review*. The excerpt from Iren Rozdobudko's *The Lost Button* is available from Glagoslav Publications in the complete English-language version of the novel. Glagoslav has also recently issued the complete version of Larysa Denysenko's *The Sarabande of Sara's Band*. Yuri Tkacz's translation of *Apocalypse* first appeared with Bayda Books. While Halyna Pahutiak chose not to be included in this anthology, a translation of an excerpt from her novel *The Minion from Dobromyl* can be found in the journal *Metamorphoses*.

A NOTE
ON THE ANTHOLOGY

Approximately four years ago during my four-month Fulbright stay in Lviv, Ukraine, I was particularly impressed by the extraordinary number of new women prose writers on Ukrainian bookstore shelves. Since that had been somewhat of a rarity in Ukrainian literary history, I decided to explore the phenomenon and started reading and collecting works by authors I found especially interesting as well as ones my closest literary and editor friends recommended to me. At that point in time I also decided to begin contacting writers I didn't know personally to get permission to translate their works. After I published several shorter prose works in literary journals and began to work on larger projects of individual novels in translation, I grew determined to promote this wealth of Ukrainian women writers to the English-speaking world in the form of this anthology. I knew I couldn't accomplish a project this vast on my own, so when I decided which authors I needed to have translated, I engaged a cohort of translators and several of my former graduate students in the project. All their hard work and cooperation has really made this anthology possible.

All anthologies, of course, are shaped by the tastes of the compiler. This one is no exception. And all anthologies can never pretend to be complete. I am certain I have overlooked some authors who would have been just as worthy of inclusion here. But all anthologies have their limitations, too, so certain lacunae are inevitable. I do hope that this anthology gives a representative taste of some extraordinarily talented writers from a largely undiscovered country, who are very deserving of a wider readership in the English-speaking world.

The arrangement of the authors presented here is largely chronological according to the age of the various authors except in one instance — the poet Lina Kostenko, whose work appears at the end. Although she is the most mature writer represented in this group, she is the "youngest" prose writer in the anthology since her first novel in prose appeared in 2010 at the age of 80. I also decided to include two still-living older writers, who began writing long before the period of *glasnost* that began in the mid-1980s and Ukrainian independence in 1991. The surrealist poet, prose writer, and artist Emma Andijewska made her name in emigration in the United States and in Germany. And Nina Bichuya has been a prolific prose writer from Lviv in Western Ukraine, who for decades has been quite influential on women's prose. Most of the remaining writers began their prose writing careers in the 1980s and after.

The anthology offers either complete shorter works or excerpts from novels and novellas to give a representative flavor of each writer's writing style. A few works have been chosen for inclusion based primarily on their historical and cultural significance, but most have been chosen for purely esthetic reasons. The novel has been the dominant genre for most of the Ukrainian women writers of the 1990s and into the new millennium, although the short story and essay have had their extremely talented adherents. Tanya Malyarchuk can be singled out as a particularly notable short story writer, though her latest work is a novel. Many of the authors included here have also distinguished themselves in the genres of the literary and philosophical essay (especially Oksana Zabuzhko), in the New Journalism genre of the travelogue (e.g., Iren Rozdobudko), and in memoiristic writing (e.g., Maria Matios).

I suggest that readers not necessarily read the book from beginning to end, but rather peruse those works and authors they find the most intriguing. Some readers may be attracted to the unreserved abandon of some of the younger authors. Others may find the more traditional writers more appealing. Readers hopefully will find a cornucopia of interesting choices in the volume while they glimpse into the heart and soul of some of Ukraine's finest women writers.

I want to particularly thank Myroslava Prykhoda for assisting me over the years with advice on the project and for helping me to collect books by a number of the authors. My special gratitude to Svitlana Bednazh for her assistance as a perspicacious editor of several of my translations. Her drive and positive energy have been invaluable in helping to complete this volume, especially with the final push. I am also thankful to Olha Tytarenko for editing several of my translations and to Alla Perminova for sharing her expertise and answering many of my translation questions in the final stages. Thanks also to Mariya Tytarenko for all her boundless energy and for providing support for the project in myriad ways. I am extremely grateful to Ukrainian artist Oksana Zhelisko from Lviv, Ukraine, and now residing in Edmonton, Canada, for allowing us to reproduce her exquisite painting for the cover. Extra special thanks to Yana Kovalskaya of Glagoslav Publications for the incredible amount of work she did in arranging for all the permissions from authors, literary agents and publishers to make this volume possible.

This book is dedicated to the bright memory
of Daryna Zholdak, a wonderful young Ukrainian
woman and mother of two, who died far
too young, to the sorrow
of all of us who
knew her

EMERGING UKRAINIAN WOMEN PROSE WRITERS: AT TWENTY YEARS OF INDEPENDENCE

by Michael M. Naydan

IN THE UKRAINIAN LITERARY TRADITION THERE HAVE BEEN SCORES of women poets, several of them reaching extraordinarily prominent status. The most renowned of them include: the legendary seventeenth-century singer folksong writer Marusia Churai, the poet and dramatist Lesya Ukrayinka at the turn of the nineteenth to the twentieth century, and the poet Lina Kostenko in the Soviet and post-Soviet period.[*] Larysa Kosach at her mother's suggestion wrote under the pseudonym of Lesya Ukrainka, which, at least, was a female one. Thus in historically patriarchal Ukrainian society, poetry was first accepted as appropriate for women, perhaps, mostly because it is an art form linked with emotion, with concomitant stereotypical sentiments associated with women. Prose fiction prior to the twentieth century in the Slavic world by and large has been a genre in the domain of male writers.

The tradition of women's prose fiction as opposed to that of poetry has been considerably less developed. Language Lanterns Publications in Canada includes the following women authors in their Women's Voices in Ukrainian Literature series: Ukrainka's mother Olena Pchilka

---

[*] Kostenko's works include a novel in verse entitled *Marusia Churai* (1982) that is dedicated to the theme of the first great Ukrainian poet-singer.

(1849-1930), Natalia Kobrynska (1855-1920), Dniprova Chayka (1861-1927), Lyubov Yanovska (1861-1933), Olha Kobylianska (1863-1942), Hrytsko Hryhorenko (1867-1924), Yevhenia Yaroshynska (1868-1904), and Lesya Ukrainka (1871-1913). Only Olha Kobylianska of this group has garnered prominent stature as a prose writer, particularly with the publication of her novels *The Land* (1902) and *On Sunday Morning She Gathered Herbs* (1909). Kobylyanska initially wrote in German and switched to Ukrainian as her literary language as she became acquainted with civic-minded Ukrainian literary circles, especially the eminent writer Ivan Franko. One other woman prose writer Marko Vovchok (1834-1907), the pseudonym of Maria Vilinska, gained prominence in the nineteenth century under the guise of her male mask. She has been called the Ukrainian Harriet Beecher Stowe for her realistic, ethnographic short stories on peasant life in Ukraine, first written in Ukrainian (Vovchok's acquired language following her marriage to Opanas Markovych), which were translated and introduced into Russian literary circles with considerable success by the great Russian writer Ivan Turgenev in 1859.

The Soviet period, unfortunately, experienced a dearth of influential Ukrainian women prose writers, with the best women writers opting to write poetry. Just the émigré poet, prose writer and artist Emma Andijewska (1931-), who was born in Donetsk, stands out with her surrealistic prose works in the genre of the novel and novella, all written in emigration. What might the reasons be for the lack of significant Ukrainian women prose writers from the 1920s up to Ukrainian independence in 1991? One can only provide conjecture. Prose fiction requires cultural and societal stability, yet the repressive and congenitally patriarchal nature of the Soviet system may have stereotyped women from working in prose fiction. Simple biological issues (child bearing and rearing) may have kept some women writers from having adequate free time to write lengthier prose works. Poetry, of course, takes shorter spurts of concentration. The same social conditions in greater Russia during the Soviet period failed to produce any Russian women prose writers of note until The Thaw in the 1960s when I. Grekova (the pseudonym of Elena Venttsel) began publishing, and in the mid-to-late 1980s when, Ludmilla Petrushevskaya and Tatiana Tolstaya emerged. Petrushevskaya's prose, though accepted for publication as early as 1969 in the leading Soviet journal Novyi mir (New World), was initially withdrawn because of its stark characters and negative depictions of Soviet realia.

The period of Soviet leader Mikhail Gorbachev's *glasnost* (openness) in the mid-to-late 1980s and the period of post-independence Ukraine following 1991 has seen a conspicuous blossoming of women prose writers. Two female writers in particular bridged the transitional period to Ukrainian independence: Eugenia Kononenko (1959-) and Halyna Pahutiak (1958-), who were publishing their short stories and novellas in Soviet periodicals. The Kyiv-based Kononenko was publishing mostly in literary journals such as the liberal Suchasnist in Kyiv, while the Lviv-based Pahutiak, besides publishing in the periodical press, managed to publish several books of collected prose works in Soviet times including *Children* (1982), *The Master* (1986), *To End Up in a Garden* (1989), and *Mustard Seed* (1990). Kononenko's early works, mostly short stories, largely deal with quite realistic scenes of Soviet life that often present Ukrainian women in crisis situations, particularly in dysfunctional family settings, and often with abusive and drunken husbands and boyfriends. In her choice of topics, she shares an affinity with Petrushevskaya in that respect. Her book-length feminist essay *Without a Hubby* (2005) comprises a lengthy, confessional autobiographical essay. Pahutiak's prose tends much more to be in the vein of magical realism and fantasy. Her vampire novel *The Minion from Dobromyl* (2009) fuses folklore and folk belief in witches and vampires with actual historical events including the Nazi invasion and Soviet rule in western Ukraine. Maria Matios, one of the most prominent Ukrainian women writers writing today, published her first prose work in 1992, a year after Ukrainian independence.

A watershed event for Ukrainian women's prose occurred in 1996. That is the year of publication of Oksana Zabuzhko's *Field Work in Ukrainian Sex*. The semi-autobiographical novel, based on Zabuzhko's travels in the US on a Fulbright grant, focuses on her disastrous liaison with a Ukrainian artist. That failed relationship leads to a profoundly intense psychological self-analysis and examination of her Ukrainian identity and her identity as a woman, over the course of which the writer, among many other topics, candidly depicts sex and sexuality, which were completely taboo topics in previous Ukrainian women's literary discourse. Male writers had been writing about sex and sexuality from a male perspective prior to this. Of particular note is the erotic prose of Yuri Pokalchuk. Note also Yuri Vynnychuk's *Ladies of the Night* (1992) about two Odessan prostitutes and their pimp as well as Yuri Andrukhovych's novels *Recreations* (1992), *Moskoviada* (1993) and *Perverzion* (1996), all of which contain highly charged sexual scenes. *Recreations* contains a brutal rape scene, *Moskoviada* — the hero's sexual encounter with an African woman in the dormitory showers at a literary institute in Moscow, and the provocatively titled *Perverzion* — a threesome sex scene toward the end of the novel as well as a considerable amount of sexual content throughout. Zabuzhko's novel, currently in its ninth edition, differs by the fact that it dealt with these issues of sex and sexuality for the first time from a *female* psychological perspective. This particularly galvanized a women's readership in Ukraine and broad support for the novel based on gender. The novel elicited considerable negative reaction in the press when it appeared, but mostly, perhaps, for its provocative title. While foregrounded in the title, sex is actually a secondary theme in the book. Negative reactions tended to come from more conservative circles as well as from the opposite sex, though female critics such as Nila Zborovska took Zabuzhko to task over her writing. Zborovska's attacks, however, may have been based more on personal issues. Certain writers such as Natalka Sniadanko, who presented sexual content in her prose but without an openly feminist stance, were presented as the "anti-Zabuzhko." Zabuzhko's novel, in fact, is more about the failure of mutually pleasurable sex (one might also call this true intimate love) to happen in the heroine's love relationship with her Ukrainian artist lover and her inability to foster a child with him, as well as the psychological reasons for that failure, both intrinsic and extrinsic. With the novel's publication Zabuzhko immediately created the persona and the paradigm of a self-promoting feminist writer in the Western mold, breaking social barriers for other women writers to follow. The novel also fostered lengthy discussions about women and feminism in the Ukrainian periodical press, as well as literary discussions on whether a bestseller was possible in Ukraine. The novel has been translated into a number of European languages and has put Zabuzhko into a dialog with Western literary and feminist circles.

Zabuzhko, just as many other writers of her generation, tends to try to always be cosmopolitan. There is no bucolic simplicity in the style of her works and little focus on village life. Her characters are virtually all intellectuals and city dwellers. Her prose writing style is also by design quite complex. Perhaps this comes from her training in philosophy and scholarly prose. All these aspects of her prose, either subliminally or intentionally, work against the imagined stereotype of Ukrainians as being singing, smiling pig lard(*salo*)-eating rustic villagers, a stereotype fostered in the Tsarist, Soviet and even post-Soviet Russian empires.

Essential to Zabuzhko's method in *Field Work in Ukrainian Sex* is her psychological, nearly confessional candor. The book, in fact, reminds me considerably of Sylvia Plath's *The Bell Jar*, in which Plath's life experiences are thinly veiled in the guise of her novel. That sometimes painfully candid and personally focused aspect of Zabuzhko's writing has been taken up by a number of other younger women writers including Svitlana Pyrkalo, Natalka Sniadanko, Irena Karpa, Svitlana Povalyaeva, and Sofia Andrukhovych. All these younger writers, who currently range in age from 29-37, just as Zabuzhko does in her pathbreaking novel, focus on urban life, use scatological and substandard language, tend toward the confessional, and in a quite frank manner describe their sexual experiences (largely ironically) as well as their inner emotional life, usually in turmoil. Most of this group have been trained as print or media journalists and have dual or even multiple career tracks. I should point out that the degree requirements for journalism majors in Ukraine focus heavily on philology and literature, often in comparative contexts, so it is not the kind of narrowly focused journalistic background as found in the US. Pyrkalo and Sniadanko work as print and media journalists, and Karpa and Povalyaeva as radio and telejournalists. Karpa served as the host for the Ukrainian MTV channel and also works as a model, having done numerous nude photo shoots for Playboy and other sex magazines. She also is the lead singer for the Kyiv-based band called Quarpa (previously named *Faktychno sami*). The works of these writers, just as Zabuzhko's novel, are largely autobiographical. The stories they have to tell are stories about themselves. This need for psychological self-revelation at an early age, particularly in their first works, seems in general terms to differentiate these writers from their contemporary male counterparts. Their background in reporting (except for Sofia Andrukhovych, who just has a literary background and is the daughter of prominent writer Yuri Andrukhovych), seems to influence their writing style.

Another strain among younger authors is a self-reflective kind of philosophical prose such as that of translator-author Dzvinka Matiash, particularly in her first novel *A Requiem for November* (2005). The novel is confessional, but in a spiritual way, and comprises a deep meditation on death. Her second novel, *A Novel about Your Homeland* (2006), relates the stories of women's lives in Ukraine's past. The author's sister Bohdana Matiyash also writes in a philosophical vein, particularly noteworthy in this vein is her book of prose-poems *Conversations with God* (2007).

The writer Larysa Denysenko (1973-) also has a considerable amount of autobiographic content in her prose, but is considerably less confessional and more restrained in her writing than her contemporaries. Hers is a measured prose of everyday life situations. She is the prototype of a rare breed of woman who has managed to have it all in Ukrainian society. Having grown up a speaker of Russian with training in law, Ms. Denysenko learned to speak Ukrainian in her job with the Ukrainian Ministry of Justice at the age of 23. While she still practices law, she also hosts a culturological program Document+ on the "1+1" television program. Besides her seven novels and three children's books, Ms. Denysenko also has done a number of photo shoots as a model for fashion and women's magazines.

Three of the most interesting writers to have emerged since Ukrainian independence include Maria Matios (1959-), Iren Rozdobudko (1962-) and Tanya Malyarchuk (1982-): the first two from the older generation and the latter from the younger. Matios comes to literature from a philological educational background and Rozdobudko and Malyarchuk from the field of journalism. One is particularly struck by the prolific nature of all three authors. Matios has published fourteen books of prose and six books of poetry, with her first book publication in 2001, nineteen years after her first book of poetry was published in 1982. One of her primary foci has been the fictional reconstruction of her past in rural Bukovyna where she was born and raised. Rozdobudko, originally from Donetsk in the Russian-speaking Eastern part of Ukraine, is the author of 14 books of prose and 2 books of poetry. She began her second career as a prose writer at the age of 38 with the publication of her first novel. And Malyarchuk, at the age of 28, has published six books of prose. She, too, like Matios, often deals with memories of village life, though in the Carpathian Mountains where she grew up.

Rozdobudko has become a master of the detective novel and psychological thriller. She focuses on story telling, and her writings are highly accessible to a mass readership. And many of her works are being turned into movies, thereby increasing her popularity as a writer. She often authors the filmscripts herself.

Several aspects of Matios's and Malyarchuk's exceptional prose works are striking to me. Rather than concentrate exclusively on the urban environment where they both live and work (the city of Kyiv), they both focus on their past and rural life in the village. Matios's writing in particular recalls the novels of Toni Morrison and Alice Walker, who, in works such as *Beloved* and *The Color Purple*, recreate a colonial past and find aesthetic beauty and philosophical depth in it. Both Morrison and Walker seek authenticity in their portrayal of the past and use a considerable amount of dialectal speech to achieve their aim. Matios's postcolonial masterpiece *Sweet Darusia* is an engaging character portrayal in the microcosmic world of a small village in Bukovyna. Her villagers speak the local Bukovynian dialect, which she regularly glosses with footnotes. Matios's writing style is rich and complex, yet still quite accessible to the Ukrainian reader. Instead of reacting against rural stereotypes, Matios revels in the unique individuality of her ancestral villagers, and shows the humanity and the psychological depth that can be found in their lives.

While Matios tends to write longer works in the genres of the novella and novel, Malyarchuk's strength as a writer lies in her vignettes, in shorter prose forms, although she has written several novellas. Like her younger contemporaries, Malyarchuk was inclined to be more self-revelatory in her first novel in 2004, *Adolpho's Endspiel, or a Rose for Liza*, while her later collections tend to have more of an authorial distance and restraint. While Malyarchuk's style is more terse and more transparent than Matios's, she is a talented and engaging storyteller. She seems to distance herself from contemporary postmodernist trends and has an impressive acumen for presenting the psychology of the characters that populate her stories. Her prose pieces, many drawn from childhood experience, avoid copious descriptive detail and comprise vignettes that, despite their seeming simplicity, give significantly deeper insight into life. Her story "A Village and its Witches" delightfully reverberates with life and the seeming natural order of things in a land that is both somehow familiar yet strangely different from the one most urban contemporary readers grow up in, a land whose collective psyche is still populated by witches, superstitions, and deeply seated supernatural beliefs. Instead of rejecting her rural roots in her writings from her now more sophisticated urban perspective, Malyarchuk often returns to and embraces her past with the life lessons it harbors. Those lessons, sometimes self-directedly ironic, seem to form an integral part of her own sense of being as well as that of her people. She also experiments considerably with narrative, often taking the point of view of male characters.

The writers Sofia Maidanska (1948-), Natalka Bilotserkivets (1954-), Liudmyla Taran (1954-) and Liuko Dashvar (the pseudonym of Irina

Chernova; 1954-) are worth noting as a phenomenon, with three of them born in the same year. They all have come to writing prose fiction late in their careers. Maidanska, Bilotserkivets and Taran are well-known poets and essayists who have begun to write prose in their mid-fifties. The Russian-speaking Dashvar, who was educated and worked as a journalist and later as a filmscript writer, began writing and publishing in Ukrainian in 2006, earning the 2008 BBC Book of the Year Award in Ukraine for her second novel *Milk with Blood* (2007) about village life in southern Ukraine. Her works, quite accessible to a wide audience, sell the most copies of any woman writing in Ukraine today. Bilotserkivets, one of the most prominent and well-known poets of her generation, has shifted to prose and has been working on a novel for several years. Her first novel has not yet appeared, so we are unable to include an excerpt of that in this volume. Taran has shifted mostly to writing shorter prose works, though she does continue to write poetry.

Three of the most important recent works in women's prose have been Oksana Zabuzhko's lengthy novel *The Museum of Abandoned Secrets* (2009), Lina Kostenko's *Notes of a Ukrainian Selfmad Man* (2010), and Maria Matios's *Torn Pages from an Autobiography* (2010). Kostenko is Ukraine's preeminent poet, a revered figure, who turned 80 in 2010. She is one of the leading representatives of what has been called the Poets of the Sixties phenomenon, a group of Ukrainian writers who sought personal creative freedom from the state-imposed literary requirements of socialist realism. Her first foray into prose fiction at the end of 2010 met with critical reaction; in fact she canceled a visit to the city of Lviv for promotional appearances because of it. The novel, told from the perspective of a 35-year-old male protagonist computer programmer (Kostenko's son Vasyl Tsvirkun is trained as a computer programmer), has sold extremely well. Zabuzhko's 832-page novel, introduced with a considerable amount of hype, has had responses ranging from high praise to reactions that focus on the opaqueness of Zabuzhko's style. The book won the 2013 Angelus Prize for best Central European prose work. Matios's candid and often ironic memoir recounts growing up in the Soviet Union and the transition to Ukrainian independence. It received a book of the year award in Ukraine for 2010. On December 17, 2010 Matios reported that the offices of Piramida Publishers in Lviv were searched by members of the Ukrainian ministry of internal affairs, who tried to remove copies of the book from circulation.* The essence of the complaint against her book was the fact that Matios called the gigantic titanium sword-wielding statue of the woman defender of the motherland in Kyiv a giant phallus.** Her comments apparently irked some Soviet army veterans of the "Great Patriotic War" (World War II), who made charges of defamation to the authoritarian Yanukovych government. Matios indignantly reacted to the illegal search with an open letter to the general procurator of Ukraine.*** While there have been no further repercussions, freedom of expression has, unfortunately, once again become dangerous in Ukraine.

All in all I see two general trends in the phenomenon of emerging women writers in Ukraine. One comprises urban writing, which is a backlash against previous Soviet colonialism and stereotyping. These writers seem to need to express their cosmopolitanism, to be a part of the larger culture and cultural trends of the world, and at the extreme end — to be chic and cutting edge with no holds barred. They, of course, tackle real issues and challenges presented by today's modern society and women's place in it. The other trend is toward a new retrospective rural prose tradition, a return to one's roots in village life in both the recent and distant past. These women writers (particularly Matios, Malyarchuk and Dashvar) revel in the past and its lessons, though they, too, at times also deal with urban characters in urban settings. Most interesting will be to see if some of the younger women urban writers continue on the same track after bearing and raising children.

---

* An article in *Ukrainska Pravda* (The Ukrainian Truth) describes the situation in detail: *http://www.pravda.com.ua/news/2011/01/12/5775945/*.

** A link to a picture of the monument can be found here: *http://miraimages.pho-toshelter.com/image?&_bqG=2&_bqH=eJyriIgIMwnzqvLxDyv2SgoMj8ovCU9Ky 8rKzE63MjIwsjIoMABhIOkZ7xLsbOuSmpaaV5yqBubFO_q52JYA2aHBrkHxni- 620SCV3iWFhT75ERmhiaFq8Y7OIbbFqYlFyRkA_MIhdA--&GI_ID=.*

*** *http://life.pravda.com.ua/columns/2011/01/12/70243/*

TALE ABOUT THE VAMPIRELING WHO FED ON HUMAN WILL

by Emma Andijewska

Translated by Uliana Pasicznyk

THERE ONCE APPEARED AMONG THE VAMPIRES A FLEDGLING SO puny, tiny, and feeble that its parents worried greatly whether their long-awaited offspring would ever succeed them in carrying on the fame and honor of the vampire race. For when it came time for the vampireling to try its wings, it became apparent that the young thing was not only too weak to attack humans but was scarcely able to maintain its balance. Its spine, arms, and legs were so soft and light that the slightest wind or even a draft through a house was enough for the vampireling to fall to the ground like an old rag doll, unable even to lift its head on its own. But what caused its parents the most travail was the terrible, inexplicable fact that even after their child lost its baby teeth and the permanent ones grew in, these were more like gelatinous scales filled with grayish fluid than teeth. Such teeth could not scratch, let alone pierce the skin of a human.

The claws on the vampireling's front legs were no better. Instead of being able to help the jaws do vampire's work, they grew as tender cartilage, resembling rose petals. Looking at them caused the parents to suffer as though an ashen stake were being driven through their hearts.

But even this did not cause the hapless parents the most anguish. Their deepest grief and disappointment sprang from the fact that from birth the vampireling could not bear the sight of, let alone drink, the human blood that its soft-hearted parents initially brought the sickly child in a pouch made from a pig's bladder. At the very sight of even the freshest human blood, the vampireling immediately suffered terrible cramps that threatened to bring its life to a close. Lest they lose their only offspring the tearful parents, gritting their teeth, were forced to feed their child not healthful and nourishing human blood but porridge cooked from dandelions and juice squeezed from daisy petals.

Finally the vampireling's parents, who, like all loving parents, had tried every means to remedy the great affliction, lost hope that their child would ever find its way to being a true vampire. With grieving and breaking hearts, they began to consider whether to abandon their degenerate offspring to humans, so as not to bring ultimate disgrace to the vampire race and clan.

But one very old, toothless vampire, living out his days in the chimney of a stable that had burned to the ground, to whom the despairing parents had turned for some word of wisdom as a last resort, persuaded them to wait a little longer, and meanwhile to find some decisive and fearless man to serve as nanny to their child.

The parents decided that his was wise advice. Barely able to wait until the break of dawn, they immediately set out among humans. But no matter whom the vampires approached, no matter how respectfully they asked, everyone they turned to, resolutely refused to undertake any such task, crossing themselves as they spoke.

Then, in a wood, the vampires chanced across a man whom misfortune had dogged so long that he had lost any fear of them. Shunning needless hesitation, the vampires talked the man into taking care of their only child for a small remuneration, having also vowed that he would be inviolable to any other vampire. The requirements were that the man carry the vampireling out on walks; in several years it had not grown even an inch, so even now its legs folded together under it like string; and that he cook porridge of dandelions and squeeze daisy petal juice for his charge — the only food that did not bring on its cramps.

They came to terms, and the man began to care for the vampireling. Fate had not been kind to the man, and he rejoiced that things had at least taken a somewhat better turn. Now, at last, after long toil and much disappointment, the man had a roof over his head, even if it was among vampires, and he was even eating normal human food, which the vampires brought him, instead of the roots and moldy husks he had serendipitously found.

At first, truth to say, the man was wary of the vampireling, for he remembered that the acorn does not roll far from the oak. But once he became convinced that the child did not crave human blood, and that it was indeed puny and feeble, the man let down his guard. And because nothing much needed to be done for the child — after eating it usually sat quietly in a corner, rather than go to play — the man relaxed completely. And having relaxed, he grew lazy and careless.

So whereas earlier the man had fed the vampireling three times a day, now he decided that twice a day would suffice, all the more because the child never mentioned being hungry. Then, noting that it did not cry, the man began to prepare its food just once a day, a meal that seemed of no great interest to the child. And then somehow it happened that one fine day, the man just forgot to feed the vampireling altogether. Earlier that day the man had lunched especially well, for the vampireling's parents, believing that the man was caring for their child conscientiously, had brought a basket loaded with foods and wine filched from their victims. And since he who is sated never thinks of one who is hungry, the man, having eaten and drunk well, forgot about the vampireling, and soon he was overtaken by the urge to sleep.

Until then the man had taken care not to sleep in the presence of his charge. But now, deciding there was no danger — as things always seem to the satiated — and feeling his eyelids grow heavy, he made himself more comfortable, and he fell asleep.

That is when the vampireling first saw a human asleep.

If the man had fed it, perhaps the vampireling would have paid no attention. As things were, it felt hunger and began to look around to see if a daisy petal might be lying about somewhere. Laboriously it made its way out from the corner and closer to the table, where there still lay remnants of the food the vampireling could not eat. Then it was struck by the discovery that a human sleeps totally differently from the way vampires do.

For when vampires slept, there arose from them a heavy stench of blood, which made the vampireling's extremities grow numb and took his breath away, making it feel ill. During the day, when the man was active, he smelled like an old goat. But now, as he slept, there wafted from him a pleasant aroma that tickled the nostrils.

The vampireling, intrigued, came up close. It did not yet realize, of course, that what smelled so sweet was human will, which during sleep rises up from man's flesh and floats above him in a soft, round, and aromatic biscuit. And because the vampireling was hungry and had found nothing it could eat, it nipped at this aroma. Slowly consuming a bit of human will, it was astonished to find that nothing in the world tastes as sweet as this nourishment.

The more the vampireling ate of this new food, the more it gained strength from it and the tastier it became. The vampireling was so taken by this new food that it ceased to eat only when the man stirred heavily and began to regain consciousness. Grasping his chest with his hands, the man felt a strange languor and lethargy throughout his body, unlike anything he had known before.

The man peered about on all sides but he did not realize what had happened. And how could he have realized anything, when, even before he sat up and rubbed his eyes, the vampireling, to whom the new nourishment had brought previously unknown strength and agility, had quickly scurried back to a corner and in no way betrayed that it had just been feasting on human will.

For the very moment that the vampireling tasted human will, not only strength but intellect awakened in it, as well as cunning and caution. The vampireling now resolved resolutely that from then on, human will would be its only food. When the man occasionally remembered the vampireling's existence, it still pretended to consume the dandelion porridge and daisy petal juice, but when the man slept it was sure to feast on its incomparable new nourishment.

Thus, before long, the vampire child consumed all of the man's will, for a person lacking will never notices that he is a living corpse. And when it had satisfied itself that all this precious food had been eaten, the vampireling asked its parents to give the man a reward and let him go, and then host a lavish banquet before it set out to go among humankind. The time had come for the vampireling to make its parents rejoice at the realization of their dreams.

At that banquet, when the vampireling proclaimed not only to its parents but to all vampire kind that from that day forward they would feed on human will exclusively, the vampires, wonderstruck, unanimously agreed: the small, puny vampireling was the mightiest and most fearsome vampire of them all.

TALE ABOUT THE MAN WHO KNEW DOUBT

by Emma Andijewska

Translated by Uliana Pasicznyk

THERE ONCE LIVED A MAN WHO FROM BIRTH WAS DEFEATED BY doubt. No matter how he began any activity, whether indifferently or conscientiously, whether work or recreation, he would be seized by doubt. At that instant the work would become loathsome to him, or the pastime would slump into boredom and despair. Nothing brought him any pleasure, and existence itself seemed such a heavy burden that the poor fellow would gladly have rid himself of it, had not the resolve entailed effort beyond any that he could muster. For doubt did not allow him to make a final decision about anything.

When they realized something was amiss, the man's parents tried every way they knew to alleviate his distress, but all their attempts proved futile. The older their son became, the stronger his doubt grew, and all his worried parents' urgings and counsel served only to increase his despair and hopelessness, making their son weary of life.

Finally the parents became convinced that in his condition neither threats nor pleas were of any use. So they began to equip their only child with the things he would need to travel far and wide, in the hope that by being out among people he would gain the wisdom and experience needed to cure him of his excessive doubt. At last, having given him directions and bestowed their blessing, they let their feckless child go off on his long journey.

But even in far-off lands doubt continued to torment the man, and sooner or later everything he undertook ended in failure and vexation. From time to time the man came across kind-hearted people who took pity on him and gave him shelter and work. But as soon as the man took a good look at whatever he was doing, doubt would seize him again: he would abandon everything and find himself once again in the same situation as before. Yet now he was no longer an impetuous youth but a man full grown, for whom it was time to have a roof over his head and a family of his own.

And then, in his wanderings from place to place, because Providence, if not always immediately then at least occasionally, tends to even the most forsaken of men, the man somehow found a corner to call home and acquired a wife and children. Now he felt pleased that at last he was making something of his life. But as soon as his children began growing out of diapers, doubt once again seized the man, doubt stronger than he had ever known before. He left his wife and children and set off aimlessly into the world, as before.

And then one day, as he was fording a stream along his way, the man turned around and chanced to see that his doubts were seven chargers forged together as one black steed, bearing him into an abyss of no return. The terrified man, feigning calm, tried to vanquish the doubts now taking on such increasingly physical form. But his powers proved too weak to scatter them. Calling on God to bear witness that he could carry on no more, exhausted in body and soul, he dropped down at a crossroads, under a tree, and fell asleep.

As soon as his eyelids closed, he beheld a little old man standing before him, tugging at his sleeve. Pointing to a small yard made of packed clay, smooth as a finished floor, the old man asked, "Will you agree to sweep my yard? For this job I need a man defeated by too much doubt. Here are the sun and the moon; they will serve as your two brooms — and as for your pay, what I have to give you is one small seed."

"All right," said the man, and as he began to sweep the old man's yard, he immediately felt his doubts vanish somewhere. After a time the old man made him stop, saying that his job was done, and in remuneration he gave him the one small seed.

The man thanked him, and then awoke. To his amazement, in his palm there indeed lay a small, luminous seed. As the man took another look at the seed, doubt again reared up within him, with such angry force that the man understood: his end was at hand, for the chargers were racing at a gallop under him. They were galloping so fiercely that, to stop himself from falling and cracking his skull as doubt was about to plunge him into the abyss, the man grabbed the horse's mane with one hand while pressing the other, the hand holding the little old man's payment to his breast. At that instant he felt the seed fall tremulously to the bottom of his heart and immediately send forth a slender shoot. And from the way the shoot trembled, the man understood that the seedling sprouting in him was hope.

"You have become a bad horseman," the man's reason immediately admonished him.

"You will never make any headway in life if you don't pull that log out from your heart," the doubts added angrily, slackening their galloping pace.

"It's not a log but a new doubt stirring in my heart," lied the man, all the while feeling the sapling of hope within him sprouting forth new branches.

"A person is a person only when he is overwhelmed by doubt," declared the doubts, appeased. And that was the last that they said. For hope, which from a tiny seed had flourished in the man's heart into a blossoming tree, silenced the voices of doubt. For only the tree of hope, growing in the human heart, helps man vanquish the doubts that are his horsemen to the abyss.

THE STONE MASTER

by Nina Bichuya

Translated by Olesia Wallo

A TRAMPLED GREEN FIELD EXTENDS BETWEEN ME AND THE podium, which was made of rough rust-colored planks hastily hammered together, and the man behind the podium, holding a microphone in his hands, exclaims something, shouting at the top of his voice, but I don't hear a word, and this is all because someone has spread out such a boundless green expanse between us and also because of the fact that the microphone he's holding is not plugged into anything; the cord droops, stretches out, and recoils like a long black snake, and maybe the man is even hissing like a snake, and although I understand that the man cannot hiss, I keep thinking that his voice is that absurd hissing, and there is not another soul in the vast green space — only I and that man who stands behind the podium holding the microphone, although it makes no sense to hold it because nothing can be heard anyway.

I woke up from a heavy, nightmarish dream three times during the night, and, once awake, I would completely forget what I saw in that dream, but in a moment everything would begin anew — the same nightmare. It repeated itself, and I knew this was the same vision, but upon waking, I wasn't able to remember a thing.

A quiet little street, resembling a narrow stream that all of a sudden expands into a big lake, leads to the square. There is a park on the other side of the square — a damp and dark one, from which the fog always comes; it has the scent of magnolias, of last year's grass, and of the swans' autumn trumpeting — they are confined to the lake and never fated to fly anywhere, and at the end of fall, they suddenly disappeared, as if they hadn't existed at all; the fog and the street are saturated with a multitude of other odors, and you can tell which one is which as if they were notes in a chord, and they can also be loud, stubborn, and there are some that do not disappear in any season of the year, but there are others, transient and timorous, that easily flicker out, quiet down, and they are delicate and beyond compare, and among all of that, as a past memory, there rises the fragrance of a miniature, tiny and insignificant flower called "stock," and in its scent, there are countless shades, a complex palette of colors and sounds. The lanterns hang over the street; they rock it to sleep, they swing ever so slightly, and raindrops fall past them, fluffy snowflakes swim in the air, and the moonlight flows — the street is asleep, and in it, as in a crib, cars doze; once a very old, strange and delicate car stopped here for the night, it looked like it had arrived from far away, from the prehistoric thirties or even the twenties; this hunched over and comical limousine groaned like an older person and grudgingly allowed children to jump on the long worn out seats under its partly rolled down canvas roof. They were feeling every rib of the car, pulling out into the open its every vein, and, it seemed, it would fall apart the very next moment, its stiff joints that were barely holding together everything that is transitory, used up, comical and unnecessary in its body would break, yet it held up, and the children kept pressing with all their strength on its black Klaxon horn, and it moaned and groaned, and over the loud noises the children could hear nothing of what the old car could tell them, a car that partly resembled a prehistoric mammoth, for some unknown reason brought out into the street from the museum of natural history.

Three times during the night I woke up from the awful nightmare, and every time I looked down the little street, narrow as a stream, my eyes stumbled on the indistinct silhouette of the old limo, and I would forget in the content of the dream, what I saw; the street would swallow up my fear and return me to reality — an ordinary night, no awful dreams, the sidewalk tiles worn out by thousands of feet covering the black earth, and there is no need to think that at some point, under the tiles just like these, everyone… We like to cover everything up.

Why are we seduced in our youth by the romantic flair of history? Without getting deeply into it, we fish out of it various colors and transport them into our own time, which we haven't studied carefully either. And when we do manage to understand something — any-thing — the end to our own brief history comes, from which someone else already will begin to pick out something for himself. It's an age-old fable without continuation and even with no visible beginning.

It was only just before dawn, having woken up for the third time from my nightmare, that I finally realized it was no dream at all. All of this was a horrifying but completely mundane reality, an altogether mundane true story that for some reason appeared in my dream three times, and every time, changing somewhat, it terrified me with its mun-danely real horror; time in that reality condensed and compressed — that's right, compressed like a spring rather than condensed — it be-came compressed, and at any moment it could break out from under my authority and hurt me; the only thing that neither I nor time could control was a high-pitched child's voice, softly humming a melody with no words — the words, after all, seemed superfluous — a toy, a game, a speck, chaff — they scattered, disappeared, made no sense whatsoever.

The man at the podium (or behind the podium, or under it — one could barely see him, only the cut-off black cord, as if alive, flailed about and recoiled) tried to reach me with his screams, his head suddenly appearing for a brief moment over that rust-colored and hastily put together box of a podium, which I (and probably he too) perceived to be the only reality in the empty green space — his head emerged, as if it were lying detached on some sort of a base, his lips torn apart by screams, but I could neither hear anything, nor even speculate — what slogans is he shouting out over there? — and is he appealing to me? — I could not understand, and neither could I take a single step forward, get closer to the man or hear anything out of his exhausting screaming (one could see it was exhausting). All of this, however, left me absolutely cold: the scene simply reminded me of a concert I attended a very long time ago, when something extremely contemporary was being played; I remembered the elegance of the figure in tails, such a long, fitted black tailcoat, a conductor's baton, a white collar — and the conductor's knotted back, and the collar of his tailcoat covered with a thick layer of dandruff, you should never sit in the front row — then you notice things that you didn't come to see — make-up, wrinkles, sinewy hands, dandruff on the collar — no, the front row is not for me; and although I didn't hear a word of the things the man at the podium was exclaiming, I was happy that I was not too close to him and did not see the bulging strings of veins on his neck — he was exerting himself so much that they had to be bulging.

It is possible that he was also spitting while screaming, and that was another reason why I was happy not to be standing too close to the podium.

When was it? — a hundred years or so have passed — and the lights in the entire city were going out, and in the blackness behind the window, only a slight murmur existed — the sound that for me had no color, no smell, and no shape — and that is why both the city and the street were vanishing, as if they were not living anymore. There was only the spear-point of a candle flame — so hesitant and unreliable; barely suggesting a hint of existence, this wavering paintbrush of light sketched out something mysterious, a fear, a feeling of transience and loneliness, although none of these should be known to a child. Under that light, however, I read, wrote, memorized foreign German words and even played the piano a little; a small piano in the study quivered with each of its curves in that hesitant light, the black specks of notes on the sheet music's thin lines were visible under the light of two candles; these had to be inserted into copper candlesticks on the music stand, whose mysterious carvings appealed to me much more than the prospect of getting sound out of my instrument. On the day when I had to part with the piano, why didn't I think to at least keep the music stand?

My shadow is crawling on the ceiling and on the walls; it hangs over me — and the piano responds quietly, the white keys radiating warmth under my fingers: Re, Re, Mi... Or, maybe, in some other way, totally different, but it doesn't matter. My childhood has passed away, vanished, disappeared — or, maybe it grew up and out of itself? A tree grows tall, is in full blossom, and produces fruit, but then one needs a graft in order for something new to be born, something unusual. Out of a child, a seedling, or a small wild shoot a person. A person-tree.

We sat at a small round table; such tables can be found only among old furniture in old apartments; a while ago we also had a table like that at home — a round, polished one, covered with something light and lacy, it would be a curiosity, an antique gem — if it had been preserved, of course, as here, in this home — but something so light and lacy could not be preserved — it fell apart, disintegrated, but as a child I used to make braids out of the long tassels that almost reached the floor.

We sat at the tiny table, round and frail, with long curved legs, and we carefully placed our wine glasses on it. We took extra care not because of the delicate table or the crystal glasses, but because of the red wine, almost forgotten among us today — so rare and tart, it was red wine from Tbilisi — and without fear to summon a new inescapable disaster on ourselves and the entire world, we were taking the name of Joseph Stalin in vain, remembering — it will soon be twenty-five years — how each of us took the news of his death and what we did on that day. None of us managed to shed a single tear that day — it was so, each of us could swear on it, and now we howled with laughter and rejoiced that it did not occur to any of us to choke up on the occasion of that cosmic tragedy. Not that we had a reason to cry, because the eldest of us was doing at the time of the leader's death the seventh year of his sentence, meted out by the heavy "fatherly" hand for absolutely nothing, just in case, so he wouldn't make a peep; another one was doing time in the army thousands of miles from home — expelled from the university also for nothing, and also just in case; and the third among us was just a lanky sixth-grader then, and that might have been the only reason why the "fatherly" hand didn't touch his boyish head, although, having been forcibly removed together with his parents from his native land of Peremyshl, he could have been feeling not entirely at home in the new place. Truly no one was spared the graces of the almighty hand!

… "He croaked! He croaked!" My father jumped up and down wearing only his underwear, thinking nothing of the fact that I could see him like that — in his long blue drawers, with strings tied firmly at the ankles; the dawn was extremely gray, even dirty, with wet snow falling. I remember that wet snow well and the trampled black ground somewhere in the outskirts of the city, at the cemetery, where the soldiers who fought for Lviv in 1944 were buried; we were herded there with torches to lament the death of the leader — the old and cruel one whom we could never see, unreachable like God, and terrible, depraved, like Satan; and I felt terribly cold and just wanted to go home, and I also didn't want anyone to notice that I couldn't squeeze out even a single tear from my eyes — good thing it was dusk and the thick wet snow was blowing into my face and eyes, and it was hard to tell whether I was crying or not.

At the crack of dawn, as soon as I heard, still half-asleep, those words uttered by my father with triumphant joy — "He croaked!" — I knew right away who he had in mind; arching his back, my dog greeted me —happy that I was awake and that I would probably take him for a walk; "He croaked! He croaked!" My father kept chanting.

At school, they locked me up in the principal's office — to compose a poem on the occasion of the leader's death, and I spent five or six harrowing hours in that "solitary confinement" and couldn't write a single line; I was ready to cover the sheets of paper in front of me with that viciously happy and ravenous "he croaked," but I knew all too well that I couldn't give in to that temptation, I couldn't trace out even the first letter of that word because that letter could be deciphered, just like all of my feelings, thoughts, and moods; and it was unlikely that I even believed the death of an individual who could seem immortal to everyone in the world —rather, I suspected that this was the only human life on the planet that had no end because there is no end to the apprehension and the worship before that fear, the cherishing of that fear; and I startled every time when my teacher quietly opened the locked door and solemnly carried into the room her face, swollen from crying, with red, swollen eyes, and wiped her nose, blowing it loudly (how she blew her nose was really comical, but I didn't dare even smile, and, besides, I felt sorry for my teacher who was crying so bitterly) — blowing her nose loudly, she asked me softly if I had written anything yet; probably all of them — the kids and the grown-ups at school — were waiting for my poem in order to place it on the sacrificial altar, to burn it or something, the way in ancient times they used to burn slaves together with their dead master; maybe they wanted to purchase their freedom with that poem, which probably had to contain all their pain, tears and despair at the death of the leader, and, who knows, maybe they would do that to me, too — put me on the altar as a sacrifice, had somebody given them the idea. Perhaps they would have done it after all if they had had at least the slightest hunch about what I truly felt sitting in the principal's office, what words I wanted to write — maybe, they'd build a fire and burn me in it, but they didn't know anything and consequently passed by the office quietly, on tiptoe, peeking through the door almost reverently, until the principal had finally decided to lock the door, so that no one would disturb me, and I cursed that day when I shared my amazing discovery with the teacher that I could put the words together in such a way that they would all of a sudden begin to sparkle, creating a rhythm, and that I could make them resonate in rhyme, like someone's voice and its echo in the woods; I cursed both my ability to write those rhymed lines and even my general capacity to put pen to paper; I wished I had fallen ill or had been hit by a car on my way to school, I regretted having been born at all — and no one in the entire world could have helped me at that moment, and at the age of fourteen, I had to decide for myself what to do, and the education in hypocrisy, which had affected and demoralized my not-yet-guilty generation, turned out to be the only thing that helped me then and suggested a way of escape: "I can't, I can't," I muttered deceptively, hiding my eyes that were not at all red from crying, turning away my face that showed neither grief, nor sadness, "I can't... I simply can't write a single line because my anguish is so great that it cannot be measured in words, my sorrow is so infinite that I can't express it," I kept mumbling and lowered my head, afraid that someone might see through my deception, hoping that they would believe me, my cheeks turning crimson with shame not so much for this lie, but for the fact that once I did write a little poem with the name of the leader rhymed with some other exalted word; and when they did believe me, I almost jumped to my feet, almost started to dance around like father, when he chanted "he croaked, he croaked!" But my training in hypocrisy saved me once again, and I lowered my head onto my forearm, and my gullible teacher stroked my hair; and when later, in the early evening, I sloshed through the wet snow at the place where we bided our time for an hour under the torches, and my feet were wet and cold, and my head was swimming from the interminable, ever-present somber music that was drifting over the city as a dark cloud together with the torches, I still kept turning around with fear to see if anyone had uncovered my trick and whether anyone could hear how, overriding the mournful melodies, my father's chant was ringing in my ears. And I would like to know how many other young Pharisees were standing next to me, shedding false tears, and how many lunatics were mourning for the leader sincerely, crying their heart out, and how many of my peers were deviously and carefully watching the former and the latter simultaneously under the red and yellow light of the smoky torches that were every now and then blown out by wind and snow, and we had to light the wick again. Those torches were made in a very primitive way: long wooden handles were attached to empty tin cans, some sort of fuel — I can't remember now what it was exactly — was poured into the cans, a wick was inserted, and it was burning, flaring, fuming, and reeking; these kind of torches were also carried through the city during the celebrations of various military anniversaries; sometimes they'd be set ablaze at soccer games — and who knows how they managed not to set Lviv on fire at least once...

From the corner of the room, we suddenly heard a soft chuckle, and then a young voice declared: "Listen to how beautifully he writes!"

While sitting at our round table and drinking our wine, we completely forgot that the girl was there; she ensconced herself in a tiny child's rocker, a rocking chair; very slight and skinny, with tousled black hair, she looked at us as if she also just noticed the presence of adults:

"I'll read it to you, listen: 'If the sovereign is kind, if he loves his servants, ministers, the members of his family, and his favorite, it does not necessarily mean that he is devoted to his country: that is a great monarch who loves his people...' And how about this: 'Those who cannot gain the favor of the sovereign try to ingratiate themselves with a minister or, at least, his servant.' Ha-ha-ha! Do you like it, Dad?"

Most likely without even listening to what she was reading, her father, who was the one doing a deterrent prison sentence at the time of the Sovereign's death, angrily asked her:

"And what are *you* doing here? Look at her, skulking around here among the grown-ups! Go to bed — immediately!"

But the teen didn't even move a muscle in response to her father's rebuke and went back to reading again, as if he hadn't said a peep to us before.

You haven't written anything in a very long time, and it seems to you that the critics' bickering about the things you did write in the past resembles some senseless, wild dance on a still-fresh grave — your very own grave; despite the fact that you are no more, that you do not exist at all, their stomping hurts and disappoints you like hell; it also feels like something else: like they undressed you with ruthlessness, and you are all alone and naked, amid a crowd of people covered and protected with clothes, through which it is impossible to get to the living flesh, to something that can hurt. Only you can feel the touch against your wounds, and you cannot hurt anyone else, you are simply incapable of that (or don't feel the need to do so); you cannot even cry out, "Don't touch me!" But in spite of all the pain, you suddenly also experience joy; you touch the hurting body and soul and think to yourself, "So maybe I'm still alive?" And you try to move your lips after all.

Your horoscope says that some individuals born under this sign should beware of garrulousness, and this warning pertains directly to your person, for lately you haven't been able to resist that incessant stream of words, the plague of unrestraint that contains for the most part such trivial, worthless thoughts; and sometimes thoughts as such are completely absent, replaced with frankly ridiculous babble, buffoonery, for a thought can crystallize either out of solitary meditation and silence or from encounters with new, unique and interesting thoughts; your withered soul is slowly wasting away, and your entire existence has a negative rather than a positive sign about it, try at least to get rid of your debts that have accumulated and grown out of proportion while you are blubbering, having succumbed to this universal epidemic.

Burdened with sins and foolish deeds, you keep going, getting closer and closer to the inexorable finish. And yet — what finish is it? Can something without a beginning and an end be finished? A line is a sequence of dots, or points, this is what they taught you in your geometry classes. Your life is just a dot side by side with a multitude of other dots — since the dawn of time and into infinity...

My friends are laughing, having forgotten about the teen girl in the corner of the room; they roar with laughter, having set their half-empty wine glasses on the round table. Red wine — what a luxury it is today! And they keep laughing at my stories about my father jumping around in his drawers and exclaiming, "He croaked! He croaked!" — and about me being forced to write a eulogy while remembering these words and not daring to rhyme them with any other words. My God, how funny it sounds today — I didn't write such a poem! — but how truly hard it was, how frightening it was then, not to write that poem (and I am not talking about myself anymore, I was only fourteen then, it wasn't too hard for me not to write it, it was enough to put on a little show, and everyone knows how to do that at fourteen when you want to trick your parents — no, it's not about me anymore). I don't know whether my friends believe this story of mine or not, how I didn't write that poem, but they really doubt that my father was yelling, "He croaked!

He croaked!," while jumping around the room in front of a child. That is, they can probably believe the latter, but that he yelled? And yelled such a thing? Those were not the times to say something like that out loud and with a child listening — my friends shook their heads in disbelief, but I make no attempts to convince them of anything, I can't even open my mouth.

The speaker on the enormous field — maybe, it's a stadium? — is waving his arms, gesturing in some direction, but I cannot turn around as though I turned to stone. The head of the speaker dives again beneath the podium, and I begin to laugh uncontrollably, but at the same time my laughter does not produce any sounds. The toy-like speaker, the speaker puppet is gesticulating with his hands and the microphone with the cut-off, dangling cord. It would be good to point it out to him, to explain that his cord is cut off — maybe the speaker has no clue about it? I wish someone else would show up on this field, there is absolutely no one, and it is not clear how this shoddily made podium, resembling a wooden crate, materialized here, and who that speaker is, and for whom and what he appeared today.

The first variant of this real dream, or this memory, or whatever you'd call it, looks in a way that no words can express. Yet the other two are the same: squeezing them into words is impossible.

I existed with that first dream, with that first variant of it, since my childhood — for what, other than a dream, can someone else's story, someone's distant experience, someone else's life be for you? Yet I existed with it for as long as I can remember — to a point where all of it has also become my life, my experience as well as my nightmare that keeps coming back. I approach that someone else's experience, related to me by my father, by comparing it to something I know, something that resembles that someone else's experience: for instance, to the taste of pasty bread with wheat bristles — they prick your lips and your tongue, but you continue to chew because hunger drives you; or to a cup of disgusting just-boiled water that reeks of crude oil, with blackstrap molasses instead of sugar, and with nauseating baked sugar-beets. You see the bony old hands of your beloved grandmother Maria — you begin to think it possible that those ghostly people could have come to her house, too — tall, lanky, and unavoidable — one can't drive them out, get rid of them; they stretch out their enormously long arms to your grandmother, and they demand bags of grain from her, and grandmother (not yours, but she could have been yours, or maybe it is you yourself) in her aged hands holds out a slightly cracked clay pitcher with a string tied around its neck: this over here, sons, is all I have, nothing else — and they take the pitcher away from her, grab it out of her hands, the grain spills, grandmother bends down to pick it up, and they step on her fingers with their giant boots, they won't let her pick up even those few grains.

Today I don't feel any shock even at the most frightening scenes described by eyewitnesses — scenes of hunger, hunger, hunger, of blue, swollen people; I don't believe it could be knocked out of someone's memory, or that someone, perhaps, did not know about it; for if this is true, then it means that all of us are incurably ill, and no independent Ukraine can save us from this disease, as it may return; Father told me about it all when I was barely six years old, he told me, unafraid of being betrayed or of my silly little tongue — such things fall not on one's tongue but straight into one's soul; and if you haven't been told these things, I feel sorry for you and your parents; there was also Kharytyna who lived in that part of the village, she baked the best bread, no one did it better than she, I could smell and can still smell the aroma of that bread, and maybe I even tasted it in that dream, in that very first variant of my dream — I tasted it although I have never met Kharytyna herself; under my teeth, I can feel the crunch of a tiny black speck of burnt coal, stuck to the bottom of the warm loaf taken out of the oven; when someone borrowed a loaf from Kharytyna, later on that person had to make sure that the loaf to be returned was neither doughy nor burnt — no one wanted to lose face in front of Kharytyna, but no one could ever manage to bake a loaf like she did; Kharytyna died of hunger, it happened at the very beginning of that march of death, and her husband buried her and put into the coffin the towel that Kharytyna used to wrap up the just-baked bread to prevent it from getting stale, and her husband's name was Overko, he was the only one from that entire neighborhood who did not join the collective farm; when Father told me about it, he pronounced her name "Kharatyna." It's probably how Overko said it, too.

While coming out of my apartment building in Lviv, I was often afraid to look to the side because I knew that back then, in Kyiv, Father saw, right under the gate, a woman in a beautiful embroidered shirt, with beads around her neck — dead from hunger; I knew about human corpses at railway stations — heavy logs that landed with a bang, thrown by others who were still alive into the freight cars; I was that young boy who, while on a train at night, tried to move away from something heavy and cold that was pushing against him, and only at dawn, he'd see — it was a dead man, the same one with whom he had boarded the train just the night before.

Did a child really need to know all this? She did, despite everything, for it was fear — yes, fear, but a cleansing, delivering fear, it helped with deceptions, denunciations, it promoted weakness of character, and it aided in that other FEAR, the abstract, inscrutable one — not the fear of death, or of being injured, or being deported somewhere to the ends of the earth — but FEAR in more general terms, ubiquitous FEAR.

Your big, old, solid, reliable table. Its two bulky sections support a heavy brown tabletop; the sections' drawers can be moved only with effort, as if they do not want to reveal their secrets to anyone. Its persistent old-time smell, unlike any other, an incomparable smell that only the drawers of my table have; hundreds of photographs, about which each of us has good intentions — for years and years — to sift through them and sort them out — but no one will ever do it, and if everything goes well (let everything go well) — our grandchildren and great-grandchildren will either begin to decipher on their own who, where, when, and with whom is pictured in them, or will carelessly and coldheartedly throw all of it in the trash, without even taking the time to tear those photos into little pieces so that people's eyes from the pictures wouldn't stare at anyone. I once saw such old, yellowed photographs, mounted on thick cardboard — by the trash-can next to the exit onto a long, immense backyard that belonged to a theater — worthless refuse was piled up there: roughly hewn and painted plywood walls, fictitious meadows, floors, doors, and trees — the junk yard of the theater where all manner of trash was dumped. The reliability of my table may turn out to be just as unnecessary and useless later, sometime in the future, to someone who will realize its age, old-fashioned character, and bulkiness, and who will see nothing in its marks, stains, spots, its scratched-off polish, the charm, uniqueness, and mysteriousness of the pattern in its chestnut finish — lianas in the jungle, somebody's eyes, the hieroglyphs of childhood, one could hide under the tabletop in between the two bulky sections, the table's middle drawer contained things to which I had no access as a child — though I wasn't in the habit of opening that drawer, for there was nothing interesting in it: documents, papers, an old, broken golden pen nib — part of a Parker pen, Father said — perhaps that is why I have always so wanted to have a real "Parker"; however, on the table itself, there was a pencil holder, a little amber elephant, a marble inkwell and a paper weight, also made of marble, with a copper handle. All of this could be touched and played with...

My wise old table whose one bulky section now belongs to me, for it is still Father's table, its middle drawer continues to belong to him, and I still don't open it without good reason — but in my own section, I know everything: its drawers now contain my "legacy" — papers, old pens, but — no letters, no notebooks, I don't keep such things because I have no desire for someone to...

We are sitting at the round table, our wine finished, and my friends are still laughing at how my father was jumping around the room in his underpants, but I can't utter a single word. While we have been taking in vain the name of that man, HE, it turns out, has been here, listening to our conversation; he is also laughing, but with a maliciously ironic, predatory laugh — go on, keep laughing as much as you want, keep talking and chattering, I give you my sovereign permission, without my permission you wouldn't dare, he mumbles, and I hear him mumbling these words — you believe in the second coming of Jesus, but have you forgotten that Satan will come as well? You want to be free from sin, want to do penance? You desire to be cleansed? Well, go on, confess and do penance, point your finger at those who sinned and burn them at the stake — prior to committing new sins of your own, he says to me threateningly. — I am in every one of you, in every person who is close to the grave, in everyone who hasn't been born yet, I created you, there is a mark on each one of you from my grip, and no one will be rid of that mark even in the tenth generation. He takes a wine glass, pours himself some red wine, it flows and flows, although I know for sure that the bottle has been empty for a while, but he pours himself a full glass, the wine overflowing in a red rivulet, he drinks and drinks, and his glass does not go empty; my friends do not see this, they are sitting with their backs toward him and have no reason to turn around; he places the wine glass back on the table, and around it there forms a blood-red stain on the white tablecloth, and he takes off his fake black moustache, puts it in his pocket together with his fake pipe — and, jumping up like a fairy-tale devil... Like a creature from hell....

The girl in the corner bursts out laughing again and says:

"I can't believe these ancients! Listen to what he writes: 'A book tells us that once a people asked the oracle to teach them a way of keeping from laughter during public debates: our foolishness has not yet reached such heights of... *blagorazumie*...' Dad, how do I translate *blagorazumie*?"*

"You are still here? Haven't you heard what I told you?" her father says angrily, but she pays no attention to it once again.

"I have, but how do I translate *blagorazumie*?"

"What are you reading?" I ask.

---

* *Blagorazumie* is Russian for "common sense" or "good judgment." As the girl quotes from the Russian translation of the French work, she is translating the text for her listeners into Ukrainian. [translator's note]

"*Reflections and Maxims* by Marquis de Vauvenargues. According to the afterword, he 'stood at the crossroads of several different strands of Enlightenment thought in the first half of the eighteenth century.' A Frenchman... So, how do I translate *blagorazumie?*"

"Listen, will you leave us in peace?!" The girl's father bursts out in anger, and I ask her:

"Read us something else from that Frenchman of yours."

She reads almost at random:

"If you want to express serious ideas, first give up the habit of blabbering nonsense."

The speaker at the wooden podium began to grow all of a sudden. He towered over the podium and was already leaning on it with both of his massive hands; I saw his enormous fingers, red from strain, with which he gripped at the podium; the latter now looked like a toy in those hands, and his open red mouth inhaled and exhaled so that the leaves on a tree nearby, completely still a moment earlier, suddenly began moving. It occurred to me that he might lift up the podium and throw it somewhere, maybe even at me, but I still could not move even an inch, and I stood there as if chained to the ground, although it was high time to take flight — there was noise all around from that horrifying breathing, a storm could arise, or the podium could hit me after all. Despite all of this, I was very interested to know what had happened to the microphone, I did not see it; it should have grown together with the speaker — instead it seemed to become smaller or even disappeared completely, or else became invisible in comparison to the giant speaker whose words I still couldn't hear — I just figured that he was a speaker since there was a podium. The microphone had really disappeared — so there was nothing else left to do but stand there and laugh — that was the only thing of which I was capable. Tearing away from the podium one of his hands, as big as a hammer, the speaker was now shaking his fist threateningly — probably at me, for there was no one else around; or, perhaps, also at the sky — it hasn't come down crashing on us just yet.

I'm not telling anyone that this man was here, that he drank the wine, took off his fake moustache, put away his fake pipe — he was here and then he jumped up and disappeared; but for some reason, I can't stop thinking about him, all the more so since we continue to take his name in vain — have we become so accustomed to it? Or are we like children who, after they've gone through adversity, must reassure themselves by telling repeatedly how bad that FEAR, or rather TERROR, was....

His death liberated us from him, but what if he had lived another ten or twenty years? An old-timer from the Caucasus — how much we usually admire such longevity! What if he had been one of those old-timers? But, in a sense, he is, for by remembering him, we extend his life. Perhaps we are incapable of living without him — hence the memories...

"When the Germans came to our town," says one of my friends, "when the Germans came, they ordered the Jews to pull off the monument to Stalin from its pedestal. Later on it couldn't be moved even with the help of explosives, even with tanks, and here they were — forcing people to do it... They tied thick ropes around it, yoked people to it, and the people pulled so hard that their mouths foamed with blood... But it was all in vain — they couldn't move him, so they were flogged with whips...."

I'm thinking, flogged with whips to the point that their skin was cut and bleeding, but they kept pulling and pulling — and whom did they curse? The Germans or that immovable one, terrifying and immovable? Or, perhaps, they didn't curse him but rather begged his forgiveness for sacrilege, for they must have wanted to survive; but at the same time, they could have been wishing for death, afraid of his punishment for such sacrilege, since he knew so well how to punish. Even at that moment, he could have fallen and covered them all with the weight of the stone slab. And they pressed their feet against the cobblestones, slippery from their blood, and pulled and pulled him, not knowing for what to beg God — to let them live or let them perish....

The stone master. Indestructible. Eternal.

For he was there, holding the glass wine in his hideous hand; he approached us quietly, as fear itself approaches, and for some reason he stood where only I could see him, behind the backs of my friends — he stood there and drank, and wiped his fake moustache, and then he unglued it.

Then a frightening thought emerges in my head: what if he is also standing behind *my* back? And my friends see him but are silent just like I am silent? They think it's an apparition, an illusion — who knows what exactly they might be thinking — I must turn around, of course, simply turn around, but I can't, I'm not able to turn — oh, how sweet it would be to find out that the same thing is happening to the others as well, that they can't turn around either.

The second variant of my dream was from my own experience.

Thin, sun-baked little hands were stretched out towards the train carriage, and from the windows, they were thrown pieces of bread, even leftovers, and gnawed chicken bones — there were some who would throw even that, and the children would clutch those gnawed bones and suck on them with ravenous pleasure. "There is a famine in Bessarabia," they said on the train, and I heard it.*

I was drinking right at the moment when the train stopped and the children flocked to it; I was drinking orange juice straight out of a can, these were being sent to us then from America, where they took pity on our all-Union misery; I do not remember whether I put the rest of the juice into someone's outstretched hands. Perhaps I did not give the juice away, but I do remember that we gave away the bread, the meat, and the fruit.

Now I repeatedly see myself traveling somewhere, but I don't know where I'm going, I forgot where I'm headed; I insist, demand to be reminded of where it is that I have to go, but no one knows, or they

---

* Bessarabia is a region in southwestern Ukraine that became part of Soviet Ukraine after World War II. This region was devastated by a famine in 1946-47, caused by similar foodstuff requisition practices that were used by the Stalinist regime in 1932-33. [translator's note]

are all simply too busy to tell me — thin and bony little hands stretch out towards me from all directions, and I know I must defend myself against them, flee from them; but I'm in agony, terrible agony, thinking that I'm some old inept woman, but in fact I don't know who I am, or where I am and where I am headed, or why.

And then my real dream comes in its third variant, with sinister, frightening colors. On completely black snow (I definitely know it is snow and not soil, for example), there sits a little girl with a white kerchief on her head, no one in the world has yet seen or painted such eyes, the eyes like that cannot exist at all, but I do see them: and I know for sure why I ended up in that place. They were staging *Kaidash's Family* at the theater, and they would come to this village to collect all sorts of old things for props.* The director didn't want to use fake props on the stage, he wanted real spinning wheels, beer mugs, sheepskin coats, spindles, real icons — and they did find all of this here, the old women gave away everything, without pay — in return they asked for just one thing: to have somebody record all the songs they knew, for the songs could fall apart like the old sheepskin coats or even die together with the person who sang them. At the time, no one had a tape recorder, so they promised to come back later, when they are less busy, and they also invited the women to the performance —to see how their spinning wheels would look on stage.

Yet who remembers promises of this kind? So the old women kept sending us letters, begging us to think of them.

All of this was real, the dream began only at the point when I finally set out for that village; however, as befits a nightmare, I could find none for some reason, I only saw that child on the black snow, a child in a white kerchief, holding a doll; I asked her where the village and the people were, but she only shook her head and smiled, and I noticed that her mouth looked like an infant's mouth, with no teeth in it; I squatted next to her, the black snow was incredibly cold while the sky was red,

---

* *Kaidash's Family* is a popular comic story about village life by the prominent 19th-century Ukrainian realist writer Ivan Nechui-Levytsky. [translator's note]

very red, but with no sun in it. The girl kept rocking her doll, producing only some very strange, incomprehensible sounds and only shaking her head the entire time.

I put the tape recorder on the snow, the girl smiled again, touched the buttons with her finger, the tape started moving, and the girl moved her tongue convulsively in her mouth, trying to say something, but the tape recorder was probably recording only those spasmodic sighs and some strange sound between 'ma' and 'a.'

"My God, what is this?" I cried out. "It's enough to make you lose your mind! Are you here all alone?" I shook the girl by the shoulder, and because of my sharp move, from that unexpected and unnecessary move, the kerchief slid down her head and — the girl was completely bald, absolutely bald, like I don't know what....

My old table, which may be someday thrown out, burnt, sold to a consignment shop for a few roubles (or else it may be taken out to the summer house or thrown out to the junk yard, or, once again, burnt) — it is a mere used-up prop, needed in the stage design of a performance that was called my life, my existence.

And the marks from the wine glass on the white tablecloth wouldn't vanish — the red circles wouldn't disappear, although I knew for sure that none of us spilled any wine, the tablecloth should have been clean, white.

"Instead of talking about him all the time, you'd better hold a séance and summon his spirit...."

"You go to bed — right now!" the father yelled at the girl.

"...and ask him in person what he thinks about your present exceptional bravery," the girl finished the sentence and tried to get out of the kid's rocking chair, but it was difficult because she had outgrown the rocker a long time ago, even though she was still very slender.

Cluttered with all kinds of goods, a narrow and dark shop somewhere in the very outskirts of the city was crowded with old women and men who were rummaging through those goods because they could afford them: the wares were sold at reduced prices, and the shop assistant was watching the customers carefully to make sure no one would stuff some trinkets into their pockets, either forgetting to pay or having nothing to pay with. Here one could find old, thinning brooms and a gigantic plush bathing suit that could fit Gargantua's wife; there was also a wooden box stuffed with a variety of shoes in all sorts of styles and sizes — from something on enormous heels to the odd-looking canvas ballet slippers and old rubber boots; there were also glass beads, plastic dolls without arms, clay cats with scratched-off eyes, some ugly lamps and a painting called *The Steppe*....

"Don't handle this, it is not for sale," said the shop assistant to a girl who touched some strange sculpture, either a bust or a dwarf with a gigantic head. "This is not for you; did you hear what I said?"

The girl took one step back but she did manage to give the black hair mass on that eerie-looking head a furtive touch.

Meanwhile the shop assistant was watching an old hag who had been rummaging in the box with the shoes for the better part of an hour. "What's taking you so long over there?" the assistant grumbled so suddenly that the old woman shuddered, as if awakened from some beautiful dream, "Didn't you pick out anything yet?"

"I would have picked it out already, ma'am," the old woman said with sadness and confusion, her toothless mouth showing, "but I can't find the matching shoe for this left one...." In front of her, she was turning over some shabby-looking boot, which she must have liked for some reason. "Maybe you could help me...."

"I can't help you," said the shop assistant, glumly turning away. "We don't have right shoes, only left ones."

"Only left ones? How can this be?"

"That's how it is. If there had been right ones as well, the shoes would be sold in a different shop," the assistant explained with reluctance. "Don't touch that," she said to me, "it's not for sale."

I stood there, unable to look away from that eerie, black-haired head; it reminded me of something, I was convinced that I had already seen something like that somewhere, only some detail was missing, something was lacking on that face.

"What do you keep looking for? I told you, didn't I? We only have left ones!" the shop assistant roared at the old hag as the latter gazed at the shoe in bewilderment.

"Yeah, I heard you, only I would like to also know which shop received the matching right ones. Or can we get them only in the afterlife?" the woman laughed to herself.

"You can go and search there if you want," guffawed the assistant. "Don't touch that! It's not for sale!" she said to me once again, immediately wiping the smile off her face.

It seemed I was losing my mind: the head appeared to have moved a little, blinked its eyes, and gave me a ferocious, evil look; now I knew what was missing on that face: the fake black moustache was elsewhere, did he lose it somewhere or did he shave it off? Oh, what the hell!

"I am keeping that for myself," said the assistant, "I found it myself and fed it, and it already c... really, it's none of your business! I want to have my own devil and that's it! I told you once that it's not for sale, and that's enough!"

"My God," the old woman crossed herself, "how awful it looks! Who would even want to buy it?" she said. "It's better to walk around in two left shoes than to take that into your home...."

The head turned in a strange way, as if there was a sharp pain in its neck, as if the collar was too tight or something; without the moustache, it was just as frightening as with it. There was no difference.

In front of me, along the entire expanse of the giant green field, yet another metamorphosis was taking place: people were appearing here and there, like seeds being scattered in the field. There were more and more of them — the black, monk-black seeds; I didn't see their faces — it's possible there weren't any; the people-seeds kept multiplying in the green expanse, to the point that the green couldn't be seen anymore. Those people-seeds could probably hear what the speaker was saying to them from his ridiculously tiny podium, for they stood in silence and appeared to listen; only I couldn't hear anything and could not distinguish between the heavy breathing of the crowd and the heavy breathing of the speaker. At that moment, he was also clothed in all black. It was something like a judge's or a monk's robe.

I finally saw the end of the unplugged microphone cord: it recoiled like a snake right next to my feet; I wanted to step back, but at that point it was impossible to do so: the people-seeds became more numerous with every moment, they squeezed me from all sides, they silently pressed onto each other; for just a split second the face of the bald girl seemed to appear before me, a white, very white wreath was now shining on her head, and this was an odd sight — a wreath on a completely bald head; the vision lasted only a brief moment, the crowd of people-seeds quivered, sighed, groaned — and its black river swallowed me up, closing in over my head.

from ABOUT A GIRL WHO DREW ON SAND

by Sofia Maidanska

Translated by Alla Perminova

1. Prelude

I'M RETURNING TO THE SEA. JUST AS A YEAR AGO, JUST AS TEN YEARS ago, something compels me to return to this shore over and over again. It might be the power of gravity of the common salty blood that burns in our bodies.

The sea and I used to be twin brothers, born on the same day, and from the same mother. We resembled each other like two drops of seawater, and the white crests of our forelocks, faded in the sun, would be tussled simultaneously by the warm wind.

When the weather was foul, our eyes would darken all the way to the horizon, but on a sunny day, they would become so clear that tiny imps could be seen, jumping with their hands on their hips on the green bottom.

The sea and I used to run naked to and fro among the flying sparks of agile minnows, without feeling ashamed in front of either a shaggy stray-dog — a watchful lord over these shores, or old fishermen with dried up copper-colored faces, who were sitting in a circle, mending mesh in silence. No one paid any attention to us. We were grappling on the damp coastal sand, and then, exhausted, we would lie next to each other and laugh, because the sun was tickling our feet.

Now we've grown apart. The sea doesn't recognize me. It resembles a heavy tablet made of lapis lazuli with undeciphered scripts of a forgotten civilization; I, gradually growing into the ground, resemble a stone replica of a man from Easter Island.

Now every time I try to leave it at least a small part of the stuff accumulated over the years, piling up in front of my eyes, separating me from the world in which my life began. The debris of rusty victories, broken in frantic races, stick out of the pile in all directions. Heaps of paper smolder there, covered with my writing that determined my fate, together with crumpled, worn banknotes — it took me a while to learn how to save them up.

I dump all this into the sea. I even empty my pockets, out of which lottery tickets fall, along with spent cartridges, and scratched coins. I dump all this into the sea... Let it rest there in the unreachable depths of the sea, alongside pirate ships loaded with gold...

Hullo! The wave that so solemnly closed up over the giant of the Titanic smacks me heavily in the face; the wave washes my face with a sonorous slap; and here I stand again covered with my own mistakes and miscues from head to toe.

II. THE ENCOUNTER

"Oh, what have you done?! You've completely broken the sun! How is it supposed to shine now — you've totally trampled its rays! Stop! How can you tread on the trees and houses?!"

The desperate voice of a child makes me stop. I turn back and see a sun-tanned girl, as if she were carved out of a piece of amber, standing a step away from me. A warm, soft light goes through a delicate body and gently touches closely cropped blond hair with its glowing beams.

Only now I notice that while roaming along the shore I had ruined the child's drawing. The deep impressions of my footprints destroyed the entire small world drawn with a twig on the sand.

"I'm sorry. I didn't mean to... I... I just wasn't looking where I was going..."

She scrutinized me with suspicion:

"Well, you didn't! Your eyes hid behind your sunglasses..."

"I'm sure you'll make a better drawing... just let the wave smooth the sand..." I smile, sheepishly embarrassed.

"What will the sea say when the wave brings it these drawings; it will think — I've drawn a war... Because everything comes to life and becomes real there..."

"I wonder if you made up this game by yourself?..."

"I haven't made anything up..."

For some reason or other I hastily take off my glasses and meet the open look of her large dark gray eyes.

"That's true...," she adds in a very low voice.

Meanwhile, the waves rolled to and fro until they reached the drawings...

What will the sea say when they come to life?...

III. DAUGHTER OF THE SEA

Somewhere on the mainland there was a small village left behind, in one of the small houses in which I rented a tiny, low-ceilinged room called "a separate room" by the landlady.

And here at the very edge of the split I'm alone. I'm overwhelmed with the desire to dissolve in this air, brewed from the sea grass, in the water growing into my skin with its sharp salt crystals.

When I was a little boy my parents moved from one land to another. In a year I forgot the language of the people with whom I spent my childhood. And now, listening to the way it sounds, I painfully strain my memory, because I used to know all that, because every word that got into my blood long ago, calls me back to this language, the way odors of a wild primeval forest call a tamed animal back to its savage nature. I'm trying hard to cross the line of oblivion, but I can't.

The same way with this air, sea, with these fish and birds. I can't get along with them. They don't understand me.

Shells, combed together by the sea, are scattered all around me. I can't avoid them. Stepping on them I hear a dry crackle as if I were walking on lime-covered bones of tiny animals, bleached by the sun, who long ago left my planet for good.

After billions of years, the shoreless chalky hollow of this sea will be covered with feather grass, having compressed the shells I crushed. There won't be any trace of my footprints though…

Thus, it turns out I'm not alone here on the split. The girl, who draws on the sand, is approaching me. Her bare feet touch the wave that splays her with large drops. A tender breeze slightly lifts her white nightgown, and the girl seems to be floating like a small light sailboat.

"Good morning!" She greeted me. "Do you have any secrets here too?"

"Not any more… I gave all my secrets away to people long ago."

"Why are you here?"

"I love solitude"

"Solitude?… What is that?"

"That is when you're alone in the whole world…"

"Are you alone here?"

"I was."

"What about the sea?"

"The sea's not a human being."

"That isn't true, the sea's a human being… Just bigger and stronger than you."

"The sea may be stronger, but it's not a human being."

"But I say, it is. It's human in all ways."

"Really?! How do you know that?…"

"I know, because I'm his Daughter…"

"You're making things up a bit…"

"You don't believe me, do you? I'm not lying to you…" And suddenly she asks: "Tell me, do you have children?"

"No, I don't."

"He didn't use to have children either."

"Who?"

"The sea. It never had any children, and I never had a father… Then I asked him: "Be my daddy, and I'll be your daughter." The sea was so delighted that he gave me five stones with holes in them as a present."

"Who's your mother?"

"My mom is very beautiful. She went far-far away to make some money. Granny said that I was found there. Granny said I was so pale, so translucent, maybe like glass, that she took me to live with her; and my mother stayed there to go on making that money. Why would she need it if I had been found there?..."

The Daughter of the Sea lowers her head and becomes silent. Two teardrops run across her cheeks and fall onto the sand, burning it with flying sparks.

"Don't cry. Your mom will come back soon..."

She can barely stop crying:

"The sea says so too... He knows... He delivers letters I write on the sand to my mom..."

"Do you already know how to write?"

"No... I don't know the alphabet yet... but the sea knows how to read... Once I asked my mom in a letter to send me a doll wearing a garland with ribbons. The sea passed the letter over to my mom, and I got a parcel with the doll I had been dreaming of for so long..."

The girl starts drawing some signs, known only to her, on the sand. They interweave like seaweed or a vine... Her lips move uttering something barely audible. First I catch separate words out of this whisper, then — whole sentences: "Come... Never ever abandon me. I want my hair to be as long as yours... And when I'm ill, don't let granny lie to me telling me you've come... In reality, a nurse pricks me with a needle... I know — you would never hurt me..."

Meanwhile, a wave folds up the letter with its calm thin fingers, and I see those quaint characters resembling seaweed or a vine nimbly spread over the emerald surface of the sea...

The Daughter sits down on a stone near the water and takes a long look into the distance; her eyes follow the letter that disappears behind the skyline. Suddenly she says:

"Since we're alone here — I'll tell you my secret. But you have to swear by the blood of the sea, that you'll never tell it to anybody, even to your granny."

from THE EARTHQUAKE

by Sofia Maidanska

Translated by Alla Perminova

A TINY GOLDEN LION FROM THE CIGARETTE CASE, FORGOTTEN BY Daniel and attached by me to the foyer mirror, froze in anticipation. With a sharp turn of its head, menacingly bearing its fangs, it stands there lonely and proud right at the edge of a looking-glass desert with its eyes following the flickering human shadows floating through like ghosts, leaving no trace...

Daniel. Just as in the ancient Armenian legend, he would cross the dark and treacherous lake every night to get to the lighthouse on my rocky, deserted island.

It was I who extinguished the light in the lighthouse.

I

"...The problem is — we've cut the umbilical cord. During the nine months before birth a human lives in a mother's womb, feeding on her juice just like a tree does on the sap of the soil. After birth and the first experience of food, day-by-day humans devour more and more of it, and their appetite grows together with them. The human body turns into a food-processing factory, with only a hundredth of it being useful, while the rest of it — this includes tons and tons of shit, pardon the expression, excrement is flushed into toilets and dumped into outhouses. The brain toils at hunting for grub, as well as inventing a perfect machine, a kind of perpetuum mobile for a total waste-free depletion of natural resources. Everything is consumable here: bread, meat, milk, the forest, stone, water, coal, oil, gas, uranium, ferrous and nonferrous metals, and lots of other assorted stuff, not to mention alcohol, tobacco, and drugs. Fancy that! This "factory" works round the clock without weekends and vacation off, with the only purpose to digest overnight what was eaten and drunk during the day (and while digesting to contribute a little something to the propagation of the species). Our "combine" is made of the liver, spleen, heart, kidneys, stomach, and so forth. It's burning out right before your eyes. Look at yourselves — at these bags under your eyes, sagging chin, wrinkled turkey neck, premature gray hair, mouth full of artificial teeth — doesn't it testify to the fact that the game maybe isn't worth the effort? If humans could invent a way of feeding on the pure energy of the soil and the sun, just as trees do, they would be able to prolong their lives by hundreds of years and they would actually become immortal. This is the topic to which my science-fiction novel is dedicated..."

"Don't you think it's high time to cut the umbilical cord?..."

"Hey girls, don't go. The most interesting part of the story is coming up — as a biologist I'm going to tell you about the experiment now..." Yagdar's narrow eyes throw two laser beams at us, transfixing immobile Grazhyna and me to the wall next to the door.

"Yagdar-boy, don't forget about us when you do your experiment, use us as guinea pigs. I hope we'll be the first to live by the Holy Spirit alone," Grazhyna warbled, tilting her curly auburn-colored head. "But for now let us go, we're starving. All the cafeterias will be closed in half an hour, and you'll lose your great experimental subjects for good."

Yagdar kills us with the lasers of his contempt:

"I won't tell you anything, go — you're missing a lot, but now it's your problem. I wonder why they pay you a stipend..."

"For the harmful nature of certain literary works," I snap back, and Grazhyna and I find ourselves outside the door.

There's dirty December slush outside. The gloom mixed with thick suffocating smog, erupting from the exhaust pipe craters of eight-wheelers and refrigerated trucks wrings out caustic tears from our eyes.

Bespattered cars dash by, stubbornly not avoiding any puddle; a heavy wave rolling over the curb reaches the walls of the buildings. Grim people lining up to buy oranges and lemons suspiciously watch every new customer — to make sure that by chance someone might trick everyone and grab stuff out of turn while scrutinizing the "colonial goods."

To get in line or not to get in line… — that is the question. Greek gods damn these Greek oranges, it's too crowded here. Moreover, it's beastly cold.

There is another crowd at the trolley-bus stop, there's the same grim patient waiting overloaded with bags and "avoskas" [net shopping bags], out of which oranges and lemons (evidently the ones from the line) peer.

"Let's go by subway because we won't be able to get on a trolley-bus here." Like a fluffy pussy-cat Grazhyna squeamishly jumps over big deep puddles, trying to shake off slushy snow stuck to her boots.

"I've had two pairs of boots ruined here this month. What do they sprinkle their sidewalks with? No pig's skin can survive it."

Again there is another line near the subway station; this time they're lining up to get ice-cream. People covered with the blizzard, grabbing several chocolate ice-cream cones, start scarfing them down right away. Pablo Neruda was right when he claimed that a people capable of eating so much ice-cream in the cold was destined to win World War II.

The thin serpent's tongue of an escalator draws a bustling human swarm into the branchy maw of a giant underground hydra. Pushed by the passengers behind us, we push the ones in front of us into the sausage skin of the wagon. Here, as always, are exhausted women, who nap while sitting, swaying like Chinese huts in the wind.

"Next station!..." As if tossed up by an invisible spring, one of them leaps to her feet like a sleep-walker shouldering her way through the hearts, livers, and lungs of others to the door on which there's a sign that says: "Don't lean against the door!" Even if everybody were *lean,* there wouldn't be enough room here!...

Sodom!... Sodom!... There lies murdered Pazolini on the beach. Whores run the world.

I can feel a young man behind my back, pressing himself against me more intensely than might be expected in such a crowded place. It's good that we're getting of the train at the next station. What a maniac! He did squeeze my butt...

"You know, Grazhyno, a walk is better than this kind of trip. After these kind of "hugs" I feel like a bitch in a pile of shit."

"You do too?... It's group sex on wheels then."

* * *

We're dreaming of being invited to a restaurant. Meanwhile a counter lady is making coffee for us in a small coffee-shop.

"Faina-baby, do you happen to have a box of chocolates? I desperately need it!" A waiter comes running up to her.

"Nothing other than this junk was delivered today." The counter lady gives a fierce glance at orderly ranks of chocolate bunnies wrapped in colored foil behind the showcase.

"Check with Sima. She may have something left from yesterday."

"She's got the same bunnies."

I feel someone lightly touch my elbow. I turn back and see Daniel.

"I saw you enter, let's go — there's a seat next to us."

A lost country boy with the pose of Paris. Though, Paris also used to be a shepherd.

"Daniel, there are two of us..."

"Oh, I'm sorry — You're with Grazhyna...anyway, that's ok, come on, I'll take care of it."

A bright brunet with eyes half the size of her face, which under the weight of long lashes seemed to be about to close up like mussels, cast a glance, thickly flavored with Oriental spices, at us. Her cigarette had just gone out, and several hands with lighters flocked together to her narrow wrist with a heavy silver bracelet wound around it. Grazhyna and I sat without stirring opposite to her, staring at this wonder of Armenian modern.

"Cleopatra has come back from Australia today," Daniel embarrassingly stammers. "He...she performed for our...there...there a big and affluent community lives there... These are my countrymen...they came to meet Cleopatra..."

Daniel glanced askance at me and, perplexed, turned his eyes away from me.

Poor boy, he must also be in love with this cow-eyed beauty. Can you compare yourself to those three sitting next to her? Just look at the shrewd silence of their perfectly sculpted masculine faces. Speechless, they keep gazing at her, piercing with the depth of a thought untainted by a word, showering her with old-testament passion. What a powerful confidence in every move, what an impeccable casual style of clothing, this checkered kerchief showing from under an unbuttoned dazzling white shirt. No, Daniel, you've got no chances, and I'm sorry...

"Anna, don't you recognize me?..."

I am taken aback, since one of those three with a kerchief on his neck is reducing me to ashes with an anthracite gaze.

"How could I fail to recognize you?..." Oh Lord, who is he, where did we meet; my visual memory is playing mean tricks with me again. If no one calls out his name right now, I'm lost.

"Armen, give me another bottle to celebrate the occasion." A sudden rattle escaped the shrewd and silent bowels of one of Cleopatra's vassals — a stout bearded man.

"Such things are unforgettable, Armen," I sign with relief...and suddenly upon recollecting the incident can hardly keep from laughing. I seem to have overdone it, since the black fire in his eyes flared up so violently that the corners of the kerchief on his neck began to smoke.

"You're on fire!..." Cleopatra cried out in fright.

"It's nothing." Armen carelessly replied. "I stroked a lighter by accident."

Having extinguished the fire on his chest with two fingers, he nervously takes a cigarette to his lips and inhales.

"Can the moment I've been looking forward to for so long be defiled with their cheap swill? Daniel you seem to have a bottle of ours, a vintage one. Don't begrudge us, your editor will do with their raw Moscow vodka, they don't know much about refined drinks. The only thing that matters to them is to get trashed."

"Do…I begrudge you…I was going to offer you this myself…" Daniel obediently pulls a bottle out of his bag. "Here it is…" And in a very low voice: "How can you say that… have I ever begrudged you?…"

"Give it to me. I'll uncork it," Armen deftly uncorks the bottle. "This cognac was aged in barrels made from the planks of Noah's ark, the remains of which were found by scientists at the top of Mt. Ararat." While joking, he pours the liquor into glasses. "Right after you sip it, you start feeling *every living thing of all flesh, two of every sort* kicking, swimming, and flying in your blood. Oh, Almighty God of pairing! Anna, you used to be so unapproachable then. Oh these subtle women's tricks of yours… Do you remember us together as a whole group of students going to buy a doll for my little Maria? Everybody advised something different, but I bought the one you chose, Anna…"

The waiter comes up to our table.

"What would you like to order, girls?"

Armen hands over the menu to us; he is a gem; he is the embodiment of exuberant generosity.

"We were going to buy the full three-course dinner," Grazhyna shyly mumbles.

"Come on! What three-course dinner! We're free from any three-course complexes! What will we have for an appetizer? Pressed caviar?… Red caviar?… Pressed is better, and crabs, and "stolychny" salad, and champignons in Polish sauce. Thank you! What will our main course be? Do you mind if I order a brisket? It's very delicious here. What? It's too much for you. Don't say another word! Two briskets, please, besides the ones we've ordered. For dessert? Do you have "Prague" torte? A torte, ice-cream, fruit, champagne, and, of course, Turkish coffee, please.

Grazhyna loosened up after a small glass of Armenian cognac. Now and then her ringing laughter, like the sparks of a sparkler, strewn over our table. The bearded man was trying hard to hit on her.

"Do you mean to say, ha-ha-ha, that Black guy is also Armenian!? You won't say that about me. I'm one of the pale faced. Did you use to have green eyes like me? When did they turn black? Genocide?.... well...I see...am I a paragon of pure beauty? Oh, no. I'm Polish girl... ha-ha-ha. I'll think about it... but...everyone eventually returns to their own Ararat...

The bearded man makes Grazhyna laugh again, and once again she strews out the sparks of the sparkler...

Cleopatra puffs out thin strands of smoke, which, upon expanding, coil into Secession-style bouquets. She languidly pecks cornelian beads of caviar out of a crystal bowl.

Sprawling on the chair, and sipping champagne, Daniel pretends sweet boredom. Only from time to time, when I look at him, he embarrassingly casts down his eyes. No, Daniel, you still fail to fake the satiety of a joyful life. It was only yesterday when you came down from the mountains. But, that's ok. You'll catch up all you've missed among those impertinent? guys.

"Anna, I still remember your talk about the poetics of folk laments. It's been ten years since then...Does it say anything to you?..."

A nationwide folklore conference in Moscow. Ten years have passed, and I want to lament.

"I'll lean against a cold wall, but it won't make me warm..."

"You even remember quotes from my student-day babbling, don't you?..."

"Anna, I remember you... I was longing to become your wall then..." He grabs me by my hand..."

"Let's get out of here. Let's go to your place. We shouldn't part like this..."

"Armen, have you forgotten that the old man is waiting for us?..." Suddenly Daniel wakes up and, switching into Armenian, rapidly and excitedly says something to Armen.

"Stop that, another time..." Armen also switches into Armenian. The clanking of crossed swords could be heard in their conversation.

66

The closed mussels of Cleopatra's eye-lashes shuddered. She looks at us with eyes of otherworldly indifference.

Those two, sitting next to her, every now and then butt into the conversation, repeating the same word. It's weird, but all this combined together gradually acquires harmony and even the euphony of a quartet.

"I'm sorry, thanks for everything, but I've got to go now…" I elbow Grazhyna's side. She seems to have taken a liking to the bearded man.

"Do you…want to go now?…"

"They're waiting for me at the radio station studio. Haven't I mentioned it to you?…"

"It seems to me you haven't…"

"I must have forgotten then. The recording session is in half an hour…"

"And I'm free today…"

"Ok. See you at the dormitory."

Only now Armen noticed that I was leaving the table.

"Wait. Where are you going? I wanted…"

"I'm sorry. Gotta dash… Hope to see you again…in ten years…"

"You're kidding! We've just agreed with Daniel to come to your place tonight… together with Cleopatra and my friends…"

"Have you? You seemed to be arguing…"

"Come on. We are just in high spirits. See you in the evening, then. Do you hear me, Anna? I'll come over…get the coffee ready…"

I'm stumbling my way among the tables heaped up with bottles and dishes in the posh restaurant. The gaggle of geniuses is in full swing. They happily plunge into intoxication mixed with obscene curses, poetry, cigarette smoke, and syncopated rhythms of a cachectic pianist pounding out a ragtime swing.

"I drank from my father's skull — eff your mother!…" A drunken poet sobs and falls onto the bosom of a gorgeous young woman.

I leave the Masonic Lodge…

MY AUTOBIOGRAPHY

by Liudmyla Taran

Translated by Michael M. Naydan

I'M IN A VERY TOUCHY SITUATION: THE PUBLISHERS OF THIS BOOK asked me to write an autobiographical piece for it. It's as though in a clear-cut way it will prepare the reader for reception of the later texts.

At first I refused to have anything to do with their idea. I was motivated by the fact that all my short prose pieces in this way or that are autobiographical and, as they say, let your American readers, when they take the book in their hands, simply take the trouble to read the texts themselves. However, the publishers insisted and managed to convince me anyway. Of course, when in my prose works I can in this or that way hide behind my main characters, enter into the changing shadow of images, then in an autobiography I need to define certain things in a straightforward manner — and this, it turns out, is not so simple.

So, a bit about myself. I was born within the borders of the historical Ukrainian lands, in the Lviv region, in the small town of Brody, known also as a settlement of not just Ukrainians, but also Poles and Jews, of whom there were a lot till World War II. As a monument to the latter, there remains the so-called Great Synagogue, built in 1742 and destroyed during the war.

My family was not entirely typical for this area. My mother — was of local stock, a Ukrainian, a Galician woman. Her ancestors come from a village near Brody. And my father — was of Russian origin and among those who, after that war, remained here.

That's a separate story — the acquaintance of my mother with my father. She at first feared him like fire because he was a "Russky." I need to explain a few things in this context. To put it in simple terms, Western Ukraine, Galicia, which was part of Poland till the war, was annexed in 1939 to the Ukrainian Soviet Socialist Republic that was part of the Soviet Union. At first the Galicians were joyful over that declaration, which was proclaimed a "unification" that had been dreamt about for centuries. However, when the punitive organs of the USSR destroyed and tortured the people after that "golden autumn," after the end of the war thousands of Ukrainians, the Galicians, were afraid of everything linked with the land with its capital in Moscow.

In order to increase its influence in Western Ukraine, the authorities called for a mass migration of people here not only of those born in Soviet Ukraine, but also from Russia, giving the latter certain privileges. In this way my future father ended up in Brody. He together with his friends had been sent here from Saratov to work. He turned out to be an affable person, tolerant, and not some kind of wild beast of prey, and after protracted hesitation, my mother, who couldn't withstand his youthful persistence and her own feelings, married him. Her parents weren't entirely supportive of her choice, but they were fearful of objecting to it precisely because they were afraid of repressions. In time after getting married, my Russian father learned our language and began to speak it nearly without an accent. Though the attitude to him among the local people was cautious just because the regime's repressions continued. Thus, as usual, ordinary people suffer because of the sins of others.

As for me, I grew up in a particular atmosphere: children of the local inhabitants on the street would call me "Russky girl," and children born from the marriages of the Russians imported to our town called me a "Banderite." Bandera was the head of the Organization of Ukrainian Nationalists, who was in charge of the national liberation movement in Galicia against Hitler's and the Soviet armies.

So, from my early childhood, it was not that simple and easy to form my self-identity. In fact, my sensitivity made me feel alien both among the "aliens" as well as among "my own." Later, at a more mature age, much went by and was overcome. In early childhood and my youth, that bifurcation of me, thrown onto me by society, often led to me suffering, the reason for which I couldn't then grasp. It was precisely these nuances you can read in several of my prose pieces.

In the end I'm writing this autobiographical piece also because my "history as a woman" is quite typical for my time. The American reader through my story can at least partially grasp how women lived in one of the lands of Eastern Europe till this day, crossing into the twenty-first century.

Another key, dramatic and sensitive moment of my biography is linked to later times.

At first my life after completing high school was more or less happy. I received my degree from the Department of Philology of the University of Lviv and returned to Brody where I worked in a library for adults. This was the time of the so-called stagnation — homogenization, when the average population existed approximately under equal material conditions with a minimal amount of social support.

I married in 1984, and the next year, exactly one year before the Chornobyl catastrophe, I gave birth to my first child, a girl, and right at the beginning of the existence of independent Ukraine in 1991 — a second girl. My husband, with whom our relationship turned out to be extremely taxing from the very beginning, left me at a very difficult and painful time: I was still breastfeeding my younger girl. He left me for another woman, abandoning me with two children without the means to survive. In Ukraine at that time aid to mothers was so paltry that I wasn't able to feed my two children or myself in even the most modest way. For the first year of my younger child's life, my parents helped me survive, though they also could barely support themselves. And I was forced to go to work as a cleaning woman at the train station cafeteria, which may have been the last one left in our town. Though I had a higher education, the job in the library didn't let me make ends meet, and the job in the cafeteria not only gave me a steady salary, but

also the opportunity to bring food home for my children. That food —
was mostly *nedoyidky* (leftovers). This is a Ukrainian word that means
not completely eaten food. These *nedoyidky* were left sometimes by
the customers. I scooped them off from plates into jars and at home
I heated them up or recooked them. I gave them to my children and
ate them myself when something was left after they had eaten. For me,
an "A" student in my studies at school and at the university, work as a
cleaning woman, whose job was to wipe tables, wash dishes, and wash
the floor in the entire building, including the kitchen, after closing
time, was, of course, not just stressful, but a catastrophe. This was the
hopelessness to which the situation had driven me, a difficult time for
everyone, my fate. Ukrainians in general often submit to fate: most
often first and foremost this means doom.

To this day I don't know how I survived. Just thanks to my parents, to
the help of friends, and to the children, whom I couldn't let die. I was
never a fighter: I didn't have that kind of character, I wasn't a certain
type of woman — something like the well-known Scarlett O'Hara
from *Gone with the Wind*. To survive at any price — that wasn't in my
nature. Not dignity, not self-affirmation, not the spirit of competition
with fate governed me, but elementary fear. Even fear before suicide,
about which I, of course, sometimes thought, but which I, in the end,
could not allow, just taking my children into consideration. Their
eyes always stood before me — joyful and sad; often they were the
eyes of hungry children. This — is especially intolerable. And in
those moments when I recollected my school years and study at the
university in the wondrous age-old city of Lviv, where I had many
friends, where I wrote poems and had dreams that someday I would
become a writer — it seemed to me that it all happened not with me;
it was as though I had read it about someone else, because I already
was hopelessly weary of life, like a hundred-year-old woman. I felt like
falling asleep and not waking up, or falling asleep and waking up in a
completely different, happy life. Ukrainians are dreamers, even during
the most unsuitable time for that. And maybe it's just a myth....

And here, when my younger daughter turned two, and the older one was already eight, I finally grew bold. Again, out of hopelessness. That was 1993, thousands of Ukrainian, if not the majority — of Galicians, legally and illegally, made their way across the border, with the majority working there illegally.

I left my daughters with my parents, borrowed some money. I had to pay for the tourist trip, a foreign passport, and a visa, and also for the future job arrangements — and I went to Italy. I was given instructions about it, that's why I knew: as soon as the Austrian border guards and customs officers returned my passport after stamping it, I needed to keep it with me and not return it to the tour group leader. You, esteemed readers, may be surprised: what am I talking about here? The fact of the matter is that according to our unwritten rules, all tourists need to turn in their passports to the guide for safekeeping. He or she returns those documents to each person only when they return to the homeland. Yes, this is a violation of human rights, but it apparently is supposed to restrain pseudotourists, potential economic migrants, from running off, from the attempt to remain abroad illegally.

So, I didn't return the passport. Our group leader kept threatening that she'll report me to the police — but she couldn't do that while the group was on the trip. You can imagine what I endured until we all made our way to Rome.

From my childhood, the dream image of the Eternal City will always remain clouded for me. I should have been overjoyed from the realization of my longtime dream, and saw everything and perceived it all through my inner tears.

No one met me at the Piazza di Spagna as had been arranged earlier, and for which I had paid big money in advance previously in Brody. No one answered the phone number they gave me though I called every ten minutes, even during the evening. Fear and despair shackled me.

Our tour group had a hotel paid in advance for two nights in a little town near Rome. The owner turned out to be a Pole. Crawling on my knees, I begged him to hire me for any kind of work.

I prayed that I just wouldn't end up in a bordello. Though, it seemed, it had to have been frightening just to look at me: I was exhausted from lack of sleep and hopelessness. At home I had heard something about stories of women cunningly and insidiously lured into traps. The disenfranchised were kept in "white slavery," forced into prostitution and into taking drugs, ultimately leading to suicide. Every other young woman, which I only discovered later through the La Strada organization, who went to find work abroad, who agreed to work as a waitress or dancer, ended up believing all kinds of "agents." And regarding the tragic stories heard in Ukraine about "white slavery," almost every other woman thought this way: bad things happened to someone else, naive and stupid, and nothing like that will ever happen to me. But — it did happen. Those who show resistance, unsubmissive ones, are brutally beaten and raped — just to break their will. The female clients of some or other seemingly legal company called Fortuna can end up on Cyprus, in Lebanon or in the United Arab Emirates — and disappear, often forever, from their family. I found out about all this later. If I would have heard about these kind of instances at home, I hardly would have traveled abroad for work: I'm timid by nature.

I won't relate the details of my "work arrangement" in an entirely different hotel, where the aforementioned Pole seemingly assisted me in getting a job. I'll only say that difficult trials awaited me. I didn't give up my passport, but it ended up basically costing me rape by my "Ukrainian brethren." These two, whose faces I want to forget forever... what didn't they do to make me hate men for my entire life. They did everything to me that came into their heads with their dirty hair. The scent of sperm haunted me long after — I couldn't eat certain foods: it seemed to me that they reeked of it, along with their urine, sorry for the naturalistic description.

I survived only because right away, because right away when the violations began, it was as if I turned myself off and seemingly with someone else's or dead eyes I looked at what they did with my body.

Really, it seemed to me that my soul was above me, somewhere from the ceiling watching over my shell, my abandoned body, that was "being worked over" by two unshaven, reaking types. The most horrifying was that fact that they were "ours," "kith and kin."

I later recalled the stories heard from my fellow Ukrainians especially about our Galician women, who, after the "second Soviets," that is after 1945, ended up in prison camps just on suspicion for being messengers with our "forest brothers," the Organization of Ukrainian Nationalists, who fought against the Soviet regime. And then I understood — only God knows what they had to suffer through there, what kind of violation of the body and soul, and not only hunger or heavy labor. "Ours" were also there... The history of my people caught up with me in the most dramatic moments of my life.

Already later, when I kept turning my thoughts to that rape scene, I understood: in order to neutralize it somehow, I first needed to draw it out "into the sunlight," and not shove it into my subconscious where it would ruin me from the inside. I had to gradually and completely "redigest" it, "cook it again." Moreover — it was necessary to treat what I had endured... with irony, with humor. Only in that way would the opportunity appear to survive as a being of full value, a person. It was unbelievable, impossible. But little by little I achieved some of that.

First, I remembered that when my girlfriend and I during our university years fell in love with the same guy, we began to dream about "amour de trois." Here you have your "amour de trois" and two "suitors" — I said to myself many times, sadly laughing. Dreams come true, but somehow in a topsy-turvy way — like the negative image on an antediluvian roll of film.

Later I taught myself to see my body in the rape — as though it were a little frog with long stretched-out front legs, crushed by the wheels of cars. There its empty carton lying on the highway — even its innards long ago have dried in the sun, and nothing hurts the little frog any more.

An original picture, you'll say? But I laughed till I cried, when I imagined myself to be like this little frog, who already doesn't care any more. This kind of depersonalization came later, of course. And in a strange way it saved me from death. But I was depressed — that's another story, described by me in the short story "Flycatcher."

Actualized recollections about the fact that one of the family members on my mother's side from central Ukraine endured German captivity also saved me. His seemingly already forgotten stories came to the surface: how, driven to the West, he spent the night in half-ruined hole-filled stables without a roof — in the rain and frost. Many times he had to sleep standing up, and then walk in a column that the Nazis kept driving forward. My relative relayed all that with a certain amount of pride that they only trusted him to divide the rations –when each one had only a little bit of half-baked bread with bristles.

And my uncle, my grandmother's brother, had the experience of surviving a concentration camp, after which he had two-thirds of his stomach removed. "But he survived," I thought, and I decided to survive for the sake of my children.

The history of my people caught up with me at every step, like the Holodomor, the annihilation of Ukrainians by starvation in 1932-33. Galicians only heard about that awful death "under the Soviets," and already in the 1990s all our newspapers were writing about it. Some of the communists to this day assert that it didn't happen... But first to speak about the planned and executed murder of millions of Ukrainians was the Congress of the United States, where a congressional committee examined it.

All of this, as strange as it seems, helped me survive and not lose my mind. In my search for work, my basic bread, I was ready to take on any kind of work and never got sick. It was that way, they say, during the war, when even chronic illnesses disappeared....

In the end I got lucky. Or I simply implored God, on whom alone my hope remained. When I'll write about this separately: how, when being brought up as an atheist in Soviet schools, I was baptized in the Greek-Catholic Rite, I truthfully started to believe in God over there, abroad, in my hour of hopelessness. A usual, typical story.

However, I ended up in a villa of a certain family in a village near Milan where I had a traditional job for female Ukrainian migrant workers: I was caregiver for an old, sickly Italian woman. After all that I had experienced earlier: rape, hunger, sleeping on a park bench — to end up under the roof of a respectable Italian family was paradise! It turned out it was not difficult at all for me to take care of the old woman. Here experience and knowledge obtained in the university, where we had obligatory nursing classes, came to good use: I even had a certificate for specialization in nursing.

I got settled, learned the language — basic conversational Italian, of course. The Italians were very pleased with me; they were sincere and open, just like Ukrainians. I finally began to send more or less decent sums of money to my parents in Brody. (A system worked out by the migrant workers, until official channels for the transfer of money, is worthy of separate attention: I speak a bit about that in my short story "Undergarment").

And here — joy and unpleasantness at the same time: the son of my signora, who had hired me to take care of his mother, fell in love with me. When I understood this, I strove to keep myself as far away from him as possible. He had a family: a nice wife and four children. But because of my thirty-three years of age and the fact that I was a natural blonde (I inherited that from my father), in the end, his passion and my understandable need for feelings made our heads spin. Though I don't know how we hid our affair that remained unnoticed for nearly a year. As everyone knows, everything secret sooner or later becomes obvious. I was forced to leave that family — in scandal and in tears. However, it was Marco himself who took me to a different home where I took care of an older woman in the same way.

Somehow after returning from Italy to my native Ukraine, I was vacationing at a certain landlady's place in a resort town in the Carpathians. And there I came across a strange couple: a swarthy man, who was constantly silent, following after his wife. I exchanged greetings with the man in the morning, and he just laughed and nodded his head. The landlady explained: that the husband of the nice Ukrainian girl — is an Italian, whom she brings to Ukraine every summer. She married him, laboring in Italy in the same way as I did. Her Sergio divorced his wife, though it cost him a pile of money, many problems, and his nerves.

And I could have had a similar happy ending! — I remember I thought that with a mixed feeling of envy and sorrow.

The two years working in Italy flew past, despite the fact that at the very beginning of my working "career" I only thought about returning home. It's possible, I would have remained there for some more time, but I already was missing my daughters. They were growing up without me, though with my parents, and I was afraid they'd become estranged from me. So many dramas, and even tragedies, every second or third family in Galicia endures just because of a lengthy amount of time spent apart! Several of my short stories, especially "Greetings from Naples" and "Life on Video" were written under the influence of events that I witnessed.

My story in this respect is also very typical. However, today my advantage is in the fact that I have a good job at home. It gives me the opportunity not only to receive a decent, steady wage, but also to travel around the world. However, in a certain way, my previous unhappiness or the unhappiness of others favored me. Or, as the saying goes — there's no bad without some good. In which way?

I'm working in the regional office of the international organization La Strada, which is charged to prevent human trafficking. For this kind of work I turned out to be a useful figure not only through my knowledge of Italian; my management qualities, which appeared unexpectedly to me; and also by the fact that I myself was in the skin of a woman who endured it. However, as they say, in order to know what boiling means, you don't have to dip your hand in boiling water... But my presentations during training sessions before women turn out to be very effective precisely because I endured what I want to warn them against.

For me personally my advantage turned out to be in the fact that from time to time I can sit at the computer and express everything that has seethed in my soul. That is, I began to write prose. Once long ago I dreamt of becoming a writer... Several of my books came out in Ukraine. And today I finally can allow myself to write not just about women migrant workers in Italy....

...This summer I was in Portugal as a tourist. On one of the central squares of Lisbon I unexpectedly met two Ukrainian women from Chernivtsi (that's a stylish city in Western Ukraine with an unusual history, where Ukrainians, Germans, Romanians, and Jews coexisted, and where afterward, until World War II, a particular multicultural aura had been created, which, in fact, no longer exists today).

I spoke with those women for over three hours, without immediately admitting that I'm affiliated with La Strada. But they were working in Portugal legally. They had been in the country for seven years already. Their grown-up children came to visit them. However, the women from Chernivtsi assured me that they're planning on returning home.

I felt ill at ease because of the fact that I was lucky enough to "jump" into a different status than they were in. After meeting them, I already couldn't look at Lisbon, at Porto, at the Atlantic Ocean, or at Cabo da Roca just with the eyes of a tourist. Everything I endured revealed itself as if it happened yesterday. I cried, and people often asked me why I looked so sad.

My life story is typical, though not entirely. It seemingly has been a trickle or veins in a stone; it absorbs the past of my people, and the *transitional* situation in Ukraine today — even when I don't reflect on it.

I write in order to brush away my pain and also, possibly, to bring comfort to someone else.

Hope truly dies last.

To lay it all out — this is an attempt to understand your life more deeply, to look at it as though from a bird's eye view.

THE RETURN

by Liudmyla Taran

Translated by Roman Ivashkiv

No matter how hard she tries, she cannot return to herself, into herself: she's carried like a codfish in the dirty, oily current of time — no chance to stop, catch a breath, think, or even simply look out the window — to look for a long, long time, long enough for everything, touched by that gaze, to start getting blurred, washed-out; long enough for that luminous wisp of her sight to dilute and melt into whatever it lands on: a tree, a bush, a leafy branch, or a little bird. And then she will certainly become a tree, a bush, a leafy branch, or a little bird. This blessed feeling of diffused being, the feeling of mutual blood circulation and indivisible tenderness.

But then — she's like a codfish in a dirty, oily current... It's because her soul isn't in the right place. Thus her body doesn't belong to her either: she can't feel it, can't see it, although when she glances in the mirror before running off to work, everything is still there: here are the eyes, here is the nose... but her, there is no her. Because of this she's irritated and keeps biting her lips not to evince, God forbid, any reproach or dissatisfaction. So she was taught: always be courteous with people, no matter what; be nice to every single person; be good; be polite; after all, you're a well-bred girl, from a nice family, unlike...

— *"Hey, where is the dishcloth? Maryna, where the hell is the dishcloth? I'm asking you! Are you deaf?"*

79

No, better keep quiet, I beg you, keep quiet, stay calm. It'll all blow over. Your husband will calm down, and your neighbors will finish their home remodeling, sooner or later. The banging and clanking noises will go away. Nobody will be cutting your skull with a disc grinder. Nobody will be drilling into your brain. Everything will get back to normal. Just be patient. You've put up with this over the last five months, haven't you?..

I want *in angello cum libello* — to snuggle up with a book…

I don't want to suffer! I'll either rip everything apart or I'll blow up myself like a gigantic bullet. I can't stand this anymore. I can't return into myself. Like a rabbit in headlights. Taking off simultaneously in different directions.

— *"… I'm talking to you, are you listening? Anyways, I'm out of here."*

The lock on the door clicked. Relief. She'll have to run off soon too. Always in a hurry, always rushing, trying to catch the wind, handfuls of sand, sand in the ears, sand filling up the very core of her hidden innards. Is that really her?

Monday through Friday, Monday through Friday, and the week's gone. It was literally yesterday that summer was still here. But today, it's severe winter, snowless, bald-headed; the wind carries plastic bags along the asphalt; they catch on bare bushes and hang like sails on leafless, orphaned branches.

It's cold: look at the orphans on her hands. Yet she doesn't feel her body. Or her soul.

Do I drink my life? Or does it drink me up? Here's an empty chalice with a golden brim. And just at the very bottom a sweet-scented circle is left. What used to be there? Chocolate liqueur? Nectar? Ambrosia? Love? A desire to tear oneself away from the earth and…

And that's all it is? I want… Oh Lord, how desperately I want… To go where? Not even to warm lands, but someplace where — … here's a motorboat, white, joyful, shiny; you can take any seat you want, it'll fit everyone; gentle sun; tender breeze, playing with the little pennants; we move away from the shore, and the placid mountains, as though covered with a green velvet overlay cast down from the sky, reflect themselves in the blue waters of the fjord. You keep silent because of this quiet, austere beauty. The words are swallowed or they simply don't come. The seagulls, conditioned to follow boats, hover right above your head as though they were tied to it, with consummate ease and no waste whatsoever catching tiny bits of bread or cookies on the fly.

Still from afar you notice it, its fantastic blue color, this truly incredible sky-blue color, as if from a glossy postcard. Could it really be a fake like a cheap souvenir? This glacier, this iceberg that has descended from the mountains and froze here, standing still like a gigantic beast? You're getting closer and closer, and it grows, and spreads, and expands. It's huge and real. It's naively sky-blue, but in its deep wrinkles, it is deep-deep blue, as if somebody had poured blue dye on it so that visitors would shake their heads and couldn't believe what a marvel it was.

At the glacier's foot there is a lake of melted water that flows and gives itself to the endless current, carrying the sky, the purity, and the transparent wrinkles of such gentle crisp air that you begin to feel dizzy and turn into a tiny blade of grass or twig.

In the evening — back to a hotel in the mountains, following snakelike paths, passing by little houses of trolls, small neat red wooden buildings. Your things, unpacked, are still nestled in the suitcase. Crammed, cheap, funny things that absorbed and imbibed the air of your homeland, but enough about them, those silly clothes. You hurry to open the sliding glass door and step out on the terrace with little boxwood shrubs all over the place. Everywhere are the unmercifully green grass and daisies. They appear to be on the edge of trespassing into your room that overlooks the mountains. You can reach the velvet mountains by just stretching your hand. The top line of the mountains is soothing and dreamy. Live your life.

You can't get enough of the green. You want to eat your fill for the rest of your life. This live, clear, innocent green. You can't breathe in enough of this air. But how do you believe that you are actually here, and that you are actually yourself, and not a dream…

— *"Where is the dishcloth? Jeez, I'm trying to talk to you here."*

… Isn't he gone yet?

Why not sit in front of the window in your plain little *khruschevka,*[*] a box of an apartment, and look at the windows across the street. What an interesting life people lead! Behind those lit windows an entire performance, a theatrical mystery: that's where real life is. People know what they want. They don't torment themselves by reflecting too much, don't aggravate themselves in vain or reopen old sores. They're wise and value every moment of life. They know how to enjoy it.

What I know is that I want to sit in the dark and watch the light from their windows across the street reaching the windowpanes of my window. On them, as though on a screen, bare, leafless branches are swaying under gusts of bare wind, which don't care what they stir or sway. I'd sit there and watch these shadows of branches, and it would feel as if the moment had been seized, and life no longer trickles through your fingers like sand, Monday through Friday, Monday through Friday. Only yesterday it was high summer, but today it's restless winter.

— *"How can one think about oneself when such terrible things are happening in the world?"*
— *"To hell with politics. Who gives a damn about their games? I lose sleep over them and get a splitting headache. My heart's aching. I want to live like I'm in a normal financially successful country. Where I can just think about all things lofty and eternal. And here it turns out I don't belong to myself. It's as if it wasn't me."*

---

[*] A mass-produced apartment built in the outskirts of cities under Soviet leader Nikita Khrushchev to help solve the Soviet housing crisis.

— "Ah, who are you kidding? You aren't the only one playing somebody else's part. Everyone has calmly got used to lives that are not their own. That's everlasting, and you're no exception."

The camera lens is almost torn apart by the panorama. She pans the camera slowly across the lake — it's either Loch Lomond or maybe even Loch Ness — as if she really wanted to capture "Nessie," in whose existence she doesn't believe, in her viewfinder. But the lake is truly impressive, and not so much because it's received such widespread publicity, but because of its deeply ingrained eternal serenity with a barely discernable breath of universal sorrow.

And suddenly she does something — a simple, most ordinary thing — that hasn't occurred to anybody before her: she focuses the camera on the middle of the lake. The waiting is attentive, milky. After some time the powerful lens captures and brings closer the unknown bottom, the deposits of the untouched depth, dating back either to the epoch of mountain formation or maybe even to the times when dry land was separated from the oceans...

It immediately occurred to her: why not try and do the same with the ancient lake of Brebenskul when you go to the Carpathian Mountains... One, after all, doesn't need to travel to some exotic faraway land to see a wonder...

That thought had barely flashed like a meteor in her head when the camera lens unexpectedly — through some reverse perspective — captured her own self as a little girl, sitting near her childhood home. The sun is shining right in her eyes. She's wearing a cute little polka dot dress and white, slightly dusty sandals. She bends down to wipe them off with her saliva-wetted fingertips, but in a few minutes the sandals are covered with dust again. You should have cleaned them with milk, she thinks, and squints in a funny way because of the sun. She is 5 or 6 there. Her whole life is ahead. Can you imagine that? It's like an entire eternity, like this gigantic, *bouundless* field, and all of a sudden an apple loudly falls off the branch and lands almost at her feet. And the juicy sound of how it bounced off the ground as well as the green trajectory with red trickles of its short fall became reflected in the pupil of her camera. A whole life lies ahead.

In about three years she will get a dress as a New Year's gift. It'll be red with a white embroidered collar and a pleated bottom. A summer dress on New Year's Eve, and it's still ages before spring or summer comes. She'll hang her new dress on a chair, the pleat falling down on one side and the white buttons and embroidered collar showing on the other one. She's looking and looking at it and thinking dolefully, almost in tears: am I going to make it by spring or summer to wear this dress? You can't really tell anyone that you're afraid to die before you can finally put this thing on, that's so luxurious she may be afraid to wear it… "How beautiful she is," everyone will think seeing her in that new dress. And she will feel awkward, maybe even a little embarrassed.

— *"Where's the dishcloth? You can't find a darned thing in this place."*

To return to herself, into herself. What's going on there? What's happening? Why does the dislike of one's own self exceed the limit? Why am I irritated with myself and the whole world? I torment myself more than anyone else. That's love.

I reproached myself for not being a good housewife like everyone else. All the borsht I've made my entire life could easily make a sea. Well, if not a sea, then a lake, for sure. The Loch Ness of borsht! That'd be something! A borsht lake.

If I only had just half a lake of peace, no haste whatsoever, no fuss, as if only eternity were ahead of me. As if there was no need to jump out of bed at the first scream of the alarm clock. I'd rather have it the way I used to when I was a child: you're lying in bed quiet like a mouse, and then quietly, gradually, slowly you unswaddle yourself — your heart sinking — from sleep as though from a silk cocoon. And your look is transparent and rounded. Like a magnifying glass, this look encompasses everything it touches. Very slowly you inspect the closet and its light unvarnished doors. You've looked at it so many times, and every time you can clearly and distinctly — as if on a painting — see

... a horse's muzzle. Here are the ears, the eyes, and the mane. Here are the mother-of-pearl arches of lips, a star on the forehead. You can see them all so clearly that your patience gives way this time: you are born out of that warm cocoon of the sleepy bed, get your leather schoolbag, feverishly open the nickel push lock (clack!). Your hands are shaking as you uncap the wooden pencil box — there it is, a simple lead-pencil, soft and ductile! Without wasting a single minute, impatiently and vigorously, you draw the contours of the horse's muzzle that you've seen so clearly on the closet. You step back to look at it from a distance.

One can't help burst into tears! And you start crying! Why now, when you've finally pulled it out, when you finally captured this very thing that could only be guessed intuitively and pulsated with hints in the texture of wood, alluring you to imagine itself more distinctly and manifestly, why is it now that this horse is gone, not even close, nothing similar! How could it be if it was there! You've seen it yourself. You'd better not even get started: something not manifested definitely, not outlined specifically turned out to be clearer and more expressive than the obvious.

Now your parents will make you erase the pencil drawing. The graphite will smudge, and the dirty tracery will damage the doors, see what you've done, you freaking painter, go to the corner, you'll be punished so that next time you know better than damage furniture with your drawings.

"Hey, Maryna, rake up the hay here and do some digging on that side. Oh, and also spread the manure at least down there on the low end of the garden. There's so much work. Why have you arrived so late?"

Mother wraps herself up in a bulky velveteen bathrobe, and her whiskers are angry, dissatisfied: the hairs, which she stopped shaving a long time ago, stick out in different directions. That's a bummer — women's whiskers. A sign of old age; life's flown by: Monday through Friday, and then it's over. *And what have I had? I've not seen a single good thing in my life. Struggling to make both ends meet all the time. Now I'm getting old and sick, waiting for my daughter to come visit — and she... There's so much work to do in the yard, in the garden. But she won't rush.*

Her own work is more important, of course. I only wish I could... — her finger joints are dark, thick, and swollen from arthritis.

They keep carrying some knickknack boxes, decorated with seashells and filled with all sorts of buttons made of metal, plastic, and even bones as well as all sorts of pins and other trinkets that no one will ever remember. But you can't just throw them out — no way. Let them be, because who knows, maybe one day you'll need something and it won't be there. You look at the knickknack box and feel as if some unwritten wisdom jumps at you from it: when you sew on a button, make sure you put the end of the thread in your mouth so that your mind won't be sewn up.

And then another simple bit of wisdom comes from that knickknack box: in order to sew on a thick coat button without a shank so that you can easily fasten the coat, you need to insert a match and sew the button on like that. Once you're finished, you pull the match out.

All this wisdom about the mundane minutia of life, the little tricks, and tiny bits of wisdom. Monday through Friday...

Heaven forbid you tear yourself away from the earth. Yeah, as the saying goes, the higher you fly, the harder you fall.

— *"Where the hell is the dishcloth? I'm talking to you!"*

It feels like you are all wrapped up in these never-ending dirty dishcloths. And in addition plastered with kissel, a hot jelly-like fruit drink that makes it difficult to turn around because it's stuck to your body — here it is, the body, finally found! Aching, twisting, shivering with fever... Will any one even offer a cabbage leaf to put on your forehead and alleviate that terrible pain?

No, nobody will. Instead, someone is sticking a rod with a fierce fiery tip right in your eyes — your eyeballs burn, catch on fire, and pour out. Your breasts wither; your hands and feet shrivel, turning into thin threads: your gender disappears; your body disappears; you turn into a sexless creature. All that remains is fever. All throughout you become encapsulated fever. Illusion. Delirium.

And who is this, having her ears pierced? Here's the right ear pierced with a fiery needle, that passes right through her head, her cheeks and jaws to pierce the left ear. Once the needle comes out, it's not followed by blood, which should scream in a shrill inhuman voice through the hole, but it's followed instead by a silk scarf. The scarf doesn't hurt. The head, though, is splitting as if it were on fire.

Suddenly though, you escape all the hustle and bustle of the raucous centipede-like street, you get away from the scorching hot sun and gasoline and asphalt fumes. You end up in a cool and quiet temple of God. The bodiless and weightless petals of light are dripping down at an angle from the high, elongated windows. The images of Saints are glowing in the golden twilight. They radiate tender hope that embraces you. Tranquility oozes from everywhere. Finally, she, Maryna, rediscovers herself. Things have fallen back into place.

Mother-of-pearl hasn't formed yet. Pain and sorrow sink into your soul. It hurts. It hasn't yet had time to drown the grief in glittering tears. It'll take time before they must get cold and solidify. It'll take millions of tears to enwrap the sorrow with their glitter.

You can feel the powerful and joyful wind blowing over your head. You look up into the sky and notice that a silk ladder, unexpectedly dispatched, is descending from the night sky almost right to your feet. Light and airy, it's hanging down from a shiny night helicopter. Its body is shaking above your head and invites you to go somewhere over there… over there… All it takes is to climb the silk ladder and to reach the sky. And then — hover over the earth.

from A VILLAGE IS NOT ITS PEOPLE

by Liuko Dashvar

Translated by Yuri Tkacz

KATERYNA WAS AWAKE. SHE LAY IN HER SMALL ROOM, AND FOR some reason stroked her glassy-looking pink coat with her hand. What use was it now, if she couldn't leave the house?

She heard a scratching sound coming from the tiny window, but it didn't frighten her. She jumped off her bed and pressed against the window.

"Uncle Roman...?" And she burst into tears. He was standing outside and imploring her:

"Hush, don't cry... Open the window, my Little Sprite."

Her hands began to tremble; she could barely turn the latch. Opening the window, she stretched out her arms:

"Uncle Roman...," and she fell into his embrace.

"You'll freeze to death..." He was trembling himself. "Wait, I'll wrap my jacket around you."

"Uncle Roman..."

"Wait, my love. Let's move away from the house a little."

"Yes, yes..."

They settled down behind the house, when suddenly her mum emerged from the shed unnoticed. She must have had a premonition or simply wanted to take a peek at her daughter... She had heard voices and hid in the shadows. Kateryna and Roman heard nothing.

"Uncle Roman," Kateryna embraced Roman's neck and sobbed. "I can't stand this any longer. I simply can't, no matter how hard I try. And they say bad things about me in the village. It's all lies! Every single bit is a lie. Do you believe me?"

Her mum had forgotten to breathe, standing there motionless.

"I believe you, I believe you, my Little Sprite. I can't live without you either. Wherever I look, I see you before my eyes."

"Uncle Roman, I'm afraid... I'm afraid aunt Rayisa will kill me."

"Eh, no!" Roman whispered, stroking the girl's hair. "I won't let anyone take you away. No one will hurt you, my Little Sprite."

"You're up on the haystack there, and I'm here... It's frightening... I'm even scared to tell anyone that I love you. Even my mother, and she's the best..."

"Don't worry. Don't venture outside anymore. Until they stop talking nonsense in the village. And don't come to the haystack either. I'll visit you myself."

"Uncle Roman! I'm ready to stay inside the house all my life, as long as you come to see me..."

"I won't stay away, don't worry. And you won't have to stay indoors all your life."

"True?"

"We'll go away somewhere. Just let me organize the ninth-day wake for my Sashko, and we'll be off. Somewhere far, far away..."

"You're not lying, are you?"

Roman laughed — there was a smell of wormwood.

"I love you, my Little Sprite. I can't live without you."

"Me either... Me either..." she chattered away. "How happy I am..."

Roman kissed the girl on the cheek and walked off. He bent low as he moved behind the fences, so no one would spot him. Kateryna ran up to the tiny window. Meanwhile her mother remained standing behind the house, as if carved from stone. Her hands were clasped over her mouth, for she wanted to scream for the whole world to hear.

In the morning they said their goodbyes to the visitors. Her mum had cooked up a feast of a breakfast and everyone had crowded around the table: mum, dad, Kateryna and Denys with Ihor. Denys had raised a shot-glass:

"Thank-you for everything. You're wonderful people! We'll always remember you."

Dad didn't know where to hide his eyes. No one ever praised him to high heaven like this… And for what?

"Drink up, come on," he said, and upended his glass. Ihor had a drink too. He rested his shot glass on the table and said to mum:

"Maybe we should drop in on the militia station at the district centre?"

"What for?" Mum's eyebrows knitted together in a circle.

"Your dear Katya is being threatened here," Ihor said to her.

"We'll sort that out ourselves," mum said. And she was not herself. Even dad noticed:

"Why are you spinning about like a top, Daryna…?"

"The things you come up with, Lyonchyk!" Mum dismissed him.

"No, I'm serious," Ihor insisted. "Please agree to it. We'll pop into the district militia post and tell them that the girl's being threatened with physical violence… That she can't leave the house."

Before mum could answer, Kateryna threw down her spoon, her eyes glowing.

"There's no need for the militia to be involved. Everything's fine…"

Denys couldn't believe his ears.

"Are you sure everything's all right, Katya?!"

"It's all good," she said and laughed. "I'm happy…"

Dad frowned. "What makes you so happy, you little twerp? That people are spreading gossip about you around the village?!"

"Let them! Mud doesn't stick to me," Kateryna retorted.

The scholars became lost for words, dad spat on the ground, and mum hid the bitterness in her eyes.

"That's enough said about that," she said. "We'll sort it all out…"

After breakfast they exchanged kisses and the visitors set off. Dad offered to carry the scholars' suitcases to Kylymivka; mum saw everyone to the gate, while Kateryna did not venture beyond the doorstep. Ihor turned around and sighed.

"Hold on a minute," and he came up to Kateryna.

He offered her his business card.

"It has my phone numbers in Kyiv and my address. If things get nasty, you can come and stay with me. I'll help you whichever way I can."

Kateryna took the card and smiled:

"Well, goodbye forever, then."

"Why?"

"Because you're inviting me to come along, if things get bad. But I'll be fine."

"May your words come true," replied Ihor Krupka and left the yard.

That day the Shanivka residents did not blockade the house. Only old Mrs. Nychypor came up to their yard and yelled out:

"Kateryna, you bloody whore! Happy now that you've ruined the life of a young lad? May you remain behind those four walls till the end of time! You'll regret it, if you come out."

Tamara's younger son Taras, a first grader, joined in. He screamed loudly:

"Katka's a whore! Katka's a whore!"

Mum went outside and launched a tirade at Mrs. Nychypor: "Get outa here, you old witch! Didn't look after your own daughter! She gave birth to two bastards god knows from who, became a drunk and choked to death! And you, you ugly old bitch, you didn't even take the orphans in! Handed them over to an orphanage! My daughter's not like that! She's done no one any harm… Now you, Mrs. Nychypor, you're the whore here! Because you believe other people's malicious lies!"

"I'm the whore?" Mrs. Nychypor rested her hands on her sides and began to pace the street. "Eh! D'you hear that? Things have changed in Shanivka now! Those that speak the truth are bloody whores! And those that do lads in are goody-goodies and angels."

Mum spat at Mrs. Nychypor and came back inside the house. She could barely move her feet.

She sat down in the kitchen and burst into tears. Kateryna came up to her:

"Mummy dearest, my darling… How I love you! Why are you crying? There's no need, no need for that. Everything will be fine. You'll see…" Mum wiped away her tears and grabbed Kateryna by the arm: "Sit down…"

Her daughter made herself comfortable and embraced her mum.

"How happy I am, mum! How I love you…"

Mum remained silent for a while and then said:

"Last night I came out of the shed…"

Kateryna froze. Mum continued:

"What's wrong? Didn't you hear me? I said, last night I came out of the shed…"

Kateryna covered her face with her hands:

"Don't scold me, mum! I'll tell you the whole truth…"

"Then hurry up, while dad's still out. Because if he finds out, he'll break every single bone."

"Whose bones?" Kateryna whispered, without removing her small hands from her face.

"Yours, my dear. And… Roman's, the old scoundrel."

Kateryna fell to her knees at her mum's feet:

"How can he touch uncle Roman? How can he? He's suffering so much… Because of Sashko… And you… you're saying such frightful things."

Mum lifted Kateryna from the floor:

"Tell me the whole truth or I'll die of grief!" She whispered so bitterly, that Kateryna became frightened.

"There's nothing to say, mummy dearest. I love him. And he loves me. That's all there is."

"How's that?!" Mum asks. "You're a young girl, and he's an old man. Tell me the truth, did he molest you? Where'd it happen?"

"No, mummy dearest! He didn't! Not once since we fell in love…"

"God Almighty!" mum burst into tears. "What are you saying, my darling?!"

"The honest truth, mum!"

"And when did you manage to fall in love with him?!" Her mum still couldn't come to her senses.

"I'm not sure myself. But I don't fancy anyone else apart from him. As for Sashko… Could I have hurt Sashko?! Never! He kept pestering me, saying: 'Soon as I turn sixteen, I'll take you for my wife, Katya.' But I kept my distance from him… By god, mummy dearest!"

"I heard you say you wanted to run away? To leave me…"

"Mummy dearest! I'll never leave you. No matter where I am… I'll come to visit you and bring you lots of presents!"

Her mum seemed to recover. And slapped Kateryna on the cheek!

"I see you've already thought everything through…"

"Mummy dearest, you've never hit me before," and she began to sob uncontrollably. Her mum took her in her arms and burst into tears too:

"My dear little daughter, what have you done?"

"Mummy dearest, you can beat me if you like… It will make no difference. I love him. You said yourself a girl needs to belong to someone. You're with dad, and I want to be with uncle Roman."

"But you're still young. You know nothing about love."

"What do you mean? I do, I do…"

"Child…"

"I should run off to join him! And be done with it."

"God…"

Her mum wouldn't let go of her, as if she were about to run away from home:

"Darling… D'you hear me? What if I tell you not to go with him…? Will you listen to me?"

Kateryna broke away from her mum and looked into her eyes:

"I will… By god, I'll listen to you… But don't you want me to be happy?"

Mum wiped away her tears.

"Dad will be back soon and we're both blubbering away…"

"Mum, tell me… Do you want me to be happy?"

"I do, darling. Only… Let me think about it… Don't ask me for advice just yet. I'll tell you later. All right?"

"Good. And I'll talk it over with Roman."

"Why?"

"You want to do everything on the sly? You can't do that. You'll never escape public opinion."

"Don't tell dad for the moment."

"I won't. And you too… Don't tell anyone for the moment."

"All right. And tell Roman not to come around. Just for the moment. The whole village is abuzz as it is."

"All right."

Mum was about to go off to feed the chickens, but could not refrain from saying: "And how would the two of you have lived?!"

Kateryna did not catch the barb:

"In happiness, mummy dearest!"

Zaluskivsky came across old Mrs. Nychypor ensconced on the monument pedestal, where she habitually sat, complaining to the neighbors about stupid Daryna and Lyonka and their good-for-nothing daughter Kateryna.

"What's all the commotion about?" He asked, and the old women responded in a chorus:

"Oh, the things that are happening here! Lyonka's Katka is responsible for Sashko's death. The damned slut!"

Zaluskivsky was surprised.

"What are you women carrying on about? What kind of slut can she be?! Her tits haven't even popped out yet."

"Her tits mightn't have popped out, but she's already got the itch between her legs!" Mrs. Nychypor argued. And then she inquired: "And where the devil have you been these past two days, Vanya?" But Zaluskivsky was not offended.

"I've got heaps of business to attend to, old woman. Unlike you lot… wagging your tongues all day long. Is that clear?"

"Of course it is! You've come at a fortuitous time, though: you can come along with us tonight."

"Where to?" Zaluskivsky looked the old woman in the eye.

"To Lyonka's place. We'll be smoking the whore out of their house."

Zaluskivsky thought a moment and scratched his nose:

"I might just join you. What do we need whores for in Shanivka?"

"That's the way!" old Mrs. Nychypor said, delighted at the unexpected support. "You're made of gold, Ivan Zaluskivsky! What a kind hand you lent Roman and Rayisa! What a dashing funeral you organized. Music, and a priest as well. I could do with the same…"

"You'll outlive us all," Zaluskivsky brushed her off and set off for home.

He wanted to rest. He was tired.

There was good reason. Two whole days Zaluskivsky had scoured the city and finally found some odd stranger, whom he had secretly brought back to Shanivka. He dropped the fellow off at one of the abandoned houses and commanded sternly:

"Venture out of here and I'll murder you. Do everything as I told you, and the drink will be on me for a month."

"Give's at least a hundred grams now!" The fellow whimpered.

But Zaluskivsky was implacable:

"Suffer, you piece of shit," he hissed. "I'll be round in the evening."

Daddy was drunk. Not the way he was when guests came round, for example, downing three shotglasses with food. This time he was blind drunk. He had carried the scholars' suitcases to Kylymivka and they had stuffed a heap of money into his pockets. And daddy… Either he had been overjoyed that mum knew nothing about the money. Or he had been distressed by the scholars' words; they had kept pontificating about village life along the way and had finally come to the conclusion, that…

"Lyonia, there's no reason in the world for people to live the way you do!" Denys ranted. "You're living in the Stone Age. Going to the toilet behind bushes, washing in a basin, cooking in wood-fired ovens…"

"Washing everything by hand," Ihor added, recalling how Daryna had changed the sheets every day.

"Life's all right here," daddy retorted. "What's so great there in that big city of yours?"

"There's culture!" Denys, a lover of folk songs, assured him.

"But you said that you came to us to collect true culture?" daddy asked in surprise.

"No, we didn't come here for the culture," Denys clarified the point. "We came to record songs and modern customs... And I can tell you frankly, they're pretty savage here..."

"So traditions are not culture?" Dad pressed the scholars into a corner.

"Yeah, we seem to have talked ourselves into a corner here," Ihor acknowledged. But Denys did not relent:

"Don't be offended, Lyonia! Everything that we saw... your life... It spawns new traditions... Traditions of savagery and a lack of culture."

"How's that?" dad asked dismissively. "When it comes to songs — they're so nice, but the traditions are bad."

"The songs are nice, because they're ancient... There are no contemporary folk songs... None! Rare drops in an ocean of sideshow howling. But the traditions are bad, because... your life is bad, Lyonia. It's bad, and don't contradict us! This lad we buried... Try to explain to someone why he died... No one will believe you! Because it's savagery! The absence of elementary information... And the whole village is badgering your daughter. Over what? We are leaving, feeling anxious about your darling Kateryna."

"Nothing will happen to her," dad replied sullenly.

"And if something does?" Denys wrenched him.

"As long as I am alive, nothing will happen to her," daddy replied firmly.

"There's just one of you, Lyonia!" Denys exclaimed. "And there's a whole village of them! They'll have your entire family for lunch."

Dad dropped his head:

"Just let them try. They'll regret it..."

"There's no sense to this conversation!" Denys exclaimed. "You don't understand a thing!"

"Sure I do," dad said. "You despise us... Because we don't have an indoor bath. Because there's mud in the streets..."

They were approaching Kylymivka just then. Denys spread out his arms.

"Where in the hell did you get that from?! I have the greatest of respect for village folk! My heart aches for you all!"

Dad dropped the suitcases onto the ground:

"You respect us? Then why have I been lugging your suitcases?"

The scholars were dumbfounded.

"We'll pay you... Have no doubts about that," the two of them babbled away.

"What do I need your money for?! To buy a bath?!" Dad smiled. "I'm talking about respect... And you... you poke your money at me..."

"Lyonia, you've misinterpreted everything!" Denys said to him. And began searching through his pockets.

Dad scratched the back of his neck, but took the money anyway.

"Go to... with that culture of yours! He pointed to a tree by the side of the road. "See that? How beautiful the blossom is! It has green and red leaves. There are all kinds of branches: straight ones, crooked ones, thin ones and thick ones. That's you people. Your culture. But how things are to be — only the roots know. Those same roots in the ground, in the mud, without any fresh air, without any daylight. Immersed in black sweat. The roots work hard so that the branches and leaves can poke their eyes out at the wide world!"

He sighed.

"So goodbye then, or what..."

He walked off. Ihor and Denys couldn't come to their senses.

"God! How much power there is in him... He works like a slave, knows nothing about what's happening in the world; he's probably never read a newspaper, and yet he comes out with such amazing things... Makes one's hair stand on end!" Denys commented.

"One can spend one's whole life mulling over what he said," replied Ihor.

"You and I are mere leaves... Poking our eyes out — and nothing more? But we need to give something back to the roots. Isn't that right?"

"In botany — that's the case, but among humans..."

"You and I have yet to give anything back."

"No one gives anything back. They only take..." Ihor suddenly burst out laughing. "If we keep going this way for much longer we'll all turn into... pineapple plants."

"Pineapple plants?" Denys was unable to follow his friend's train of thought.

"Yes, we'll become like pineapples. Without any roots, neither living, nor withering away. Only sporting a spiky rusty-colored shock of leaves... And without any taste!"

"I was thinking of a terrible paradox here," Denys sat down on the suitcases and lit a cigarette. "Brother! If all the branches and all the leaves were to justly return to the roots a part of the useful, necessary, important things... the roots would still... Do you realize, that the roots would still remain in the black earth! Without air! Without light! Without hope."

"Why without air? Why without hope? The roots will become strong. The leaves and branches will send them air, light and hope. And the roots... The roots can then draw even more goodness from the earth."

"But, they'll remain in the ground all the same!"

"Why does that frighten you? Each thing has its own place. We leaves have to fly with the wind, the roots need to be firmly entrenched in the earth. But something else frightens me..."

"What?"

"That the connection has been lost. I can't sense the connection between the leaves and the roots any more, but it must be there. It has to be, otherwise there won't be a tree any more!"

"I don't understand..."

"What don't you understand?!" Ihor sat down beside his friend. "We're leaving the village afraid and in awe... As if we had spent time in the Amazon jungles. No, had we gone there, it would have been understandable. But we rubbed shoulders with our own roots and... we're running away scared. Running away, as if from a plague! No, as if from a UFO! Everything here is foreign to us and incomprehensible. Everything! Not only the absence of toilets in people's homes, not only the mud in the streets, the abandoned houses and farms, the tumble-down fences... People's thoughts and actions are foreign to us! We no longer understand them. That's what is frightening!"

"Maybe because this is no longer the earth... These are no longer the roots..."

"What then?" Ihor looked at Denys.

"The start of geography without history... The start of the wild steppe. And they... They're like the last of the Mohicans. They'll all die out and no one will take their place..."

"Then the leaves are kaput," Ihor retorted.

"Yes, kaput," Denys agreed. "There won't be any more trees."

He recalled something and said to Ihor:

"So what about the cow shit? Is it better that it slops onto the asphalt or sinks into the mud?"

"I have no idea..."

"Well I do," Denys exclaimed.

He had made a discovery!

"I've been collecting folk songs for many years," he said. "And I've come to the conclusion... People create songs only during glorious periods in their history. And Ukraine's glorious period was the Cossack era. So that every second folk song is about the Cossacks."

"You think that asphalt, computers, hospitals, schools and hair-dressing salons won't destroy folk traditions for milkmaids?" Ihor inquired.

"I'm convinced," Denys replied.

"So we agree," Ihor stood up and grabbed his suitcase. "So what do we do with our conclusions?"

"As they say in American action novels — shove them up your ass!"

"You're a pessimist, my friend!"

"No, I'm a realist," Denys replied. "The enlightenment of two people is nothing for the rest of the country."

He burst out laughing.

"I really like the analogy of the tree!" He said to Ihor. "We... We're two stupid little leaves... When we mew, a whole pile of leaves will come down on top of us! Completely burying us! Pressing us to the ground. And we'll start to rot, my dear brother... We'll start to rot..."

"P'raps we'll set forth roots. Begin sprouting," Ihor sighed.

"Not in our lifetimes. Not in ours. If God permits, our descendants will be allowed to sprout. But us... We'll simply rot."

Dad reached home on all fours as the moon was setting in the night sky. Kateryna was overjoyed. Now mum would certainly not reveal her secret to dad. And she could dash off to the haystacks.

"Mummy will let me go!" She thought. "I'll tell her I want to warn uncle Roman not to come round for the moment. She'll let me go. She's a gift of gold."

Her golden mum was taking care of dad. She pulled off his boots, wiped down his face with water, covered him with a blanket, and dad began to snore away on the floor in the middle of the house.

"Oh, what a villain you are, my Lyonchik!" Mum whispered. "How will our child and I fend off the entire village?!"

The village seemed to have heard mum's words. Kateryna glanced outside through the small curtained-off window: old Mrs. Nychypor was waving her arms about outside their front gate; the womenfolk were crowding around her, a few of the men were standing nearby, and Tamara was egging everyone on.

"Let's show some respect for Sashko," she called out, "and tear that strumpet to pieces."

Everything disappeared from Kateryna's face. Only the fear remained. She dashed up to her mum:

"Mum, I'm scared..." People were buzzing in the yard outside. And her mum was far from being a mum. She was a veritable Joan of Arc. There was a glint of metal in her eyes.

"Know what, Katya..." she said, her eyes glued to the windows, "get out of here..."

"Where to?"

"Hide somewhere... If our house isn't burnt to the ground by morning, you can come back. But come back through the backyards, so no one sees you."

Kateryna hugged her mum:

"What are you saying, mummy dearest?! I can't leave you! I won't go anywhere!"

But her mum was beside herself. She grabbed her daughter by the shoulders so hard that Katya let out a whelp from the pain. "Go..." she whispered resolutely. "And don't come back till morning."

Kateryna kissed her mum all over, slipped out of the house through the window in her bedroom and dashed off. Making straight for the burial mound.

Where the haystack stood.

Once she was certain that her daughter was a good distance away, mum crossed herself and gave her drunken husband a swift kick.

"Eh, my dear Lyonia!" She grabbed an icon, slipped a kitchen knife into her pocket, and stepped outside.

"A good evening to the kind people of our village!" She yelled out ferociously. Tamarka even stopped egging the others on.

The crowd got its back up and grew silent.

"What's with the icon, Darka?" Zaluskivsky called out. Mum raised an eyebrow.

"Oppah! Here we go! So Zaluskivsky is here too!"

And she made her way straight for the Shanivka people.

"I swear by the holy Lord and swear by this holy icon...," she shouted. "You've entwined an innocent child in lies! Clear ripped her innocent soul into pieces! You've hurt her, like a homeless puppy! You want to tear her to pieces? Here, take me instead! Grab me, you damned lot, because I can see your hands are itching to do just that! Grab me and repent straight away, because we have no sins behind us! Neither my child! Nor me… Nor my husband…"

"And where's your Lyonka?" Fedir called out.

"That damned husband of mine's asleep! Stuffed his face full and fell asleep! If you like, I can drag him here too! Take the two of us, because we'll either die in the name of our child, or we'll slash open all of your throats. And you — you're all the same… All the same!"

Mummy stopped. All of a sudden she roared at the top of her voice:

"Rayisa-a-a! Rayisa! Can you hear me?! Would you give your life for your son? Or would you hide? Why are you silent?"

Black as death. Rayisa stirred in the crowd. She took a step forward. And screamed madly in answer to mummy.

"No, I wouldn't hide! I'd die if I had to, but I would punish that harlot of yours! She… The damned bitch did my Sashka in…"

"That's a lie!" mummy answered hoarsely. "That's a lie, I swear on this holy icon!"

"Then tell her to step outside," Rayisa moved toward mummy. "I want her to look me in the eye…" But mummy retorted:

"I've come outside to confront you, because you've scared my child to death. Kill me, if you don't believe me!"

"Serhiy has owned up…" Rayisa continued yelling at mummy. "Your harlot talked Sashka into it, and Sashka talked Serhiy into it…"

"Sashka?! Talked Serhiy into it?!" Mummy laughed. It was not a full chesty laugh or an exhalation, but a nervous outpouring. "Did you all hear that? Sashka talked Serhiy into it?! Everyone here knows that that troublemaker Serhiy had only foolish thoughts in his head! While Sashka was no idiot. He was a good child!" And the two mothers stood facing one another. The Shanivka people moved to one side.

They were silent, like a bunch of mutes. Even Tamarka didn't put in a good word for her son.

"Yes, he was good! A good child," Rayisa burst into tears. "A lad of gold! And your… your…"

Mummy pressed the icon to her chest. She stretched out her hand toward Rayisa:

"My Kateryna is innocent, my dear. Don't listen to lies." And she pulled the kitchen knife from her pocket. The Shanivka mob didn't even manage to exhale a sigh. Mummy offered the knife to Rayisa:

"Don't believe me? Then kill me! I will let you be my judge…," Rayisa fell to her knees. She didn't take the knife.

"My darling little son… My darling son…"

Mummy glanced at the Shanivka crowd.

"We need Serhiy to come here!" She called out. "Get Serhiy! We'll get the truth out of him."

The Shanivka crowd began to buzz.

"Maybe Tamarka's lied to us? Serhiy's known for being a varmint. He's afraid of all the shame and so he's blamed everything on Katka… And Katka… Hey, Katka's a fine girl! And she's friendly. And no slut either." And like mummy, everyone called out to Tamarka:

"Hey, bring that son of yours here! Come on! There's no need to hide him in the hospital there … Yeah, they're curing his willie… But he's the one who did Sashka in, and the louse is lounging about in hospital… And meanwhile Tamarka's feeding the gossip mill!" old Mrs. Nychypor was thinking out loud. "She's made it all up! She wants us not to think ill of her Serhiy!"

"What are you on about!" Tamarka answered, and began to retreat step by step. "Have you all gone mad? I've told you the honest truth, and you start spitting in my soul?! My son's suffered as well. He won't be able to have kiddies now."

"And a good thing at that," old Mrs. Nychypor exclaimed. "Why multiply bad seed?!"

Tamarka spat at the crowd and raced off.

"May you all go to hell!" She yelled as she raced off. "May all of your arms and legs become paralyzed! May you all…"

And the crowd made off after her. Only Tamarka's Fedka spread out his arms, as if to say: there's no need to run after her.

A moment later Rayisa and mummy were alone. Mummy fell to her knees before Rayisa:

"Don't cry, my love. Don't tear your heart to pieces…"

"Forgive me," whispered Rayisa.

Mummy wiped away a tear.

"Oh-ho-hoh!" She sighed. "If only it was all so simple…"

"If only… Get up, my turtledove. Let's go… Let's go to my place. We'll have a stiff drink and remember your Sashka. He was an angel…"

Rayisa got to her feet and followed mummy.

"Where's Kateryna?"

"I've hidden her well away from sin," mummy said, while Rayisa burst into tears once more:

"As you can see, I wasn't able to keep my lad out of harm's way…"

The Shanivka residents were at each other near the monument pedestal.

"Liar! Liar!" old Mrs. Nychypor screamed. "How could we have believed you, Tamarka?! Everyone knows that Zaluskivsky is the father of your little Taras, and you lie to everyone that he's Fedka's."

Alla Zaluskivska grabbed hold of old Mrs. Nychypor on one side. And Tamara's Fedir on the other:

"You old piece of shit, let your own daughter hit the skids, and now you're slandering others?! Old Mrs. Nychypor tried to break free:

"Don't go gutter crawling! Stop traipsing about behind bushes, and no one will gossip about you!"

"Did you see anything?!" Alka yelled. "Were you there holding up a candle?"

"I was!" Struggled old Mrs. Nychypor.

They would have killed the old woman, had Zaluskivsky not brought a rifle out of his house:

"When I fire this thing you'll crap in your pants," he boomed at the top of his voice.

The Shanivka people settled down. Zaluskivsky was reestablishing order:

"If only you would put as much effort into your work as you do into raising a revolution here... Head back home, the lot of you!"

Old Mrs. Nychypor was the first to obey him. She made to set off home and turned around to face Zaluskivsky. Suddenly her lower jaw dropped and she slapped her cheeks:

"Va-a-ania!" She suddenly hollered. "Vania, look! That's your haystack burning! Your haystack..." Before Zaluskivsky had managed to swing around, the whole village began in a chorus:

"The haystack's burning! The haystack... The haystack..."

"The haystack's alight," Zaluskivsky turned pale. "Those bastards!"

The Shanivka people were already racing toward the haystack, even though all of them knew that it would finish burning before they even reached it. But they ran toward it all the same.

Kateryna had dashed off faster than the wind to join Roman. She hadn't even glanced back at Shanivka. Only her heart almost popped out of her chest out of fear for her mum: how are you, how are you, how are you back there, mummy dearest...

She was so breathless, that she fell on the ground. And the haystack was over there. A little bit further on. At that moment mum hadn't even shown Rayisa the kitchen knife.

Kateryna got to her feet and slowly kept walking. Even if any of the Shanivka people had wanted to chase her, they wouldn't have found her in the darkness.

No sooner had this thought entered her head, than she saw a dark figure approach the haystack.

Kateryna stared wide-eyed, unable to take a step. "It's the Shanivka people chasing me!" The words pounded inside her head. She squatted behind a bush and stopped breathing.

Roman heard a rustle, and spread his arms apart: "What are you doing, my Little Sprite?! Why did you run here? I would have come myself..." He got up on the hay and pushed a cigarette into his mouth. He struck a match and raised it above his head — trying to spy Kateryna. Another rustle seemed to come from behind.

Roman looked about. And came face to face with someone. Thump! He jumped back and stared into the darkness:

"E-e-eh, these are not local bastards!"

That's all he managed to utter. From behind there came more than a rustle. Someone struck his grey head full-force with a rock.

The world cracked apart. Roman remained standing. He did not fall. The blood poured into his eyes.

Suddenly there was another blow to the head. Only then did he fall.

He soon came to his senses. He was a strong man. He was able to open his eyes. But he couldn't get to his feet. There were stars in his eyes, but he could see that the bastard of a stranger was not about to steal the hay — he was running around the haystack, liberally dousing it with petrol.

"What are you doing, you bitch? Better to steal it… D'you hear?" He whispered, and the tears washed away the blood from his eyes.

Roman saw a match ignite. He saw the flame quiver in the darkness. He fell onto the hay, and the haystack caught fire. And he heard a rustle as someone ran off. Further and further away… The figure stopped near the bushes and called out to Roman:

"The hell with you, you mangy old rooster! You'll burn to death now!"

Kateryna was hunched up under the bushes. Grabbing hold of the ground, she was afraid to move.

She regained her senses only after the fellow who had screamed out the unusual words 'mangy old rooster' was far away. She crawled out of the bushes.

"Uncle Roman… Uncle Roman, my love… What's with you?" And she seemed to be watching a horror movie.

The haystack was engulfed in fire. A bright male figure was moving among the flames.

She tossed aside the burning hay and again threw herself at the haystack.

"You're lying, you bitch! I don't intend to be burnt alive! And the haystack won't burn down!"

Kateryna jumped to her feet and rushed up to the haystack:

"Uncle Roman! My dearest one!" She kept running around in circles, screaming in terror. "Stop that! I beg you, stop that! Uncle Roman!"

But he didn't hear a thing. He only swore profusely and kept throwing hay around.

And his voice grew ever more softer and softer:

"Just think… people strained their backs… to have something… f..k him! Couldn't just grab it… The bitch! I won't let 'im have it! I won't…" And he fell into the fire. He was no longer burning. He was black. Kateryna was screaming and dragged him away from the haystack by the feet:

"Uncle Roman!" She sobbed. "My little ray of sunshine! What have you done?!"

She dragged him away from the fire and fell down onto the ground beside him.

The haystack was burning so brightly, that it was clear as day… Roman's eyes were closed, he had no face — it had been burnt away, his clothes were still smoldering. Was he breathing?

The young lass got to her feet, not knowing what to do, but she did what she could. She wrapped her long plait around her neck and bit into the end with her teeth to stop herself from crying. She grabbed Roman by the back and carefully lifted him, manoeuvring him into a sitting position. She pressed her back against his chest, tossed his arms over her shoulders and tried to stand up — but it was no use.

"Can it be…?" She whispered as if she were mad. "Can it be…?"

She tried once more, but simply did not have the strength.

She looked into the night and crawled off on all fours. She bore along Roman on her back like a tiny ant carrying a giant crumb of bread. The burning haystack was beginning to die down.

Grandma Kylyna crossed herself before the icons and crawled out of her mud hut:

"Rudy! Chubchyk!" She called out to her dogs. "Off you go… I can sense misfortune. Misfortune is aflame, burning everything around it."

She came across Kateryna with Roman on her back in the grove that had overgrown the deserted farmstead.

She didn't utter a word, dragging Roman off to her hut. Having ordered the dogs to stand guard over the girl.

In her hut she washed Roman's body and shook her head:

"He won't survive…"

She rubbed dried herbs between her hands and added them to water, continually talking to Roman:

"Don't be afraid… It won't hurt too much. I'll do my bit. I'll make sure you won't suffer…"

She fetched a small bottle from behind the icon:

"This is precious stuff," she whispered and poured some liquid into Roman's mouth: "Sleep and don't wake up. No need for you to feel pain, my son. Time to be on your way."

She immersed a thin white sheet in the herb-infused water and completely wrapped Roman's body in it:

"I'll be back soon…," she said and left her hut.

Kateryna lay there in the grove, as if she were dead. She had turned over onto her back and stared into the blackness of the heavens, as if into misfortune. She didn't even blink.

Grandma Kylyna leaned over her, raised the girl's head a little, removed the plait from around her neck. She ran her trembling hand over the girl's thin arms:

"Don't be alarmed, child. Lie quietly. Rudy and Chubchyk won't let anyone near you. I'll be one moment… I'll be back…"

The dogs rushed around Kateryna and kept staring at the retreating figure of Grandma Kylyna. The old woman was off to Shanivka.

Mummy drank glass after glass with Rayisa, but the alcohol affected each of them differently. Rayisa couldn't stand on her feet, they kept buckling under her. Meanwhile mummy's head kept spinning and she felt so sorry for herself… She just wanted to cry!

They emptied the bottle, and both nodded their heads at Lyonka, who was snoring away on the floor.

"I'll be off then, Darka," whispered Rayisa. "I feel bad wherever I am. And I won't get better here."

"Go-oh then, my dear," was all mummy managed to utter, and only now did she realize why she felt so uncomfortable.

"Oh, why am I still holding onto this icon?" she asked herself.

Rayisa left and mummy collapsed on the bed, falling asleep immediately. She dreamt that there was a festival in the village. And such a loud one at that, so stunning and intense. The Shanivka people were all beautifully dressed. More beautifully than people on television. And they were so well behaved. Each of them came up to mummy and greeted her: "Good day, Daryna!" And mummy answered them: "What's this great festival we're celebrating here?" And the Shanivka people laughed: "It's a wedding!"

"And who's marrying whom?" Mummy inquired.

"Your Kateryna's the bride. And the dress she's got on... It's as if it's covered in flames!"

"Where is she? I want to see her dress," mummy yelled at them and tried to push her way through the Shanivka crowd to see her Kateryna. Suddenly she heard someone crying... And so bitterly... "Katya?" Mummy pushed the Shanivka people aside and saw Kateryna standing on the pedestal. And she looked so frightening! Instead of a dress, she was completely covered in hay. Like a scarecrow. And Zaluskivsky was circling around the pedestal. "This really is a scarecrow!" He yelled. "I'll place it outside the office. It'll scare away the crows!" Mummy tried to rush up to her daughter, but the Shanivka people stopped her. They grabbed hold of her hands. "Such a lovely dress! It's as if it's covered in flames!" They repeated. Mummy watched — and the hay on Kateryna caught fire. "Katya!" She screamed... And woke up.

Her eyes were open wide.

"Lordy-lord..."

Grandma Kylyna was staring down at her. Mummy began to shake:

"No, no..."

"Come with me," said grandma Kylyna. "She's alive. But you have to bring her home soon as possible. When we get to my place, you'll understand why…"

The sky began to turn gray. A little longer — and it would be morning.

When it came to rescuing her darling daughter, mummy's legs were like perpetual motion machines. She ran ahead of Kylyna and kept urging her on:

"Walk faster!"

The old woman stopped:

"You run along, I'll take my time… I have other things to attend to anyway."

"What happened?"

"The haystack caught fire during the night. Kateryna dragged Roman on her back to my place. He's burnt all over. He won't live, but I won't let him suffer either. I know various recipes… The Shanivka people needn't know about Kateryna. It's none of their business. I'll tell them Roman reached my place himself. And the poor soul won't deny a thing… Run, Daryna. Drag your daughter home. Go the back way through the gardens. You hear?"

The news was like a blow to the head for mummy:

"Lordy-lord…," she began to shake and made off for the copse. First she saw the dogs Rudy and Chubchyk. She headed for them. The dogs moved away, lowering their heads.

"My dearest darling," mummy fell upon the ground beside Kateryna and began to kiss her little arms, choking on her words.

"Mummy dearest…," the young girl whispered.

"Katya, Katya…," and she couldn't say anything more.

"Is he alive, mum?" Kateryna asked.

"He's alive, he's alive," mummy's words stuck in her throat. "We have to hurry off. Can you get up, child?"

Kateryna sat up. She looked about with surprise, as if not recognizing where she was.

"Of course I can. Where are we?"

"Come, my dear, we'll talk about everything at home."

Mummy helped Kateryna get up. They took a step, then another… And hobbled off through the backyards toward Shanivka.

When they entered the house — dad was not on the floor.

"What grief!" Mummy led Kateryna into her bedroom and looked about. Where could her husband have gone?

She put her daughter to bed.

"I'll be back shortly…," and she slipped outside into the yard.

Dad was in the shed, taking swigs of moonshine from a bottle.

"Lyonia!"

Dad didn't even turn around. He merely waved an arm, as if to say: leave me be! And finished his drink.

from SWEET DARUSYA: A TALE OF TWO VILLAGES

by Maria Matios

Translated by Michael M. Naydan
with Olha Tytarenko

THE DAILY DRAMA

"Where, Maria, who did you get the georginas* from that are so bright and puffy?" Vasyuta asked her neighbor over the fence. "No matter how hard I took care of mine, they were wiped out by some kind of disease. They became curled like snails; you can't do anything about it. Maybe I gave them to wicked people, or maybe Varvara plucked them out at night, it's not for me to say to you what kind of witch she might be. God only knows what happened to my flowers? They're gone — and you can't do anything about it. And this weed is useless. I love it when flowers are big and puffy, and not teeny tiny,"and she throws out an armful of asters onto the path.

"Fie on such a miracle! Everybody's asking who'd you get them from, who'd… they'll hex my harvest," Maria answers without straightening herself up from the garden bed as though she were angry. "It was sweet Darusya who gave them to me. Both the lilacs and the rose bushes. She brought them to me in the spring."

"Before things got bad with her again?"

---

* Georgina (colloquial) means dahlias. In Bukovyna georgina isn't a Russian word. It's even a woman's name. [author's note]

"No-no, it was already after that. She, poor orphan, carried around the dug up roots all over the village as if they were her child. She wrapped them up in a blanket she used to cover herself with, pressed them to her breasts to warm them up, and brought them — unswaddled them just like a child. I'm telling you, Vasyuta, my heart began to ache so much then that I thought twice about even quarreling with my Slavko, and he's not handicapped after all... I wish lightning had struck him in my bosom, he'll make me die before my time with that damned vodka of his, God grant he burn up..."

"May boils cover my tongue for saying such things!"

*

...And sweet Darusya is sitting in a flower bed among the asters, three steps from Maria and Vasylyna, she's braiding and unbraiding her hair that had thinned out and turned gray long ago, she's listening to the tender conversation about her, just quietly smiling to herself.

They just don't have any brains in their head or God in their belly, her neighbors, 'cause they think she's foolish in the head. But Darusya's not foolish — she's sweet.

So what if she raked the dahlia roots into a blanket? It was right at the time the snow had disappeared, and the frost hadn't yet let up. Darusya passed the flowers out throughout the village because she had dug up so many in the spring, even more than there were potatoes in the cellar. And so she carried them to the houses that didn't have flowers blooming around them. Would she have carried a bare root in such a chill? For some reason Vasyuta doesn't carry her grandson to the garden in just his pants, but wraps him up in a little blanket, and then takes him in her arms and rocks him through the village. A child is just like a living flower.

Darusya is sitting on the warm, still almost summery ground, she's stroking the cheery little heads of the asters, with the palm of her hand she's tousling the fragrant locks, speaking to them, telling them what she wants, laughing — and what is so foolish about that?

How can she be foolish when she *understands* everything, she knows what everything is called, what today's date is, how many apple trees have borne fruit in Maria's garden, how many people have been born in the village from one Christmas to another, and how many have died?! In the Village Council they look up this kind of knowledge in a book, but Darusya keeps everything in her head. She's better off talking to chickens than to people. The trees understand her, dogs don't bother her, but people — no. People can't leave Darusya alone.

But she doesn't want to talk to people, because then they'll just *give her a piece of candy* they know will make her sick.

And what can you think about this when there's nothing to think about? People in the village sometimes do things that even make Darusya pull her hair out, but for some reason they don't call them foolish, but about her, who speaks with the trees and flowers, and who just lives the way she wants, and though she doesn't do any harm to anyone, they think of her as foolish.

And if she's really foolish, can you tell she's handicapped by looking at her?

...Fedyo put a saddle on his ram and carried his son to school on it, and no one said that Fedyo was foolish, though from that day on the nickname "ram-boy" stuck to his son.

And Stepan one day came from the city on the village church's yearly holiday celebration and brought with him a big shiny washer of immense proportion. Near the club the boys were playing "dare," and Stepan bet a bottle of beer he could put the steel washer onto the *foolishness* under his pants, and after half an hour remove it, with no harm done to his *foolishness*. But *the foolishness from under Stepan's pants* didn't take heed of Stepan, swelled up, and nearly broke off in the skirmish with the washer. So Dmytro the welder ended up cutting off the washer on Stepan's shame with some kind of saw. It took so long that his hands shook because he didn't want to cause damage to Stepan's goods, because Stepan was supposed to get married soon. They laughed it up in the village, lamented a bit — but they didn't call Stepan foolish.

In the village they think Darusya doesn't understand, so they use the word *sweet* in talking to her instead of calling her *dim*.

Maria's son Slavko somehow once got so drunk that he carried out an entire yearling pig, stabbed it thirteen times in the chest with a knife, threw it into the pond near the house, and banned his household from going up to the water. "Let the damn bastard swim!" The drunken Slavko screamed so loudly that he could be heard countywide." And whoever doesn't do it my way will be catching frogs in the pond!" The pig floated for two days in the water, and it was really getting to be a hot summer, so it started to stink, and no one of Slavko's household dared take pity on the mortified soul, fearful of the crazed drunken temper of the master of the house.

But it was Darusya who waited things out until his entire household had gone their separate ways. She took a pitchfork, found a new rope for the cow in Slavko's barn, brought a stone from the river, carried the pig to the banks with the pitchfork, tied a stone around it, made a sign of the cross over it — and the poor killed thing began to gurgle its way to the bottom.

In the evening Slavko stormed in the yard and roared like a bull across the fence at Darusya, baring his rotten teeth:

"Fool!!! Fool, don't you want a candy? Here's a candy for you! A candy!" And he threw a handful of barberry flavored ones right near the door to her house.

*

It would have been better if he had not mentioned the *candy*. In the village no person with half a brain mentions or gives Darusya candies: they know that her head aches from *sweets* and she vomits terribly from them. So terribly that by morning not even a tiny sliver of life remains in her. And it takes her a week to come back from that other world.

It happened that way after Slavko's words.

Darusya didn't leave the house for two days — her head ached so much that she couldn't even look at the ceiling, she just tied her head up with scarves, covered herself up with a pillow and turned away toward the wall. She didn't eat, didn't drink, didn't get up to go to the bathroom — she just waited until the iron rings that were pressing her head broke, as if they had wanted to completely crush her.

A few times Maria took a look in on Darusya. She silently put a half-liter of milk on the table, and then she unwrapped Darusya's head and rubbed it in badger fat. On the top she put on a cabbage leaf, onto the leaf — a small handful of coarse wool and tied it up again with a white scarf.

Darusya, wasted away, quite entirely without strength, dwindled like a little child, silently let herself be turned over, and then sat down, holding her head in her lap until Maria rubbed badger fat on the crown of her head with her cold hands. She didn't have the strength to say a word. Her head had been blown off somewhere so far away that she held it all the more tightly with her hands as though she were defending herself from a thug. If that thug would have been so kind as to call some butcher, maybe Semén, who chops up pigs for people, and if Semén could have cut out the pain from Darusya's head, then she would have been overjoyed, and, perhaps, finally would have begun to speak.

But the thug was nowhere to be seen, just a sharp unbearable knife tears along under the crown of her head — and from despair Darusya at that very moment would have given her head to be chopped off. She doesn't have the strength to endure that infinite pain. She doesn't have the strength even to listen as Maria quietly sobs at the table and sniffles. It would have been better for her to go to her Slavko or to anybody she wanted to go to, so the sobbing would not torment her. Maria's sobbing seems like the blows of a hammer in a gypsy forge. And Darusya all the more strongly presses against the wall, yearning for just peace and quiet.

It was this way every time when the pain knocked her down. Maria, crying a little and grumbling inaudible words under her nose, walked on further. And Darusya remained with her head ripped apart from the pain in an empty house until *something* hit her with a knife in the heart — and then she got up and went following her eyes.

*

…And this time her legs carried her to the river. Darusya went into the water up to her knees — and she felt better right away. The cold water floated through her somewhere to the very edge of the sky, and with eyes shut Darusya rocked side-to-side, sensing the rings that had been pressing her head for two days and nights had loosened up. Somewhere there, deep inside, they cracked so loudly that it seemed like sparks were strewing themselves into the river, but Darusya didn't open her eyes, knowing that, just as she opens them, the rings again will plait a nest in her poor little head, the way that snakes on the Feast of the Holy Cross wind their lair into the ground for the winter.

When Darusya's head hurts, she has to wade into the river up to her waist in the water. Otherwise the pain cuts her into tiny little pieces. It's good when it's summer and the water is warm. Then no one forbids her from standing in the water. When it turns cold, she goes into the water just up to her knees. The colder the water, the quicker the pain would let go of Darusya.

The first time after having attacks of pain for several days, something told Darusya that she needed to look for *cold water*. At first she looked for a long time into the well in her yard. But it was far down to the water, and Darusya didn't have a long ladder. The one that led to the chicken coop had rotted long ago and wouldn't reach the bottom. Then Darusya stumbled to the river, with both of her hands holding her head as if at any moment it might roll off her neck, with her drunken gait frightening the village women in their flowerbeds and vegetable gardens. While she was slowly entering the water in her bare feet, nearly half of the neighborhood gathered.

"Mother of God, she's come to drown herself! Tie her up, Maria, she'll only let you come up to her!" Varvara the crook said to Darusya's neighbor from the riverbank, waving a twisted rope from the wash line.

Maria looked for a long time as Darusya with eyes shut rocked from side to side, having gone up to her chest into the icy water. Quietly she finally said:

"Leave her be, girls… She won't do anything to herself. As God grants, so it will be. And you don't have to tie her up, Varvara. It's better if you tie up your tongue with that rope… Go back to your homes, ladies, and I'll sit a bit near sweet Darusya and then

I'll go home to my stupid…."

*

Since that time no one would go with Darusya to the river any more. She wouldn't even have gone there if she didn't have to rinse her wash. But wash is wash, your head is more important. So, when just after the attacks of pain something drove her out of bed, she would go to the river, and no one held her arms anymore; the women just followed her movements with their eyes, placing their palms over their brows, and one of the school children quietly chuckled: "Just look, sweet Darusya is going swimming again." For that time and again he got a poke in the back of the neck from another schoolboy who was a little more intelligent than he was.

It's good until the river freezes up. And the first time that Darusya stood on the ice and it didn't break, she wanted to break it with her head because she needed to go into the icy water, even if it would have cost her her life. She got down on her knees, hit her brow once or twice on the ice — and quietly began to whimper: the ice was hard and didn't give in. Darusya stamped her bare feet along the river's frozen floor, her legs weakened from several days of lying down, she struck the ice as though she were kneading clay, and wrung her hands from despair.

And here from somewhere, as if he were following in her footsteps, Maria's Slavko appeared. And Darusya's head immediately stopped hurting: *Slavko was sober*. It seemed to her that since birth — perhaps only during childhood — she hadn't seen Slavko sober, and now he was steadily walking to her to the middle of the river with a trembling outstretched hand. Always with a mouth full of words, Slavko this time was as silent as a mute.

And Darusya also stretched out her hand to him.

So they walked along the bank, with hands stretched out to one another, as though they were being led to a marriage ceremony or on a rope leash. Slavko didn't utter a cutting — or any — word for that matter, and Darusya obediently followed him, not feeling the wintry cold.

Slavko brought Darusya to the village greenhouse. A small, almost round little lake with a handful of fountains that were unceasingly pulsing up from under the earth hid behind the fence of bare willows by the bank. The clean water pulsed in front of Darusya's eyes, and she, immodestly rolling her skirt up to her bellybutton, stepped into the abundant gurgling.

When she stepped onto the bank, Slavko wasn't anywhere to be seen. But she knew the way home herself.

*

...So now Darusya is standing in the cold bath of autumn — and fighting with the nails hammered into her head by some kind of heavy, heartless hammer. A certain amount of time passes — the black iron of pain finally settles on the river bottom, and then spreading one of her headscarves, Darusya sits down on a stone. The pure transparent water rinses her bare legs and further down all the way to her ankles. She feels it finally easing for her. The gurgling of the river finally calms Darusya — and again she returns to her endless thinking.

She *doesn't know how not to think.* Perhaps it's because she doesn't say a word to anyone, but isn't mute, that's why she thinks incessantly. So she thinks about everything in the world — and from that her head is always aching.

...Darusya is surprised that no one ties up Slavko when he gets drunk and debauches all over half the village. On Easter Sunday he got so loaded that he wanted to burn down the barn, and then a blue flame shot out of his mouth.

Her head uncovered,[*] Maria ran to her neighbors screaming and crying: "Good people, help! Christ is Risen! Slavko's dying!"

Mykola the forester, without getting up from the Easter table, peacefully told the disheveled Maria, who looked like a madwoman standing at the doorway:

"Maria, piss into his mouth, he'll get better right away. If you don't have any piss, dilute some horse dung with water and pour some of

[*] According to village custom, married women should wear a scarf on their heads as a sign of their respectable status.

it into his mouth... There on the path near Sokil the collective farm horses have left droppings, nobody's planning on gathering them up.

That poor Maria... So, the way she was dressed in her Easter skirt, she lifted it up in the middle of the yard and pissed into the blue flame coming out of her son's mouth. His father and some visitor from outside the village held down Slavko, who had fallen onto the ground like a pig getting ready to be stuck.

Darusya started to feel bad for Slavko, who might burn up for nothing from the *horilka*,* and in the evening she brought him the last red apple from her cellar and gave it to Maria in silence. To which Maria's husband sighed:

"People take *pysanky* to normal people,** but sweet Darusya brings her last apple to the roaring drunk.

Maria sat on the chair near the bed near Slavko's head, who was clearing his throat from beneath the quilted coat that had been thrown on him. And she was holding her head with both hands the same way that Darusya would hold it when she got an attack of pain, and she staggered back and forth exactly the same way, as though rusty rings were tearing her head.

And which of them now was stupid, Maria, her son, or both of them at the same time, Darusya truthfully didn't know.

That's why she goes to the river, sits on the bank right on the green grass that already reaches up toward the sun, and gazes at the water. Her head isn't hurting today. Today is Easter Sunday, and she put on really old shoes, but nevertheless her Easter best. And tomorrow Darusya will take them off till the next Easter Sunday and will walk barefoot until the river freezes over. And when it freezes over — she'll pull on her father's felt boots.

---

* Ukrainian vodka. Its root word *hority* means "to burn."

** The famous colorful Ukrainian Easter eggs with geometric patterns and symbols. The word for them comes from the verb "pysaty," which means to write. They are literally "written" in beeswax with a stylus before they are dipped in various dyes.

When she walks barefoot, the pain bothers her less. She sometimes even digs a hole in the middle of the garden to the height of her lower back, she lowers herself into it, wraps herself in the living black cover that tickles her body with broken roots, worms and rotted leaves, and she stands or sits in the living earth this way for hours. The earth takes away her pain and gives her the sap of life. It rises up along her body to her brow, as if along a tree trunk, and inside herself Darusya again feels strength that had been taken from her head by the red-hot iron of pain when it seemingly crawls out even through her ears and skin.

Then she thinks: is it good to make fun of her when at times she spends the day half buried in the earth while Tarasyk had been saved in the village this way when he was shocked by electricity? They buried him up to his neck, and the earth pulled death out of him. But no one made fun of Tarasyk's father, or his brothers who had placed him in the dug up hole as if it were a cemetery grave.

Why has the village made fun of unfortunate Darusya for years? Electricity struck Tarasyk *just one time*. But the pain strikes her head almost every day. What, should she wait for someone else's help? They can't even help themselves, why would they care about her? They should be happy for Darusya that she doesn't cause them problems. But heck... let them make the crazy sign with their hands. All the same, just stupid ones make it. If they would just stop reminding her about the candy.

*

People don't understand that Darusya saves herself any way she can. Sometimes with water, sometimes with earth, sometimes with herbs. Because more than anything she wants to live in *this* world, which is such a happy, colorful and fragrant one. When she is healthy she makes up for the lost time when she writhed in pain. She doesn't want to remember because she's already so wracked with pain that she doesn't know how she can walk on her legs.

But Darusya never complains about anything. She takes a faded little ball of colored wool threads, several scraps of wide tinsel folded in four, ribbons from the wedding wreath of Maria's daughter Anna, and she goes into her golden orchard, among the pear and apple trees planted by her father's hands. The apple trees already don't bear very good fruit. They're old. But the fruit still shines here and there among the sparse gold of the leaves. And the pear tree has completely dried up. It already has as many leaves as the hair on Pitryk's bald head.

Darusya shimmies up the pear tree and begins to tie tinsel strips around the sad branches. Why should the tree be sad, when the autumn sun warms up, when Darusya isn't wracked with pain in her brain? On Sunday Darusya always puts on her mother's embroidered blouse. And what, the pear tree can't have a blouse today, sewn by Darusya's hands? The tinsel shines in the sun, the wind rocks the colored threads on the red leaves — and Darusya wants to sing. But someone might hear. Singing also causes harm. Ivanna and Vasyl sang so much about a red guelder rose* that they carted them off to Siberia where they keep them to this very day. Or maybe they're not keeping them anymore, because there's nobody there anymore?!

---

* A national emblem of Ukraine and the central image in a patriotic Ukrainian song. During Soviet times Ukrainians could be imprisoned for singing it.

from MOSKALYTSIA, THAT RUSSKY GIRL[*]

by Maria Matios

Translated by Michael M. Naydan

For every woman individually…

For certain, Panska Dolyna[**] knew one thing: Katrinka had named her daughter not for her biological father, but rather just to deflect people's talk from the truth, and to protect the child — from judgmental slander.

But it actually was this way.

Petro Severyn, Ivan's son, stopped dating Katrinka the day right before the feast day of Maccabean Martyrs.[***]

On that feast day in 1914, Petro Severyn, along with a score of village men, was taken away to the tsar's war.

---

[*] The word "moskal'" in its masculine form means a Russian soldier or a Russian, both with pejorative connotations. The feminine version of the word also has derogatory connotations.

[**] It can be translated as something like "Noble Valley" or "Splendid Valley."

[***] Called "Makovei" in the popular tradition. It is the feast day of The Seven Holy Maccabean Martyrs. The Orthodox church holiday occurs on August 1 according to the Gregorian calendar and on August 14 according to the Julian. For more information on the holiday see: *http://www.holytrinityorthodox.com/calendar/los/August/01-03.htm*. Ukrainian village life often revolved around the church as the center of the community and the church calendar, and was a typical way of telling time.

And a week before the Beheading of John the Baptist,* for the first time during this first war, a foreign army dashed into Noble Valley on gray horses. It was mostly a Russian one.

In time the army, ravenous for someone else's property and ferocious regarding the damages it would cause, would dash into Noble Valley two more times. But that already would have nothing to do with Katrina's fate.

And the first time, until the army had cleared out of the frightened village, its soldiers managed to do plenty of harm to the people. All in just a little more than a month.

Some had their agricultural implements cleared from stables and threshing barns as though they had been shaven clean with a razor.

Some were orphaned from a milking cow or fattened pigs, not to mention the chickens.

Some prematurely — only because of their innocent blood and unbridled power — were shown to the next world.

And some of the locals were spared from pillaging and massacre — and were left even with their offspring.

So, when on the Feast Day of Saints Peter and Paul** in 1915 Katrinka unexpectedly bore a child, Noble Valley gave her a name quicker than the village priest.

Katrinka, for several months was gossip in the teeth of the chaste young married women in the village, like prey in the maw of a hawk, and after all of that — purified and confessed in the church, didn't think long and asked no advice from anyone, but immediately baptized the baby girl...Severyna. As if she were directly indicating the last name of her father. The fact that the child had the same last name as Petro, the son of Ivan Severyn, there was nothing to be surprised at: half of the Lord's Valley had the last surname of Severyn, and the other half — Polotniuk.

---

* Celebrated August 29 in the Gregorian calendar and September 11 according to the Julian. Known as "Holovosik" (the Beheading) in the popular tradition.

** Celebrated June 29 in the Gregorian calendar and July 12 in the Julian.

But the boneless wagging tongues in the village, long before the church baptismal record book did so, ascribed the newly born child her lifelong name — Moskalytsia. As though directly, but already aloud, calling to mind last year's overnight stay in Katrina's house of three black-haired soldiers — Russians, after whose retreat the door from the porch to the entryway swayed for a day, opened wide, and the orphan girl didn't show herself in the yard from Thursday till Saturday.

When during white Saturday* Katrinka stood by the well in her torn white blouse with thick brown bloodstains on it, she first poured a bucket of water on her head, without even moving her eyes, in case one of her neighbors would see this.

She further carried out into the yard all her household goods and set about to whitewash her squat house.

Each wall three times.

Both outside and inside.

To which her attentive and wide-eyed neighbors still shrugged their shoulders: it was a long time till Christmas, even longer to Easter, but the girl was overdoing it, as though preparing for her wedding: she was certainly still waiting for Petro Severyn from the war.

When Katrinka made her baby, no one thought anything of it or particularly shrugged their shoulders: each house had its own problems. And in some — it was even worse.

Unfortunately, Petro Severyn, just as the five other men from Noble Valley, perished in Serbia. Therefore, there was no one to confirm or disprove his fatherhood. And in the end there was no need to.

On the signet seals of this story some of the more gracious and softhearted tried to soften the name of the innocent bastardess, call-ing her a Russian girl (*rusachka*) behind her back. But the nickname Moskalytsia stuck to the child no worse than if she had been intention-ally tarred with a brush made of straw or branded on her skin.

---

* The Saturday before Easter and the end of the Great Fast (Lent). It is the day when baskets filled with Easter eggs (pysanky and colored eggs) and other Easter foods are blessed. The holiday probably gets its name from the white robes neo-phytes wore as they went to be baptized on the Saturday before Easter.

The father of the deceased Petro Severyn — Ivan, who received a government pension for the loss of his son in the war, one day brought Katrina thirty krone. He didn't say a lot. He just looked over the house for a long time as though he were trying not to meet the gaze of the young woman, who herself resembled a child, and not a mother. And he further gazed into her pale face — and stared this way until he said everything that he wanted to say, almost without breathing:

"You'll buy yourself some shoes, poor thing. Because I can't look at you walking barefoot in the village. I know this isn't Petro's child. You were an honorable maiden. But it would be better if the child were Petro's… we'd at least have a remembrance of our son. But what can you do — that's fate… And the war, if it could only have disappeared from our sight, God willing…"

So as not to anger a good man, in whose eyes stood autumn slush and inexpressible pity, Katrinka bought women's shoes for 24 krone, though she hesitated for a long time: she could have worn leg wrappings till her old age. Even on Easter Sunday to church.

But the new shoes funded by Petro's father a needless time superfluously confirmed before the village population Katrina's honest maidenhood, and also the good opinion of her in the eyes of old Severyn.

Katrinka put the rest of the money behind the icon of St. Catherine the Great Martyr — her kind intercessor and patroness — into the house.

So the mice in the house didn't devour leaving bits of that once valuable tsar's paper, which Katrinka, through her lack of knowledge, failed to exchange for the new money — Romanian leus. Since with her village wisdom she was not capable of grasping the reversals of fortune of greater world politics. For great politics as always rumbled through lands and people with a merciless cart, and after the war and the next repartition of countries the politics of the tiny Noble Valley (Austrian from time immemorial and Ruthenian in essence) was now being written by the Romanian.

As always in such situations, whether it was just or not particularly, nature made the law, all the same its own, among the people. Impartial, nearly indifferent, it canceled all human debts and forgave minor offenses that over the course of life are collected among people in a small territory.

Thus the natural law now was momentary and cruel: in 1927 a sudden nighttime flood in the blink of an eye sealed the great drama of Katrinka's innocent soul, carrying off into the world along the water several homesteads from Noble Valley, and together with them — Katrina's white body with her squalid house, with icons of the Lord, and the no longer legal six Austrian krone behind the icon of St. Catherine the Great Martyr.

The nighttime catastrophe didn't leave a trace of an entire human life.

And it didn't carry a recognizable body to the shore.

Thus, it was as if a person had never lived… had never jubilated and had never cried, and just existed only to fertilize the earth with her decay.

There's the entire worth of a person for you.

God continued the days for Katrina's daughter Severyna, because at that time she was already hiring herself out among the people. At the time of the flood she was rocking a baby at the Travyany Homestead owned by the Polotniuks — Andriy and Paraska.

Suddenly the orphaned child had nowhere to turn to, and after several years the Polotniuk's neighbors — the childless homestead owners Dmytro and Maria Onufrichuk — took poor Severyna in as a foster child, finally finding peace in knowing that there would be someone to bring them a glass of water before their last day. She was hard-working. The way her mother Katrinka was. Except for her disposition…how to put it more precisely? Well, somehow…different.

Katrinka for the girls was a funny girl for all of Noble Valley, until misfortune happened, unexpectedly pranced into the house on horses with weapons.

But Severyna had to be paid to utter a word.

Even for that harsh, like the blow of a whip on the back, word — "Moskalytsia," she would never respond to anyone.

She did her work silently — as though she were keeping a secret behind her teeth. And she didn't particularly have anyone to talk to. Travyane Farmstead was far from the village: by the time you reach the farmstead on Easter from church from Noble Valley — chicks will hatch from the *pysanky.**

---

* Ukrainian Easter eggs
NB: Moskalytsia was published in its entirety in Yuri Tkacz's English translation by Bayda Books in 2011 as The Russky Woman..

from APOCALYPSE

by Maria Matios

Translated by Yuri Tkacz

I

ON SUNDAY, BEFORE DAWN, AFTER DAWN, AND EVEN AFTER THE SUN had set, before the church service, during the reading of the Gospels and after the priest's thrice-repeated blessing, the whole of Tysova Rivnia spoke of nothing else, aloud and in hushed whispers, but the fact that

there would either be a new war,
or some other pestilence would descend upon the land,
and peaceful times would come to people
only after they had died –

for there was no other possibility and it could not have been otherwise.

For neither in Tysova Rivnia, nor anywhere else where soldiers and traders had ventured from this village, a village hemmed in by mountains and fanned by winds, a village which had taken on the name of the hardest wood in the world — the *yew**, never before had such a miracle happened to either the tough or the timid, or indeed any type of person; a man who had been completely healthy in the evening was found to be comatose the following morning, and then had lain in bed for three more years like a log, lying there without

---

* Tysova is Ukrainian for yew (feminine adjectival form).

waking, and then suddenly one fine morning, not even on Easter Day and without any shamanic rituals having been performed, after three years of non-existence, right before the eyes of his daughter-in-law who had nearly taken a turn, he had simply sat up in bed, looked about without recognizing a thing and, very unsteadily, but nevertheless on his own two feet, had made his way to the door, as if going off to the toilet after a good night's sleep.

After that, the *whys* and *wherefores* were passed on by those eager to communicate other people's fortunes and misfortunes, and the hair of the timid stood on end, while tears welled up in the eyes of the tough.

But, Lord, forgive all those with their rumours, lies and tall tales.

The only truth was that one Saturday morning Tymofiy Sanduliak actually returned from the other world, from where no one had yet managed to return safely.

The fact that Sanduliak had been in the *other* world was evident even to small children in Tysova Rivnia, let alone the moss-covered righteous and the respected healers, together with the hardened thieves and utter fools.

"Who are you?" Tymofiy glared at his daughter-in-law, Sofia, with drowsy bulging eyes. He rose from the bed with such unexpected certitude, that if an outsider had been in the house at the time, it might have appeared that he had barely had time to catch a quick nap, and that already restless wolfhounds or the ubiquitous cloud-chasing devil were spurring him on to do some small mischief on the farm.

At that very same moment, Sofia was pushing tins of bread dough into the oven. In utter surprise, even had she wanted to, she could not have fallen further than the cold bench top in front of the oven. The iron poker dropped from her hands and struck her toes, but scared to death, Sofia failed to notice this. For a brief moment she looked insanely at the stark-naked skeletal figure; a veritable grey-haired beggar with flabby dry skin, straggly greasy hair and a long white beard. Wordlessly, but purposefully he made his way toward her, ripping the thin clear plastic tubes from his nose as he advanced.

The daughter-in-law sat down as if glued to the floor; however, a moment later she jumped to her feet and dashed into the entrance hall so quickly, that the old man, who looked more like a ghost than a living person, was still struggling to yank out the tube stuck in his throat. Meanwhile the woman's frightful screams filled the empty morning yard.

"*O-o-oh, help me, someone!!! Help! It's the end of the world!!!*" Sofia hollered deliriously, waving about the white scarf, which she had pulled from her head together with a large tuft of hair, and dashed from one side of the fenced yard to the other, as if lacking the wits to open the gate into the street.

...Few people were interested in what happened next.

The residents of Tysova Rivnia, from the mill at the *near end* of the village to the mill at the *far end*, were all shocked by the incredulous news, but, after all the lamentation and wringing of hands by the women, and after the silent actions of pacification by the men, everyone was interested in only two things.

The first was: what would become of the Sanduliaks now? The second concerned those who were more informed about the ancient and strange history of this reclusive family. Still others were unnerved by the niggling thought of God's retribution, which finally caught up with people, just as they had stopped thinking about the possibility of such punishment ever being meted out.

And at the very bottom of people's minds, somewhere even deeper than where their tiny soul cowered in terror, everyone was tormented by an engorged twisted grub of disquiet: "What if suddenly... maybe... something similar... God forbid... was visited upon me..."

2

From about the times of Franz Josep in Pisky* (since ages past this outlying corner had been dubbed thus in Tysova Rivnia, despite its soil being unusually choice for a mountain location), but definitely before

---

* Literally "Sands."

World War One, only Austrian colonists had lived here, set apart from the rest of the village. There were perhaps a dozen or so households. These were for the most part former impoverished townsfolk from the alpine regions. Unlucky fate, wanderlust and a craving for adventure had driven them here amid the black and densely forested mountains of Bukovyna, which, from afar, had promised the dreamers limitless wealth, true peace of mind and quiet twilight years after their passions had died down.

Among the hard-working Austrians and *Schwabs**, who were quite savvy and resourceful, quite by chance, or, perhaps not, three Jewish families somehow ended up in Pisky. They had found no comfortable place to settle in the neighbouring town, that is in the *shtetl* of Vyzhny-tsia, an exceptionally crowded Jewish colony on the banks of the deep waters of the Cheremosh River.

Or perhaps Schlioma Buchbinder, Abram Mashtaler and Leon Reich, each with their own continually replenished *kahal* of old and young family members, themselves had decided either against multiplying their own poverty, or to stop annoying their less successful relatives or fellow Jews. So these three families had chosen a place removed from busy thoroughfares and countless envious eyes.

In any case, the mix of people in Pisky differed little from the mix in Tsaryna, near Mlyny or in Luhy, that is, in all the other corners of Tysova Rivnia, where life proceeded sometimes peacefully, sometimes violently.

The newly-married village miller Tymofiy Sanduliak settled on a block of rich land which was as flat as a pancake and located immedi-ately behind the Jewish gardens. By a stroke of luck he had managed to purchase seven *falchi*** of land from Abram Mashtaler, upon which he had erected a house with two rooms, an entrance hall between them, and an open porch facing the road.

Behind the miller's place, a little closer to the Cheremosh River, where the village cattle grazed from spring until autumn on the

---

* *Schwabs* — name given to the Germans by the local populace.

** *Falcha* (plural — *falchi*) — an old unit of land measurement equal to 263.5 m2.

commons meadow, the aspen reached up to the sky. Or *trepeta*, as the locals liked to call it. The trees were so high, that if one were to clamber into their tops, said the old people, one could see the snow-capped peaks of Chornohora.[*]

However, even the greatest hooligans in Tysova Rivnia — the children — for some reason never dared skin their knees on the very tops of the white, eternally-trembling trees. They didn't even try to grab hold of the branches, which bent almost to the ground — not even to have a bit of a swing over the meadows, which were fragrant with lungwort, yarrow and clover.

From early spring until just before winter the *trepeta* tirelessly rustled its timorous leaves and glistened with its white, almost cream-colored trunks for all of Pisky to see, rising well above the other trees, which were by no means diminutive, in this populous corner of the village.

No tree could compete with the aspen in exuberance of growth.

Neither in Pisky, nor anywhere else in Tysova Rivnia.

From this lonely rural stand of aspen began the unraveling of Sanduliak's life, until then so very ordinary.

Early one autumn Tymofiy had decided to cut back the lower branches of the *trepeta*, which were drooping like a man's untrimmed mustache, and to use them to make a floor in the barn. He had already raised his axe, was gauging where he needed to make the cut, when Mashtaler's wife, Ester, practically leapt out from the river's turbulent waters — she was thin as a splinter and pale as buttermilk, and was carrying her washed rags draped over her left shoulder.

"Don't you touch it!" she exclaimed at first, and then continued in hushed tones: "This tree is damned...," Ester spoke as if she intended to shield the tree with her body, but she looked Tymofiy straight in the eye as she spoke.

"It's just ordinary old wood... Good for flooring," the cringing Tymofiy replied uncertainly, and lowered his axe.

---

[*] Chornohora (literally: *Black Mountain*) is the highest mountain range in the Ukrainian Carpathian Mountains. The highest peak is Hoverla (2,062 m).

"Little do you know! Your people say it's an evil tree. When Joseph and Mary hid from Herod under it, all the other trees became silent, except for the aspen, which kept rustling its leaves... and gave them away."

"Don't carry on...," Tymofiy shrugged his shoulders.

"...They also say Judas Iscariot hung himself on an aspen. The rabbi used to tell us he was 'Ish krayot.'* He called him a man of the outskirts. The squalid part of town... They from the outskirts know not what they do, when the will of the Lord is being done...." Ester seemed not to notice that Tymofiy was cowering. "From that time on the *trepeta* always trembles with fear. And they say that you shouldn't use aspen to build a house, or else your whole family will tremble day and night with disease, just like the tree. You can't use an aspen stick to hit cattle or people, otherwise they'll become contorted as hell." Ester herself seemed to be trembling, as if she too was made of aspen leaves or simply trembling from the cold. "You can build an enclosure using *trepeta* around where your cattle sleep. And no witch, or she-devil, or she-werewolf, or any other evil spirit will visit your cow at night to suckle the milk from its udder if there is an aspen stake driven into the ground in the yard."

...Tymofiy heard out his neighbour's soft, although challenging monologue, but he chopped down the accessible branches all the same, and cut away the trembling leaves and burnt them beside his house, using the aspen wood to line the floor of the barn.

Some time after this, on St Andrew's Day, the two close neighbours gave birth at the same time to children: Tymofiy's wife Maria gave Sanduliak a son — the blond Andriy, and Ester bore Mashtaler a black-haired little girl, who for some reason was named Andrea. 'Maybe the Jews have a name like that too,' Tymofiy thought, but asked no questions.

And afterwards came the war. Sanduliak, together with many others from Tysova Rivnia, was conscripted into the Kaiser's army.

To avenge the death of the crown prince.

---

* Iscariot is Greek for *Ish-Krayot* or man of the Krayot (outskirts).

3

When Tymofiy returned from Serbia, Mashtaler's Ester, burdened with two more children, was already a widow. Although the Russian Circassian Cossack unit had been stationed in Tysova Rivnia for a short while, it had left behind a frightful legacy of plunder and murder of the Jews.

Among the dead had been Abram Mashtaler, who to his own and his family's misfortune happened to be in Chaim Melamed's tavern buying some Hanukah candles right at the moment a pogrom took place there.

In addition the Circassians had left a few of the village women with rounded bellies after raping them and provoked evil curses from the old grandpas, bent double with age, as they left the village on horses that were forever tired and forever hungry.

Eighteen months after the departure of the Circassian Cossacks, during the Brusilov Offensive of 1916, Tysova Rivnia was again host to another detachment of Russkies, no less wild when it came to robbery, but who nevertheless did not perpetrate any great pogroms against the people, even though they had as good a nose for women as a musket had for an Austrian soldier debilitated in battle.

After her husband's sudden death, Ester had gone about dressed in black for a long time, just like the rest of her fellow village women — be they Hutsul, Austrian, German, Polish or Jewish — whose husbands had been scattered about the near and distant corners of the Earth (and no one knew whether they had left forever or only until the conflagration of war was over). And then Ester began to wander about the village with her head uncovered for some reason, accompanied without fail by her children — Andrea, Yosyp and Yudit. This caused the tongues of certain respectable farmer's wives to flap: "Has the widowed Jewess lost her mind?"

Sanduliak's little Andriy, fidgety and restless, joyfully teased the elder Mashtaler daughter, calling her a *sister*, pulling on her long plaits braided tightly to hide her pitch-colored curly locks. Or else nervously, although without malice, he tousled Andrea's thick plaits, fixed crosswise around her little round head.

In reply Andrea unfailingly struck little Andriy's brisk fingers with disdain and each time, with the same enmity, she repeated through her small chipped clenched teeth:

"While your dad was away at war, the Circassian Cossacks killed my daddy," contemptuously shrugging her right shoulder and moving away from little Andriy, disappearing into the dense bushes of jasmine growing on the boundary between their two yards.

After each of these verbal altercations Ester gave her daughter a good hiding with a thin cane either across her bare legs or her buttocks. But this did not stop Andrea from starting each conversation with the young Sanduliak boy with words, which she seemed to have learnt by rote: "*While your dad was away at war....*"

Mrs. Mashtaler acted if not warmly, then at least courteously, toward the Sanduliaks. As happened between neighbours who were close territorially, but not in spirit.

Meanwhile, the childhood friendship which had at one time blossomed between Andriy and Andrea, when they had been divided only by a fence, had evaporated, as if it had never existed.

4

...Little Andriy already had bum fluff growing above his upper lip when late one afternoon, for the first time since her childhood confrontations, Andrea appeared on the doorstep of her neighbours' house dressed in a white linen shirt with jasmine and linden flowers, wild rose and tight heads of yarrow pinned to it, her cheeks unusually rosy and with a strange glint in her eyes.

"What can I do for you, darling?" Maria Sanduliak raised her forever sad eyes at the curly-haired child, resplendent, like a poppy in flower and fragrant from head to toe — and was amazed at the unusual beauty which streamed from the small girl's face. She would very soon become a maiden, or perhaps she was one already.

"My mum Ester invites all of you to come visit us for Purim. And she also said to bring your own dress-ups from Malanka*, because we don't have enough costumes for everyone."

"For Purim?!" Mrs. Sanduliak wiped her wet hands against her apron and feverishly tried to recall all the Jewish festivals, which were fewer in number than the Orthodox Christian ones.

Even with her limited female mind, she recalled that Purim never seemed to fall in the middle of summer. Besides, the Jews of Tysova Rivnia had already celebrated the current year's Purim a little over a month after Christian Christmas.

Maria would sooner have thought that Ester was inviting the male members of the Sanduliak family for a Mourners' Kaddish: 'The Jews also have heaps of their own prayers. Just like the Orthodox Christians, they have prayers for every major and minor saint.' However, Maria also knew that the Jews mourned their dead for only seven days. They called this *shiva* — the family sat on the floor and the men didn't shave for seven days.

After that the Jews did not hold any memorial services on the ninth or even the fortieth day. Except perhaps, reading a memorial Kaddish during the ensuing eleven months and each year at *yahrzeit* — the anniversary of a person's death.

But there was no synagogue in Tysova Rivnia. And so in a single moment everything became all mixed up in Maria's head from the shame of not knowing the Jewish tradition, and even more — from the unexpected invitation she had received from Mashtaler's child.

5

Maria first year the Mourners' Kaddish when the surviving Jews of Tysova Rivnia — from the mill at the *near end* of the village to the mill at the *far end* — assembled in the Mashtalers' home after the Circassian pogrom

---

* *Malanka* — a Ukrainian folk festival celebrated on January 13. On this night carolers traditionally go from house to house playing pranks or acting out a small play; a bachelor in women's clothing leads the group. Malanka capped off the festivities of Christmas and was often the last opportunity for reveling before Lent.

in Melamed's tavern to read a mourners' prayer in memory of the slain Abram. For the most part these were impoverished rural Jews. They had not been conscripted into the army, nor shipped en masse out of Buko-vyna, as had happened to the Galician Jews, who had been deported to the distant provinces of Russia. They had not become refugees either: these people had nothing left to flee with. Except for perhaps their old age.

That time Maria came to Mrs. Mashtaler's straight after the family had returned from the Jewish cemetery at the edge of the village, where they had buried Abram only hours after he had been killed with a Circassian saber. The one-armed Marko — a cabinet-maker from the Tsaryny corner of the village — had hastily nailed together the simplest of wooden coffins made of roughly hewn planks of different types of wood, since it had been hard at the time to find anything else. And the body of the once comical Abram Mashtaler, who for some reason used to wear a Hutsul keptar made of thin goatskin over his *lapserdak**, was assiduously washed by the same one-armed Marko and Shlioma Buchbinder's son Yehuda, for they couldn't let the distraught Ester see her husband's body, which had been chopped almost in half; and they buried Abram without any tears or lamentation, having first wrapped him in a linen burial shroud, the *tachrichim*.

Dressed in black, Maria stood in the doorway of the Mashtalers' home. Ester and her three children were sitting on the floor. The men had black skull-caps.

Mrs. Sanduliak also squatted against the wall under the window. For a long time she hesitated whether to sit wordlessly and silently pray to her Christian God for the soul of the deceased Abram, or whether to cross herself at all.

The people in the house spoke softly to one another. Shlioma Bu-chbinder cut the edges of their jackets, vests and shirts with scissors. Maria offered Shlioma the bottom of her *keptar*. Shlioma sighed heav-ily and made the cut, but in the very corner, and on the underside, so that the cut was barely noticeable.

---

* Long black coat worn by Hassidic Jews.

Then Shlioma read a Jewish prayer for the dead man, although it did not carry the despair so common in Tysova Rivnia. After this, in words that Maria understood, he spoke about faith in the Lord, redemption and salvation, and then he glorified the holiness of the Almighty.

When Maria made ready to return home, Ester, who was overcome with grief, said quietly to her:

"Thank you for the *mitzvah*, Maria…"

"Who thanks people for the dead?!" Maria almost exclaimed.

"E-e-eh, no… In our language *mitzvah* means a good deed. You did a good deed, Maria, visiting us in our suffering."

One time when the two of them were on the riverbank hammering away with their wooden battledores against wet linen steeped in ashes, Ester complained to Mrs. Sanduliak that the war had not yet ended and a year had already passed since Abram had been killed, and there was no one to erect a gravestone on his grave. Yet she did not want any old gravestone, only a proper one, which could be made only by master Kogan from Vyzhnytsia. That is if he was still among the living…

6

…Master Yankel Kogan of Vyzhnytsia listened to Mrs. Sanduliak distractedly, but briefly:

"You beg me much longer about Abram? Better send me your boy and I teach him to carve stone. Because I no can do anymore. My hands cannot make all gravestones. People dying, only priests happy, because much work."

…Mrs. Sanduliak thought awhile, and then thought some more, and two days later she arrived at Kogan's workshop on horseback, ready to help him. She had left her son behind to guard the family farm. Who knew what might happen? The Circassians and the Russkies did not kill only Jewish men.

Yankel shook his head for a long time, hearing that, rather than being offered a male assistant, he was being asked to place the chisel into a woman's hands. He brought his hand down and said:

"Yankel not so heartless that he teach woman to write on stone when her husband not return from damned war. How many not come back, *oy!*" He grabbed his head with both hands: "Better look. Little bit at me, because woman's eye no more look at old Yankel, but better you look at stone. Stone always say more than man. And say only truth."

And he took the chisel in his hands.

...When all those quaint chimerical symbols, chiseled out so conscientiously from right to left, snuggled up one against the other under Kogan's chisel, Maria wiped her sweaty brow with the sleeve of her shirt, as if she herself had been adjusting this mute grief for Mashtaler onto the stone.

"What does it say, Yankel?" Mrs. Sanduliak asked timidly, after all the dust was blown away from the gravestone and the letters were wiped with a dry rag.

"O-o-oh, woman...," Kogan worked some rubbed tobacco into a piece of yellowed newspaper. "Abram's name here, in letters it give day when Abram killed, look," he moved his tobacco-stained finger over the convoluted letters, "in year five thousand six hundred and seventy-five. But most important it say here: *There are three crowns in the world. The crown of the Torah, the crown of priesthood and the crown of kingship. But the crown of a good name rises above them all.* This is written here, woman. But what not written here, but I tell you from me, the last crown is the hardest to wear. Old Yankel Kogan tells you this, man who remind living about the dead, but they not always hear him."

"I hear you," Maria placated the master engraver for some reason. Afterwards they loaded Abram's gravestone onto the wagon, which Mrs. Sanduliak had borrowed from the village priest, and then she took hold of the reins: "I need to be in Tysova Rivnia by nightfall. At the Jewish cemetery."

A KISS ON THE BOTTOM

by Eugenia Kononenko
Translated by Michael M. Naydan

"HOW MUCH DO I HAVE TO TELL YOU NOT TO KISS THE BABY ON her bottom, you vile old thing, you unrefined hag! How often do I have to repeat it to you! You're showing the baby unhealthy tendencies!"

"Who told you I was kissing the baby on her bottom?! Where'd you get that from?! I'm not an idiot!"

"You trying to say I'm an idiot?!"

"Ask the child! Sunshine, do I really?!..."

"Don't teach her to lie!"

"I'm not teaching her! You're teaching her God knows what! You smoke in front of her, you drink!...."

"Me?! It's you who's teaching the child all kinds of perversions! I barely managed to wipe the lipstick off her bottom after you gave her a bath yesterday!"

"I didn't kiss her on the bottom!"

"Even so she had your cheap lipstick on her bottom!"

"Listen, you came home yesterday at 4AM! I stayed with your child the entire night! And then I ran to my place all the way across the whole town when none of the public transportation was running! Where were you that night?"

"Don't knock me off the subject! What's the difference where I was?!"

"You promised to come in the evening! At nine! You were planning on tucking your own child to bed! It cost me dearly to have to tell her that her momma had met a fairy from the land of butterflies, and the fairy will tell her all kinds of new children's fairy tales!"

"Oh God, what an idiotic imagination you have! What's this have to do with a fairy from the land of butterflies! You couldn't just tell her that her momma's at work!"

"What kind of work can you be doing at night?"

"Don't you know, you old jade, what kind of work I do?! I had to go see a nightscape right away — just like in Syuchenko's painting! How can I write an article about the painting if I haven't seen the nightscape?!"

"It's dark at nine already! Why do you need to go at 3 AM?!"

"Just ignoramuses like you think that it's the same at 9 as it is at 2 AM! But really, after midnight the colors are completely different! Every fourth grade art student knows that!"

"Good God! You were out of town at night!"

"Not out of town, but at Shchekavytsia!* I've said this to you a hundred times! Syuchenko's an urbanist!"

"No, I'll just end up hanging myself with you!"

"Then hang yourself! Should I bring you the rope?! Or would you like to use a belt?!"

"You went all the way to Shchekavytsia where all the drunks live? An older person like me is afraid to go there during the day! And you're still a child!"

"What kind of child am I to you? I have my own child!"

"All the more, you should take care of yourself and not run around at night all over Shchekavytsia!"

"Really, you old roach, do you think I was there alone?"

"Who were you with there?! With Syuchenko?"

"What's Syuchenko got to do with anything?! What kind of idiotic ideas do you have?!"

---

* One of the oldest parts of Kyiv beyond the Podil region in the center of the city. It is named after Shchek, one of the three legendary brothers who founded the city. In more recent times it became the center for illegal activities and the new Ukrainian mafia that emerged after independence in 1991.

"As a matter of fact, Syuchenko's wife once was looking for him here! She even took a look under the bed!"

"I've told you that your head is full of holes! That wasn't his wife, it was his mother!"

"No, it was a young woman!"

"How many times do I have to tell you! Syuchenko doesn't have a wife! That was his mother! She looks really young! She's an accomplished graphic artist! Not everybody who's 48 looks 64!"

"With you I'll soon look like I'm 74 or 75! Sweetheart, I should know who you were with last night in Shchekavytsia!"

"I spent last night at home with my child!"

"Do you understand what I'm saying! Who were you with last night in Shchekavytsia?!"

"Isn't it enough for you that I wasn't there alone? Do you really think that I — I'd walk around there at night alone?!"

"But that Syuchenko is so thin, so short, he won't be able to protect you if robbers attack you!"

"What's Syuchenko got to do with this?! Why are you harping on poor Syuchenko?! What do you want from him?!"

"What do you mean, what's Syuchenko got to do with this?!"

"Just what I said, what's Syuchenko got to do with this?!"

"But isn't it Syuchenko's painting?! Isn't that so?!"

"Which painting?! What kind of painting are you talking about here?"

"Well... The painting... The night... Shchekavytsia... Two AM...."*

"My God! She's gotten into writing poetry!"

The night... Shchekavytsia... Two AM...

---

* The words and subsequent lines of poetry recited recall the second poem of Russian symbolist poet Aleksander Blok's "Dances of Death" cycle:

The night, the street, the lamp, the druggist's,
A senseless and a dim light.
You live at least a quarter century,
All stays the same, no exit in sight.

You die, begin again anew,
And all repeats as in the past,
The night, the icy rippling surface,
Canal, the druggist's, street, and lamp.

The autumn evening burns your eyes,
And we crawled into a dark garret
To drink a fifth for three!

"A fifth! For three of us! And you were drinking?!"

"And I was drinking! Do you know how cold it was then! You want me to catch a cold?! Do you always wish misery on me?!"

"I wish her misery! I? Wish misery?! Sweetheart, I'm speechless!"

"Then shut up if you're speechless!"

"I wish her misery! Who wishes you happiness then? Syuchenko?! Or that third guy?!"

"Who is the third guy?! Which third guy?! What are you prattling about?!"

"Well... the third one from the garret!"

"No, you have the thought processes of a genius! Or that of a total retard!"

"That means, in your opinion, if they say it's red, then it's red?!"

"It isn't?! I've gotten used to it this way!"

"My God! And she spent her whole life with an artist! And she never learned to understand the language of colors, of light, of shadows, of semi-tones!"

"The main thing is that I've learned to wash away your colors and semi-tones from everything in the world!"

"From a painting she sees only the floor spattered with colors! And this is someone with a higher education!"

"Right! Who needs to wash the floor! And the walls! And wash clothes!"

"That's not it, that's not what's needed! Try and understand with your empty head!"

"And what?! What do you geniuses need?!"

"Don't mock us! My father and I aren't geniuses, just gifted people! Don't mock us, that's what we need! Don't *mock* us! Clear?!"

"Really, when I wash your sweaters, do I mock you?! And do you, like your father, have to stand next to the easel only in imported clothing! You can't dress in clothes made in this country! You swiped the last

decent dress from me and went off to prance all around Shchekavytsia!
Pretty soon you'll tear off my pants!"

"I need your stinking knits that drop all the way down to my
ankles!"

"For sure! They're not needed! You show off your bikini bottom to
all of Shchekavytsia!"

"Have you gone off your rocker?! What bikini bottom?! Which
people in Shchekavytsia?!"

"And why were your underpants all tattered?!"

"Grandma remembers when she was a little girl! That was in the
summer! In the sum-mer! I fell down! I was riding downhill on the
bare ground! It was good I came out of it alive! And you just remember
one thing — my underpants were in tatters! Everyone understands
according to the degree of their own depravity!"

"You just accused me of depravity! Anything you want to accuse
me of, but just not of that!"

"Of course, who'd dive a damn about you then?! You'd want me to
be the same kind of nun as you! That was your dream!"

"Why kind of monastic life could you have? I've endured your anti-
monasticism since you were fifteen!"

"O, what words! What neologisms! Anti-monasticism!"

"At eighteen you needed a separate apartment — we arranged that
for you! For creative inspiration you needed to take an academic leave
and travel around Tataria! I endured that! I sent you extra money!
Plus, for your creative inspiration you needed a child from God knows
who!..."

"I'm asking you not to refer to the father of my child! I'm asking
you not to mock me!"

"Mocking is good for you! I'm taking care of your child! Day and
night! While you're running around Shchekavytsia!"

"Listen, by the way, I've been thinking about giving the little one
to daycare! I've had enough of your rebukes! You don't give the child
anything anyway! You're not helping her grow the way she should! You
feed her miserably You just kiss her on the bottom!"

"To daycare! Have you gone nuts! Where they're fed unsanitary food that's irradiated! Where they sit naked children down on chairs! Right next to the garbage collector's children!"

"You should sit down naked on a chair in front of the garbage collectors! There you'd be a Venus de Milo!"

"You can stick me anywhere! But the child!... You gave birth to a child for daycare?!"

"How much can I take listening to you saying you're taking care of me and my child?! You should be happy that I let you get close to her!"

"I'm happy! I'm the happiest person in the world! Such a lovely daughter! Such a wonderful husband! I'm extremely happy!"

"Doesn't even your husband suit you?! Have you been to at least one of his shows?!"

"I haven't! I don't need to. But all the cognac at his show openings was bought with my money! I save all the clippings on him in a folder!"

"But you asked if he needs this?!"

"And you know what it cost me to get you into the Art Institute! It wasn't he, but me who arranged things for you! Without me you'd have been studying in the oil and gas institute along with the garbage men!"

"And that wouldn't have been so bad! There are people in the oil and gas institute! In Tataria I was at an exhibit of oil workers' paintings! Great expressiveness!"

"There you go, you'd be sitting with your expressiveness, and your father with his bottle! You'd see that kind of landscape! You'd see that kind of art criticism! How did you say it?! A bottle for three and a dark garret!"

"Extraordinary memory! Simply fantastic! So you know what to feed the baby?! Give her 150 grams of puree, just don't give her 200, one meatball, and grate an apple on the carrot grater, not on the beet grater! Read to her for a while about the turkey! No, you don't need to read about the turkey, it's not a particularly artistic fairy tale!"

"I'll figure out what to read to the child!"

"She'll figure it out! And last time you read about skeletons to her! You put two and two together, you old clothes hanger!"

"Are you going to Shchekavytsia again?! Haven't you seen everything there?!"

"She knows what I saw and what I didn't! It was a cloudy night, and I need a starry one!"

"It's raining right now! Where are your stars!?"

"Listen, have you decided to finish me off today?! You've been mocking me since morning! At two the clouds will blow away, it'll be a full moon!"

"When will the clouds blow away from my life?! And when are you getting back?!"

"No, this is impossible to endure! You jabbed into father his whole life with this "when are you getting back?" — and now have you started in on me?!"

"Sweetheart, put on a warm jacket, don't run around in a raincoat!... Do you hear me, when you get back, change your jacket!... Well, if you catch pneumonia, I'm not going to take care of the child! You'll watch after her yourself!"

"Why are you screaming across the whole courtyard! Yowler!"

Downstairs the door slammed. Grandma disconcertedly returned to the apartment. Refrains of the argument seethed in her chest, but she had to make dinner for the child. She dragged her way to the kitchen.

"Where's momma?"

"Momma went to work."

"To lork? Why were you scleaming at her?"

"I wasn't screaming. We were just talking."

"Just lalking?"

After dinner they read some books. Then went off to bed. They began to change into their pajamas. The child was oh so sweet, the most adorable one in the world and the most beautiful, just like a tiny cupid from a foreign book. Grandma couldn't hold back, quickly wiped the lipstick from her lips, and...

"Who do you wuv so much, gwammy?.." And the little one began to chuckle.

IT JUST DIDN'T WORK OUT

by Eugenia Kononenko
Translated by Nataliya Bilyuk

I WILL REVEAL THE WILDEST DREAM OF FEMINIST WOMEN TO you. One to which no one normally confesses. What can it be? For her to earn more money than the whole lot of men in the world? To make love to her heart's content and leave in the morning without saying goodbye? To force a man to carry and bear her child? To soil her husband up to his neck in baby food and other things, and make him look after three children, while she enthusiastically takes on three jobs, running to meetings, symposia, and receptions, and spends time with her lovers during breaks? All these pictures can seem unattainably attractive to many women at particular moments of their lives. But these pictures aren't their most cherished desire. Their most cherished desire is to meet a man for whose sake they can toss away all the experience of feminism they've acquired in their lives.

God created this world so that there are very few of these kinds of men. At least there are fewer such men than women who are ready to meet them. Because for many women, feminism began at that moment when the impulse to follow a man to the end of the world was laughed at by him or by life itself. And then it turned out that it was unnecessary. It turned out that it is more important to secure one's house and home, to cook a three-course meal, and always be in the mood for sex. And the alternative to all this — is woman's loneliness or another man of the same kind.

At those times when the world was harsh and stormy, the dominance of a man was determined not by legislation and stereotypes, but by the logic of life itself. Women were ready to see men off to war, wait for them, meet them, and love them during short breaks between the battles. At least the general idea of such gender stereotypes of the past is still present in our modern culture. And today men don't go off to war, but rather to some safe place, further from battles in the home. And the world, if you get down to it, is just as mercilessly stormy and as ruthlessly harsh as before. But it is different. And a woman little by little has become equal to a man both in nobleness as well as in loathsomeness. A woman stopped being a domestic guardian, and a man stopped being a protector.

Real men exist only in mainstream films, in which they are primitive, simple, monotonous nothings. In so-called high culture, extreme psychos with complexes figure. In everyday life we can meet average men with various levels of intellect. And in the souls of many women, especially feminist women, lives the unspoken longing for those real men. For feminism — it is not a desire to humiliate a man and be superior. It is pursuit of the world in which, contrary to all the traditional prompting, a woman does not have to play dumb and weak in order to get the man she loves.

Who are these real men? They are, probably, people who are not afraid to look directly into the eyes of fate however difficult that fate may be. Or look directly at their epoch no matter how awful it can be. And those who are able to find strength in themselves under any circumstances and find reason and courage to act in such a way as to preserve their dignity. But why real men? Why not real people? Women are also capable of showing their courage, reason, and countless talents. In our cynical, money-rules world, not everyone has lost the ability to admire the incorruptibility of either sex. God alone knows which women men secretly dream of — do they also dream of courageous, incorruptible, extraordinarily gifted ones? And at the very bottom of women's souls lives the dormant romantic dream about meeting with a real man.

And finally you sit down in a restaurant with a real man. A little oil lamp's light flickers at your table. Outside on the main street of a small American university town, one of the four streets of the so-called downtown, your colleagues are walking and notice you. They wink at you, express with their gestures their admiration when they see the kind of wine you have there at your table — certainly the dishes are also of an appropriate quality.

It is impossible to describe good wines just in words. They speak for themselves, when they reach your mouth. This kind of wine must, probably, be sipped in silence. But you haven't reached a state of comfortable silence yet. You're talking. It's interesting for you, and, it seems so for him, too. Inconceivable fate must have brought you together with this man. A photographer for one of the leading American political journals, he's visited almost all the countries of the world. After the slideshow of his photographs while some people were admiring his work, and another blaming him for awful corruptibility, you came up to him and asked:

"Do you work for history or for today?"

"Good that you asked precisely about this, almost nobody asks about that. Usually people ask who pays and how much — the truth, which is disadvantageous to some people, can be advantageous to others."

"And it may be disadvantageous to no one."

"That's absolutely right. But history favors only the truth; otherwise it's not history. It may be difficult for the coming generations to understand what is happening now. I've spent much time sorting out photos of World War II. What is useless for politics is also of no use for history... If all this is interesting to you, we could have a dinner together, if you don't mind."

Numerous travels to distant countries comprises the dream of many people.

That kind of travel involuntarily is associated with meetings at the airport, expensive hotels, and buffets for breakfast and dinner in restaurants. And this guy often had the opportunity to travel to countries where explosions and gunfire greet you, where there has long been no electricity, water, warm food, or anything to drink. Where he can't reach the next spot to make his report. But he has to press the button of the camera all the way and take photographs that no one else will take. And protect the film more than his own life.

"I always want to tell the truth about the places where I've been. Although the well-known political magazines give me accreditation, my employers never go to the "hot spots" themselves; they only give hints about what to emphasize. I don't want to serve any kind of politics when I shoot pictures of the miseries of people who were predestined to be born and live in the region of yet another cataclysm. I don't work for anyone when I take pictures of the eyes of refugees who go who knows where, or of the unclosed eyes of those killed. But, of course, my pictures are used for one or another political project. Or they remain unnoticed if they are of no use to any of the projects.

"Aren't you tired of such a frantic life? Don't you want to sit at home and write your memoirs about your crazy travels?"

"At the moment, no. I'm 48 and I still have the strength for this kind of life. I have a very acute sense that I'm living my own life, the one I'm predestined for. I don't know whether I'll write my memoirs some day. I say everything with my pictures.

The man sitting opposite me in a Japanese restaurant and pouring expensive wine into my glass has not just traveled all over the world. He has been right in those places on the planet and right at the time when events, with which all the international agencies start their news reviews, happened. He was in Beijing when a student demonstration was broken up by gunfire, and saw blood on the pavement of the Chinese capital. He was standing some five steps away when *Ceausescu* and his wife were executed.

He was in Baghdad during the conflict in the Arabian Gulf. And in March 1985 he stood at *Staraya Ploshchad* (Old Square) in Moscow — there wasn't any bloodshed, but, as it turned out later, the world's destiny had just been decided right at that moment. He took some pictures of the Muscovites and the guests of the capital of the USSR, who busily were hurrying to Moscow's grocery shops, not knowing that an event had already happened that would soon radically change their fate and the fate of the world.

This year, of course, he has been to Iraq. His photographs make your blood freeze. You can see women near the road, who've just seen death. On another picture, you can see an American soldier, who put his foot on the body of a killed Iraqi. Why this savagery? Information is spread all over the world that this is the most peaceful war campaign, that Iraqis are being saved from their burdensome heritage, that from now on everything will be good for them. Now he is prohibited from visiting Iraq. His reports do not meet the requirements of the presidential administration of the US.

The pictures that appear in the reportage of the leading American newspapers absolutely do not reflect what is really happening in Iraq. They portray a false picture that they want to sketch for the world.

He takes pictures not only in hotspots of the world. On one of them you can see lovers in a park in Paris, on another young girls near a fountain in Rome. And we're not doing an interview for one of the Ukrainian newspapers. If it had been an interview, he would have invited me to a bar for a glass of wine or a beer, and not to a Japanese restaurant in the town. Not everything in this world is measured by money, but the price of that dinner is a sign in a system that you don't yet comprehend.

This will be explained to you in the morning, and at the moment you don't know how it will go when your leisurely dinner comes to an end. But now it's over; he pays and you go out into the cold dark street with him.

A strong wind is blowing, and you walk to your hotel slowly. You don't feel the cold. You're afraid to do something wrong, since this is the first time in your life you're moving to uncertainty with a man. He takes you by the arm only when you cross the street and then he puts his hands in his pocket again. You reach your hotel. There's no one in the lobby. In general it doesn't bother you what your colleagues would think if they saw a man in your hotel room. A real one or an unreal one. But there is no one there, and that's good.

You stay in the lobby, and he tells you that he was in Ukraine in 1990 and saw an unsanctioned meeting broken up. He took some pictures. But he doesn't have them with him at the moment. And what happened later? You've been talking for almost an hour in the lobby of the hotel where you have a separate room. You're starting to get feverish: maybe this man and you are on the threshold of some particularly exciting moments. But he says goodbye, it seems to you, reluctantly, but he says goodbye and leaves. Let it be so. Why did you think he wanted to stay with you alone? You've spent an interesting evening with an extraordinary man — isn't that enough? And you had that superb dinner. Then you return to your room. Outside the wind is howling. The tipsiness from the expensive wine is gone. It was white California wine. American wines differ from the French ones; they're good only when they're very expensive.

And in the morning you meet your colleagues, who ask about your rendezvous with the photographer that didn't take place. They explain to you that as far as all this took place in the territory of the US, you should have invited him to your room. If he had been the initiator, it could later have been seen as sexual harassment. He invited you to an expensive restaurant, and the salmon steak with Pacific Ocean seaweed plus the expensive wine should have meant that if you give your consent, he does as well. He walked you to the hotel and talked with you for a long time in the lobby; he might have been waiting for an invitation from you that didn't come.

So, to spend a night with a real man, at least in the territory of the US, you should not have forgotten all the achievements of feminism. Just the opposite, you should have shown yourself to be an even greater feminist than you actually are. You regret you lost a rare chance. Maybe it could have been some incredible new experience. How does he behave with a woman, this man unafraid to tell the truth in this world full of lies, and who even has enough courage to extract this truth in the most dangerous corners of the planet? But you feel sorry not only about a lost romantic adventure. Your experience — your life experience and work experience at the Center for Cultural Studies also force you to ask other questions, in this case rhetorical ones. To what extent should a woman show her interest? Okay, she can invite a man to her room, and what next? Should she also do all the things that a man traditionally does? Should she hug him first? And maybe the laws of civilized countries, adopted with consideration of women's rights, has already led to deep changes in the strategy of sexual behavior, when a woman needs to ensure transition to the most intimate?..

It's like this. Two worlds — two ways of life. In your life there were bad moments when you were left badly protected from sexual demands. You had to act on your own, relying only on the strength of the word, hands, legs, doors, and bolts. But overprotection can also not lead to the better.

You don't believe in fate at least because you don't consider yourself worthy of a substantially better fate. You are certain that blind chance decides quite a lot in the vortex of people's life paths. Chance brought you and this man together. You've met not in one of those wild countries where he goes regularly, but on the territory of the country where he is a citizen and where he rarely visits. You will not see each other again. He doesn't have your contact information, and you don't have his. Though, on the one hand, everything is so complicated in the modern world, and on the other — everything is very thoroughly structured. Of course he has a website on the Internet with his email. It seems you have the opportunity to write him to say you have fond memories of that dinner and you feel very sorry you didn't know how a woman should have behaved herself on the territory of the US in that particular situation. But such a missive already will be, despite the modern means of communication, an attribute not even of some distant past, but our notion of it. And we have to live in the present world here and now.

THE LOST CODE

by Eugenia Kononenko
Translated by Natalia Ferens

IT'S PAINFUL FOR ME TO WRITE THIS TEXT. IT'S PAINFUL TO SPEAK in detail about an extremely painful situation. On the surface everything remains calm. The pain comes right from the inside. No one knows about anything. No one asks about anything. It's as if there is no need to seek a word for these tribulations that have been laid to rest. There's no need to talk about anything.

Maybe this should remain unspoken. That unspoken nature always has been an essential part of our strange shared space; that was its special charm. "So that no one will ever think something really happened here," you used to say as you hastily grabbed and hid the bedding on which we had just made love. Relationships that never were made clear seemed in the greatest measure close to real. It seemed to be a way out beyond the borders of unconquerable mundanity, an undeniable way of expanding the limits of a gloomy existence.

And it really lasted for quite a long while. But then the code started to become ruined — a code with the help of which a man and a woman find common ground, as only very limited people operate in this sphere, those who say everything directly when it comes to a relationship. This code doesn't work at all now, but it keeps convulsively gathering, causing ghostly pain. Certainly it would be most sensible to stop tending to this pain and search for another code to open some other eternal gates. But there exist spheres of life where the laws of reason simply don't work. The old code won't let go, and the gates remain stubbornly shut. And so necessity invincibly takes us by the throat to speak about the unspoken for years. To name the unnamed. To attribute features of life to something that seemingly never was.

The decline of our relationship corresponded in time with the common and inevitable fading of the female body. The man who seemed so uncommonly tender and wise turned out to be no more than a commonplace lout, in whose eyes a woman is first and foremost a plaything for his eyes and hands, and who refuses to accept a woman as an equal to him, and whose corporeal shell also is subject to the changes that age brings. You don't see your own protruding belly, as it requires bending down your head too far and thus taking the risk of breaking your neck. It is much easier to look at a woman's bottom to ascertain the inexorability of time and to dream consciously or subconsciously of a younger babe.

It is only when her woman's body starts to lose its looks that millions of women come tragically to realize how utterly physical a man's love is. And millions of women in despair rush to make themselves look younger, raping nature. You can take a guided tour of Baykovy Cemetery to look at numerous gravestones of beautiful women who, at finding themselves on the wrong side of fifty, madly rushed to correct their bodies and torment their flesh with barbarous things such as "alternative massages" and "hot wraps." This didn't lead to a new youth — they only got tumors. Women, trying to salvage their love, ended up in the arms of death. And the men, for whom these bloody sacrifices were made, simply took younger women to replace them....

The flesh, though, doesn't particularly disturb me. You can make fun of it, as there are men who are not particularly sensitive to deviations from standards of physical beauty. There are men who prefer mature women to younger ones. We — you and I — had other dates during the long while when the secret, never quite real common existence of the two of us was trying to emerge on the brink of being and non-being. As I reveal it, I'm not trying to boast about being a real modern woman who can have as many partners as she wants. I'm just trying to say that our secret code wasn't a mere encoding of fleshly symbols. It also had some spiritual element to it. Though sometimes the union of our bodies was so inspired and sweet to the point that my heart seemed to stop beating, but I always knew that it was so because of an immaterial dimension, even beyond the material.

I've just mentioned the unity of the spirit and the body now only to divide them. Since time immemorial the very union of two bodies — a man's and a woman's — has been considered particularly sacred, closer than anything else. But there also exists the exchange of innermost thoughts, which true friendship between two noble souls equal in the eyes of God gives; it brings two people incomparably closer than the closeness of lovers in moments of lovemaking. The revealing of souls in an intimate conversation is much more innocent and titillating than all the titillation, and all the innocence of the nakedness of lovers.

I have always ironically pitied those who live in the space of an overripe melodrama, who try desperately to grab unhealthy, used-up love by the tail, hysterically dragging it where it doesn't want to go. If the one you love refuses to go to bed (or to a cot, depending on the situation), we let them go. I have always been able to look at the whole thing ironically, as it is laughter that helps us to survive. But it's been many, many years that I find myself incapable of laughing when I hear you say again and again "I'm busy, busy, busy, I'm living in a frenetic rhythm, where I have no time for your neurotic hysterics, I'd be happy to help, but I'm no expert, call, he's not a bad doctor, say I recommended him…"

It would be a sin for me to complain about that man. He really did a lot of important things for me in the outer hypostasis of my life. How many friends there are, who are ready to listen to all our confessions and bring to light a deep understanding of all our problems, but they never do anything practical for us; for the most part they can't or, sometimes, they're unwilling. This man, however, can help — and he really does. He did a lot for me. He hardly ever gave me presents, and the ones he did give, he didn't invest in the objects any sacred sense of a true gift; they were just things he came across. But it was he who gave me money when I needed it desperately. I was deeply touched in each of those cases and doubt that I will ever forget it. And now, too, he'll do if not absolutely everything, at least everything he can — if I ask for his help. But after saying just the essentials, he breaks off the conversation; I'm kind of busy, busy, busy, we'll chat another time, have a nice day, tell me if you need anything, but right now sorry; I have to write an obituary of a good man. Why can't I just take advantage of him as a "valuable person" who has a certain sentiment for my previous merits as a lover? Why do I want something else from him? Can it be that I just feel — that world that so firmly holds him, the world that makes him so "busy" is a bad, unhealthy world that irreparably ruins his personality?

When we still used to have conversations somehow, I noticed you were afraid to talk about any breakdowns, mine or those of my relatives. You'd always interrupt me decisively. My memory keeps a careful record of all the interrupted sentences, those phrases broken in the middle. "Better to write a story about that," you said. You seemed to be afraid of my revelations. Why? What frightened you so? Did you really think I was just attempting to provoke a reciprocal frankness from you to reach your forbidden zones that for someone like you don't exist? In your public life you're known as a perfectly balanced, sober, well-mannered person.

Last winter you interrupted our phone conversations several times, and it felt as if you had slashed a razor across my face. Since that time, I've never dialed your number again and won't. I quiver, I shiver like hell because of the horror I feel when I think about hearing you again say "Sorry, I'm busy." "We'll chat later." "I need to write an obituary." Just promise that in case I pass away earlier than you do, you won't write any obituaries for me!!! And you won't deliver any funeral speeches over my casket!!! Yes, I'm talking about death now, but don't speculate, this is, so to say, to provoke pity because I'm dying. This is evidence of the fact that the frankness of my words now has reached a point when you do see death. Or the devil. Or God — though you can't comprehend His will at all.

...I'm not going crazy (apparently), although I've been taking antidepressants since last winter. Do you know how they taste? I don't feel an addiction to them yet. I'm in a quite good emotional state. And when I don't, it isn't tied just to you. But all the time the pain of the lost code smolders in my being. Its embers sometimes nearly go out — but suddenly it's enough for a tiny spark to set it all on fire again, flaming up to a burning, hellish fire. And so I don't go mad, I just have to talk for some time about our unspoken, strange space. There's no other way to get out of the murkiness of those imaginary dialogues that burst into me at the most inopportune time. For several years little by little they have been ruining my bodily shell with their wild vibrations, causing horrible black spasms of unbearable despair.

In answer I hear your despairing (and I know there will be a dash of anxiety in your voice as you'll say it): you have to understand, I'm incredibly busy! I don't know how I'm managing to live. I'll soon forget my own name. I have to be in several places at once. I have countless things to do at the same time. I'd be glad to talk to you. That will happen without fail, just another time, but right now I'm really busy, understand this, please understand this!.. And I have to write the obituary too!

I DON'T UNDERSTAND, DO YOU HEAR, I DON'T UNDERSTAND!!! DON'T YOU KNOW: "LATER" NEVER HAPPENS! "ANOTHER TIME" MEANS JUST IN THE NEXT LIFE!!! IF SOMEONE ELSE IN THIS WORLD IS WAITING FOR SOMEKIND OF WORDS FROM US, THEY MUST BE UTTERED **WITHOUT FAIL!!!** IT WON'T TAKE MUCH TIME!!! YOU JUST NEED TO FIND THE RIGHT WORDS! YOU KNOW THEM, YOU DO, YOU JUST HAVE FORGOTTEN THEM FOR THE MOMENT. AND YOU NEED THEM AS MUCH AS I DO!!! IF YOUR WAY OF LIVING LEAVES NO SPACE EVEN FOR A FEW GOOD WORDS, YOU **DON'T** HAVE A LIFE, BUT A MISERABLE EXISTENCE FROM THE DEVIL WITH A COLLECTION OF SELF-QUOTATIONS AND TOTALLY UNFUNNY JOKES!!!

IT IS IN YOUR BEING AND NOT IN OUR SPACE WHERE THE CODES OF GOODNESS ARE RUINED, BECAUSE, AS THE ANXIOUS CORE OF LIFE DECAYS, LITTLE BY LITTLE ONLY A HIDEOUS LIMESTONE SKELETON IS LEFT!!!

I've been living with the silence of these words for several years. I'm ready to accept your refusal of my body. After all, as the Ukrainian classic* exclaims: "Don't be concerned about the body." But I can't bear your refusing my soul. And I keep searching maniacally for those changes of the code, so that it can open the eternal gate above, because today with the help of the ancient code, just a meaningless black abyss opens below.

I do know what can happen next. "Sometime" will come, and "another time" will take place, but there will be no joy. The woman, powerless, will feel the urge for revenge for all the years of fruitless waiting, and she'll throw away the good words that came late and will answer with malicious words, because her tenderness will be gone. And not just with malicious words, but fatally unkind words. I pray for fate to spare me from such an outcome.

But the monster of uncontrollable black aggression walks this world, cruelly striking those whom their friends have abandoned. Not lovers, but friends. Once you used to awaken unbelievably good feelings in me. And can it now be that the apocalyptic destruction of the eternal code is just what God wants?

---

* Lesya Ukrainka is the Ukrainian classic. The character Mavka says this in her last monologue in Ukrainka's famous verse drama *Forest Song*.

from WITHOUT A GUY: FRAGMENTS OF A 'CREATIVE' AUTOBIOGRAPHY

by Eugenia Kononenko
Translated by Michael M. Naydan

MEN BUILT THE WORLD IN WHICH WE LIVE. THEY BUILT IT FOR themselves and without taking women into consideration, set up their laws in it, unleashed wars, built the machinery to oppress and stifle. And women are forced to live under inhuman laws, which men thrust on them. There is truth in this, but not the whole truth. This is the so-called raw truth, for it transforms truth into life not under just any conditions. In the world, created by men for men, there is a large female subsidiary, a state within a state, under the laws of which an immeasurable number of women live. The world that women created for themselves and in which they established their own laws. A world into which, as much as possible, they do not allow men and from which they do not release them.

By birth you are from just such a world. It has been in it that the decisions of your life have always been taken, though, as feminists say, women are not permitted in the sphere of decision-making. For us the country of men existed somewhere really far away. Let them hang up the portraits of the decrepit cretin men of state on national holidays, and those were exclusively men. We had nothing to do with them, and they had nothing to do with us. Not in any way did we touch the greater world of men. Caregivers in kindergartens, teachers in schools, female doctors in clinics, saleswomen in stores and pharmacies — they were all women, intelligent ones and some not so, qualified ones and some not so, nice ones and some not so. With them and only with them could one live and build relationships.

We don't look more loftily. Certainly, one of the main unwritten laws of our female world was not to push our way into the Soviet elite. Not into the party elite, not into the artistic elite, not even into the scientific elite. Because you can't go there without a guy. And we live the weary life of our female-manless subsidiary of the so-called middle Soviet intelligentsia honestly.

"Lord don't you marry a professor's sonny boy! He'll disgrace you, humiliate you and toss you out!" My mother used to say. She began to say that about fifteen years before the problem of the choice of a marriage partner would become a reality. About his conduct in the case of him being the sonny boy of a general, a party member, an artist, or a store manager, they don't even give you any instructions — something like that can't happen with you by definition. It's worthwhile to avoid not just those kinds of sons, who reside in the higher echelons of the Soviet hierarchy, but also the sons of exotic nationalities of the peoples of the USSR — Georgians, Uzbeks and Jews. And in general, men, even those of your social sphere, even of your own blood — are as a rule bad, we are unable to cope with them. When you get married, you need to look well at whom you'll be divorcing — a brilliant phrase that you hear almost from your early childhood. It's good when right after the birth of a child the guy disappears to not mess up your nerves anymore. And there are awful examples of those with whom you can't live, and it's a problem to divorce.

Men are bad. Men are grief. A lonely life isn't a pot of honey, but it's a reliable defense against black eyes and abortions. Your teenage years and youth passed in a woman's monastery with roughly that status. The hideous walls of a one-room apartment surround you, where the three of you traipse, you, Momma and Grammy. Three babes. Three babes without a guy. Grammy is always at home. They tell you you're lucky for that. She feeds and keeps watch over you. She makes sure you don't have Kuprin's *Yama* under your geometry textbook.* She makes sure you don't draw girls without clothes on and don't secretly get acquainted with the vulgar, pernicious, but so enticing world of cosmetics.

"Why are you hiding? Who so does nothing bad, has no reason to hide!"

And if she sees that you're bent over diligently working on your polynomials, she'll gently praise you, and will ask if you need help. Everyone assumes that you've really lucked out with your Grammy. When Grammy ends up in the hospital for several months, they give you to a family of well-to-do relatives. They don't miss the opportunity to remind you that you are their poor little relative. Momma knows all too well how that family treats you poor relatives. But what can you do? You can't leave the child home alone under any circumstances! Because she'll suddenly get pregnant! And we are respectable! Though WITHOUT A GUY!

Let it be WITHOUT A GUY, but with a sense of your own self-respect. The revolution gave women divorce. It was worth having the revolution for that sake alone. And in tsarist Russia they legally could return a wife to a wicked husband from whom she had run away. And what would it have been like to be forever tied to the father of your child? You can't even imagine other possibilities of a guy in the context of our women's world. There can only be one guy in the life of a woman and no more — maybe less. But it doesn't work out that way. Invariably the time comes when you go crazy and you pick up some lout. Everyone thinks that it won't be like that with them, but it turns out the same with everyone. Certain women live with their husbands.

---

* One of Russian writer Alexander Kuprin's last major and most popular works written in 1915 just before his death that with great sensitivity describes the lives of fallen women in the den of soldiers, criminals and prostitutes where they lived (Yamskaya Sloboda). The title means "hole."

But all of them pay for their clumsy guy in the house with heavy-duty humiliation and women's diseases.

"What kind of diseases?"

"You'll grow up and find out. With just one man in the time it takes till your first child is born, you'll find out everything! It happens that you get so befouled, that it will be enough to the end of your life!"

Does it happen that there are normal little men with whom you can live and not get befouled? It does. Somewhere in the unreachable distance there are honorable men, who abide in unparalleled moral heights, battlers against the untruth of this world, following them you can walk wherever they go, abandoning everything. You can even give yourself to them without getting married, because they'll never deceive girls they have given their trust. But they were all killed in the war. Or they were tortured in Stalinist prison camps. But if you dig deeper, it turns out anyway that there is a small percentage of men with integrity. And whores instantly pick and choose them. They have a nose for the best boys, those nimble accessible babes with pre-marriage contacts in the past. In our times the whores don't sit around with yellow tickets or with red rights. They encircle the best men and take them away from good women. But that's not a reason to become a whore! Mainly — this is a maiden's honor and a woman's dignity, and not a guy. Men don't even come to visit us. Except for your father. And he doesn't have the qualities of men.

"A hideous, enslaved babe!"

"A dust rag in the hands of your own mother!"

"Your mother's!"

But, if you don't let him come into your house, he will meet you alone in school, will teach you to hate your mother and grandmother, in short, it will be awful. And you'll have to tolerate him here. You used to live with him in a two-room apartment. You slept in one room with your grandmother, and your mother with him in another. Then momma moved to your room, and he was left alone. That is, the three of you have been in one room for a long time. When you moved to a one-room apartment, things in general became better. Now you can *not* lock yourself in your room, and go, when you need to, to the kitchen and to the bathroom. When you lived together, you often sat there, locking yourself in on a latch until he'd go through his temper tantrum and leave. Or sit in the bathtub printing photographs.

Mother had many female acquaintances, the great majority of them also WITHOUT A GUY. Divorcees, or those who never got married. They would come visit us, and we visited them. Those who are still with their guy come to us without their dunderheads. All the "husbanded" women from the number of mother's acquaintances don't live, but suffer.

"Why does she live with him? Why doesn't she get divorced from him?"

"I've said it many times: this isn't life. And after every argument she runs to him again. There are three large categories of intolerable guys: drunkards, players and momma's boys. Your grandfather on your mother's side was a drunkard, the deceased husband of your grandmother. She's been a widow for a long time. The drunkards with black eyes gather next to the liquor store. Grammy likes to observe them from her window. In absentia she recognizes them the way other grandmothers identify tame pigeons in city squares. Players are those who hit on one after another, even entirely decent women. The kind like we are. One of the representatives of this disgusting breed once came over to our house. He was the former husband of mother's girlfriend. He slobberingly kissed you on your twelve-year-old shoulder. Mother later wiped you off with cotton and eau de cologne. And then there are mother's, momma's, mommie's little boys. Yes, women comprise the better half of humanity, but there are creatures from the women's half that are even worse than men. These "mothers," "mommas," "matriarchs" are women who gave birth to little boys, from which, in time, men grew up. The sons of single mothers comprise a particular threat. This in general is worse than atomic war. You're a teenager, you're twelve or thirteen years old, but "mommies" and moms arouse in you uncontrollable horror. Your father is a momma's boy. She has magical influence on him. It is she who forced him to beat all three of us, it was because of her that we locked ourselves in our room on a latch, fearful of even going out to the bathroom. And now we live in a pathetic one-room apartment, because he, for spite, wouldn't agree to build himself a coop apartment and leave you the two-room. That's what *she* ordered. The main aim of "matriarchs" is complete control over their little sons. Woe to girls who fall in love with the sonny boy of such a "mommie!" Because "mommies" to their dying day give their married sons a bath in the tub and vice versa. At night you pull out your awful scraping sofa bed, put out the light, and in the darkness, first before going to sleep, ridicule guys. And during recent times a new type of male intolerability has appeared: not drunkards, not players, not momma's boys, but jobless loafers who live on the money of women workaholics. One of my mother's friends won't get divorced from just such a man.

from FIELD WORK IN UKRAINIAN SEX

by Oksana Zabuzhko

Translated by Halyna Hryn

FEAR CAME EARLY. FEAR WAS PASSED ON IN THE GENES, ONE WAS to fear all beyond the immediate family circle — anyone who expressed any degree of interest in you was in fact spying for the KGB to find out what's really going on at home and then those bad men will come again and put Daddy in prison. Especially suspect were those who tried to strike up "liberal" conversations. Around grade nine, at the city-wide Creative Writing Olympiad, she met a whiz kid in big glasses from the math school. He had the skin of a freshly peeled peach, rare for an adolescent, and glancing at him sideways she could see, behind the abnormally thick lenses, dark feminine eyelashes as thick as silk, and when he laughed his whole body contracted as often happens with very nervous intellectual boys who aren't allowed to go out to play by themselves, but are let out only when sitting on a sled bundled up in a wool shawl to well above the bridge of the nose. Such boys inevitably fell in love with her, that much couldn't be helped, but in spite of it they were avid readers and liked to discuss what they read. And so one day the whiz kid from the math school, holding on to her elbow awkwardly and old-fashionedly (as if with an artificial limb) while he guided her around the slippery spots — it was winter then and the snow-covered sidewalks glistened with treacherous black mirrors — had the indiscretion to ask, by the way, had she read the banned Ukrainian author Vynnychenko? Instantly she felt her head pound: this is it! This is what mother and father warned about — and with that shrewd Lenin glint in her eye (she did sense it quite consciously to be Lenin's), accompanied by oh, such a languorous pause as if to say, okay, let's play with this, I can see right through you, she replied, "No, can't say that I have," and, having waited it out until the whiz kid confessed all he knew — about the democratic Ukrainian republic that waged war on the Soviets, about the Ukrainians living abroad (as she listened, practically swooning at such flirtation with danger, she no longer had the slightest doubt *who* this was talking to her) — she doused him with a bucket of ice, tapping out each syllable in precise Pioneer Girl fashion ("Attention!" "Right face!" "Forward .. . march!"), informing him that she hadn't the slightest interest in émigré counterrevolutionary trash, especially at a time when the international situation is as tense and complicated as it is and demands our vigilance, she has always been outraged by young people who listen to Voice-of-this and Voice-of-that radio broadcasts — he, staring wildly at her with both pairs of eyes, seemed to forget all about breathing ("Little hedgehog, where was your head? Forgot to breathe, and now you're dead!") — that'll teach him! She was more pleased with herself than ever before: her first test of maturity and she passed it without a hitch! No, she had always said she would never want to re-live her adolescence, those desperate, unconscious attempts to BREAK OUT — out of the dull concrete walls, out of the family nest choked inside, amid billows of pungent fear, miasmic haze, where one false move, one ill-considered revelation, and you splash into the murky waters to your death. On the radio that father listened to every evening, squeezing ear-first into the speaker that sputtered with a deafening scrape and occasionally burst into a sharp, dangerously increasing metallic whistle — on the radio came memoirs of the dying Snegirov, lists of surgically removed intestines, ruptured kidneys and bladders, insulin shocks, forcibly inserted feeding tubes, puddles of blood and vomit on cement floors — summary reports from the slaughterhouse, a carving of carcasses: Marchenko, Stus, Popadiuk, every few weeks more names, handsome young men not much older than yourself with thick manes of hair brushed back stiffly. You dreamed of them the way your girlfriends dreamed of movie stars, any day now he'll come out of prison, scarred, matured, masculine, and you'll meet — except that they never came out and the airwaves groaned with their agony, while father sat on the other side listening helplessly, year after year, ever since the day he himself was thrown out of work and began just sitting in the house, listening to the radio. There *was* no breaking out — all around nothing but Communist Youth League meetings, political education classes, and the Russian language. One only ventured OUT THERE (like a four-year-old to a stool in the middle of the room to recite a poem for aunties and uncles) in order to reproduce, in ringing tones and tape recorder accuracy, all that had been learned from them and them alone, and only this guaranteed SAFETY — a Gold Medal upon leaving high school, a Diploma of Red Distinction at university, and then ever so carefully along the tightrope — my God, all the garbage she had let pass through her brain! — and at age fifteen tumbling right into a depression, complaining of mysterious stomach pains. Daddy ran himself off his feet dragging her from doctor to doctor who found nothing wrong, for days she tossed in bed crying hysterically from the slightest sharp word — Daddy's girl, apple of his eye, it was he who hovered, wings outstretched, over her first menstruation, calmly explaining that this is very good, this is what happens to all girls, just lie and rest, don't get up. He brought her thinly sliced apples laid out on a saucer, as for a real sick girl, and so she lay there, curled up and very still, frightened by this new feeling — on the one hand shame at her secret being revealed so openly (but then how can you have secrets from Daddy?) and, on the other, a kind of searing vulnerability, a wary uncertainty — a feeling that would reappear at the loss of virginity (which she only manages after Daddy's death), and then every time after that, the same eternal sense of daughterly duty, ultimate feminine submission from which men, not having a clue as to its source, would necessarily go wild ("you're such a great fuck!") and then she would leave them.   Break loose, that's all she wanted to do, break loose — all elbows from spontaneous adolescent growth, pimply teenager in tears at her own awkwardness, one pair of pantyhose speckled with brown knots where she tried to sew up the runs and one dress, the school uniform worn lily-white at the elbows. She went to school dances religiously — every Friday without fail, like a Moslem to the mosque! — in a borrowed blouse and too-short skirt from her Pioneer Girl days (white top, black bottom), consuming herself with bitter envy at the sight of her classmates in all-grown-up clothes, with grown-up haircuts done at the stylist's, in full bloom like the proverbial cherry orchard, glistening in high-gloss lipstick and black Lancôme butterfly lashes. Ten rubles was what that blue tube of mascara cost and mother's monthly paycheck, on which the three of them lived, came out to 150 rubles, so what was there to do but steal it, in the coatroom, from a briefcase thoughtlessly left open by a beauty queen from the senior class. True, it was a pretty cheap tube, from Poland, half used up, or so she consoled herself, and not such a great loss for the beauty queen, but nonetheless there it was, nineteenth century, the classic Jean Valjean loaf of bread and Cosette staring at the doll-store window: shame, fear, a secret, both despicable and exciting, like her exhibitionist exercises alone in front of the mirror. She applied makeup badly in the school bathroom, painting crooked lines under her eyes, and after the dance she would fiercely scrub the mascara from her red eyelids: it was frightening to think what would happen if Daddy saw — Daddy, who was always so afraid for her, who ran around collecting dossiers on each of her girlfriends: they were all spoiled, smoked and kissed boys, Daddy screamed, face turning beet-red and she, you have to hand it to her, screamed just as loud in return, and then sobbed in the bathroom — especially after that memorable evening when he slapped her face right out on the street, at the trolley stop, because she had taken off somewhere and he decided that she was running away from him — but she came back, because there *was* nowhere to run to, and he, not saying a word, slapped her as hard as he could across the face. Of course, later there were hugs and kisses, forgiveness-begging, and the like, "my baby," "my golden girl," all this after several red-hot hours of pandemonium, wailing, sobbing, slamming of doors, accompanied by the shuffle of Mother's feeble attempts to intervene — because Mother was quite beside the point in all this; mother was, in fact, frigid, and obviously out of it, a black window pane deflecting all light (later on, one morning in the early months of your marriage, she would poke her head into your bedroom with an alarm clock merrily ringing: wakey, wakey, breakfast is ready! — precisely at THE moment — and after the ensuing explosive scene she would weep like an orphan in the kitchen, frightened and helpless: she was just trying her best! — so that in the end you, having calmed yourself and shaken the rest of the shivers from your startled body, will be apologizing and cheering her up). And what else could she have been if not frigid, a child-survivor of the Famine (a three-year-old in 1933, she stopped walking, while Grandmother made her way to Moscow in freight cars, switching from train to train, in order to exchange her dowry — two thick strands of Mediterranean pearls — for two bags of dry bread). A child nourished on single stalks of wheat stolen from the field, for which the Collective Farm guard, catching her once, cut her across the face with a whip — you can still see a thin white thread of a scar even now — and it was lucky to have ended with that, because her father, your grandfather that is, was already up in the Arctic panning gold in a slave-gang, and about fifteen years later *your* father, her future husband, would be up there doing the same. And as for her, she made out okay, she got over the stolen ears of wheat and finally got enough to eat, twenty years or so later, once she graduated from university and found a job. And American Sovietologists still can't figure out why there are so many fat, shapeless women in this generation, they read Fromm and Jung up and down and between the lines — *Eat,* that's what these babes wanted to do when they hit twenty — *eat, that's all!* — stuff their faces with meager bread rations in student dorms, both hands, picking up crumbs, what a clitoris was they never did get to find out (it hit you for the first time standing in line at a pharmacy: they had brought in some sanitary napkins and a queue made up entirely of young women was busily stuffing shopping bags — the grannies, meantime, walked up shyly: "girls, what's in those packages?" — "They're women's packages, for women!" the girls snarled back: not for the likes of you, in other words — and the grannies stared back blankly, not understanding). So mother was as innocent as a lamb, or rather the Virgin Mary (there really was something Madonna-like about her in those photos from the late fifties — the time when they all finally did get enough to eat — she glowed with such gentle innocence, a girl in curls, you couldn't take your eyes off her! — delicate, long face with a slim, tapered nose — a now-lost, quiet kind of beauty illuminated by an inner smile, the Cossack Baroque portrait three hundred years later: Roxolana, Varvara Apostol, Varvara Langyshivna — yup, those were the days, now gone for sure! You still get to see the full-faced, embroidered, fresh-off-the-farm-let's-go-dance-in-the-cherry-orchard variety, but not the true Cossack ladies, forget about those! And even your own good looks are already by two exponents coarser, more vulgar (let's not forget to make that *were*). And so mother, gentle songbird, sacrificial lamb, slaved over her dissertation in a Khrushchev communal housing project, while in the kitchen her neighbor, a cook from the local working-class diner — one of those that Lenin had ordained to rule the state — single mother of five from five different men, threw rags and teeth into mother's borsch *(baby* teeth belonging to one of the progeny, perhaps?). But mother did finish her dissertation despite it all, right in time for 1973, when as the spouse of an "unreliable" she was booted the hell out of grad school, so that the day of *your* dissertation defense (which you needed like a hole in the head) was in fact *her* day, she was as happy as a child. "Ah, if only your father were alive to see this!" — and *how*, in God's name, by what means was he supposed to have stayed alive, pitched to the very bottom of the well but catching hold of a beam on the way down and clinging desperately (anything but back to the prison camp), buried alive in four walls, listening to the radio, blowing cigarette smoke out of the tiny pilot window and watching with horror as the only woman of his life, his own flesh and blood, irrevocably slipped away, pushing out through the trap door, propelled by the sheer force of natural growth: *"Lift up your nightie, I want to see how you've been growing."* And would it not be the same kind of both concerned and authoritative intonation twenty years later — *"Turn around, I want to take you from behind now"* — that would awaken in you that long-forgotten feeling of home? And it won't matter that you never liked it from behind, it won't matter that at first you refused to lift up your nightie, flushed with an un-child-like feeling of insult — only to hear in response a quiet and unfamiliarly moist, deeply felt "My child, it's me, your Daddy!" — the end result of which was that the nightie did in fact go up (what else could you do?) — that anxious, obscene feeling of exposure, the first experience, far stronger than any of that knee-touching under the classroom desk — and yet you yearned to break free, God how you yearned to break free, like a condemned soul from under the executioner's axe, but — *where?* To your teenage friends, any dance in sight, rock bands, soccer games, and the first groping of body parts in the darkness of the school gym — what a joke! You couldn't even tell any of them how in the third year *they* finally showed up, father's fear came to pass, because fear — it always reifies in the end. They burst inside the family's four walls like a tornado with a luscious creak of leather holster belts and a vigorous outdoor wind behind them and suddenly filled the room to capacity: three huge males, rosy-cheeked from the sub-zero temperatures, slapping the covers of their identity cards, "Pack up, let's get going!" Father scurried around looking for papers, sorting something on his desk, hands trembling, stunned and pathetic, and then *you* jumped out at them from the corner of the room, pimply pale-green adolescence trying to unbend its back — squelched and squeaky, long bangs swinging across your nose, you screeched, "How dare you, what right do you have!" It didn't come off too well; actually it didn't come off well at all: the guys shut you up as easily as kicking a puppy aside with one foot (young junior officer, moustache the hint of a thin line, was trying real hard, piece of fucking shit on his first responsible assignment — no piddling matter, catching a real-live anti-Soviet! — "Not your business, sweetie, you're a little young for this aren't you?"). And anyway, your parents, dark-faced with terror as though someone had slipped Polaroid paper under their skin, began hissing-shushing-flapping long before you even rushed forward. But the first failure didn't stop you, because it's true what the man said, you're a brave lady, that you are, darling. Some years later, as a student in the eighties out on a date with the latest cutie-pie, you decided to head for the theater with a group of friends to see some hit show in from Moscow. Just a random attempt since nobody had tickets, laughing your heads off the whole while, quips flying back and forth like snowballs, you began storming the ticket office with a mob of similar revelers, the crowd having grown quite sizable by then: New Year's Eve, after all, you're young and alive and who wants to go home and that's when the cops showed up — a squadron of paddy wagons revved up, gray coats plowed into the throng sending furrows of breaker waves crashing in all directions and who the hell even knows how it happened, just a moment ago there you were, well, having fun — so, if you hadn't gotten in, big deal, you would have headed over to Khreshchatyk for a cup of Turkish coffee! When suddenly there was cutie-pie's friend, the most persistent of the bunch, light and slippery as quicksilver — in fact, one more push and he just might have squeezed into the theater! — there he was, identified and fished out from the huddled, bellowing herd and now being dragged under the arms by two gorillas in uniform. He couldn't even reach the asphalt with his feet; the rest of your coterie followed in confusion, not having the foggiest where to begin, and he was already whining to the gorillas: "Come on guys, let go of me, let me go, please, come on guys," legs twisting in the air independently of his torso, and your cutie-pie, dumb jerk, shuffling behind like a somnambulist, mumbling, "It's okay, they won't do nothing to him." Meantime the paddy wagon was standing ready, rear end wide open, and then you once again — brave lady! — with a panther leap of a by-now considerably stronger and better-looking body landed smack in front of the wagon, a two-legged lightning streak in a short sheepskin jacket, scattering them to both sides (by that time they were already pushing the poor schmuck into the van): "Boys!" — your voice sent sparks through the air like a piece of flint — "What are you trying to do here, huh?!" And you sprang the captive free: the boys (more like mating bulls, really) opened ranks, became somehow softer around the edges and more malleable, stepped back, mumbled something in defense along the lines of, "Well, how come he . . . ?" — oh yeah, he resisted arrest and said something rude — and then cutie-pie stepped forward and you scooped up the victim and let's get the hell out of here! (And wouldn't it be like that on your first night with that man, when he boldly zoomed up the no-exit ramp and the cops pulled him over — and he, puny and stooped in an unbuttoned leather jacket which suddenly drooped on him like a used condom, was explaining something to them out there, flailing his arms about: "Come on guys, what did I do, I didn't, honest? — and you, tired of waiting in the car, swung the door open, stepped out, click-clicked your heels down the sidewalk, tossed your curls, absorbing the ravenous glances of the holster-swinging males — one could light a cigarette on your scintillating laugh: "What's the problem gentlemen? We didn't break any rule." — and the tempest somehow dissipated all at once: well, okay then, go ahead, but watch yourselves." And in the early morning, fixing his fiery eyes on you as you lay half-draped on the couch, he muttered slowly, smacking his lips and relishing his triumphant smile, "Ah, you're a tough broad — jumped right out to plow the cops in the kisser. . . . I could do some jobs with you," and you were flooded by a surge of childish pride: finally, finally somebody noticed — because he was one of those who could have come out of the prison camps, and you met, after all these years — for he was more than a brother, he was Fatherland and Home.) Fear oozed in from the outside like caustic fumes, but inside the house it was warm, sultry in fact, teenage depression, no, neurasthenia, some kind of stupid pills, fever stuck at 99.2, tears umpteen times a day. The lady doctor told you to undress and asked Daddy to leave the room — "She's a big girl already" — and you were shocked that Daddy, rather than defend his paternal right — after all, it was *his* child that was about to be examined! — shuffled to the door in humiliation, flustered and dwarfed as if caught red-handed. (The curious thing, she tells herself with the imperturbability of a surgeon, is that he really was a good-looking guy, talkative, witty, and ready to embrace life, and women liked him, and there would have been absolutely no problem finding some action outside the house, so why did he guard his chastity like some Galician old maid? Was it not because mother had married him before he was "rehabilitated" and he spent his whole life cowering, afraid he'd hear her say aloud what he was secretly tormenting himself with: that he'd ruined her life? But to be left alone, *without* her, he was afraid of that, too, wasn't he?) And by the way, this time they only charged him with "willful unemployment," keeping him for only twenty-four hours in the district jail and sending him out after that only as a night watchman to a construction site where he sat in a glass booth, opening gates for dump trucks and the rest of the time reading Bruno Schulz, about whom he was going to someday write a book but never did get around to it (he had pretty good taste in literature, except that, like the Catholic Index, he couldn't stand any hint of eroticism). His panic at her unrestrained growth — "Hey, stop that!" — settled into his insides and slowly sawed away at them like a dull blade, but they only diagnosed cancer when it was too late to operate, his whole reproductive system affected: prostate, testes. (Every day Mother grated carrots for juice and squeezed them by hand, twisting the ball of mash through a piece of cheesecloth; her fingers, which had once strummed a guitar, acquired a permanent yellow color and could be straightened only with effort, and at night Daddy's girl would run to the phone booth down the block to call the ambulance, and so when mother, her eyes white with horror, returned from the hospital one day with news of the diagnosis, which at all costs was to be kept a secret from Daddy, the first thought that flashed through *your* head [for which you would never ever forgive yourself] was a cold and merciless one, hissed through clenched teeth: Thank God!) In fact, it was nothing less than war, in which there could be no winners because, having exhausted all means to get his way (pin 'em down with your knee, shove 'em into the crib, "she's just a child," we wanted a boy, but that's okay, she turned out a smart tough cookie and she'll show *them all!*) — having done all that, the man resorts to the ultimate weapon, death, and that does the trick. You lay down your arms and you go over to his side. And your adolescence, which you swore you would never again re-live, it catches up with you twenty years later, releasing from the darkest recesses of your being a tearful and frightened teenage girl who takes over completely, and then it laughs at you long and hard: "What, thought you could get away?. . . Didn't get too far, did you?"

* * *

Maybe it's true that slaves should not bear children, she muses, staring dully out the window: yesterday the first snow fell, but now it's melted; only the windshields of cars parked up and down the street look like wet spots on newborn calves. A man — black skin, bright red jacket, blue baseball cap — bounces down the sidewalk with his hands in his pockets: it must have gotten colder. Because what is slavery, if not infection by fear — she draws towards her an open notebook half-filled with lukewarm aphorisms that move you about as much as a textbook in formal logic. Slavery is the state of being infected by fear. And fear kills love. And without love — children, poems, paintings — all is pregnant with death. "A+, girl! You have completed your research."

* * *

Ladies and gentlemen — no, for now it's just ladies or, more precisely, one lady, Donna from East European Studies, one of the few friends you've made during this time, half-Irish, half-Slavic mix, a rather pleasing combination: golden hair, warm hazel eyes, high cheekbones, skin sprinkled with fine freckles like a good sesame seed roll. You can't smoke in the university cafeteria, where you've arranged to meet for lunch, and Donna, having finished her cup of the dark brown liquid Americans for some reason insist on calling coffee, stuffs a stick of chewing gum in her mouth: sublimated nicotine. This chewing of the cud comes off as not at all offensive, perhaps because Donna laughs so often and so sincerely, which gives the impression that she keeps tasting something funny. She's writing a dissertation on "Gender in Post-Communist Politics," she is quite honestly interested in knowing why in those politics there aren't and never have been any women — a question that stumps you every time, no matter how often it's posed to you by Western intellectuals (hell, how am I supposed to know?). It seems that Donna suspects that this is the root of all our problems: like all feminists, she is convinced that men are "full of shit," and the minute you let them loose you've got wars all over the place, concentration camps, famine, natural disasters, someone starts shutting off the hot water and electricity; then there are budget cuts in the department for the second year in a row and her dissertation defense is postponed yet again. And so Donna takes your story perhaps not so much to heart, as directly into her files. Ladies and gentlemen, let me go on. "Whaat?!" Donna thrusts herself forward so that her golden curls bounce in the air and settle into the deep cut of her sweater. "How?!" Donna is outraged. "How could he do that? And how can anybody treat a woman that way?!" "Oh my!" Donna nods her head sympathetically and with completely uncharacteristic domesticity begins straightening out a non-existent tablecloth with the palms of both hands: a gesture that indicates complete bewilderment and a loss for appropriate commentary. No, she had problems with her last boyfriend, but nothing like this! "Listen," says Donna as her face clears up with the discovery of a solution: "Looks like this guy is severely sick, don't you think?" A short course in psychology, the road to mental health: find the reason and the problem goes away. Why hasn't anyone thought of doing this with nations: you neatly psychoanalyze a whole national history, and poof, you're cured. Literature as a form of national therapy. Hmm, not a bad idea. Too bad that we happen to have no literature. "I just don't understand one thing," Donna says judgmentally (it's obvious that a fundamental aspect of her worldview is at stake here). "I don't understand, why did you put up with it? In bed, I mean? Why didn't you just say no?" The conceptual approach: women's struggle for their rights. What can I tell you, Donna-dearest? That we were raised by men fucked from all ends every which way? That later we ourselves screwed the same kind of guys, and that in both cases they were doing to us what others, *the others*, had done to them? And that we accepted them and loved them as they were, because not to accept them was to go over to the others, the other side? And that our only choice, therefore, was and still remains between victim and executioner: between nonexistence and an existence that slowly kills you. After throwing the vestiges of their lunch into the cafeteria trash bin — plastic trays with paper dishware, cups and plates all in bright spots from different sauces: soy, ketchup, mustard, plum (vermilion, carmine, ochre, umber) — palettes, props from a theatrical performance (act one: an artist's studio; act two: a room in a student dorm; act three cancelled for technical reasons, tickets not returned and prayers not answered) — they head for the exit. Donna pushes the glass doors, a sudden burst of frosty air joyfully zaps the lungs, cars drive by, young men in jackets sporting emblems of their university walk past laughing, a disturbing electric-blue sky blazes overhead, and on the corner a tall, shaggy, grey-haired Leonardo da Vinci stands wrapped in a blanket, stretching a paper Coca-Cola cup toward them and rattling coins, "Help the homeless, ma'am!" — "I'm homeless myself," she shakes her head, not at him, out into space. "But you know," Donna turns to her suddenly as she pulls her fine leather driving gloves on and happily chews on a new stick of gum, "these East European men of yours may be brutal at times, but at least they're passionate. While ours ..."

* * *

And you'll be staring out of the airplane window watching the suitcases go up the conveyer belt of the ramp loader and disappear into the bowels of the plane, one after another, and then it will be just empty space floating by, and the man with US Air written on his cap will hop into the blackness of the baggage cart tug, and the bag carts will move out, and while you follow them with your eyes the ramp loader will be taken away and only a gray puddle of melted snow will remain on the cement: "Well, that's it," will resound in your head, like a cry in an abandoned church, that's it — it means they have battened down the hatches, and in a moment you will hear the dry crackle of a microphone, "Ladies and gentlemen" the flight attendant will purr, and the plane will rumble and shake as the engines warm up, and soon you will be in a different reality, a different life, with the bitterly searing pain of unfulfillment of the life lived thus far ("And what, what have you done with your life," a far-away voice will ask — ah, let's drop it, this topic is as old as humanity: you're always waiting, dreaming, thrashing about, hoping for something up ahead, and then one day you discover that this indeed *was* your life) — better for that pain to shut its mouth and never poke its head out again. Pass me the microphone and I'll say, "Ladies and gentlemen, we have created a wonderful world, and please accept, on this occasion, sincere greetings from US Air, and from CNN, and from the CIA, and the Uruguayan drug mafia, and the Romanian Securitate, and from the Central Committee of the Communist Party of China, and from the millions of killers in all the prisons of the world as well as the tens of millions still at large, and from the five thousand Sarajevo children born of rape, who will, after all, grow up some day, and — onward and upward, brave new world, and that, actually, is all I wanted to say, thank you for your attention ladies and gentlemen, have a good flight." When I was young, I dreamed of such a death: plane crash over the Atlantic, an aircraft dissolving in the air and the ocean — no grave, no trace. Now I wish with all my heart that the plane lands safely: I like to watch the tall, sinewy old man with the hooked nose and deeply furrowed lines running down from his eyes, the way he takes the nylon bag with a tennis racket on its gut and pushes it into the overhead bin; and the Spanish-looking brunette with the unbuttoned leather coat — she's on board with two children, and while she removes the smaller one from her backpack and sets him on the chair, the other one, a girl of about five, narrow, tanned face in a baroque frame of promisingly capricious curls, flashes her eyes and smiles up and down the aisle in all directions, glowing with excitement — her first trip! — and her eyes stop on me: "Hi!" she shouts happily. "Hello there!" say I.

GIRLS

by Oksana Zabuzhko
Translated by Askold Melnyczuk

DARKA SAW HER IN THE TROLLEY, THE SWEATY, JUNE-SOAKED trolley, brimming with people and their smells: sweet, almost corpselike, female, heavy, equestrian, yet oddly palatable, and even stimulating, sexual, distinctly male. Suddenly all the smells switched off, leaving only a girlish profile on the sunny side of the car, angular as a Braque: abrupt, soaring cheekbones, a fine pug nose, mulatto lips, and a sharp, childlike fist of a chin-a capricious, fragile geometry which occasionally seeps from an artist's pen, piercing the heart, as when in childhood you pick up a new Christmas ornament (I remember it: a blinding white ballerina, tutu frozen in an upward sweep, an inconceivable liquid legato of arms and legs, so delicate and small-fingered that touching them with your brutish five-year old's stumps seemed blasphemous), such faces catapult into the world in order to reawaken us to life's fragility. She had the disproportionately long (instead of Braque, Modigliani) neck of a wary fawn (Fee, Fi, Fo, Fawn chanted the other girls, but Darka couldn't bring herself to say it: the fawn was simply Effie and none other, because these slopes and angles, lines pushed to the breaking point, suggested something else entirely). It was the same kind of neck that had emerged from the open collar (stiff, angular, extending over the shoulders in that style from the seventies) of the school uniform, flashing cleavage. Ah, Effie the fawn! In the chemistry classroom her spot was near the window where the light fell on her face and neck that same way, trailing down the trench between her breasts. It deepened as she bent over, giving the sun her downy left cheek. Only, Darka realized now that this couldn't be her childhood friend, that the real Effie would be well over thirty, and yet amazingly enough, it was her, newly returned in her incomparable-not-quite-twenty-year old prime: every woman's beauty has (like every figure, its ideal size, where one pound more or less makes all the difference) its own moment of perfection, one in which everything opens to the fullest, and which can change in a minute like the bloom on a desert flower or may, in happier circumstances, depending on care and watering, last for years (so, optimistically, thinks Darka, whose expenses for moisturizing, for creams and lotions, have recently begun exceeding her outlay for clothing) and Effie at the start had been junior-sized. Yet who knows what life turned her into eventually? Effie: ephebe, the word exactly.

Effie or non-Effie, on the sunny side of the trolley senses she's being watched and turns her head (the butterfly brush of lashes), glance sharp as an elbow: Look, look, said Effie, sweeping up her sleeve, see how sharp, want to feel it? And here too-thrusting forward her neck and, already disheveled and spooked, pushing out her collarbones: held breath, the gaze dead, strange, a little frightened, whether through its own daring trustfulness or because of your unpredictability: she loves me, she loves me not (or, as she played it: love, kiss, spit)-of course it's not her, and neither is this one as young as she looked in profile — Darka turns her eyes away, and looks politely out the window where at this moment out of the dappled green of Mariinsky Park rises the monument to Vatutin-dull, bald, and smug, a sculptural epitaph to Khrushchev's era: a peer, Darka sneers (the monument went up the year she was born) — and at that moment she decides about the school reunion (a stiff envelope with a gold seal, an invitation, removed yesterday from the mailbox, and uncertainly set aside — there will be time to think about it), dammit, she'll go to the reunion though the prospect wearies her: what could be interesting about this pathetic act of self-assertion before the face of one's own adolescence, what's intriguing about the gray and the bald blissfully morphing to boyos again, and artificial, elaborately decked-out women who sneak glances at your wrinkles, hoping they have fewer themselves? But she'll go—whatever happened to Fawn-Effie-Faron? Suddenly, she needed to know. Once Darka read an article by an American gender-studies guru which claimed axiomatically that boys tended to be competitive, girls cooperative. Only a boy could have blathered such nonsense so glibly.

The struggle for power, not for its dividends in the form of grades (suggestive of subsequent financial achievement), nor for success with the opposite sex (which had not defined itself as being opposed to anything yet), and not even for the applause meter running high at the Christmas Pageant (which principally feeds the vanity of one's parents, and only later flexes the muscles of your own), but for power in its nearly unalloyed pristine form, like the sweet narcotic of pure, dry white spirit, and all the more intoxicating: the exclusive right to lead the class either from the schoolroom to the playing field, or after class to what they called a "recital of cats" — below a window where you torment the tub from the front row, the one who chews her sandwich wrapped in wax paper from home during the break and then leaves hideous grease stains on textbooks — to lead the class no matter where, no matter whether for good or ill, because the difference between good and evil doesn't exist, just as it never exists in the presence of absolute power — this struggle, aside from its earliest form in tribal war, you see precisely among girls from ages eight to twelve. Later, thank God, they develop other, more civilian concerns.

By fourth grade, when Effie appeared in their class, Darka already had the rap sheet of either a budding criminal or a political leader (the boundary between them is of course narrow, and depends not on nature but nurture): at least two girls from her class had to change schools, one in the middle of the year, black-haired Rivka Braverman with bluish-white starched bows in her glistening braids, whose father's chauffeur drove her to school in the company's glistening black Volga, and after school drove her to music lessons.

Rivka had a plump, confident ass and a disdainful mouth melding into folds of flesh. She smelled of homemade vanilla cookies, vacations

at a spa in the Caucasus, third-generation antiques confiscated during
the Revolution, and a five-room apartment of the sort reserved for
only the most privileged of Soviet families, in a building erected by
prisoners-of-war for the new Soviet elite. Such a start in life does little
to encourage an instinct for self-preservation, so that Darka, whom
Rivka carelessly attempted to treat with all her studied arrogance
toward others, none of whom had ever darkened the threshold of such
a five-room apartment in a building erected by prisoners of war, forced
on Rivka her first lesson in survival training in a society sufficiently
transformed that neither her grandfather the Prosecuting Attorney,
nor her father the Director of X, were able to secure for her what
was most valuable: a more bankable nationality to declare in that
fifth blank on her passport. After Darka sicced on her a group of
classmates, including red-haired Misha Khazin and Marina Weissberg,
who chased her from school to the entrance of that apartment building
built by prisoners of war, in one breath chanting Kike, kike, running
down the pike-and Rivka really did run like the Wandering Jew of all
Treblinkas, her plump bouncing ass suddenly, pathetically deflated, and
the next day in class the whole group murmured to themselves so that
the teacher facing the blackboard heard only a monotonous hum as
though the room had been filled with bumble bees-Zhid, zhid, zhid,
the word sounded especially greasy, thick, repulsive, Let the damn bee
out, the teacher snapped, at which point the bee fell silent, and then
Rivka suddenly leaped up and shouted Again! There they go again!
and ran out weeping. After this, no matter how Braverman the Elder
threatened the school, no matter how many parents were called in for
meetings, it was no longer possible for Rivka, proudly upholding the
propellered bows of her braids, to stay in class.

Darka herself was shocked and frightened by Rivka's unexpected
collapse. Her hysterical crying had aborted their game of King of the
Hill and for a few days Darka herself lay in bed with an inexplicable
fever. Her principal sorrow lay in the fact that Rivka, arrogant and
hateful, with her muscling into the class presidency, with her hideous
pouting mouth (a clear legacy from her grandfather, an agent of the

Cheka, the brutal secret police, a fact Darka could not have known at the time, though she registered it instinctively) with which she talked her way into the coveted position of sanitary inspector, where she would examine her classmates' hands and send the ink-spattered back to the washroom for a scrubbing, with her methodical nerdiness and unblemished faith in her own perfection, who had once dared to point out reluctantly that Darka too was an A student (it's you who's an A student too, Darka blurted back), with her glistening elbow sleeves, and that second pair of shoes in a special pink bag, real pumps, delicate and also pink, like a little princess's, with heels: You don't have any like this and you never will. My daddy bought them for me in Copenhagen — that Rivka suddenly appeared to be a child, just like Darka, and because of her, because of Darka, that child was screaming with grief. Her mother and father also grew worried as Darka began groaning in her sleep. She'd gladly have made peace with Rivka, would have apologized, made it up, cheered her up, had she only known how. Her experience of peacemaking involved only her mother and father who, no matter what happened, always found themselves in the pastoral position: Go and sin no more, they'd say after a time, and it was possible to skip out with a leap, lighthearted, with quickly drying-as-in-a-sun-shower tears. Here, however, something had broken irreparably, in Rivka, in the world, in her very own self, and through the break, as in a fence, there crawled a thick, hot, brown darkness, and when Darka's fever finally fell and she returned to school she found that Rivka was no longer in her class.

The remote consequences of these events revealed the mixed feelings of guilt and shame which from then on dogged her in her every encounter with Jews and which only faded on closer acquaintance. The direct, immediate consequence was that Darka shrank, grew subdued, and dove deep into books (that began the period of intoxication by reading) right up to the end of the school year.

Then, the following year, a new girl appeared.

Darka remembered her first meeting with everyone who'd played any real part in her life, even though it may have been hidden — the bottom of memory's drawer, a snapshot of another-other-stranger, who God knows why your eye alighted on, cutting him out of the chaotic backdrop that became the rest of the world, like a promise, that when laid out in a row, with the rest of the sequence, reveal various unexpected poses, from the lightning glance of direct eye contact, creating a voltaic exchange across the short distance between two points (blue eyes, gray eyes, green eyes, each with the same enchanting glassy gaze of antique crystal, men's eyes, but who knows how hers looked to them?), to those taken as though with a hidden camera, when the object has not yet noticed you and not begun to suspect that he or she will soon be someone in your life, profiles, three-quarter shots, even shots from the back of the head: napes can be outrageously singular. Yet, no matter how she rummaged through her memory, she could never find that first shot of Effie.

Effie hadn't come from the outside; she'd unfolded from within Darka like one of her own organs. Like the dormant gene of an inherited disease.

What Darka remembered were Effie's panty hose — most of the girls in the class still wore white and brown cotton ones, wrinkled, droopy-kneed, and for some reason eternally sagging too short, oh this damned command economy (did socialism set as one of its goals the breeding of short-legged and suspiciously tubby little girls?), with the crotch always sagging out from under one's skirt so that everyone, above all the wearer, expected that any moment they would fall off, and so our childhood passed, in the Land of the Falling Panty Hose. Toddlers were constantly hiking up their skirts and purposefully yanking up their stockings. Once tubby Alla from the front row did it in fourth grade when she was called up to the blackboard, the most natural gesture, the same as rolling up your sleeves or smoothing your hair, but in fourth grade this made her a laughingstock (or: they mocked her mercilessly), the boys practically fell out of their chairs, pointed their fingers, and the treacherous girls too yukked it up, and maybe because of that Darka remembered Fawn's legs, those of a long, vulnerable, lanky newborn fawn, but covered smoothly with a fine transparent wrap. In the sun-drenched classroom they looked golden. It was as though Fawn had no childhood, nothing to outgrow, all the barely visible, minute women's ways of sculpting, transforming themselves into women, which take one's entire adolescence to master (some even dedicate part of their youth to it), all that plucking of eyebrows, trying on various haircuts (the shag, the flip, Sassoon-bangs — a chirping already incomprehensible to boys), nail polish with glitter and flowers until settling in tenth grade on, thank god, one's natural color. She seemed to have been endowed with everything at birth, a fully drawn, breakable gold-legged figure: Braque? Modigliani? No, Picasso, Girl on the Ball.

Effie, Effie, my love.

And she remembers something more about the legs — that unbearable internal burn which you eventually learn to recognize as jealousy when the English teacher (and really as though copied from life, from the grotesquely bland, flat-chested, formless, ageless English women of de Maupassant whom Darka was already devouring surreptitiously) makes Effie stand in the corner: teachers, that is, female teachers (there was only one man, who taught Phys Ed), somehow teachers did not love her, but why? And Effie stands there in her uniform, in front of the whole class, lightly rocking on her golden fawn's legs and Marinka Weissberg whispers to Darka: Doesn't Fawn have nice legs, Darka pulls back, this isn't a subject for discussion, but Marinka keeps on, Long, too. Mine are twelve centimeters shorter. We measured. You know how you measure, here, from the hip, the blow seems so strong that Darka inadvertently opens her mouth to catch a breath and then under her breast the burn spreads with a slow fire, just yesterday she and Effie sat late on the lake in the park, first feeding the Effie-necked swans, and when the swans went to sleep the girls watched the sun set on the burning, splintered, intense dark purple streak of water, wide-eyed as though frightened. Both gazed with Effie's wide-open eyes: so much beauty, she said, her thin — so thin they looked shadowed with blue — eyelids butterflied: So much beauty in the world, how to grasp it all? You know, Dar, sometimes

I can't sleep all night, I keep thinking, my head goes round and round, how to hold it, this world's so huge? And you know, the lids dropped, along with Darka's heart, mulatto lips puckered as though for a kiss sprinkled with dewdrops, the result of an extraordinary internal effort, You know Dar, I think either something very beautiful or very terrible will happen to me, her knuckles squeezing the bench turning white. Something, some way in which I'll finally be able to capture everything, hold everything, contain everything, you understand? Darka trembled within, not from the cold, because her cheeks and mouth were hot, but from the feeling that in her cupped palms fluttered a butterfly, because from childhood, because everyone knows that if you blow all the pollen off the butterfly's wings, it will certainly die. Never again in her life would she so desperately want to protect someone, before no one else did she feel such numbing awe as then, with Effie, all later connections were mere shards of this sensation, like those splinters of purple fire on the water (a bit like loving a man, bodies dissolving, and after a few minutes you hungrily move toward him again because you don't know what else might be done with this flesh, impenetrable as a wall, aside from taking it one more time, because there's no way to come together so as to never part again — but that's coarser, more primitive. For that matter, as you develop your self-conscious flesh, everything becomes simpler and more linear, or maybe, Darka assumes now, being a sister, an older sister, is the same as being born with the instincts of a mother, and it was her sisterlessness which had been an absence swelling inside her for years and at the right moment shifted onto Effie, Effie who in fact needed something different) — deafened and blinded, Darka bent low over her notebook, trying not to look at Fawn standing in the corner though she smiled wanly in her direction as if she knew what she and Marinka Weissberg were whispering: that Effie yesterday entrusted to her the most precious part of her inner self meant to Darka a kind of vow to eternal and absolute fidelity, so, aside from the shock that the beloved turns out not to be transparent, that she leads a separate life and can have secrets from you (measuring legs with silly Marinka, giggling, hiking hems to press their hips against each other — she never did such things with me, not even a hint of it). In addition to that shock, there was the grief of insulted love which demands everything at once, unsatisfied with bits and pieces, and therefore is destined to doubt that which it has actually received: is it possible she lied to me yesterday? How is it possible to be so, so hypocritical — Darka remembered she'd used just that word; during recess, she passed by Effie in proud silence; it took her stupefied senses an entire class to recover from the shock, while at the next recess Effie herself approached her: What's up? You mad at me?

I have to talk to you, said Darka in a tight voice she didn't recognize herself, a lump in her throat. After school they again sat in the park at the lake, wrapped like fairy-tale heroes in a cloud, an air of Shakespearian thunderstorm, a tempest — the sweet sorrow of parting — Effie, flashing eyes full of wobbly tears, passionately assured Darka that the thing with Marinka had happened long ago, implying that it was before her friendship with Darka, that it was all silly and meaningless and didn't matter and Darka brightened, the sky cleared, as though pulled out from under an avalanche, yet for a while she still pretended to be offended, partly from an innate sense of form and partly out of an unconscious bartering with Effie for new concessions, new guarantees of undivided and exclusive affection, a scenario which Darka later on inevitably repeated with men except that with them it was much easier, while Effie was about as supple as Picasso's acrobat, dodging to avoid Darka's onslaught, from despairing repentance to a sudden collapse into a complete and trancelike absence and a self-absorption, to half-hysterical recitals of poems meant to explain everything (that year they buried each other in poetry), until, exhausted by the endless back and forth, Darka heard her own voice cry: Forgive me! then sinking to her nylon-warmed golden knees, embracing them and at the same time greedily snorting in, through tears, their surprising smell of bread, the odors of home reached after long travels: in the bedroom under your parents' door the light pours, let me fluff up your pillow, the ticklish scent like a kitten's on her hair on your cheek, two girls cuddling under the covers, hugging each other, whispering, sudden outbursts of laughter, stop you're deafening me — like you, but different, that's what a sister is, that's what I'm embracing, tightly, so tightly that it can't be tighter, never to let it go — two wildly intertwined girls on a bench in the park of an evening, her swollen breasts under her school uniform thrust into yours, her lashes tickling your neck, like in that myth where the cloud of the gods rendered the lovers invisible to mere mortals — nobody walked down the path, nobody rustled the fallen leaves, there was nobody to be surprised when Effie began kissing the trail of tears under Darka's eyes and then pressed her lips to hers and gasped, Effie's heart beat inside Darka's chest and both froze, not sure what to do next, and then Darka felt between her lips something quick, wet, salty, and very large, it floated in her mouth like a naked hot fish blacking out the rest of the world and she did not immediately understand that it was Effie's tongue but once she did she was seized by another, incomprehensible sort of sobbing, inhaling her tears and Effie's tongue, squeezing the skinny body even tighter: shoulder blades sharp as wings, the keyboard of the vertebrae under the coarse uniform, suddenly brought to memory her first realization of what it meant that something was alive. She was three years old, standing speechless above a basket full of tiny fluffy white rabbits, unable to step aside or turn away, until one of the adults said from above, Would you like one?

She struggled to come to terms with the idea that such an astonishing creature breathed and moved, and then with the equally astonishing news of what one could do with such a miracle: one could possess it (at that most honest of ages, possession meant just one thing: it meant that, out of an excess of feeling, one could put the thing in one's mouth and swallow it, as one did the petals of the prettiest flowers from the courtyard garden which you plucked and chewed, your saliva turning bitter and green when you spit, and over years that original meaning of the word doesn't change, only gets clouded over). It takes a lifetime to understand that long ago the grownups fooled you, that in fact nothing living, neither a flower, nor a rabbit, nor a person, nor a country, can in fact be had: they can only be destroyed, which is the one way to confirm they have been possessed.

* * *

And here too, said Effie, but it was another time, at home, before a large tarnished mirror in a dark-brown frame, she first unbuttoned her dress, exposing two bra straps on a cubist shoulder of protruding horizontal bones, she'd long ago begun wearing a bra, Darka saw, when they changed before gym class Effie's expensive snow-white underwear unavailable in any store though there amid the smell of mats stacked up in the corner which were old and rough to the touch reeking of old sweat, there, in the middle of it, it was just underwear, but here, when Effie, not turning her hypnotized, dark eyes — pupils dilated — away, slipped off her bra — a tender, pearl-pink nipple popped out of its cup like an outthrust tongue and at the same time Effie's fingers stumbled over buttons as though asking permission, began cautiously unbuttoning Darka's shirt and she saw, alongside Effie's, her own nipple only darker, redder, like a cherry pit, here blood rushed to Darka's head and everything grew blurred, Effie leaned lightly over her breast and Darka felt her wet gathering mouth, and goose bumps, and her own rapid breathing, and everything began flowing, was it her, Darka, who was slipping into the unknown, something heady and hot, something forbidden and tempting, compared with which all of Darka's steady will to power, being first in her class, academic triumphs, captain of the volleyball team, all this was small and insignificant as she went down and emerged new, dark, dangerous, and big as the world — oh Effie Effie, two girls with their shirts undone in the depths of the mirror where Effie touched her kissed breast with her own and said: Here too, pointing to the other one, and that was how it began.

And so it whirled, sweeping all away. All their school recesses spent together on the windowsill, wandering through the park after class, drunken talking talking talking, insatiable as two mutes who'd suddenly discovered the gift of tongues or infants who'd just learned to talk, but they really were just learning to speak, learning to translate each other into words and speech different from what the adults had expected — about the meaning of life, the future of mankind, will there be war, about their own childhoods, it was frightening to see how many reflections surfaced at that age — I remember when I was little — and then you don't remember a thing until you're old, when, they say, the sluices finally open again, you can't even remember what those things were — you spent hours gushing at each other so that the day felt too short, except a few splinters, of poems for instance, So Long Had Life Together Been by Joseph Brodsky (Effie), Lady with Eyes Larger than Asters by Kalynets (Darka), but that was passed on from the grownups, it was the frigging legacy of the sixties generation that was passed on from family to family in a thin stream from a closed tap, while all of one's own content that filled the cup to overflowing had drained away somewhere, leaving only silt after the passing of a stream — the memory of a bench, of a windowsill in a school corridor, a memory of Effie's concentrated face — did she know how to listen with shiny eyes and half-open mouth, and all that in the shadowy, autumnal light of sad, nostalgic longing for the long-gone unreachable heights — that whole visible daily aspect of their friendship (sixth grade: just as, among kids, that boiling process of clinging and dissolving molecules begins, friendships forming and dissolving several times a year, so that none of the teachers ever paid these two much attention), it all continued, this material world, yet invisibly tightening and shrinking the dress (now pinching her armpits) under the abrupt combustible wind of that suffocating, heady element of their friendship which unfolded without witnesses and gathered strength — to be more precise a lot more energy, at least with Darka, went into supporting it because all their trembling falling into each other, all their hot kisses and more frequent, growing caresses exploded not on their own, not from a purely physical compulsion, as later occurred with boys but each time moving to some kind of emotional resolution, a little drama, the improvisation of which they were wonderfully adept at: in the feat of peacemaking after a new argument that took them to the edge of break-up (regular as storms in July), in an ecstasy of simultaneously recognizing the music of the Doors, to which Effie responded by collapsing onto the carpet and pounding her forehead into it, shouting, I can't stand it, I can't stand it.

And Darka, seizing that dear warm downy head (smelling like the fur of a kitten), her whole body trembling at the unfathomable mystery of feeling things, at how far more subtle and spiritually richer Effie was than she (that was what Darka wrote in an essay titled My Friend: My friend has a richly subtle and spiritually rich nature; she was stuck for a long time on the repetition: one of the two had to be crossed out, yet neither was willing to leave), really, it's quite puzzling, Darka now wonders, how on earth did they manage to study that year, where had they found the time for it, or, to be more precise, where had Effie found the time, since she never managed things as well as Darka, yet succeeded in passing all her classes, even earning A's, and not only in music and gym (honor students, which, as the Vice Principal said during the PTA meeting about her, a girl from an honorable family, because that was what she was, with divorced parents who spoiled her competitively: stereo, French linens at twelve), where did she find it, the time and strength?

And they read, insatiably, with all their might, living through the work as though it were their own inner life — their own times fit them like a glove: these were the years of the book boom: the hunt for hard to find books from Moscow (special access), bound in smelly fresh leatherette the color of dark amber or bottle green or marine blue, all spines gilded like the epaulets on an officer's uniform (yet looking for all that like the expensive cognac boxes next to which these books were meant to cohabit on Yugoslavian shelves symbolizing lives of cultured leisure and the ever-expanding well-being of the Soviet people), and Darka, whose family connections gave her access to risky mimeographed samizdat materials, borrowed from Effie high-ranking uniform volumes of Akhmatova and Mandelstam, as well as *The Master and Margarita,* which Effie read first, before loaning it, rehearsing for her most of the first chapter up to and including the part where the head's cut off by the tram but Darka never managed to memorize the final chapter: as she was finishing the book she was called out and interrogated by the police, and in one moment her childhood came to an end.

Much later, as a grown-up, Darka finally risked asking her mother just what horrible thing had been discovered at that point (oh if only it hadn't been) and which had stormed through the entire school for over a month? To an adult, the story seemed utterly banal: a girl from a well-to-do family, not yet thirteen, secretly, without anybody knowing (not even me!), hangs around with sexually mature seventeen-year-old boys, goes with them Sundays to the deserted Trukhaniv Island, and later the mother of one of these boys (you can imagine this mother, someone should have drowned the bitch!), raises a fuss across the whole school (idiot!) because her dear little boy had the bridle on his penis torn, or rather, bitten through (so what's the big deal? It would heal before the wedding!). Darka's mother was only able to tell her about the torn bridle because the story had been an unforgettable lesson in anatomy. OK, I agree, said Darka insincerely, hoping to coax more information from her, the story's not pleasant, certainly not for the girl's parents, but when you think about it, there are many worse ways to lose your virginity, which don't always lead to broken lives, and a girl with such a turbulent debut might, in twenty years, why not, surface as an affable matron with a decent university job, while the poor mangled boy may to the delight of his mother, yet become a Ph.D., an oceanographer, a celanographer, or a stylographer, why not?

(What Darka herself remembered was her first glimpse, through a crack in the principal's office door, of Effie's mother — young and dazzlingly beautiful, sheathed in leather, draped in pendulous Gypsy jewelry, in sheaves of turtledove-gray veils of smoke which swirled like burning incense round an unknown goddess — apart from the brief shock at the fact that someone had the nerve to smoke in the principal's office, she remembered it as the first time she became aware of a different species of human which somewhere, no, here, beyond the glass wall, though you can't get there, thrives — a richer than rich, glamorous, movie-idol with an unfathomably intense life who has been given the world for her pleasure forever.) Darka's mother, however, also remembered the arrival of a detective, something Darka barely noticed (maybe because the children were questioned in their parents' presence and parents were, to kids at that age, more significant than any strangers, so Darka retained the vague impression that it was her own parents interrogating her). A detective? That means it wasn't simply a matter of children's games under clear skies. What else was up? Chewing gum, American jeans (the height of luxury) given or traded by these kids near the, oh god, Intourist Hotel (where all foreigners stayed), that terrible word — the most terrifying word there was — for saling, because trading with foreigners was, after all a crime.

What had all this been about? Were they plotting entrapment at a later date, or hoping to keep the kids from racing into the future with extravagant appetites, teaching them instead to sin in secret?

Did you see, Skalkovska has (Effie immediately become, and remained, Skalkovska) that badge with the American flag? Did she tell you where she got it?

Chills, my god, what a nightmare, plus the reek of political informers — was it the mother of the victimized, unbridled, half-circumcised boy who'd used this as a way to break up the circle once and for all?) What could Effie, her Effie, have to do with this? And above all how could she have maintained her life on such parallel tracks, as invisible as panty hose without a wrinkle, without ever giving herself away to Darka?

(There was, however, one moment during which Darka, with the sudden jealous clarity of all lovers, did get after all, one barely visible splinter: Ihor M., from tenth grade, passing them in the corridor, the red-scarved peons whom the upperclassman shoved aside blindly like ants, suddenly stops: Fawn, he says, with an unusually intimate, creepy, utterly adult tone, and a strange smile on his lips, and Effie steps toward him like a ballerina, leg suspended in the air, heel to toe — and while they exchange a few hushed words, Darka sees nothing but the bent leg, toes lightly pressed to the ground, and her heart breaking out of the pain of uncertainty, suspiciously asks Effie after she returns, Where do you know him from?

We're neighbors, says Effie, puckering her mulatto lips into a chicken's ass — it was the kind of grimace she put on when called on in class, driving the female faculty wild. This was the single glimpse, brief as a scratch, of a distant and incomprehensible, beautiful and frightening — and could it be otherwise — secret: because she was all mystery, that's what she was, and neither I nor to those hideous boys whose brains leaked out in their sperm, not that there was much there to begin with, could have dreamed of holding her for more than a moment, a moment brief as the flutter of a butterfly's wings.)

At the time of course Darka knew nothing about any bridle, and for that matter neither did anybody else, except for the parents, of course, among whom the news might even have caused a surge of sexual activity: the atmosphere was electrified. All Darka knew was that Effie had been dishonored, irretrievably thrust into some dark nightmare, into a muddy bog suddenly opening where the ground was supposed to be hard and well-lit, and Darka's parents loudly complained about the little prostitute and even went in a delegation from the PTA to the school director insisting that Effie be immediately removed from school and that the rest of the children, implicitly tender and pure, be forever segregated from her immoral influence. (What Bolsheviks they in fact were, what monsters, Darka discovers, with cold surprise, twenty-five years after.

The entire generation, the Orthodox, the Orwellian newspeakers, and the dissidents, the thinkers, the free thinkers, and the thoughtless, my God!). And she also knew that Effie had betrayed her, this time not childishly, but in fact.

Forever.

(Shameful, and frighteningly obscene, and at the same time so unsettlingly grown-up, the head spins: with boys, with the thing that dangles between their legs which just two years ago they'd spied on in gym class, elbowing each other: you can see everything on B! And exactly what was it they saw? with big boys who knew everything and therefore do with her who-knows-what and she lets them, the strangers and grown-up, and they look at her as did Ihor M. It's curious that no images from their own Sapphic games flashed before her, only this: how could she, with strangers? How could she let strangers take off her panties? Never mind what followed, which blurred in her imagination. But the worst thought was: Effie, what about me? What about me? A mixture of feeling ignored, disrespected, for her gender, her age, and of course for her sex: no matter what, Effie was chosen, this was obvious, chosen by those boys for a different sort of life, while me, I'd metamorphosed in a stroke into one of those comic, clumsy, hunched honors students accompanied everywhere by parents, even to the movies, as though by bodyguards: she didn't let me in, didn't let me touch something essential in her, which means that everything about our friendship was a lie because under the best-lit, most ecstatic explosions of our union, which seemed so transparent, there always hid this gigantic dark cave full of sealed shameful treasures, oh what an idiot I was! And nightly tears into the pillow, deeply buried so her parents wouldn't hear.) And therefore, when at the class meeting, as the chairman of the Pioneer unit (Tovarish Chairman — the drumbeat as before an execution, the red flag carried in, red plush with yellow fringes) and as a former friend of Skalkovska's, sure because there was no getting around the need for distance, as she was told by everyone, the vice-dean, the class tutor, and all the king's men, otherwise Effie's fall might drag her down so low she could hardly imagine, when she had to announce the Case of Comrade Skalkovska and be the first to speak (and again at first the strange resonance of a voice squeezed by your own throat so you can't swallow, it echoes inside your head, you're constantly aware of the feel of your own head) then she turned Effie in in a way no one would ever have imagined, she least of all.

This must have looked like the unbridled attack of a mean little dog, nipping at her ankles, drawing blood, and again, to the meat: Remember! Remember what you said about all the classmates, that they're all narrow-minded nonentities! (Naturally these good-for-nothings closed ranks and Effie wound up completely isolated.) You put yourself above the class! Above the collective! You decided you were better than the others, that you were allowed more than the others were, and look where this has led you — your friends (no: first you gather up the unit, then you speak in its name) — are now ashamed of you! And so on, A+ and !!! but alas there's no such grade.

And it was not an excess of administrative zeal (as it might have appeared to a dull outsider), and even less was it a desire to save her own skin (as it might have been appropriate to say had they not been children) but rather an ardent, overwhelming drive to possess Effie, even if for the last time, to have her back, begging forgiveness, repenting her betrayal. (And because Darka didn't have that power over her, she pursued instead the one path offered her by the adult world: Tovarish Chairman of the Unit Council — and the drums beat, oh how they beat, a chill went through her, this Shaman's drum and tympani, that's right, all turning points in life should be staged as solemnly as tribal initiations, and what is one's first act of collaboration if not a kind of initiation?) Consequently, Darka's words should have been read like a secret message, revealed in ultraviolet light: Remember! Remember how you said I was your only soul mate, the only one you could talk to. Remember what I said about the Doors as though the doors were really opening, and you immediately understood, those cast-iron doors! Heavy as those at Vladimir's Cathedral. And I really saw them as that, and I screamed with joy that you, you too — we stood before the doors together, we breathed as one, Effie, why did you slam them in my face?

But Effie-Skalkovsky stayed silent. And didn't intend to remember a thing, nor to repent, nor to beg forgiveness.

She didn't even look at Darka — she looked out the window, at the playing field lined with poplars, occasionally biting her lower lip, she cried — and it was clear it was something very personal, something a galaxy away from Darka, her fiery speeches, and this endless meeting. The doors, which Darka hadn't been asked to enter and tried to break down, remained shut.

Maybe, Darka speculated now, she'd been pregnant? That, thank God, I'll never know. Because you won't find everything out at a reunion over a glass of wine with a semi-stranger whom you can't exactly ask: Listen, remember, then, at the end of sixth grade or at the start of seventh, did you have an abortion?

Now out of this dull bare plateau which is called experience, Darka could assume something else: namely that Effie with her innate vulnerability was like a package, its contents bubble-wrapped, stamped Fragile on all sides in runny ink and sent on its way, yet without an address, this perfidious, secret, gracious, spoiled, truly vicious and irresistibly attractive, inwardly aflame Effie-Fawn, simply had to find, at an early age, her own way of protecting herself, especially from the suffocating Darka, defending herself with what was most obviously hers, her body. Putting it between herself and the world like a cardboard shield: take it, take it, feel it, you want it?

(I certainly didn't leave her any other options — why should others have?)

For one, two, or three years after that — in seventh, eighth, yes, and ninth grade too, they passed each other like planets on separate orbits, greeting each other with a nod, though for a long time Darka avoided Effie's eyes and was careful not to get stuck alone with her: the awareness of her betrayal, which couldn't be undone, poisoned her, lying somewhere on the bottom like an immoveable rock raising up muddy miasmas so that in the upper grades Darka even had fits of nausea, something approaching morning sickness, problems with her gall bladder, and she had to take a spoon of sunflower oil in the morning and a heating pad for her side — and then she noticed, with embarrassed relief, that when they were in groups Effie began to answer her remarks, calmly, almost warmly. She stopped pretending that Darka didn't exist, so Darka decided finally to risk speaking with her one on one, politely and purposefully — what's the big deal, really, let's get over it — asking Skalkvoska when she'd be on class duty, and Skalkovska politely answering it would be Thursday, and so it went, sideways, as between strangers, and by that time they really were strangers to each other, having outgrown their childhood episodes along with the panty hose and splayed children's shoes, snub-nosed, which get tossed into closets or storage spaces, where they gradually air out the pigeon-toed warmth that once filled them, and all the falls, scratches and bruises they witnessed, the jump rope, hopscotch, the sand carried into the house (while mother scolded), and sticky as lacquer (to be pulled off with fingers) traces of jam, and after some years, when you find them again, amid the dust and the cobwebs, you drag them into the light to see they have become old rags.

No, they weren't girls anymore, they were ladies and young women, sighing, well well.

Lies, because in fact nothing passes — no matter how deeply you bury it, what happened keeps growing darkly under the skin of years like an indelible bruise-hematoma.

Somehow, the turmoil passed. Maybe some influential parent from the Bad Company managed to turn down the heat or maybe the school wanted to protect its own reputation — the school had a fine one! — and who needs it, the endless meetings, commissions, inspections, good Lord, enough, and so it all dried up. Dried up. For a while Skalkovska suffered her isolation but it too slowly dissolved. Only the teachers, or more precisely the female ones, continued to rage (rumor had it only the gym teacher — a man — tried to defend her at the meeting but it sounded silly, what kind of defense could he mount?) — treating her badly, really badly, which she definitely did not deserve, standing straight, expressionless, an honor student to the end, and she was once even sent to the regional academic tournaments from her English class probably. And yet a teasing, seductive spirit seeped out of her like that slightly nauseatingly sweet, yet barely noticeable (except up close, along with the body's warm smell) and thus all the more lascivious (so they thought), scent of what must have been her mother's perfumes, it tickled their noses, entered their bloodstream, darkened their faces: Skalkovska, leave the room! (Shaking her head like a pony with its new mane, biting her lower lip, whether getting ready to cry or to laugh, concentrating as though she were leaving forever, she would pack her books and notebooks in her bag: a long narrow back with a keyboard of buttons running down it, a short skirt, walking down the aisle between the desks to the door never turning around: Darka could never keep from staring at her back, as though she were expecting something, but her back was buttoned tight as the door that had just closed quietly behind her, which teachers were eager to take as a provocation, repeating her punishment, again and again: Leave the room, Skalkovska, that'll teach her.)

And in ninth grade, before the end of her last term, she finally did leave for good. And after her, the gym teacher, an Olympic medalist in swimming, a forty-year-old with burly gray hair (why do sportsmen so rarely go bald?), with acidy sweat and hair sticking out of his nostrils, was also let go. It turned out that he and Effie had been carrying on an affair all spring. Someone had seen them.

Heaped in a corner of the girls' gym room, the old mats, rough to the touch as though steeped a long time in brine, and a dry, sunk-in smell, familiar as the odor of old stables, the smell of children's sweat, or not only children's, but also that other, violent and acidy?

All the time, somebody is living your life for you, one of its possible, never-to-be-realized versions. All those feelings that really do bind us to others, from love to envy, grow out of this half-secret longing for other lives intuited, recognized, our lives which we will nevertheless never have. And somebody defends us, something shields us, lives them out for us.

And we sleep without nightmares.

Of course, said Darka's mother, it's all the fault of the parents: one look at Effie's mother tells the whole story. She said this while cutting her nails with a sharp, whipping sound: she was using a tailor's scissors, because they didn't have a manicurist's pair. Her triumphant voice a monument to motherhood, utterly beyond reproach. And something apart from this, which even then forced Darka to get her fur back up, though keeping it to herself: faceless and impersonal, with all the pressure of the ten atmospheres at the bottom of the ocean, the truly terrible eternal righteousness of the community — against all breakers of the rules.

Darka's mother also had her most intense life experience at thirteen. She'd stood at the top of a hill with her sled, red and gasping, awaiting her turn to go down — and suddenly she saw how the snow-covered slope was flowing underfoot in the lilac-colored shadows of the trees: in the sun the snow glimmered with billions of sparks and each one was a planet. The planets burned, shimmered, and as the poet whom she had not yet studied at school said, spun into alignment.

The girl stared while the light grew brighter until she could almost hear the ice tinkling. She didn't know that that sound had once been called the music of the spheres. That this was the voice of the infinite. She knew only that she had to look away otherwise something terrible and irrevocable, otherwise it's all over, I'll go mad! a bolt of black lightening flashed a boundary marker: get back, get back!

And she turned away.

Everything that followed in her life was fine with her: marriage, poverty, children, sickness, work she didn't like, as well as the little joys, like a new apartment or a leather coat. It's true, the leather was only pigskin, but had been well tanned.

It could have been worse. Much worse.

THE EXTRATERRESTRIAL WOMAN

by Oksana Zabuzhko

Translated by Michael M. Naydan

B UT PARDON ME. WHAT'S FREEDOM GOT TO DO WITH IT?
"You are elemental forces." Dreamily, Valentyn Stepanovych
let the words drop, calmly shaking ashes together with his words into
a heavy crystal ashtray. His speech smoldered, enveloping Rada with a
slight dizziness, "freedom emanates from you."

Everything in the study was ponderous — an ancient desk on
bent gilded legs, a velvet armchair, the padding pressed in so deeply
it seemed as if a bear had been sleeping in it just a moment ago, dark
cherry-colored window drapes, hanging in the corners like some giant
mythical bird's wings (the window occupied the entire wall). And if
not for the space beyond the window, broken up by the rooftops and
the distant ceiling, it might have been impossible to work then amid
this heaviness of settled things. Rada preferred empty places, suffused
with the bareness of parquet floors, balcony doors thrown completely
open, a wafting echo, the clearly doleful sense of scenery taken down
and packed suitcases: in just such surroundings she could think best;
however this didn't keep her from absorbing with a deep sensuous
love the borrowed coziness of chance places where you could dip your
bare feet into a puffy carpet with pleasure and, filtering the coffee
hospitably prepared by the hosts (especially when it had cognac!),
filling herself with soft, tepid assurances that tomorrow without fail

she would create something outstanding, "and freedom for a writer is the main thing," Valentyn Stepanovych recapitulated. In Rada the instantaneous reflex of protest weakly shuddered: this phrase was already superfluous, it was just the way Valentyn Stepanovych wrote — drawing every flash of an idea to a final, single-meaning resolution that, with a slam, shut up the inner space of a work, screening the reader's vision with his haughty infallibility. Certainly freedom for a writer is the main thing, how can you object to that, and nobody needs your objection anyway. She felt slightly embarrassed, catching herself on this disagreeable independent thought; anyway, whatever you say, Valentyn Stepanovych was an undoubtedly distinguished writer, and she leaned forward with exaggerated devotion to him shining in her eyes. He dominated the desk, leaning back on the chair. He was a stalwart, robust, middle-aged man with a wild, savage mane streaked in the light here and there with tiny sparks of gray. And his motionless, slightly slanted eyes gleamed like an animal's, or like two precious stones — with the pure, autonomous luster of matter that reflects light according to the laws of optics. Before this unblinking gaze, Rada, swooning, sensed how in the depth of her stomach softly, cat-like, a restless paw was turning upside down and, at the same time — how his heavy hand imperiously pressed Rada's thin manuscript to the top of the desk. Yes, it was as if that hand were lying on her shoulder. "I'm very thankful Valentyn Stepanovych, I've wanted to show you this for a long time, and, honestly, I was a little bit afraid." A thought was dangling like the end of a rope in front of her, but she stumbled and it slipped away before she managed to grab it and throw it to him, but I *have* to grab it on the spot, right now, "I was a little bit afraid," why she was afraid, quick-quick, her face stiffened just as it did in front of a camera — "it was so quickly written that it was amazing even for me, because usually this isn't my kind of topic — death, this entire gamut of feelings — it's as though it came from outside of me." Ah, it seems she's surfaced from the water, "and in the process of writing, it grew by itself like crystals," to demonstrate she flicked out the fingers of her hands — and again she got burnt: his gaze, that wrapped her body in plastic without penetrating it, now returned to Rada her unconscious gesture, suffused with the rapture of reflection: delicate thin wrists, long nervous fingers with the protruding precious stones of lustrous fingernails, the hands, fluttering like a captured butterfly's wings. Involuntarily enchanted, she softly giggled: in the end this was the gaze of not just a man, but of a writer artist as well — the most prominent one in Ukraine today, a divinity, a living legend. When first permitted into his study, she slid as though she were on ice, yearning only to get to an armchair, a shaded island of velvet dry land from which she wouldn't have to stick out her nose until the end of the visit, limiting herself to listening and yessing to the host's own monologues. Valentyn Stepanovych ignited himself, and this bonfire did not need the skimpy brushwood of anyone else's intellectual participation. He was a delightful speaker with his baroque manner. He wove dense, curling thickets of complex picturesque sentences, from time to time in appropriate spots he graciously inserted illuminating pauses, rousing the content with the breath of artistic intonations: light irony, skepticism, the sad reiteration of upsetting human imperfection — these were his brilliant oral novellas: episodes from life sprinkled with witty psychological observations, bright, perfect, like gold ingots, recollections, at various spots dotted with the epically intricate thoughts of a true humanist — about society, about the essence of art, about human relations — "and in 1974 when I already was (a glimpse of a sad but contemptuous smile) a p r o h i b i t e d writer, I came across N., who just then began to beam so full of himself (indulgently anticipating Rada's questioning surprise): well no wonder, a knight of the Golden Dog's Tail — why are you laughing? (in feigned penitence he wagged his head side to side). Ah, these youngsters, nothing sacred for them — yes, so I came across N." Rada, hiding in her armchair, took it all in like a sponge, saturated with devout consciousness, that she — first hand — was being offered a bit of living history of literature, filled with the all-penetrating glow of Valentyn Stepanovych's presence. All these tales were like stones polished to a luster, which the unfathomable sea of himself, with kind generosity, tossed onto Rada's shore. Once, when she was telling some friends an anecdote that Valentyn Stepanovych had shared with her, she realized that she was unconsciously imitating his manner of speaking. She discovered, much to her bafflement, that all these precious details he'd entrusted to her really had no value of their own outside Valentyn Stepanovich's electric presence — thoughts, scalded to brittle crystals of bare prose, became common places, observations lost their original hypnotic freshness. Only his life, soaking into their minutest pores, saturated all these images with the underwater glimmering of myth: as when an ordinary remnant of porous, chalky stone takes on a palpable charm after the host explains that he found it in the ruins of the Roman Forum. Rada thought that in the end Valentyn Stepanovych could afford to create an authorized legend of his own life, and she even felt a little flattered that of all the young writers, he chose her, Rada D., as his confidante of this legend. After her third or fourth visit he, slightly smiling, said: "Your armchair," and with this he instantly turned Rada's chronic intimidation at the sight of this study where books, already crowned with the nimbus of the classics, were written, into a sweet detail of her personal habits, capable of interesting a future biographer. Rada, stirred by the warm influx of gratitude, attributed this to Valentyn Stepanovych's authentic means of remaking reality, of making everything that he touched a prominent cultural fact. Just like her, he was constantly experiencing the gaze of an alien force aimed at him, but unlike Rada, he knew well the name of that force — History, and from time to time, like an actor in front of the camera, he took up the most inviting position in front of it.

Freedom — this is the main thing for a writer, and it did not matter at all what Rada jabbered in answer about how she had come to write this particular clump of freedom, now pressed to the top board of the desk with his massive, peasant-like flattened palm. It did not matter and could have been easily crossed out — in fact, it was erased already, as though it were a cassette, because above flashed the heavy beaming strength of his two staring, bright, barely slanted eyes, and Rada, willingly or unwillingly, her own husky agitated laugh sounding conspiratorial, gave a tune to *something* hanging between them in the smoky air of the study and waiting to be reified. It was Rada's laughter that started this reification: it was she who took this step, thus taking away from Valentyn Stepanovych the authorship of the further possible courses of events — and by this she protected herself from them with the unmistakability of primal woman's intuition. What happened dazzled Rada like the flash of the sudden possibility to put her life into the course of the transrational, spontaneous logic of an artistic work, like the vibrating approach to a brightly-lit *completeness of existence*, already beforehand cut into the magical gem of a masterpiece by the very personage of Valentyn Stepanovych. Rada felt a need to protract that moment in time — not to weigh this unexpected vertiginous chance on the scales of common sense, but to appropriate the authorship of that prospective masterpiece, woven with the fabric of their two fates (once she strove in vain to accomplish a similar situation in her marriage with Arsen, but the marriage fell apart, unable to endure the high temperature of Rada's demiurgic endeavors) — in order to step out of the role of a theatrical extra, drawn into a game, as though into a dark memory — resilient to words. Valentyn Stepanovych meaningfully smirked to her and returned to his penciled notations on the shores of her manuscript: certain places had to be shortened, others, to the contrary, expanded, and Rada had one more serious drawback — an excess of abstract lexicon.

Freedom emanates from you, hmm.

No, I didn't have any kind of freedom. And never did. And what people understand as freedom, when during rush hour, inattentively jingling coins in their coat pockets, they descend into the sonorous, inhaled metallic stench of the subway womb, with the blissful calmness of vacationers pondering whether to go today after dinner with Tamara to the movies or, maybe, to set off for the Yakhnenkos to play preference — that minimum of freedom to manage your own body: whether it will perform its respiratory, gastronomic, and sexual functions, leaf through the pages of the newspaper, fill out questionnaires with its right hand and to speak into the black net-like eyelets of a microphone in this or that building, among these or those people, in this or that city — this is just hopeless, drab and helpless — like a depressing desert landscape — the freedom of the graphomaniac to exchange whichever written words for others, or not to write at all: the superfluity of actions. Socrates' students asked him: "Is there a difference between life and death?" "None," he responded. "Then why aren't you dying, teacher?" "For this very reason." That's it. It wearies you, that false freedom, and in order to make do with it, people avidly demand that reality prompt them: O Lord, give us a sign whether this campaign will bring victory; listen, Rada honey, how would you have acted in my place, would you have applied for alimony or not? — these are not searchings for approvals from reality, for your own, already accepted, decisions lay claim — but attempts to verify your choice with the awareness of its final necessity. And the graphomaniac with the directedness of the insect-parasite stuffs every unhappy ear with its verbal eggs, and it's impossible to stop him, for the only thing he painfully demands — is to silently be listened to: as soon as a reader opens the book, he involuntarily gives the author proof of the intention of his work in this world.

No, what kind of freedom is here.

This freedom betrayed me every time I tried graphomaniacally to build my life according to plots I've drafted myself, my pretensions to authorship returned to me, like crumpled and greasy letters, crossed out with arrogant red letters "Moved — No Forwarding Address." It was that way the morning in the wretched room of the southern hotel where Arsen and I the day before happily managed to squeeze in for a vacation, by that time our marriage seemed to have stabilized on the quite ordinary level of mutually accepted peaceful alienation, and only the curved line of nocturnal madness crawled up steeply, like the temperature of an organism otherwise showing no signs of trouble. We exhausted each other to the point where we existed in a full 24-hours at a time semi-real state, as if desperately striving to solder the snake-like edges of an invisible chasm with frenzied coupling. This was some kind of unslakeable obsession: exhausted, cooling off my entire ponderous immobile body, I began to fall asleep to Arsen's rustling whisper (once I dreamt of someone faceless jabbering about me with the boring righteousness of severely limited people: "She has a wonderful husband, what the hell more does she need," well now, that's true, everything's fine — this was the only time I'd looked at my own marriage from outside and I was dumbfounded by its saccharine yuppiness — awake I was never able to see so clearly); Arsen was tormented by insomnia, and after a while his hot hands once again pushed aside my sleep, with a moan I turned to him, and once again every one of my veins swelled, once again a pinching tremor raked through me thoroughly, and again ocean waves were crashing through us — once, twice, a third time — no couple of love birds is able to make love the way a couple does during the premonition of the end — and then, opening my eyes in the morning, I saw the gray barracks ceiling, the plaster walls painted a joyful bright green, a milky light filtered through the white blinds. In front of us there was a shared vacation, but after that — an entire life together, the same as it was right now — and, lying on my back on a narrow twin bed, I began to cry. "Did something happen?" Arsen asked sleepily, burying his face into the pillow. I shook my head, slanting the angles of tears flowing along my cheeks: "Nothing. Sleep." He sighed heavily and didn't say anything else. We shouldn't have gotten married. And the worst part of it is that I always knew that we shouldn't have, long before the wedding, and Arsen, must have also figured it out, at least he didn't repel my doubts in any way like a ball off a wall; but each of us thirsted to unlock his or her life with this act of free choice. Eh, free choice. Like hell it's free.

How can you talk about the heavenly kingdom when you don't have the power to add one cubit to your stature?..*

---

* A reference to Matthew VI: 27 from the Sermon on the Mount: "Which of you by worrying can add one cubit to his stature?" The immediately following paragraph of the story echoes Matthew 13:31-32.

How can we talk about freedom when we can't change even a grain of mustard seed in our own soul?..

But I knew another level of freedom!

Writing "under dictation." Words that strongly flow by themselves — not a single one of them can be arbitrarily changed. Every paragraph, flowing, falling down on the paper, discloses the next — as though you're advancing along an unknown corridor without the slightest idea of where it will lead you, but there is an easy, joyful certainty to finding the path — if only you don't lose your way, because then right in front of your nose the dark halves of the armored doors come together, and you remain on this side, crumpling in your hand already displayed in the text bits of a somewhere existing, living work that was opened up to you, that allowed you to approach — and there — all of a sudden: it turned off, fell into the darkness — and until the end of the world it won't appear from there to anyone, ever. And you can grumble as much as you want at your family, flinging your books on the floor, lamenting that in this house no one understands you, aha, the phone! — who, who? — send him to hell! — and you don't want their tea, why the hell do you need it, when they finally comprehend that you want just one thing — for them all just to leave you in pea-ce! see? in peace! only in blindness when senseless words have disintegrated into letters, can you reread what you managed to jot down, straining to find in the thickets of your own handwriting an unnoticeable opening, a hint at continuation, a flashing and disappearing outline of lost entity — the leaves of the doors, as soon as they closed up, deathly keep the mystery. You can — why not, imagine — make up the further direction of a work — not so? no, it seems, better this way... or maybe I should develop this line, here it's gotten weak (when before it had promised a shimmer of meaning!), and this way — it's also not bad, and in that direction — it's also knock on wood, and all this is already shit. Beg your pardon.

I never imagined anything. I *knew* what to write, or I didn't know (and then I didn't write).

Two levels of freedom. Helen and Cassandra.* "Don't you ever see that what happens is inevitable, inexorable? Doesn't a voice in your heart speak to you: 'Yes, it will be so, yet! Will it be so and not otherwise?'" — Helen's goodhearted calmness in response: "Having said in all sincerity — no, never." — "How do you prophesize? What do you tell the people?" — it's not that she's accusing him, nor is he getting shocked, she quite sincerely inquires — by which signs does Helen guess what exactly to say, for when you "don't see" that one thing that really will be (but does that mean it is? Does it mean, somewhere there, beyond these doors where constellations of uncreated works of art turn, it breathes, concealing, "the inevitable and inexorable," already-existing, just not yet slipped through the chink of the visible "now"?, when it's closed to you, then it doesn't matter — "not a rat's ass," as Arsen used to say — what you tell.

And what you write.

And where you go.

And whom you kiss.

And whom you turn in to the guards.

....

Forces that govern the world, fate, God — what a miserable language mankind has produced in this realm over its entire history. The result is particularly striking when you compare it with the tens of words to differentiate shades of blue or green in some languages! And who will tell me — what these thirty-seven or whatever many designations for the color green are good for, when there's not a single word to answer who I am in this world?..

What Rada admired Valentyn Stepanovych for in some murky part of her being was the fact that for him the world was clearly and firmly fixed, like crystal gratings. "Ethics," Valentyn Stepanovych kept saying, and this word of his always resonated: every vowel fully

---

* The quotations that follow come from Act VI of Lesia Ukrainka's verse drama *Cassandra*. The play has been translated by Vera Rich into English in: *Lesya Ukrainka: Selected Works*. Toronto: U. of Toronto Press, 1968.

consumed its ration of air, "the ethics of a writer's behavior," Valentyn Stepanovych kept saying, — at this point each time Rada shriveled inside, as though watching him demonstratively turn a New Year's tree in front of her, with all the ornaments swaying threateningly with the melodic glass-like tinkle of bells. "The ethics of a writer's behavior," Valentyn Stepanovych kept saying, "this is what literature stands on, just look what pernicious results," Valentyn Stepanovych kept saying, "are perpetrated by the even the most innocent attempts to sell out one's own talent — take a look at X, and at Egrek, and at Zeta." Thus spake Valentyn Stepanovych. "And they still have the balls to complain about readers. Believe me, Rada, here we've got the kind of reader," Valentyn Stepanovych said, whose books came out in million-plus print runs, "Western authors could only dream about." In the study from time to time the telephone warmly purred. Valentyn Stepanovych picked up the receiver, and — for a single moment — holding it in the air first before putting it back on the phone, maintained on Rada that expressive, costly flash of the two precious stone rings — of his slightly slanted eyes: a small sacrifice in her honor, a hook thrown on the door before...; Rada was sprinkled with glowing coals, as though her skin were being titillated by thick fur, in his presence she lost her strength, unlike anyone else he was able to envelop her, to make her powerless. Ah, Radochka.

"Lord," she said to him — at first just not to be silent, and then little by little getting dragged further and quicker into the magnetically darkening maw of his consuming attention, "Lord, how awfully we live, Valentyn Stepanovych. I was just walking along the street and tried to catch with my look at least one face open to the world, the way flowers open up in the morning, and children also know how to be this way — when they stand and trace white scratches on a brick wall with their finger or look at the sun through a thin yellow leaf — and you know, I failed to find one: every face you meet is burdened as though with a grave stone, with some kind of daily trifling problem — every one is rushing here or there at such and such an hour for something or other, buying something on the way, calling somebody. Lord, how worthless this all is — in this way you don't see the world where you live, you attenuate it to a narrow strip of things with which you operate!.. But every leaf on a tree, every apple on a plate, every insect under your feet — they all are unique," she claimed, as though lighting her way with her own speech and following it with increasing speed. "And this chain of cigarette smoke of yours weaves like no other smoke on earth. Artists who paint still lifes know this, but we fence off for ourselves the horizon with the blinders of trifles we have invented ourselves and don't dare look around till our death!.." Valentyn Stepanovych contemplated her growing ardor, moistened by a strange, uncertain smile, that was groping for the focus, swaying between tender condescension and unwanted discomfort — or maybe she just misunderstood? — "Here, write about this," — she grew quiet as though she had bumped into an invisible obstacle in mid-flight: what? what the hell?.. Valentyn Stepanovych grew serious, he always grew serious when the conversation touched upon *work*. "Look, Radochka, you still aren't quite aware how much these impressions, even fragmentary ones, which to you the writer seem insignificant, and even creatively uninteresting, so you're just dropping them on your way, you still don't understand how much people might need them." Rada bit her lower lip, a hot wave of resistance rose within her, it was as though Valentyn Stepanovych suddenly without warning had begun to speak in ancient Hebrew or something else, and tensed up she listened to the splinters of foreign words, straining to get the sense — how could you write about something that was "creatively uninteresting?" Is this what real work is about, to spend six hours a day at a desk, to neatly rake together all the crumbs onto a piece of paper, people need this, hair combings and nail clippings, old villagers till this very day don't throw them out in the trash, but collect and burn them to make sure that no sorceress would be able to cast a spell on them. Rada remained silent, tensing up inside, unconsciously squeezing her legs together. Maybe she's just not a professional writer, and that's it, she has always waited for the work itself to call her out from non-being, with that powerful, reverberating hum, and who cares who might need this, maybe the work itself, maybe the souls of those who were writing beneath this sky prior to her — with an engraving tool on clay tablets, with a goose quill pen in candle light, maybe this very hum sadly clenched their hearts, but for some reason didn't reach to the words of their language, — and, who knows, maybe it's Rada D. who no one needs, one night some drug addict might bash her on the head, and here we go — in Berkivtsi Cemetery two square meters, an iron fence and a laurel wreath on her head, in case she's lucky with the parceling of plots, because it's not permitted to fence off everywhere, of course they'll cry, they'll mourn, but no one will go into a pit after her, while with Valentyn Stepanovych, things are quite different. Like an asteroid, in every reader's head he'll leave a hole, what an irreparable loss, who can say how many unfinished masterpieces we have been deprived of — that's why they publish him in millions of copies, and his wife, a quiet transparent woman with the illuminated look of a nun or a nurse, one day serving them coffee in his study, recounted, slightly lisping, what a tough business it was for her to maintain her husband's creative peace and quiet — a steady flow of people incessantly push into the house, some for an autograph, some just to take a glance at their divinity, one woman thrust out her wallet with pictures in front of his wife's eyes : "Here, look, I carry his picture with my children's photos!" — how terribly difficult it was to reject these people, but could you imagine how little Valentyn Stepanovych would have written if he had begun to chit-chat with everyone? — that's why his wife keeps guard at the door. Rada mindlessly led her finger along the chimerical Arabian patterns of the sofa throw as in a children's lead-the-rabbit-out-of-the-maze game. She just couldn't understand whether this tirade meant she should get her buns out of there on the spot, or, on the contrary, she should be puffed up with pride that she, Rada D., had been allowed through that guarded door, and thus that she in some way — what is the way? was considered to be a part in Valentyn Stepanovych's work. "Not everyone who says to me "Lord, Lord," — for some reason flashed in her head, but she crushed that thought like a just lit cigarette in an ashtray. Any kind of doubt darted away from Valentyn Stepanovych, he seemed surrounded by a mighty energy field, and in the end, hadn't he written at least one undeniably great novel, and one more that was pretty good, both when he wasn't allowed to publish his works. Back then Rada was a school girl, and the devout whispers of the adults — "Valentyn Stepanovych is writing something extraordinary" — rose around her like vertiginous smoke from hundreds of incensers, creating an elusive atmosphere imbued with the anticipation of a miracle, with fragments of secretly circulating hearsay stories. Which were true, which were made up? — Valentyn Stepanovych had given a slap to a high ranking bureaucrat (a duel!); Valentyn Stepanovych was under house arrest; Valentyn Stepanovych was attacked by unknown assailants; the wife of Such and Such, madly in love with Valentyn Stepanovych, had poisoned herself, yeh, the very same Such and Such guy, they barely managed to revive her, they say she's a beauty. From those dazzling bits of mosaic stones a silhouette was erected, wrapped in a golden mist. It was impossible to focus your eyes on him closely, just like when you look at the sun. And his novel back then turned out really well: warm. Like a conversation with a nice guy: nothing special to recall afterwards, just the usual trifles in life, but somehow it keeps you warm.

"Wait," she said, stumbling into the ladder he had pushed to her feet, "but how can you write this way? All kinds of fragmentary impressions, even images, don't make art, they occur to everyone," — she paused as though sticking her hand too close to a fire, she jerked back so as not to get burnt: here, that's it, I always knew Valentyn Stepanovych was writing too much! — he was too meticulously recording all his impressions in a row, instead of *writing* he *describes*. Valentyn Stepanovych with readiness closed a pause: "Well, first of all, I don't think it occurs to *everyone*," — at this point his eyebrows mockingly rose, "and secondly, if so, it's all the better: for isn't it about their experiences that you tell people your stories?" Once again his unshakable logic, smooth as marble, knocked her off her feet. "Wait," Rada shook her head, "wait, but why do I need to tell people what they already know?.." "What do you mean — it's known? who knows it?.." He resolutely threw back his wild pagan mane, and the shadow of a murky enmity crawled between them. "On the whole — *known!*" Rada was getting lost, painfully suffering from her own inarticulateness: Lordy, what's the difference exactly who and how many know it, what kind of sociological interest is there…finally the articulate words came, but the proper moment to utter them had slipped away: art begins at the point where some new entity shows up! *En*-tity — every time it's singular and unique in the universe, inaudibly it breathes beyond the braced doors: so open them, break the latch, because the world is different from what it appears to be, it plays peekaboo with us and, perhaps, only madmen know the way it really is, so what kind of fun is it to trace your finger along a drawing on those doors and to reiterate to people in 37 different ways that the grass is green, and in forty or so, that the sky is azure?.. What if both the grass and the sky just pretend they are this way, and the very moment we turn around, the sky gets covered in red grass, swaying, like water plants, and the grass crawls along in myriads of silver snakes from place to place?.. Rada didn't tell all of this to Valentyn Stepanovych — so the two of them reverberated in their own corners like billiard balls.

However these conversations in a strange way devastated Rada. Afterwards she experienced some insane verbal obsession, rambling along the streets all alone, seeing nothing around her, and incessantly mumbling to herself ideas that had come too late and unwinding new monologues addressed to Valentyn Stepanovych, but destined never to reach him — and from time to time she moaned, stiffened up, and lost her thought beneath the instantaneous impulse of recollection: Valentyn Stepanovych crosses the study to take an album of reproductions from the shelf — and behind her armchair he suddenly stops, as though he's hanging in time, holding back the hands of a clock, she seems to hear his exhalation on the nape of her neck, and swooning with her entire, momentarily all-seeing body, — no, oh no, he's about to stretch out his hand, not a movement as yet, just an intangible stretch of muscles, and — here, the shuffling of footsteps along the rug, the wave breaks away, the gurgling foam sinks into damp sand — it's her heart beating in her chest, so hard you could hear it behind the wall…

The fatigue showed itself through the cotton impenetrability of reality: it was as though Valentyn Stepanovych had enveloped Rada in the thick cloud of his presence. Next to him Rada felt herself forcibly taken into the shiny convex lens of an historical vision — only that lens somehow hurt her the way a glass slide might hurt a laboratory bug. From time to time Valentyn Stepanovych invited Rada to theatrical premiers, to literary soirées, once or twice to the studios of artist friends. Anywhere he appeared, he pushed the crowd aside with his ponderous form as though they were a dusty curtain, and the faces, gestures, and greetings started to swirl around him in a dance of radiant dust: soon Rada understood — everywhere he kept his own particular rhythm, the same that he always had in his study, so that in any, even accidental surroundings, he appeared to be in the position of a conductor. These public appearances baffled Rada the most, for instinct warned her that the further from the focus of the lens, the more the image distorts. When Valentyn Stepanovych started, with his usual loquacious pomposity, to praise Rada to high heaven to his acquaintances, impeding with his improvised audience the regular flow of the foyer or hallway: "Let me introduce you — Rada D. Have you read her?.. You know, this new generation emerging in literature sometimes really strikes me...," — and his friends, staring at Rada with unseeing eyes, forcibly diverted from the natural center of gravity — from Valentyn Stepanovych himself — were accompanying his talking with a politely admiring muffled murmur — each time Rada sensed that somewhere in the wind an invisible and unheard tape recorder was on: on such and such a day in such and such a month and such and such a year Valentyn Stepanovych admitted to so and so that the new generation emerging right now in literature sometimes really strikes him. She, Rada D., couldn't boast of such a tape recorder. Neither of million copy printings. Nor of the love of an entire nation.

Standing like a post by him she saw clearly with the eyes of the gaping and stirring throng what she really could boast about — the body of a fashion model, pear-like skin, and luxurious wavy hair with a honey-colored shine, — and, as if on children's "x-ray" pictures, drawings where stick-like arms and the legs of a human figure are taken into the rectangle of sleeves and pants, she saw through the garments her straightened shoulders and sexy bodice — and her cello-shaped thighs and long legs, and her juicy bulging buns. A cute babe. Have you read her?..

Freedom emanates from you.

What emanated now from her was the dislocated sound of a puppy's whimpering, that failed to touch a human ear, still sadly resonating in the air in its despair. Everything that she now wrote seemed to breathe with this miserable sound.

Rada began to avoid people.

However, it was impossible to avoid Valentyn Stepanovych: he caught her by phone, invited her over: "I feel empty without you, Radochka," the phrase broke up the conversation with the suddenly opened abyss of silence, and stayed hovering over it like God's edict: rise and go to him. Once again at night while gradually falling asleep — laying on her left side, twisted up in a coil, she jolted back to consciousness with a shout of "No!": near her bed from God knows where Valentyn Stepanovych suddenly appeared (all the time Rada clearly was perceiving as though from the corner of the room, the diaphanous, gleaming greenish yellow of the contours of her own, twisted-into-a-coil, body). Kneeling down next to her, Valentyn Stepanovych encouraged her with such lustful, sensuously tangible physicality — with a stifling touch, with the moist taste of a kiss. With the deep influx of caresses, Rada grew nearly torpid from delight, and it was this very readiness to give in that brought her to her senses: the shout of resistance carried her out from her semi-sleep. It's bad, she thought, burying her face into the pillow, oh how bad it is. The most oppressive was the astounding sensuous reality of what she experienced. For Rada knew: Valentyn Stepanovych needed her every day all the more insatiably, but she also knew the fact that at some turn her own openness before him was being buried.

But then his new book appeared in print. And Rada read it.

Valentyn Stepanovych presented her with a press copy. "To a dear person, with love" — in large tranquil, erect handwriting: each separate letter formed with love.

She read it.

The book was called *The Art of Living*. With an epigraph taken from Pidmohylny* — there where over a glass of beer the poet Vyhorsky revealed his classification of the arts. The art of living.

When Rada had turned the last page, her face blazed. For some reason like a stupid fish in a frozen pond an obscene ditty lurched in her brain:

On this side of the river

A fig tree was burning,

Dad made love to Mom so hard

They both turned red from squirming.

This was *my* book: the one that I didn't write over that time. My point of view. My twist of the theme. *My* target. And even more: with guiltless impudence it was shimmering with *my* favorite words and turns of phrases, *my* observations dropped in conversation, suggestions, trifles — "she absentmindedly picked up the fork and with an unconscious gracious movement dipped it in the borsch," — of course, all that was translated into his steady, perhaps just a little bit decapitated, respiratory and muscular rhythm, poured out like a heavy syrup, with the covered peaceful clarity of his solitary, polished, fluid language: it was as though I were holding an x-ray of my own chest cage: mine, although all the same, it's unrecognizable. The book turned out nice — written in a single wave; after those earlier novels, perhaps, it was the best.

A blistering clot of her life was sucked out of her through an invisible catheter — instead a harsh whistling void broke in. As though Rada

---

* Ukrainian prose writer of the 1920s and 1930s Valerian Pidmohylny. Author of the novels *The City* and *A Little Touch of Drama* as well as a number of short stories. Pidmohylny was repressed by Stalin's regime during the so called "Executed Renaissance" following the Ukrainian cultural revival of the 1920s. Most of his works were banned in the USSR until Gorbachev's era of *glasnost* and ultimately Ukrainian independence in 1991.

had been locked in a ward with the portrait of Valentyn Stepanovych above her bunk, and she was doomed with the look of a fly to crawl unceasingly along his features. Finally it occurred to Rada how deeply he managed to possess everything that in her was his own, transferring the stereoscope of her inner life into the hard impenetrable surfaces of his perception. Any kind of thought now caused her pain other than getting up out of bed, walking to the tub, opening up a new tube of toothpaste, squeezing out onto her brush a fat white worm. Shoes! Polishing shoes. Before leaving home she diligently and meticulously picked out her clothes: clothing was something belonging to her; taking panty hose without a pattern, plain red, and above her wool skirt a tight wide red belt — with a sleepy vegetative satisfaction — the way a well-fed stomach seems satisfied despite the oppressive state of mind — she stared at herself in the mirror, as though concluding a contract with someone: this will be me. But the moment a more vibrant, searching thought attempted to move inside her, yearning with its feeble fingers to push aside this besieging burden, at once the invisible Valentyn Stepanovych announced his rights to it: his deliberate voice switched on beneath his skull, incessantly dictating immense, densely packed sentences, which immediately deprived the poor thought of its immanent strength, — words, words, words, the dry rustle of paper: what you are now saying, Radochka, is quite familiar to me — in 1978 when the publisher rejected my *History of a Single Defeat* with the editorial decision saying the work (here his sarcastic accentuation was about to begin) was ideologically pernicious and there was not a single human being who could remember what literature was — then I experienced the same hermit's life aversion to the world. I turned off the telephone and said to myself: that's all. That's all, and for good. For good, everything he touched upon turned out to be "very familiar."

First Rada didn't realize, whose moaning was she hearing?.. It was her own. She was breaking herself against his unstirring historical rightness, like a swallow against a window pane. And oh Lord, how unbearably skillfully and inexhaustibly his speech flowed, as though he were telling yarns: he was knitting. The art of living.

IF I HAD MASTERED THE ART OF LIVING, THEN WHY WOULD I NEED TO WRITE?

The critics were preparing to initiate a discussion about a new period in Valentyn Stepanovych's writing, but Valentyn Stepanovych called Rada, interrogating her: how did she like his book?.. "Great, — Rada squeezed the words out with her disobedient lips, "I'm sure it'll be a wild success." He'd have had success, however, even if he'd scratched three letters on the fence with a crayon, because everything scratched by his hand pulsated with the bright aureole of his *name*: no one saw the bare text, everyone had a blinding black disk jump into their eyes, as though after looking directly at the sun. She, Rada D., who saw the bare text — and she always did, she always silently knew that description isn't real art, that except for those old novels, the rest of his books (six hours daily at his writing desk, people need this, the directed lens of an historical vision, the author especially succeeded in the image of the heroine, and who else would be able to depict so sparingly, just with several brush strokes, a full-fledged impressionistic landscape) all these books smelt of paper, and it was exactly this stubborn silent knowledge of her that was rising in front of him like an unconquered territory. "Really?" — he asked happily into the receiver. "You *really* liked it? And when will you come to visit me, I haven't seen you in ages?.."

Run away. Run away into the woods and eat grass.

Lord, do you really have to waste a piece of your life in order to, along with the text, create your own myth — this obligatory blank interleaf between the text and the world?

from THE LOST BUTTON

by Iren Rozdobudko

Translated by Michael M. Naydan and Olha Tytarenko

The last day of August 2005

... I already don't remember when I got home, since I was slightly tipsy. And probably not just slightly... Since yesterday I felt like someone had sewn a firecracker under my shoulder blade and that I'd die from even looking at a glass of vodka or cognac. I had no way of quelling my anxiety. I had to some- how drag things out to the end of the workday. On the other hand, I wanted it to last forever. I was afraid to go home. I was afraid to sit at the computer. That's why after two not very onerous lectures in the Institute of Cinema- tography I went back to my office. I didn't have anything to do there, I could have even worked at home, making up endless plots for advertising videos, but I already noticed I was afraid of going home. So I just sat for some time in my office, putting my feet on the desk, and from time to time obliging our office manager Tetyana Mykolaivna to bring me the strongest cup of coffee she could make. I looked out through the window. My stare was so sharp and focused that I saw the tiniest interlacing and furrows on the bark of an old tree that was growing on the other side of the street. I didn't tear my gaze away from those furrows, stuffed with gray cobwebs, and they reminded me of the deep furrows of an old man's face.

Summer was coming to a close. The year was racing to an end. I don't know about other people, but the year ends with the last day of August for me. Maybe because everything in my life seemed to begin in the fall...

I made every effort to turn off my brain, not to get lost in thought. But mentally I had already been in my apartment a hundred times and made several of my customary movements: I opened the door, took off my sport coat, sat down at the computer, settled myself into a deep black armchair, and clicked the mouse.

Why in truth am I so afraid of doing all this? What is stopping me right now from taking my feet off the table, snatching up my briefcase, jumping into the street, sitting behind the wheel and in about ten minutes really pushing open the door of my own apartment? What kind of weights have been strapped to my feet? In time I understood that these "weights" were the fear of not finding anything on the monitor screen. NOTHING at all.

But with not the least fear I thought about the fact that in the corner of the screen a little yellow email icon folder would light up.

And I didn't know what was better: that nothing or the icon folder...

Close to eight o'clock Tetyana Mykolaivna began to cough pathetically at my door. And then, opening it slightly, asked:

"More coffee?"

I knew it was time to go. I stepped out into the street and at first didn't go in the direction of my favorite restaurant, the "Suok,"* though I could have... But the urge overwhelmed me on the street, I felt its fever and barely came rushing to my building entryway. Then I was afraid the elevator would suddenly get stuck and I would have to be bored stiff in it for endlessly long hours, wondering whether the icon folder was there?....

Thank God that didn't happen and I tore into the room, while I was still in motion taking off my sport coat, tossing my shoes and tie every which way. I fell into my black armchair, having enough of a fiery look. It would have been interesting what my students who have gotten used to my complete "buttoneddownness" would have said?

I calmed my breathing...

...At that time the weather was almost the same. Watermelons sat on the balcony.

Right now there's a thick layer of street dust.

---

* *Suok* is the name of a character in Yuri Olesha's fairytale "Three Fat Men." She is a girl who takes the place of a mechanical doll for a boy.

I clicked the button. In the corner a little yellow folder appeared. Everything was the way I imagined — and I didn't believe myself. Really? I clicked with the mouse. I shut my eyes. I opened it up.

"I died on the 25th of September 1997...," the first line flashed on the blue background of the monitor.

I shut my eyes again. The cold and darkness shackled me...

PART I. DENYS

I.

It happened at the end of August 1977... I had just turned eighteen then. I was dreaming about fame. And I knew it would come. It wasn't about some kind of temporary ascent onto a pedestal in the small space where I lived then. It wasn't about the applause of the audience that forgets you the next day. No. I sensed that some kind of mission was there for me, the mystery of which I needed to solve. But for the time being it was being generated somewhere deep inside me, as though beans had germinated in a damp cheesecloth — we did that kind of experiment in biology classes in school. All thirty-five students grew beans on their window sills, and after a few weeks brought the results to school. I remember well that my sprout was larger than the other ones. It happened a long time ago in the sixth grade. But after my experiments, I understood what and how things develop inside me. And I patiently waited. So patiently that I endeavored once again not to call attention to myself — while there was no need for me. In the meantime, I finished school, quite easily got into the film script writing program of the Department of Film (my exam film script turned out to be better than the opuses of already experienced and much older prospective students, and they kept it for a long time in the department as a particularly successful sample). After learning the grade, I went for a small vacation to the mountains, to a tourist hostel at the foothills of the Carpathian Mountains. In fact, this was a cinematographer's hostel to which all my future classmates would go — an announcement about unused student passes hung in the hall of the Institute. We didn't know each other well yet. We were united by the common spirit of the recent exams, during which we all jostled each other in a friendly way by the doors of the classrooms, clamorously saluting each lucky individual.

All this was behind us. We arrived at the tourist hostel little by little, without making any arrangements beforehand with each other, and ardently reveled at each familiar face. They put us up in small wooden buildings, and we immediately began to learn the territory, finding out where the dining room, swimming pool, and movie hall were along with the closest *Silpo* general store, where you could buy the cheapest strong wine.*

We felt we were grown up and experienced. We tried to communicate with each other in a loosey-goosey way and uttered the names of our idols like good buddies. We gave each other Western names, that's why I was immediately christened "Dan." My roommate, accordingly, was called Max.

Dan and Max — two cool guys, the future geniuses quickly ran over to the *Silpo* general store and loaded up on several bottles of strong "ink." We drank like fish without having a bite to eat and... in baby sips during our school days — nothing more expensive than port wine. To be truthful, a little later I was sorry I had come here...

The mountains turned deep blue in the distance and it seems they were glimmering, enveloped by the torn white silk of evening cheesecloth. And I was forced to sit on a hard bed, chugging the port wine and listening to the chitchat of my acquaintances. When we all started to get sick (no one, of course, complained and we tried our best to maintain our dignity), we began to take our turns going out "for a breath of fresh air." I finally managed to tear myself away from the smoky room and, already no longer in a hurry, to stroll along the grounds of the camp.

This was quite a quiet little spot. Or else it appeared that way at the end of the summer. Behind the curtains of the cottages a dusky light

---

* "777" wine. An inexpensive high alcohol context (18%) wine made in the former USSR and now in Russia and Ukraine.

shimmered, vacationers were sitting in spots on the verandas, from an open "green" movie hall the sound of the music from a film echoed. It seems like it was the movie *Yesenia.** Altogether it was disorder and havoc. Just beyond an old-fashioned fence in pseudo-baroque style, the shaggy black forest murmured alluringly, and from it a powerful wave of freshness and anxiety rolled onto me. It was already quite dark. Simple sculptures of girls with oars and other body builders snowily-whitely shone on both sides of the alleys like ghosts. Almost all the benches were "toothless," and all the lamps "blind." I walked up to the end of the alley, sat down on a bench, and pulled out my cigarettes from my pocket. And nearly right away I noticed the flash of a red glow across from me... If I had not been drunk then, and if, like the wine, the drunken feeling of the euphoria of an entry into a new life had not been playing inside me — nothing would have happened and would not have dragged behind it a chain of actions that would pursue me my entire life.

But I was drunk. That's why I saw *something*... A silhouette, etched by the light of the moon resembling an incorporeal, empty outline in the total darkness. A woman was smoking a cigarette in a long mouthpiece. She slowly raised the small red glow to her invisible lips, inhaled, and for an instant the silvery smoke filled her entire outline, as though it were sketching her body from the inside.

And then, with the last small cloud of smoke, it, this body, once again melted into the darkness.

Jeez!

I strained my eyes and comically waved my hand before my nose, chasing away the apparition.

"What, you got scared?"

The voice was husky, but so sensuous that I got goose bumps over my entire body, as though the woman had uttered something obscene (even later I couldn't get used to her voice: whatever she talked

---

* A Mexican melodramatic film from 1974 that was very popular as a rental video in Soviet times. See: *http://www.videoguide.ru/card_film.asp?idFilm=17763*.

about — the weather, books, movies, food — everything sounded sweetly-obscene, like candor).

"Well no… I'm fine…," I mumbled.

However, the damp night and the appearance of the mountain summits that were blackening in the distance, and this little red light, and the wind — so saturated and fresh — sobered me up. I tried to look over the woman who was sitting across from me. No use. Maybe at that moment I was already completely blinded by her. A similar thing happens, for example, with mothers who aren't able to honestly judge the beauty of their own child, or with an artist, for whom the most recent canvas seems to be a work of genius.

"Do you also live in this resort house?"

I couldn't have thought up anything more idiotic to say! It's the same as if you were to ask someone on the road after a flight, "Are you also flying in this plane?" But I itched to hear that voice again.

"Do you like it here?" I continued.

The glow flashed even brighter (she hesitated) and slid down (she lowered her hand).

"Do you know where I like it?" I heard (goose bumps! goose bumps!) after quite a long pause. "There."

The tiny glow of her cigarette flicked in the direction of the forest.

"I haven't been there yet…," I said. "I arrived just today…"

"Strange!" The fire in an instant flew into a bush and went out. "Let's go! There's a hole here in the fence…"

By the rustle of her clothing I understood that she had gotten up and made a step in my direction.

"Give me your hand!"

I stretched into the darkness and stumbled on a chilly palm. I got goose bumps again. Her hand was hearty, not soft.

"E-eh, you're completely drunk!" She started to laugh.

I got up, trying to keep steady. We were the same height. I was able to discern something more or less definite: an elongated figure, a dark, possibly black shawl that covered her shoulders… But nothing more. And I also could smell her scent.

Back then I still didn't know the scent of expensive perfumes — they got them under the table through friends, girls I knew for the most part used the overwhelming Scheherazade or the highly concentrated Lily of the Valley brands. And here suddenly a wave of a fragrant aroma — bitter and dizzying — wafted in on me. Involuntarily I clenched my teeth and pressed her hand more tightly. Giving in to her will, I swiftly moved toward a dead end where the fence stopped. There really was a big black hole in it, which I didn't notice right away. Without letting go of her hand, walking after her, I bent my head down sharply and we ended up on the other side of the tourist hostel on a wide plain that was overgrown with tall grass. We walked, buried in it up to our knees. Again I tried to look over the woman who had commandingly led me by the hand like a little boy. Her long black shawl covered her from head to toe, the length of her hair was also unclear to me — it flowed with her shawl and in full sight was just as black and long. Not even once did she turn back toward me. It seemed she was completely indifferent to whomever she was dragging behind her.

I strove not to fall and not to lag behind, so I began to look beneath my feet more often, and the wild vegetation reminded me of the sea that rolls powerful, fragrant waves and just about drags you to a depth, from which you can't swim away.

My head was topsy-turvy. The night, a thin crescent of the moon above clouds, mountains, goosebumps all over my body, intoxication, this unknown woman… Everything seemed to be phantasmagoric. I cherished these kinds of adventures. I couldn't imagine what would happen further! Maybe wild sex in a clearing in the forest? Who was this woman? Why and where was she taking me? How old was she, what does she look like? What does she want? We walked up to the slope of the mountain covered in trees that rose above the clearing like columns next to the entrance of a pagan temple. The gloom again swallowed her, and from the forest the particular thick scent of resin wafted. The woman led me beyond the fence of the first stand of large pine trees, from which the forest began, and leaned up with her back against one of the trees.

"Wonderful, isn't it?"

I barely caught my breath and looked around. Really, it was wonderful! It was as if we had ended up in the bowels of some great living organism, some fairytale fish. The trees were its twisted muscles, it breathed through the treetops, and somewhere inside, in the depth, slowly, its heart beat. I even could hear this rhythmic, uneasy sound.

"It's alive. Do you sense it? During the day it's all not quite like this…"

She clicked her cigarette lighter and for an instant I saw the semicircle of her cheek and the flash of her black pupil. Then once again the red glow began to dance in front of me.

"What's your name?" I asked, persistently thinking how this strange adventure might end.

"What's the difference? Especially now…"

The red glow traced an arc and disappeared. And again I sensed that I had been taken by the hand and dragged somewhere higher. We walked so quickly, as though we were running after an escape. At a certain moment things got uncomfortable for me. Branches of trees that I didn't manage to brush aside from time to time smacked the side of my face.

Finally, we made our way even higher and stopped. Everything repeated — her merging with the tree, the red glow.

This time with wonder I looked below: we had come out of the maw of the beast, and in the distance the outlines of the closest village were being painted by vague little lights, intersected by the golden line of the river. Thick tree tops grew below, from which clustered storm clouds stood out, along which you seemingly could walk as though along dry land. I completely came to my senses and breathed avariciously, enjoying the strange taste of the air, which I was able to appreciate just now. Together with this air, rapture filled me. How good it was that I had torn myself away from the stifling room, stumbled upon this woman, and she gave me such a wonderful stroll! I understood that two weeks of my rest will be wonderful. I turned back, I wanted to thank her…

The glow disappeared. I walked up to the tree where she had just been standing, I had even touched her with my palm. No one!

"Haloo," I hailed quietly, "where are you?"

My voice echoed unusually in the darkness. Somewhere not far away a night bird began to flap its wings. I walked around each tree, each bush. A mad thought entered my brain that somewhere she had spread out her shawl, had lain on it and was waiting, so that I'd stumble on her body more quickly

Then I became angry: what kind of idiotic pranks?! Then I began to worry whether I could find the road back. And then a little later I inopportunely recalled that his place was swarming with legends about mermaids, *niavka* river nymphs, *mavka* forest nymphs, *molfar* wizards, and witches…

It was unpleasant enough to go down the mountain myself. The entire time I listened attentively to try to hear the sound of her footsteps nearby. But the forest only breathed deeply and grabbed at me with its stiff fingers. I even fell twice.

Coming out onto a flat clearing, I took a breath and again looked around at the forest. It seemed to me that up above once again the red little glow of her cigarette was breathing. It was observing me like an eye. And maybe, it was laughing…

from FADED FLOWERS GET TOSSED

by Iren Rozdobudko
Translated by Michael M. Naydan

PART ONE
CHAPTER 1
Edith Beresh

THE MOST PROMINENT, BRIGHTEST MEMORY FLASH OF MY childhood is a rocking chair. The most hellish — from everything that was to happen later is — Leda Nizhyna!

Although, of course, there were countless adventures and problems. But the rocking chair, which I saw three times at a flea market in the middle of a town square of some small provincial little town — is a big rocking chair, whose legs an arched cross bar connected, but that bitch Leda today surpasses all the memories of my former triumphs and tragedies, deaths and wars, husbands and lovers, parents and unborn children, diamonds and dirt beneath fingernails, cream soufflé and frozen sweet potatoes, Chanel perfumes (with that unsurpassed nasty piece of work Coco; in fact we had clams together in the Pid Kupolem* Restaurant), and the disgusting soap of the Chervoni Vitryla** factory. What marvels memory conjures with us! At times you don't remember the name of some deceased person or even your own mother, and in a

---

* Meaning "by or under the cupola." A very nice retro-style restaurant on a hill overlooking the Stefanyk Library in Lviv in Western Ukraine.
** Red Sails.

moment of relative harmony of the soul, when you want to remember what is dearest to you, that wicker rocking chair speaks… And nothing else. As though it was the main thing in your life.

Back then I couldn't imagine that you could make a chair with a rocker and weave it with wicker! How could that possibly be? The rocking chair stood separately from other goods in a circle of sunlight. As though it, so elegant, could speak, maybe even read the soliloquy of Prince Hamlet. Though then, of course, I knew nothing about the theater, or even about the existence of Shakespeare.

That summer day father drove us and mother to the village, where you weren't as hungry, and I overheard conversations that this village is "ours," and that "our family property" is located there. Understandably, on hearing such words, I felt like a princess. The station, at which the train stopped, and which buzzed like a beehive, where in the middle of lively haggling the amazing structure stood that struck my imagination. My parents bought me honey in real honeycombs, which I chewed with pleasure and tried to swallow, a rag doll, and a wooden little horse with a straw tail, and forced me to drink up a small mug of warm fresh milk. But the entire time I turned my parents back to the spot where that amazing chair stood. "I want that!" I kept repeating, and the old sales guy in wide pants and straw hat intentionally and temptingly rocked that chair in front of me, and it glistened in the sun, flew up to the heavens, creaked in a nice way and… it smelled of grass, wicker, reeds, the forest, and rain.

"We can't take it with us, sweetie," father tried to persuade me.

"It's very expensive," momma backed him up. "Look, I bought you a candy rooster on a stick…"

And they dragged me to the train car. Then I fell in the dust in the middle of the square by the station and screamed deliriously until I was foaming at the mouth. I really had to have that thing! To have it or die right on the spot, near its living fragrant wood. Maybe already then I sensed that this rocking chair by some kind of miracle will be preserved in all the entangled collisions of my life and, in the end, will become my only real friend…

And Leda... She's no Leda! She's some kind of Yavdoshka from near Poltava or Kozyatyn. Strictly speaking, I'm also not Edith. But today I sometimes forget my real name. Sometime you need to have a look at the personal file kept by the director of our Building. Maybe, then something else will be restored in my head other than the memory of a rocking chair. No one called me anything other than Edith, from that time when I stepped out on the stage for the first time...

...Now I sit in this swing next to the window. This is one of the few things that belongs to me here. Also — the photographs on the wall next to the mirror. The rocking chair has darkened. Now it's almost black, all scratched up, and it sometimes nicks you with its many protuberances. Its bars attentively and repeatedly wrapped around by a sticky ribbon, have been rebandaged a hundred times. The rocking chair threateningly squeaks beneath me. And I think we'll dissipate into dust together. Like old faithful friends. My cellmates stroll through the garden. Breakfast was just over — cream of wheat with a glass of milk or tea — and they've crawled out to warm up under the last rays of the autumn sun. Ragged cats and kittens! Once all their coats used to shine. But today maybe just fleas latch on to them. Though sometimes journalists come — they bring, as though for dim-witted little kids, cookies, fresh magazines, gifts in the form of bags with sugar candies or even cooler — sets of perfumes from sponsors, who suddenly felt the urge to be charitable. One time I received just such a set. I stood waiting for it in the stinking line of these old people, who amassed next to our dining room, just because they were giving out perfume with a familiar label — "from Chanel." About the shellfish in the Pid Kupolem Restaurant I, certainly, held my tongue: the journalists had come not to see me — but to see someone else, more deft and with a sharper tongue. Look, even if they had come to me — Edith Beresh! — all the same I wouldn't have let loose even a wisp of vapor from my lips. Though I imagine, how their mouths would have been agape if they found out how Coco and I... That's why I hold my tongue.

I hold my tongue because instead of the milk I despised, I'm used to drinking coffee. Good coffee, not instant, but real Turkish coffee.

(A big can of Lavazza, that my neighbors gave me before my nephew put me in the car to bring me here, was gone before last New Year).

I hold my tongue because I ran out of my black cherry tobacco, my pipe — my favorite delicate ladies' pipe, which was thirty five years old from its birth in far-off Havana — broke.

I hold my tongue because I can't ask anyone to buy me this or that in the local store. Edith Beresh has never asked anyone for anything! And I don't have enough money for all that. To admit to be in such a predicament — means the same thing as death. And, as strange as it seems, I still wish to see a production called "How Old Age Ends." Earlier I acted on the other side of the footlights and never was interested in what was happening in the darkness, beyond the orchestra pit. Now I'm sitting in that darkness. And with a spiteful eye I look at the light, in which other characters are scurrying. I'm sitting in my chair and holding my tongue. Let others speak. Their lines aren't written by Shakespeare. And that's why it's comical for me.

I come out of my room three times a day: for breakfast, lunch and dinner.

I always try to be late so my colleagues in the Building, whom it's more pleasant for me to call my "cellmates," have managed to eat and go their separate ways. I don't care that my food gets cold, and the cook keeps arguing. I pretend I don't hear. It's a very convenient position! I learn so much about myself — for example, "old fart," "nasty piece of work," "peppered goat," "dog shit." The cook mutters under his nose, and in my time I used to say even worse out loud to the costume designers, make-up people, hairdressers, and the directors too. Just she, Leda Nizhyna, never had the opportunity to hear it. That's what I won't stop regretting till my last day. And if today I don't have as grateful listeners as that Leda, then why wear myself out on some cook?

* * *

The building in which I live now has a quite impressive name — The Building of Creativity for Solitary Actors of Theater and Film. A bronze plaque hangs above our main entrance. And below there's even a painted dove that's carrying a palm branch in its beak. As though he couldn't have brought it earlier — only just now, practically, on the grave of expectations, to this refuge. If an artist knew for whom he's painting, then he'd be better off painting a decrepit Narcissus — the symbol of vanity. There are plenty of those kind of Narcissuses here...

The building has two floors and two spacious wings, situated in a picturesque suburb — right in the middle of a luxurious park that changes into a pine woods. The air is marvelous, the natural surroundings really nice. Once this establishment was owned by the state and therefore wasn't just a place to rip off the poor, as, say, other similar establishments, but a comfortable enough place, to which future solitary theater and film stars would sign up. Even those who had a family. They signed up long before their old age, just in case...

Some dreamt of taking it easy on government food amid nature, others escaped from their other half, so as not to take care of her — ill and already unwanted, some expected to meet likeminded people here and to spend the evenings in good company, and others were simply brought here by family with the statement: "After remodeling the apartment we'll get you out of there right away!"

But no one, believe me, no one guessed that this — was forever!

A mousetrap opens just one time.

It's comical to observe how the first weeks the pomaded madams and the spiffed up (by old habit) messieurs come out to dinner in their frocks and bow ties. As they call this refuge "Bohemia," and, putting ear horns to their lips for one another or picturesquely placing their hand to cup their ear, they talk highbrow, tossing out names, they pout, they jostle before one another in front of their old posters, order pineapple in champagne, act capriciously, fight with their nurses. Until they hear that "dog shit" directed at them. Then they begin to go through all the channels, including their relatives, who at that moment are in the middle of remodeling; they write letters to the minister himself, for two days they bravely starve in their cells. And then... Then they come out to dinner in flannel robes and slippers on their bare feet. And try not to look one another in the eye. Only the nastiest pieces of work of the narcissuses sometimes can ask: "Well, how about your relatives — have they finished the remodeling? For some reason it's taking a long time..."

That's why I don't come out. Even when sponsors come, children scouts (right now they call them something else) or charitable societies with their gifts. I still haven't fallen into old age sclerosis or childhood, to jostle for candy. Except on those holidays (everything happens on holidays — on March 8 International Women's Day or Victory Day) everyone puts on frocks and lipstick...

Late in the evening sometimes I unnoticeably step out into the common room to watch TV — the news or some old movies for crazy insomniacs. One time I even heard out of the darkness, from the first few rows:

"Edith Beresh! That's Edith Beresh... From our country. Maybe she's already died in America... She was a woman of rare beauty..."

from TWO MINUTES OF TRUTH

by Iren Rozdobudko

Translated by Michael M. Naydan

...HE STOOD BY THE CORNER FOOD STORE WHERE HE ALWAYS had coffee, and was watching as the patch of dry land beneath his feet grew smaller little by little. The balcony of the second floor loomed above him, but today he couldn't hide it from the streams of water. The sudden August downpour turned the morning into night. The street that just had been alive and in motion — died. Just he, as always, was stubbornly standing beneath the balcony, drinking his coffee from a plastic cup and having a smoke, though the damp wind and droplets flying into there kept trying to douse his cigarette. He loved the rain and that feeling of solitude beneath it when you become different from everyone else. But everyone scatters like mice, covering themselves with umbrellas, plastic bags, and runs with dismay toward the first best shelter, but you keep walking along the street, wet and happy. And you talk to the water. And every droplet tells its own story. Because each droplet truly has its own story and soul, which it inherited from someone on something it had been earlier...

Today they raised the price of coffee in the shop by thirty kopecks. In principle, this was insignificant, because it was cheaper here than anywhere else in the city. In addition, right at this spot, the coffee wasn't any worse than in a first class restaurant. And, maybe, it was tasty because the saleslady had known him for many years and made this kind of coffee conscientiously, especially for him.

Shifting his weight from one foot to the other, he imagined he was standing on the last patch of dry earth, and everything else had already been engulfed by water. Everything, just everything. His building, work, the buildings of his friends, his friends, the train stations, airports, TV towers — everything. Everything disappeared. And he remained alone, completely satisfied by that. He long ago already had wanted to say go to hell to everything, but if nature does this — what benefit is there from it?

Great.

Passengers in the minibuses passing by cast glances at him in wonder, or perhaps, to put it more precisely, swimming past the corner food store. Maybe they're feeling sorry for him, he thought. Unless you explain to them that all is good for you right at that moment when the streets are empty and nearly dark from the torrential downpour.

He celebrated his birthday yesterday. It was the most detestable day of the year.

Before that — about two weeks ago — he was, as usual, aching like a drug addict. In the direct sense of the word his joints were unscrewed, he was feeling nauseated and giddy. A damned disagreeable condition. And he, to defend himself, already began to drink that week — with anybody just to deaden the aches. Everything finally receded yesterday, and ended. He had a dry mouth, his hands were trembling. Hate for himself and for everything was off the scales.

And also yesterday his wife, with whom he woke up, with whom he's woken up over the course of the last five years, said she no longer wanted him. They've always had this agreement to tell the truth. Now he was sorry he had suggested that game. It would have been better if she had lied. She could have simply said she was tired, that she needed a rest from him, to think a bit, or something else like that. Were there more delicate considerations for that to divorce quietly? And here it's like this… It was pitiless. Maybe he already didn't want her too and was tired — at least for the last few months, but he never would have dared to talk about that aloud. But she was able to.

Today's downpour was quite appropriate. The patch of dry asphalt beneath his feet uncontrollably and symbolically kept getting smaller.

It was "Queen" playing in his pocket. With his damp hand he pulled out his cell phone, surprised and annoyed by the fact that someone had been left whole, had saved themselves.

It was Eva.

"Seems like you've landed yourself into something," she said (at that moment out of boredom his jaws clenched. "You're going to be fired. Do you hear me?"

He heard her and pulled the phone from his ear. He imagined her red lips that always left imprints on a glass. It was unbearable for him at that moment to hear any woman's voice.

"Where are you? Why are you silent?"

"What do you want to hear?"

"Yesterday you nearly botched the filming — and you have nothing to say?!"

"It nearly — doesn't count. Nobody's irreplaceable."

At the other end there was a sigh.

"But I stood up for you. At least you have till the end of the month to fix things. Your last chance."

"Listen, what the hell do you need all this for?" He was surprised.

"You were the best of us," she said. "You're dying here, Dan."

"Are you sure of that?" He started to laugh.

"We'll talk about it tomorrow."

"What's going on tomorrow?"

"I lined you up for a business trip. They told me it's suicidal, but they authorized it. We'll go together. We'll talk on the way. So I don't fall asleep at the wheel. I'll drop by at your place tomorrow at eight. Get ready."

"Get ready" meant that he needed to shave, change his clothes, buy a few clean handkerchiefs and a few pairs of socks. A few bottles, coffee. And something for Eva...

He used to love to go on business trips earlier, to see the road, to grab his camera for shots after he saw a grasshopper on a leaf or an unusual flower in the field.

Right now he wanted just for something like that to happen — but without him! — so that everything would die, be covered with gloom, and never return. Though in the form of the first infusoria in the first reed that's formed in thickets after a worldwide flood.

"Good," he said. And having thought about that for a bit, decided all the same to add: "I'm grateful to you."

...She pressed the button on the phone and shoved it in her pocket. With a hopeless look she glanced at the papers scattered all over the desk and looked through the window. It was dark beyond it, long snakes of water crawled across the glass pane. They mated, created entire rivulets and again split into hundreds of small streams, and crawled onto the windowsills. The entire pane resembled a nest of transparent snakes that were shamelessly mating before her eyes...

The roads will get soaked by tomorrow. The village area will become completely impassable. But, she thought, the worse — the better. So as just not to sit here in this office.

She thought about Bohdan — she finally reached him by phone! She wasn't able to yesterday, though she wanted to wish him a happy birthday. As always, he turned off the phone. And she was concerned. Though last year on that day she had to drive to the police department to get him and shake her documents in front of the cops, to swear that this late night lush-hooligan — is the best cameraman at a well known TV station. And that, for the umpteenth time in a row, has the strange habit on his birthday of ending up at the police station.

This kind of carelessness aroused indignation in her and a certain amount of jealousy at the same time — she never could feel as free. She couldn't just not give a damn about it all and, say, not go to work. Though she understood perfectly that she herself is "nearly" irreplaceable. At least, no one of her colleagues has as many professional honors, or gets letters — five-to-seven great big boxes a day, or capable of, without anyone else's help, writing good texts for her scenarios and flawlessly editing those of others. The secret of her diligence was the fact that Eva to this day was fearful of losing what she already long ago and safely had. It was not about her position. It was about money.

Eva never admitted to anyone that she had grown up in uneducated poverty. And when she was in her later years in school and they were officially allowed not to wear a school uniform, she wanted to hang herself, because she had nothing to wear. The uniform for her was multicolored, with bright-brown frills below and with the same kind of insets on the sides. The girls used to say this looked "stylish," but the artfulness of this stylishness was known just to Eva: the uniform several times had been sewn from an older, children's one.

When Eva received her first packet of money — and it really was a packet! — a bank one, glued with a paper ribbon, and understood that this was her pay, and not quite all of it, because "all of it" was still in a separate envelope in dollars — she decided that she would "chew dirt" for that packet and envelope.

Dan was different. The kind she could have been the way she was born — a "desperate little girl," diligent at first glance and confused on the inside, with fantasies, with a carefree and easy attitude toward life, with an indifferent conceit toward fashion, with a sense of humor and affinity for adventures. But all that had gone into the past, to the kingdom of memories.

Now she was simply functioning to regularly have that packet and envelope. So that once every two or three years she could change the furniture in her apartment, maintain a car, and dress well... And the desperate little girl in a motley school uniform, who remains in the pages of an old photo album, followed this from her paper non-existence. She had nothing in common with the Eva of today...

Though in recent times all the more often the unproductive feeling of pity for herself overwhelmed her — the way she was, and envy — for the one who was on the photographs of ten or fifteen years in the past.

Hardly imagine anything worse than pity for yourself! Eva strove to strangle it in embryonic form; nostalgic memories about that damned uniform had just started... She tried to convince herself that she's young, beautiful, and successful, that she has everything, and everything is completely in order with her. Not like Bohdan, not like many others. But in the morning her first look into the mirror was overflowing with pity, mixed with a speck of hate.

...The alarm clock began to ring at six. He turned it off and turned on his other side. He had slept poorly, because he wasn't used to sleeping alone. At times it seemed there was no difference, who was lying next to him — just as long as he wasn't alone! When she, who had left, had told him this truth, he tacitly agreed. She was right. But it was also pitiless, because he had never heard nastiness from her before. He needed to wake up at seven, shave, and toss some things into a bag. Usually she would do all this. She used to fold everything tidily. He got angry and shook things out of their cellophane packets — he hated cellophane, that hideous artificial rustling.

At eight he heard a short beep beneath the window.

When he stepped out, Eva was standing there, leaning sideways against her flawlessly shining car and having a smoke. On seeing him, she tossed away her cigarette, silently nodded in the direction of the doors to the back seat, and sat down in the front. All these gestures were masculine.

Bohdan tossed his case with the camera into the trunk and sat in the car.

They briefly growled out a sleepy "Hi, there!" to each other — and Eva steered the car onto the street.

"Have you recovered?" She asked some time later.

"A bit...," he said and squinted.

The Renault Clio drove through the city for about forty minutes. Then the city ended.

...Eva wasn't named Eva. Something else was written in her passport. She always had been wildly embarrassed by her name, especially in school, where she was fiercely teased. And the teachers, who perfectly well knew about this, intentionally called her by her full name, with a particular intonation, suffused with irony. A female teacher of "life skills" taunted her the most — she was a gray mouse, who was irritated by the loose hair of her pupil, who in her classes should have worn it tied in a kerchief. Real enmity heated up after Eva, having found out about the origin of her name, explained to her about whom they were talking in front of the whole class. The teacher hadn't known that. Then Eva finished her off completely, when she pulled out of her satchel a national classic book, on which was embossed that name — "Eupraxia."[*] In several days, after assiduously preparing the topic, the teacher recounted in class the adventures of the debauched Kyivan princess, who was a participant in black masses during her marriage ceremony with the German monster-emperor Henrich… And then she forced her hushed pupil to tie up her kerchief.

Just after graduating from school was she able to easily get out of the situation, calling herself Eva. And now she was surprised how easy it had been — to name yourself a different, shortened name, as though your were shortening a the train of a dress of failures, cutting off the tail of damned poverty. Eva was the first and only woman on Earth, pure in her firstness, Eupraxia — was raped over and over and a guilty sinner without guilt…

…Bohdan's wasn't named Bohdan. Though he never thought to change his name — his friends changed it. Dan — and that's it. Short. And, as they assured, it was convenient and to the point. Dan — is a "hook" with his left hand, when there are brass knuckles clenched in his right… But he never used them. The hook with his left was always sufficient.

"Who are we going to film?" He asked. "Pre-election shit again?"

Eva smiled crookedly:

"The granddaughter of Tina Modotti.[**] She lives near Hulyai-Pole…"[***]

In the rearview mirror he showed her his bent pointing finger — "are you lying? — and they burst out laughing.

"Of course, it's shit…," she said. "What right now isn't shit? And you keep dreaming about making a revolution in art? It won't work ooo-uut… Everything's out of whack… Want some coffee?"

---

[*] For more information on Eupraxia, who was married to German king Henrich IV, see: *http://www.ukrainians-world.org.ua/eng/peoples/9oe952b1cdfed607/*.

[**] An Italian actress (1896-1942) and revolutionary activist.

[***] In Ukrainian villages there is a penchant for naming things in oddly unique ways. "Hulyai-Pole" here means something like "Dance/Stroll-Field."

"Just not from the thermos," he said. "Let's stop somewhere."

"We still have ten hours to drive. If I listen to you, we won't get there till morning. We just started…"

But she really wanted to stop herself. The city stopped strangling her, they left the great big letters with the name just behind them.

"Then, let's find a decent café," he said. "I haven't been out of the city in a hundred years."

"It started…," she said. "Nine in the morning… We need to think about work. Especially you. You're hanging by a thread."

"Don't lie to me," he said. "You want to stop too. I know you. It's just your thread is made of metal. Only a welding machine can cut it."

She started to laugh and corrected him:

"An unwelding one. But don't expect it!"

He sighed and fixed his eyes on the road. They approached the next blue sign, on which in white letters the name of the locality was traced. Dan hmmmed

"Nedoharky!"* On reading the name, he then later burst out laughing even more when a little further beyond that sign there was hanging a white lopsided sign with faded writing "Kolhosp Iskra" (The Spark Collective Farm).

They were laughing their heads off, as though they were crazed.

And further on there will be "Nedopalky" (Not Quite Smoked), "Nedoyidky" (Not Quite Eaten Up), and "Nedobytky" (Not Quite Reached)!" She said and grew more serious: "Why is it like this? Why always "not quite eaten up"? What kind of people live there?…

About five hundred meters on the same kind of blue sign "MOSKALENKY" was marked, and in three-hundred more — "PROTSENKY."**

---

* Meaning: candle ends.

** Villages in Ukraine are sometimes named after the dominant clan in the village. So in this case the Russian village of people named Moskalenko (*moskal'* was a pejorative used for Russian soldiers and Russians) and the Ukrainian village of people named Protsenko are contrasted with each other. The "-enko" suffix is a typical suffix used in Ukrainian Cossack names.

"Super!" He said. "Imagine what a happy place it is to live here! At first the Moskalenky give a good beating to the Protsenky, and then vice versa. And it goes on like that for centuries. Until the last man standing, like in a computer game..."

"It seems like no one really lives here," she said, looking around the empty street sprinkled with cherries.

"Aha... Do you know why?"

"Why?"

"Look at the next one!"

They already had passed the "Protsenky" and were approaching a taller sign*: "Cherovonopashentsi."**

Eva barely managed to hold on to the steering wheel, with tears splashing from her mascara covered eyes.

"Everything's out of whack," he said seriously, "the Moskalenky and the Protsenky were eaten up by these red maw Chervonopashentsi. Can you imagine what kind of thriller that would be?!"

"No, that's wrong!" She laughed loudly, pointing to the next sign, "Look, it's so super — 'Kryva ruda'! Lame and add redheaded to that — that's worse than these 'maws'." It was something like this: one of the Protsenky married a lame redhead, from that kind of life both of them became red maw Chervonopashentsi and gobbled up all the Moskalenky!"

"Let's stop. And take some shots of the signs," he suggested.

"Why the hell?"

"Just as a joke."

"No jokes!" She kept herself from laughing. "You don't have enough of them? How old are you, little boy? We'll soon be getting white slippers for our funerals, and you're amusing yourself. Young people are plowing the earth. Soon they'll plow under us."

"Are you fearful of that?" He asked caustically.

She glanced at him in the window:

---

* Ukrainian road signs designating villages are narrow and rectangular.
** Literally: red maws.

"And you?"

"I have nothing to lose. Just the opposite, I'd want to hurry up everything. In the Middle Ages people died at thirty-five. But how they used to live!"

"Well then, we have a little time," she said.

"For what?" He hmmmed. "Everything's happened?…"

"Good little boy, you always know how to cheer people up. In distinction from you, I still want something."

"For example?…"

Eva got lost in thought. The road went through fields with sad sunflowers, drooping under the heaviness of the seeds.

What did she really want? Work, a career, money, men? She needed to do a "high tech" style remodeling, sign up for the pool, take a trip one more time to her beloved Serbia…

She looked as the asphalt river flowing quickly under the wheels.

"I want to ditch everything," she said to herself unexpectedly, "Buy a trailer and drive off God knows where…"

"…and when the money runs out — rob the village club?" He added.

"Not necessarily. You can steal potatoes. Go hunting. Fishing. There you'll have it — the Middle Ages…"

"Look, honey bunny, at your nails…," he said. "Where will you get your manicure fixed? In Nedoharky or Kozyatyn?"

"Are you laughing? In fact, I'm being honest…"

"Me too."

"I can get by without a manicure!" She said angrily, and then started to speak, looking first at the road with a chilly gaze, as though she were talking to herself. "I'm suffering from the imperfection of the world of people. The further I live, the more I suffer. It seems sometimes like I hate people. I look them over like in a menagerie. Imagine: a woman enters the metro — one, you know, like a sweet roll — as though she were filled up with air and is happily sniffing under her armpits — a mechanical gesture that she simply got used to doing… All men sit with their legs spread widely apart… Overfed teenagers…

246

Loud conversations on their cell phones... People wearing headphones, through which you can hear their crappy pop music anyway... I can't live in this anymore!!"

"You've just gotten weary. You need a vacation."

"But I can't live anywhere else," without listening to him, she added, "If I could clear out of here... But — I can't..."

A long pause occurred. She contemplated how true what she had said was, he — again, to the point of spasms in his jaws, thought about today's empty bed and about his being affronted.

It's good that Eva had taken him on the road...

The sunflowers came to an end. The village began, but they already weren't paying attention to the name. However, they noticed a quite decent roadside rest stop. Eva stepped on the brakes.

"Chicago," she read, "Lord, look at that! And here's — Chicago. Total idiocy. Let's scarf down something. Otherwise you'll die. They'd have to bury you in the middle of the corn."

The patio in front of the coffee shop was neatly laid out in pink tiles, even the tables under a striped awning looked fairly decent. A bunch of men were sitting at one.

"Should we sit here or inside?" He asked.

"Here. Let's breathe some fresh air. Order something, and I'll go to the powder room. I expect they have one here."

"What should I order for you?"

"Coffee to start, and then — we'll see."

She went toward the door, out of which right at that moment a waitress was stepping with two red binders wrapped in cellophane...

Dan waited, thinking about whether he believed what Eva had said, it wasn't like her at all.

He pulled out a cigarette, looked for an ashtray with his eyes, and stumbled on the binder with the golden letters "MENU," which the waitress had pushed toward him. He looked at her and nodded his head. She smiled and nodded back. "Why do white aprons look so sexy on women?" He thought. The waitress stood by the table with a pad in her hand.

from JOURNEYS WITHOUT SENSE OR MORALITY

by Iren Rozdobudko

Translated by Michael M. Naydan

A CHANGE OF SCENERY
(Instead of an Introduction)

... THE END OF MAY SOME (IT MAKES NO DIFFERENCE WHICH) recent (compared to eternity) year.

I walk out with my suitcase to the taxi that's waiting by the entrance.

"Going far?" The driver asks as we ride.

"Far…"

"Where exactly?" He doesn't stop.

"Abroad…," I answer unwillingly.

And not because it's hard for me to answer or cast an evil eye, but because I imagine him dropping me off at the airport — like this, "all in white," he'll think that "here *they* are travelling around the world, seeing something interesting, and I'm just doing this, turning the steering wheel to the airport and back…"

In the evening he'll get drunk out of despondency.

And I really don't feel like dividing the world into those who are "they" and others.

"Is it far abroad?" He asks again.

I have to explain to him that I'm travelling to Malta.

And I make a note "on business." Just for a few weeks.

"Not bad…," he says and steps on the gas.

I agree mentally.

If he also knew what a double booking this turned out to be: the next day after returning, I'm on my way to America. A second packed suitcase is standing in my apartment. I'll arrive, sleep the night, and in the morning — again go to the airport.

The driver doesn't need to know that.

But, precisely in ten days, when I'm already walking (this time with a different suitcase!) to the summoned taxi — the same old guy is sitting in it.

These kinds of coincidences happen!

This time he takes me in silence, he just sniffles and doesn't look in my direction.

I toss out my "justification": "They sent me again…"

It sounds ambiguous.

I don't know why I always feel uncomfortable before those who having travelled farther away than their city. Certainly, from childhood the reproachful line from Nonna Mordiukova from the movie *The Diamond Arm* nested in my head: "Our people don't drive to the bakery!"

Besides that, I knew exactly that I'd travel on any occasion by saving on everything except on the ticket for the flight.

New refrigerators, washing machines, and just cars, furniture, and other similar things — are nothing compared to new impressions.

What attracts you most during travels? To each — their own. From the audacious desire to mark your name on a cliff "Here was…" to the possibility of not returning. But both the former and latter don't attract me.

If I were asked, I'd answer (true, just at a given instant, however, how I would answer tomorrow — I don't know): to be reassured that the "world is small," that it can fit in the palm of your hand and… what cretins we are, that, despite this, make it smaller each year with artificially created cataclysms. Soon we'll be standing on it on one leg, like herons…

But we won't talk about sad things.

There still is something that takes our breath away. Let's say, in the evening you're getting your suitcase ready and are sleeping in your bed. The way it was yesterday, and the day before yesterday, and month ago. And here today as your nodding off, you think: what will your lodging be like tomorrow? That is, an entirely simple question: what kind of roof will be over your head? What kind of air around you? What will you see from the window?

You can't foresee that.

The moment of opening unknown doors — is one of the most interesting in all journeys.

Those are doors to another reality! And the quick change of the "picture" also strikes you over the course of some several hours. In the morning you're still at home, but during the day you're already coming out of the plane, say, in Helsinki. After a half hour — already in the commuter train that's rushing across the spaces of Finland.

Forty minutes pass — and you're already in Turku, another thirty — on the eleven-deck ferryboat. And in an hour, it's already carrying you along the waves of the Baltic Sea to Stockholm. And from the porthole you watch the tall dark green waves. And the thought that in the morning you were drinking coffee on the balcony of your city becomes imaginary. Although several hours have already passed! And the impression is that between coffee on your balcony and the journey to the shores of Sweden lies something approaching an eternity.

The abyss of time.

It's hard to get used to it.

It's precisely this that attracts you in travels; jumping cross the abyss of time. And finding yourself in the unknown…

…I don't like tourism in its pure form.

I don't like walking in a crowd. I'd give up a march-sprint to the next museum or fake ruins of some palace for sitting in a tavern and looking at the streets of some unknown city.

It seems to me that right then the mysteries of those ruins and monuments — artificial or not — enter into you by themselves together with the air you breathe. At times without any assistance you find answers to those questions, to which even the most experienced guide can't.

It's worth it just to adjust yourself to those transmitting waves that surround you in each unknown locality. The main thing is –to feel them. And if you feel them, you'll swim in them like a little fish. Then even the stones will begin talking to you…

Interactions with the world are very similar to any kind of other human interactions. When you understand this, you'll stop hiding that, which… well, that one or another object didn't strike you, but rather something entirely different — even completely opposite — drew your attention. So, upon seeing the Colossi at Memnon for the first time, I was struck by a sight… piles of Pepsi cans around their feet. And the celebrated Sphinx, before which I honestly had planned to cry tears of rapture, for some reason didn't stir any emotion, because every minute I had to keep my distance from the lively Bedouin peddlers.

Here you begin to contrive those emotions — for others, for those who'll ask: "Well, HOW is it there?" And… fool yourself.

At that time when something entirely insignificant elicited the greatest impression — that, about which it's not worth even talking, returning from there, where "our people don't ride in taxis." Let's talk about the keys that jut out on the outside of all the doors in Malta.

Or about the laundry hanging on the roof of an apartment building in the very center of the Old City in Jerusalem: underwear, shirts, socks — on the backdrop of The Lord's Tomb Temple.

Or about the old woman who makes extraordinary coffee in the slums of Umag…

There is also a thing I'm afraid of in deciding to go on a journey.

It's a really strange fear: I'm afraid of not gathering the necessary and generally accepted impressions. I'm fearful that my brain will refuse to accept information. The way that happens before you take a test, when you take your textbook and command yourself to concentrate to the maximum, and then you read and… think about something of your own. And with horror you notice that just when you've leafed through a hundred pages, as though they've been read. It happens like that too when they tell you: "You just have to read this book — it's genius!" And you begin to tense up or suck out in yourself that genius to the smallest abbreviation mark, and you return again to one and the same line a hundred times. However you feel a responsibility before the general opinion that has been thrust on you.

And it happens otherwise: some kind of insignificant "little book," about which no one ever said anything to you, is swallowed in a single evening, it enters you like a hot knife through butter. Because there are *details* in it.

Those keys in the doors.

That hanging wash.

The aroma of the coffee.

Two little boys on a donkey in front of the Temple of the Chalice.

The profile of Our Lady on the bark of a tree in the Garden of Gethsemane...

When you accepted the world in details, then the "grand" becomes more understandable.

...That's why I sought out the hare in the fields of Finland, with which the hero of Arto Paaselinna's novel traveled in *The Year of the Hare.*

from A COLLECTION OF PASSIONS,

or THE ADVENTURES AND MISADVENTURES OF A YOUNG UKRAINIAN LADY

by Natalka Sniadanko

Translated by Jennifer Croft

CHILDHOOD PASSIONS
When is it Worth Starting, What it's Not Worth Paying Attention to, or How to Fall in Love with George Michael?

TOLYA WAS THE TALLEST, FATTEST, CURLIEST-HEADED LITTLE BOY in the whole class. He was really ashamed of the fact that the shirt of his school uniform popped out over his rotund stomach and that he couldn't quite button up his blazer; and that his mom made him put on knee socks instead of regular socks in the summer and warm woolen long johns that his grandma made him in the winter. I sympathized with him, because my mom, too, made me wear a lengthy pair of pantaloons made of thick wool called — for reasons unbeknown to me — "reforms," which would sometimes stick out from beneath short skirts. Or, maybe, it seemed to me at the time, they were visible. Just that awareness — that you had something that hideous on — would be enough to ruin anybody's life. I don't know what Tolya did with his long johns, but starting around the sixth grade I would take my pantaloons off at the base of the stairwell of our apartment building, stuff them into the mailbox, and then take them out again coming home from school.

At least until my mom came home from work early one day and found my "reforms" next to her *Science and Life Magazine*.

Tolya was a really shy little boy and would blush every time our math teacher would call him up to the blackboard. During recess, while all the other boys were scampering outside to play soccer or jumping over each other's back, which they called "playing the goat," Tolya would find a little nook where no one could see him and from some secret blazer pocket would remove a slender dark green little book he would read all recess, in secret, since it wasn't the kind of behavior that would be accepted by his classmates. Tolya would usually go to the top floor of the school because it was always deserted and quiet in the corner by the physics lab: the physics teacher felt recesses were not for pupils to run wild and make a racket, but rather for teachers to rest and ready themselves for the next class.

And so it was that she would make absolutely sure that nobody played the French elastic band skipping game or "leap the goat," let alone play the save-a candy-wrapper game anywhere near her office. Anyone who sullied the sanctity of that spot was risking considerable unpleasantness; this having already been confirmed by several students, so everybody avoided her office and its environs like the plague.

But back in the first grade neither Tolya nor I could have known about any of that: we hadn't taken physics yet; we didn't even have classes in multiple classrooms like the older kids yet. We had all of them in the same "Starter Classroom" in the opposite wing. Out of our whole grade it was only Tolya and I who conducted expeditions to the physics wing, both of us with a slender dark green little book that actually turned out to be the same book in the end, namely *Cosette* — excerpts from the novel by Victor Hugo — which I was ultimately able to recognize from a distance thanks to the standard Soviet cover that still graced the bulk of the books in our parents' libraries back then, when you could still get paid for recycling them afterward.

I don't know why Tolya and I both happened upon that particular book for our secret reading at recess. It occurs to me now that there was little childhood romanticism in it; it was just that the Hugo book was the smallest and lightest and — of course! — the easiest to smuggle around under a school uniform. Then, though, that coincidence struck me as enigmatic, mysterious — and filled with hidden meaning.

Tolya was the first in our grade to learn to read, and he always got the highest marks in penmanship. He wasn't a total A-student per se, and his preference for the humanities was strong. The other kids made fun of him nonetheless, as mercilessly as if he were already on the math team. They never even took him with them when they went to watch the older kids play soccer.

At the end of first grade, Tolya's mom had a talk with the principal, and Tolya skipped the second grade so he wouldn't stand out too much from his peers who were shorter and tinier than he. He made up the material over summer vacation. His parents worked with my parents, and sometimes they would all come over; once we even went on a trip together.

As it was in fashion back then, we drove down to Odessa and stayed in an inexpensive pension near the city. The whole way Tolya tried to get me to play chess with him, or checkers, or to talk to him about books. We both had such awful car-sickness, though, that our parents had to pull over every half hour so our moms could take us out in turn along the side of the road, where, with the good influence of the fresh air, we would deposit the contents of our stomachs. We would then get back in the car clutching plastic bags in our fists as a precaution in case next time we didn't manage to stop in time. That must have kept us from coming up with mutually stimulating topics for discussion; our friendship failed to flourish over the course of the trip. Tolya did try talking me into playing badminton on the grounds of the pension, but because I could still remember the details of the voyage and the fact that Tolya nearly barfed all over my shorts and would have had I not leapt out of the car with a brimming plastic bag in my hands, I refused.

Besides, I intensely disliked the yellow polka dot underwear Tolya's mom put on him instead of swimming trunks; there was also the matter of Tolya's rotund stomach hanging over the waist of his yellow polka-dot underwear. Add to that, Tolya would be held up as an example for me to follow as we barely crossed the threshold of the dining hall.

"Look," my mother began and finished every procedure in the consumption of food, "Tolya finished ages ago, and you're still sitting there thinking about your plate."

Equaling Tolya, who with an expression of bliss would devour several servings of pasta salad along with warm dried-pear compote in ninety-degree heat, and then while taking a walk on the beach would jam into his mouth the four pieces of bread with butter they had given out at breakfast to accompany the tea, was absolutely impossible.

Basically, Tolya did not arouse in me even the slightest sympathy or friendly interest, even though there was no one else our age in the whole hotel.

Even by the time I was bored out of my mind, I didn't give in, and instead of going over to Tolya, I began to read the *Science and Life Magazine* my parents packed at the last minute — my mom intentionally having brought nothing else to read — to prevent me from "ruining my eyes." The optometrist had recently recommended a break from reading so I wouldn't have to wear glasses.

It was with unusual frequency, then, that I read the article dedicated to the latest discovery in the field of chemical crystallography, maybe because the issue began with it. When for the umpteenth time my parents tried to force-feed me a piece of meat, and I discovered I couldn't take it anymore, I wound up reciting the following:

"A central place in the study of mineral evolution in heterogeneous mountain geological formations ought to be occupied by geocrystallography, as a new branch of traditional crystallography; a sizeable role ought also to be given to geocrystallography in the exploration of defined-property fluid synthesis from a crystal-energy perspective, as well as research in isomorphism and polymorphism utilizing x-ray diffraction, electron diffraction, and neutron diffraction, as much for chemical properties as for the entire aggregate of physical properties. And you all are busy with your same stupid nonsense." I then exhaled victoriously, drank the rest of my compote, and left my stunned parents to keep watching Tolya finish his cutlet and barley groats.

Tolya was within earshot of the grand finale of my monologue: he had actually just finished his lunch and was walking by our table with his mom when I delivered it. After that my parents hid *Science and Life Magazine* somewhere, and Tolya never asked me to play badminton with him again.

I regretted my youthful arrogance only much later, when in the eighth grade I realized that, for the first time in my life, I had fallen in love.

MICHAEL JACKSON, POETRY, AND TENDER MAY

Actually May that year was not particularly benevolent to the female part of our class. A particular type of epidemic had struck. The tastes of my female classmates divided into three groups: the first was head-over-heels in love with Michael Jackson, the second with George Michael, and the last — and least numerous — chose as the object of its affections the soloist of the young without exception and then-popular band Tender May. It was unclear which among us was the worst off.

Symptoms of this illness, independently of the choice of the object of love, were always identical. Every single one of them — even the most assiduous A-students — suddenly raised the hems of their school uniforms, stopped wearing the required ribbons in their hair (sky-blue on weekdays, snow-white on Sundays), pilfered their mothers' high-heeled shoes; and ignoring the uncomfortable nature of them, tied to them being the wrong size, attempted to wear them after school, and later even to class.

The next stage of the illness was characterized by the painting of fingernails in the unlikeliest pink shades as well as the application of artificial eyelashes, the meticulous plucking of eyebrows, and the use of considerable amounts of other cosmetics; some would even wear bright pink lipstick. This was in school. After school the makeup got considerably more intense and forced you to think of heroes out of James Fennimore Cooper. Skirts got much shorter, and sometimes you couldn't see them at all below a jacket, even if you were looking hard.

Add to that our mothers' perfumes that we used in excessively large quantities, and our very first cigarettes smoked at the entrances to our apartment buildings.

The final, most serious phase of our illness brought walls covered in posters that came from *Peer* magazine, to which all the representatives of a particular age subscribed, private collections of photographs from other publications and even more radical changes in outward appearance. The last depended on the type of illness.

My classmates, who were amassing Michael Jackson memorabilia, ordinarily dyed their hair black and used mass quantities of henna. The George Michael girls focused less on hairstyle and more on owning as many black turtlenecks, jeans and suit jackets as they possibly could. They would just wear their hair flatly combed back; they would also wear several earrings in each ear.

Those devoted to the *oeuvre* of Tender May didn't pay even the slightest attention to outward appearances, taking a page from their idols' book, not to mention the fact that their parents were generally less well off than the girls who were in love with "Western pop-stars." Physical symptoms, then, were less evident; the less observant might take them for totally normal teenagers.

Nor was I immune, although the epidemic cropped up in me only after everyone else already had turned violently ill. Plus it did not happen the way I wanted it to. I had already begun to worry about whether or not I was going to actually undergo the process of sexual maturation properly — if I underwent it at all.

This is why every morning I would run into the bathroom when I woke up and examine the posters of Michael Jackson and George Michael I had carefully cut out of *Peer* magazine, as well as a little black-and-white group photo of Tender May. Here, inspecting each of the men in turn, I would try to detect my heart skipping beats at the sight of any of them.

Ashamed of my belated development, I would try to artificially stimulate the process of falling in love and think intensively about each of the potential candidates for the object of my affection. At first

I consoled myself by thinking you probably had to get used to the way your crush looks before you designate him as such. Then I tried going into the bathroom twice, once before and once after breakfast, figuring that love probably arises slower on an empty stomach than it does when you're full. After a week I took up regular visits, on the half hour, which only ended up making my mom inquire as to the state of my stomach; she force-fed me two pills of something. And my heart kept beating the best at breakfast and not while I was gazing at any of the objects of my girlfriends' ardent desires.

The situation became critical when one day in the cafeteria I happened to glance at Tolya. My heart began to pound with intensity, as if I had just run several meters to catch a tram that was about to leave. I refused to believe my eyes and took a more intense look at my old classmate, who was just wolfing down a third helping of hot dogs and mashed potatoes. But the more ardently he shoveled in the sauerkraut, which was dangling down his chin, the closer I wanted to watch him, without tearing my glance away. I must admit, that in the time we'd grown up, Tolya had indeed grown, but he hadn't really changed. He was still the tallest kid in the class, his school uniform was still riding up his rotund little belly, he would still run to the cafeteria every chance he got, and he still never played soccer. He still took a book (Sir Walter Scott's *Quentin Durward*) with him everywhere he went, including to the cafeteria; he now made no attempt to conceal this from anyone. He spent every free moment reading, even the time he was waiting for the hall monitors to deliver his tray of plates heaped with steaming hot dogs and potatoes. He didn't even notice that the kids sitting with him were using that same waiting period to bang their elbows on the table in an attempt to eject the last kid sitting on the bench from that bench, nor did he notice their mad cackling whenever they succeeded in doing so. No one dared pick on Tolya, no doubt due to his powerful build: if he were to exert himself even a little, he would be able to knock them all off the bench with the whack of a single elbow. Right at that moment I was also reading *Quentin Durwood*, albeit at home and in secret, firstly because the doctor had forbidden me from reading a lot again, and secondly because the book was too heavy to drag to school along with all my textbooks. And this, which then seemed to me, mysterious confluence of circumstances, made my heart pound even harder.

I found myself in a trap, a situation out of which it was impossible to find an honorable exit. Until then I had been ashamed of lagging behind my classmates, who every morning asked me anxiously, "So? Which one do you like?" My attempts to fall in love with one of the generally acknowledged idols were being tracked tensely by the whole female half of Grade 8A for results. I would avert my eyes and wind up having to admit that I didn't like any of them. I was risking the last shreds of my authority at that school and might have been considered underdeveloped. Now, however, things had gone from bad to worse. Settling on Tolya as my love object was like signing my own death warrant. None of my friends would be in a position to understand it. Such a blatant lack of aesthetic values — of good taste — such absolute incomprehension of the essence of masculine beauty, such an absence of enthusiasm for muscles, sheathed in tight spandex swimsuits, for the very symbol of masculinity, combined with the soft eroticism of the supple timbre of their voice, a fabulous hairstyle, numerous earrings in their ears. By this choice I definitively admitted my complete unwillingness to take part in all this regarding women's solidarity, "because everybody is doing that," but it didn't work for me.

The object of my affection looked more like he had spent the last thirty years working himself to death as the Director of some establishment, it was clear that not one of his muscles had ever even heard of a chest expander, let alone dumbbells or free weights.

The worst happened: instead of underdevelopment, it was something pathological. Although it would be with great difficulty, I could imagine myself confessing to my best girlfriend my indifference to Michael Jackson, but to tell her (even having sworn her to secrecy) that I was in love with Tolya, I could never do that.

First of all, the whole school would find out about it immediately, because what girlfriend would be able to keep anything like that to herself? Secondly and worst of all, Tolya might find out. I'd never live that down.

The only reasonable way out of the situation was suicide. Before I decided to do so, however, I thought I might just pour my suffering out onto paper. My first work was titled "For You...."

> *My heart is in sorrow*
> *Rain in the meadow*
> *I'm not going to tell you*
> *Why I am crying*
>
> *The moon is shining bright*
> *But all the same it's night*
> *You are a glorious sight*
> *I am so sad*

Despite my doubts, stirred by the unsuitability of the word "glorious" regarding Tolya's external appearance, I really liked the poem, and I decided I'd wait on the suicide so as to not deprive humanity of my immortal works. The next poem was penned that very night and bore the title "You..."

> *I'll never forget you*
> *I'll always love you*
> *My sorrow is like*
> *Eternal damnation*
>
> *You don't even know*
> *You suffer nothing*
> *But I suffer so*
> *I'm not myself*

Without a doubt, this marked poetic progress. "I'll always love...like a woman damned," that was really something. Only such a rich poetic image could do justice to the conflicting emotions that came with first love. Brief, powerful, cruel. Reminiscent of Ukrainian writer Vasyl Stefanyk. I was unlucky in love, but maybe, just maybe, I would go down in history as a poet, and by breakfast the next morning I had already written "From You."

> *But for you I'm blind*
> *The world is so unkind*
> *And I can't live*
> *Without you now*
>
> *What the future holds*
> *No one can know*
> *Yet this heart cannot*
> *Be taken away from you*

There was a hint of folksong lyricism in this, and even it wasn't overly original, then at least it was abundantly sincere, and if you looked hard enough, you might just see a certain flair for style. I was extremely pleased with myself. I copied all three poems out into a special copybook, which I titled *You*.

Over the course of the next few days I filled up an entire copybook of graph paper with my poetry, and then another one, until I realized I needed to put together a larger notebook more befitting of my feelings. My work from that period was characterized by a certain stylistic unity, as evidenced by the titles themselves: after the *You* cycle I'd written a collection of five sonnets called *Me*, and then an epic poem called *You and Me*, until ultimately after three sleepless nights several poems came out from under my pen worthy of being called a collection.

I titled it *About Us*, at which point I felt I had exhausted all the personal pronouns of the Ukrainian language in all their cases.

Their extensive use in that first volume ought to interest, if not literary critics, then at least linguists. If they study "The Role of Exclamatory Particles in the Late Works of [Nineteenth-Century

Ukrainian Philologist] Panteleimon 'Panko' Kulish," why would someone not write their dissertation on "Personal Pronouns and their Case Forms in the Early Work of Olesya Pidobidko?"

LITERATURE IN NOTEBOOKS AND LITERATURE IN LIFE: MYSTERIES OF THE MALE SOUL

The days passed, my feelings increased, and humble nighttime versifying no longer satisfied me. I'd composed multiple notebooks of confessional verse, and yet what had any of this changed? I longed to share my feelings with someone, most of all with Tolya so as to get some idea as to whether or not I could count on his returning them. The only advantage I had over my girlfriends was that no matter how much less they were currently suffering, they would never have any chance for it being requited.

On the other hand, Tolya's behavior had not changed at all despite having recently become the center of the universe. Either he was concealing his feelings as diligently as I was, or he felt nothing.

I tried to tell myself that fate could not possibly be so cruel for the latter to be the case, but still I wondered, and with each passing day my desire to find out for sure increased.

I ruminated long and hard as to how to do so, until finally I discovered a way.

Over the course of the next sleepless night I translated Tatyana's letter to Onegin into Ukrainian from Pushkin's novel in verse *Evgeny Onegin* — and decided to slip the missive into Tolya's jacket pocket.

The letter begins, "I love You — what more do You need?" and ends with "I'm stopping, it hurts to read it." Afterward I put in a little P.S. that told Tolya to put his response in the pocket of his jacket, which he would hang in the cloakroom on the second coat hook from the right in the third row of hooks and not request a rendezvous or ask anything else of me. I signed the letter "Mrs. X" and addressed it to "Mr. Y."

Several feverish days passed with my checking the cloakroom repeatedly and always expecting but never actually finding Tolya's jacket in the agreed-upon spot. A week passed, and then a second, and Tolya was still taking his jacket off the same as before. His pockets were empty. I had been concerned that Tolya had mixed up the instructions and put his response in his pocket, but hung the jacket up in its old place, so naturally I had to check.

So two feverish weeks passed, with me frantically searching my "mailbox" and the attendant in the cloakroom giving me funny looks all the while, no doubt elaborating their own theories as to my motivation for digging around in other people's pockets.

After two weeks I couldn't take it anymore and wrote Tolya another letter, in which I abstained from poetic expressions of my feelings and reported everything in my own words, trying to be as clear and straightforward as possible. I was aiming for maximum sincerity, not lose a sense of my own worth, so as to make the best possible impression on Tolya. My constructs ended up with the following results as the model: "Do not think ill of me, but I believe that with the reality of the corresponding situational context, the emotional coloring of our confidential conversation might acquire a positive impulse. Given my desire to preserve anonymity, I suggest starting with a virtual-verbal relationship with the intention of transitioning later into direct contact."

Once more I asked Tolya, or rather Mister Y, to hang his jacket with his response inside it on the second coat hook from the right in the third row of hooks and not ask anything else of me.

At that point he gave up, and for the next three months he couldn't even bring himself to wear a coat to school, despite the fact that it was winter.

This might have meant either that Tolya had misunderstood my letters and thought someone was playing some kind of trick on him, or that Tolya had understood perfectly and decided to play some kind of trick on me, thereby confirming my worst suspicions.

If the former, Tolya was a coward. If the latter, I had suffered a major defeat. The next night I wrote the last poem cycle on the subject of my love for Tolya, titled "You Don't Deserve Me," ceremonially burned a piece of paper with Tolya's name on it and swore to never again fall in love unless it was reciprocated, and for the rest of my days I would avenge the male race for my ravaged first emotional feelings. I entitled the poem commemorating this ritual "An Oath." It contained the exceptionally strong, as I saw it, lines:

> *Taking a solemn oath to forget them all*
> *I seal my lips, until into the grave I fall*

from A COLLECTION OF PASSIONS

Appendix i. Theoretical Issues

by Natalka Sniadanko

Translated by Liliya Valihun

So, dear reader, you have examined the collection of passions gathered by me. Some examples in the collection will definitely seem familiar or even banal to you, such as, for instance: "Ukrainian Passions" or "Russian Passions;" some others may seem unjustifiably exotic: "Italian passions," "German Passions," or, in particular, "Aristocratic Passions."

Try to be indulgent both in the first and second cases, and don't make strict demands regarding these jottings that you are holding in your hands. Because this is nothing like a treatise, an investigation, and definitely not a literary work.

This is a simple collection, in which things are preserved the way they are in reality; and the task of the collector is entirely not to embellish or to perfect examples, as writers or authors of memoirs do with their writings.

In no way does this collection pretend to be exhaustive or all-embracing either. It's good that I don't have to write passages entitled "Homosexual Passions," "Unrequited Passions" or, even worse, "Zoophilic Passions."

First of all, I would like to dwell on the purely philological aspect of the topic I've touched upon.

So, why exactly the word "passions?" Having lived to the mature for a young lady coming from a respectable Galician family age of twenty-five, and having not even started a family yet, much less talk about the birth of a child, I had to seriously think over the reasons and consequences of such a regrettable fact.

Then I arrived at the conclusion that one of the reasons often influencing the course of our lives in a fatal way is the incorrect use of words.

Let's at least take the word "love." Every time we experience a love adventure, and when we have mild or even intense excitement at meeting with a male or female representative of the opposite sex, we mentally ask ourselves: "Is it the one?"

And in most cases the answer is: "No." In those numerous cases, when even after asking yourself the same question for the twentieth time, your heart does not stop trembling frightfully, and you already are almost ready to say: "Oh!," The Highness of doubts descends on you, and you answer: "Do I know?..."

At any rate, this has happened to me. Maybe if at least one true love had happened among numerous passions, infatuations, or just fascinations on my life path, I'd long ago be bouncing babies on my knee instead of shuffling papers. But, maybe it would be valuable at least to name one of the passions "love;" but by naming it that, and believing in what has been said, then everything would be different. Indeed, "how weighty a single word is!"

Such situations, of course, could be avoided if we precisely understood what we expect when we use this or that word. Let us take, for instance, the words "love" and "passion." What is the difference between the two, and which word is stronger or more valued? For me, by all means, it is love. What do you think?

Just think a bit yourself. A normal person can't find anything attractive in such a terrible combination of letters: "pr" * — sounds as

---

* The author has in mind the Ukrainian word *prystrast'*, which means "passion" in English.

if someone has smashed your face; "st" — is as hard as a virgin's dream; and, as far as "str" is concerned, it is embarrassment to talk about it. Such a word can only be uttered from a throat that is going to be strangled in a minute, but not from a loving heart that is full of desire and adrenaline. It is totally opposite if we compare it with the sound of the word "love."*

It sounds soft, slow, songlike, tender. It sounds rounded like a young girl's breasts. Rapid like the thirsty switch of caresses. This is a word that you want to repeat, you want someone to repeat it for you, about you, or at least in your presence.

Whatever you say, the quality of the sound differs noticeably. And, besides, if you think it over carefully, the meaning of the word "passion" is fairly obscure. It is as if a man can't make out what's going on, or, to be more precise, who is with whom. He is "passionate," she is with him, and feelings, at least strong ones, are not applicable at all. In my opinion, there is a slight difference between whether a man is "passionate" or "passionless." It is a bad sign when a person wears feelings in his or her pocket, like a wallet, a pager, or a handkerchief. For me, there is little temperament in this.

The word "passion," of course, has melodious synonyms such as "thirst," for instance, or "infatuation." However, the synonyms exist to show the differences in meanings. It seems to me the feeling that we call passion, is insignificant, but all the same it differs from the feeling one has in mind under the word "desire," not even to speak of "infatuation." Also, feelings are issues that need precision.

That is, in particular, when one talks about their quantity. Just imagine that you have to use the word "thirst" in the plural. It doesn't work. It is even worse with the word "infatuation." The word does not care at all whether it is used in the plural or the singular. But I do care what exactly I discuss with you: about one infatuation, three or fifteen of them. And if you were my husband or at least my lover, I think you'd also ask about understanding the importance of this aspect of Ukrainian grammar.

---

* "Liubov" in Ukrainian.

If we assume that language directly influences reality, then we can explain many things. Perhaps the best example will be poetic texts because, as it is generally known, the most characteristic features of a national mentality are reflected in them. Imagine a nation where a poet, making his beloved woman a declaration of love, writes: "Do not look so affably" (Pavlo Tychyna) or "Do not caress me silkily" (Pavlo Tychyna). I don't even want to mention "To run away from you to the ends of the earth" (Lina Kostenko).

The related mentality of our "elder brother" Russia has something similar: "I don't regret, I don't call you, I don't cry" (Sergei Esenin).

These are from classic poets. It seems that in the process of evolution, feelings, or, to be more precise, the form of their expression in poetry had to be polished, become more tender, more delicate. But this is not the case with our happiness.

For instance, imagine the poetic image: "… did he want love that has not been touched and that flies above the outdoor market with snouts and carcasses" (Yuri Andrukhovych). Did you imagine that? Would you want to touch that love among the snouts?

Or another image. "I thrust a tulip spear into the young lady" (Viktor Neborak) — and this is written by a poet at the end of the XXth century, having told his trusting girl beforehand: "Not a breath or a word are between us," and then finished off with satisfaction: "And I will fall happy into the grass" (Viktor Neborak). Indeed, how little we sometimes need to be happy. Another poet needs even less:

> *Princess! Take your clothes off quicker!*
> *Princess! Get on the mattress quicker!*
> *Everything is good — let's go at it:*
> *Ersatz, ersatz, ersatz, ersatz.*

Yurko Pozayak

It's true, that not all poets nowadays are deprived of romanticism to such a degree. Some are still able to have certain features of lyricism present while describing, for instance, a first kiss:

When a half breath remains to reach your lips,
when a half step remains to reach your lips,
your eyes are full of wonder,
your eyes get blue and wider.

Hryhory Chubai

Beautiful? Don't get too mellow, everything ends not so sweetly for the girl: "I forget I know how to breathe, and I forget I know how to walk," the poet confesses to her, so do with him what you want. And what if it's already dark outside, it's far from home, and the trams aren't running that late? That's romanticism for you.

The situation is not much better if we try to define the importance of passion in the hierarchy of poetic values. Just think: "Somewhere at the bottom of my heart," one Ukrainian poet says (Pavlo Tychyna). It's already enough that it's at the bottom, but you don't know where, as if they're glasses that he put somewhere and can't find them.

Another poet wonders: "Whether he wanted a girl or her cake" (Yuri Andrukhovych). "I love you Hope," — a third poet (Vasyl Stus) starts his poem and ends it this way: "And still you don't listen to me, whore." Would you listen to him if you were addressed that way?

Sometimes there is doubt whether such man is "in" passion or already "beyond" passion. Especially when you speak about such immaterial matters as dreams. For instance, what should a woman think when at first she is addressed like this: "Why do you come to me during my dreams (Ivan Franko)?" It is as if she were to blame.

However, before you even get to the end, you suddenly get: "Come to me, my dear. At least in my dream…" (Ivan Franko). Go figure that out.

To make a long story short, Ukrainian poets don't deal very well with passions. Especially when a declaration of love is concerned. Without any complexes, Europeans already got rid of this problem in the past century. For example, already during the times of Heinrich Heine's blessed memory, German did not feel ashamed to look sentimental and say:

To the wondrous eyes of my dear love
I write beautiful canzoni
I write the best tercets
To the delicate lips of my dear love.

I don't even want to mention the French, who have long since been well known for their gallantry, or the Italians or the Spanish, famous for their temperament.

Ukrainians will at the best be able to utter: "I curse. I kiss. In silence" (Vasyl Stus).

Such a situation could not help but influence the feelings and the imagination of Ukrainian women. And especially their imagination regarding happiness. Let's take Egyptian women for example. Everything linked with their wishes and imagination has been very simple from time immemorial:

And if you snuggled up
To me closely
My heart would say
"I've found my beloved happiness!"

From Egyptian folk poetry*

This woman is unlikely to understand the Ukrainian poet, for whom: "To abandon everything, all things, to die with you,/That would be happiness (Lesya Ukrainka)."

Or would Egyptian women understand the woman for whom "… happiness is woven from partings (Lina Kostenko)?"

There, in Egypt, they don't even know about us or our Ukrainian men, they can't imagine our Ukrainian life and our Ukrainian problems.

If we carefully read through intimate female lyric poetry, in the Ukrainian ones we'll find the imprint of complicated and often almost incomprehensible contradictions that we have just outlined in the male

---

* From Egyptian folk poetry

world of poetry: "Forever mine!" — one woman states with pride.* "Even in memory I will not say — beloved" — another one** promises to herself. Guess which one is Ukrainian?

It is not hard to guess that in such a manner of expressing feelings, fear is far from last place "among passions" in Ukrainian poetry: "If we were to meet again, Would you be afraid?" (Vasyl Stus)?" One Ukrainian poet asks.

"We will meet. We will be enemies. I have already prepared my sword for you" (Lina Kostenko), the Ukrainian woman poet answers.

We need to acknowledge that there is nothing to choose between them.

The Ukrainian woman is as unpredictable as Ukrainian passion. Therefore, there is no need to have stereotypical imagination about her such as this: "...you will come to me alone, frightened and sad, robbed in all 160 centimeters in your height..." (Lina Kostenko).

You can, of course, make Ukrainian woman show her weakness at some moment and make her confess: "... I've really suffered over you" (Lina Kostenko).

Or you can even find her at a moment of confusion: "... And how should I forget you now (Lina Kostenko)?"

But don't think, though, that this lasts for long. The moment of weakness will pass, and you will definitely hear something like this: "I don't like unhappy people. I'm happy. My freedom is always with me (Lina Kostenko)."

And just try to deny that. Or rather, don't even try to risk it. All the more, in written form. So that you're not answered with the famous quotation from school, which will destroy all the remnants of your masculine dignity: "Your letters always have the fine scent of faded roses, you, my poor man, faded flower (Lesya Ukrainka)!"

On the other hand, what should one expect from life, or to be more precise, what should a Ukrainian woman expect from a man, a woman

---

* Emily Dickenson

** Lina Kostenko

who has grown up in Ukrainian realia, and in the best traditions of the Ukrainian mentality not adapted to these realia; moreover, a woman who has been brought up on Ukrainian lyric poetry that is uttered from a male perspective: "The smile of love flowers once — but it wilts (Pavlo Tychyna)." The vast majority of women poets just are in despair. One even requests:

> *Bury me under a maple tree,*
> *One whose branches catch the rain*
> *Like my eyes he is green,** *
> *And in love with you too.*

Maryana Savka**

However, not everyone is full of such pessimism, thus in their disappointment one can find a way out of a situation that has happened:

> *I love you I wait for you always*
> *I've looked for you (for a long time!)*
> > *in the eyes of train stations*
> *I have not found you I kiss your footsteps*
> *But forgive me I have to run away further.*

Marianna Kiyanovska

Despite despair, some manage to find a way out, or rather the direction of a way out:

> *She will always stay at the Dominican school near Vienna*
> *Pray only in Ukrainian, to the nuns' surprise,*
> *After evening vespers write letters to relatives sometimes,*
> *Asking about their health and if their gardens are yielding.*

Halyna Petrosanyak

---

* Ukrainian words have grammatical gender, so the maple tree (klen) is masculine.

** Maryana Savka

But don't think that I'm giving all these examples in order to justify myself. Because other Galician young ladies do manage to live somehow, and even the women poets among them get married, give birth to children, although it's true after that none of them for some reason write poems anymore about the way they live. No matter.

While contemplating this way, I came to the conclusion that I'm not alone in my doubts about finding the difference between the words "love" and "passion," and also to the conclusion that my doubts have foundations; and after all, I came to the conclusion that we so often get mixed up when we take passion for love and love at face-value... However, someone seems to have already said this.

I've gotten carried away. It's time to peruse the next appendix.

from AN HERBARIUM FOR LOVERS

THE DIARIES OF AUNT AMALIA

by Natalka Sniadanko

Translated by Michael M. Naydan

IN HER DIARIES AUNT AMALIA JOTTED DOWN VARIOUS THINGS. SHE started the first notebook when she was a young teenage girl, because back then every girl from a respectable family had an album and a secret diary. But Aunt Amalia didn't want to write various kinds of silliness in the coarse folio that had perfumed pages and was tied with pink ribbons. From childhood she was neither sentimental, nor exaltedly romantic, and had no hang-ups over it, though such features contradicted the notions back then about the ideal disposition of girls.

So in her diaries, for which she always chose coarse notebooks with black covers, she would write, for example, the following;

This morning, before everyone woke up, I went outside to gather green walnuts. It's important to get them before they ripen and fall on their own, because from the fallen ones only some of them will turn out just right for you. Every fall you need to eat twenty green walnuts every day, and it's best in the morning when no one can see your hands tear them off the tree. Then a bitter scent comes from your fingers all day, and you want to eat even more; it's hard to stop, and every day your heart wrenches in fright when you clean the first walnut; you're fearful that morning that when you feel the shell's skin, it will harden and soon won't be as easy to separate, and the walnuts will turn bitter and loose their sweet-tasting semi-transparency, which is characteristic for them at first. You feel so irked and bitter from the fact that it's as if these are your years passing and just as quickly, drying you from the inside, and then from the outside; your soul is being covered all around with a hard and dry shell; you're being pinched and it gives you no peace. Every day twenty green walnuts. In the morning and the evening, so that no one sees you as your hands tear them off.

I thought a lot today about the fact that it's hard to form compassion inside you for people, who are physically imperfect. That is, not the kind of superficial compassion regarding the human eye that the rules of decency require, but truly to overcome it inside you right away for a person, who at least in the smallest feature differs from the norm. I long ago conquered in myself the sensitiveness that once constantly sparkled in me. I just recently sensed someone change their attitude toward me when they found out I had just one breast. I grew up that way since I was little, the doctors couldn't find anything abnormal about it, and my father would joke that I'm a true Amazon woman. He even liked that. But, it seemed, no man did afterward, though none of them openly admitted it. At first I was surprised at their horrified looks each time when they found out about my defect and suddenly couldn't feel anything for me that men feel for a woman. Their desire turned into fear. Maybe because my defect was so unusual. If I had had my breast surgically removed or if one leg were shorter than the other, then they wouldn't desire me like a man, but they'd feel sorry, they'd try to do something good. But the fact that I have this imperfection by nature, it just paralyzed them; and they were afraid of me, the way they incomprehensibly were afraid of someone stronger or more powerful than they were. Men aren't capable of tolerating a woman's strength. Even if that strength is expressed no more than by the absence of a single breast. But then, likewise, fear unexpectedly grows into interest, and I have already seen them like the same thing that frightened them. They want to touch the missing breast, and for them their breathing stops, it's so horrifying but interesting for them to try what it would be like with a woman who isn't like others.

A bit more about compassion. I don't know if I can maintain control myself when I see external deformity openly. I know just that I try to convince myself that it's all unimportant, that a person is guiltless in that, but somewhere in the depths of my mind, I understand that aversion, unwillingness, along with worthless and abhorrent feelings don't force me to help a misshapen beggar or give him some kopecks. Can't you overcome that instinct with common sense? We value a person and treat them, looking at their appearance. Especially women. That, from one side, gives women power, because an attractive woman can induce a man in love with her to do incredible things. But more so, this is unjust, because it chooses for us, human creatures, the right to consider ourselves more perfect and higher than animals. Because what kind of loftiness can you speak of when we listen just to our instincts, blind and uncontrolled. Just the random bad spirit coming out of our lips can ruin our sympathy to someone worthy and important, who on more than one occasion has demonstrated their devotion to us. And let even this attitude change in just an instant, then we are sorry about that, but that moment is worthwhile.

Young apples and gooseberries. I like just the green ones. It's hard to stop when you begin to eat them and sense a tart and fresh taste, hidden bitterness in them somewhere at the very bottom, as though it were just at the first moment when it singes you and pushes you away, but it's worth suffering through it, and in a minute that same water externally and from inside you burns, gives strength and elasticity to your skin, and you want to swim and not stop, not interrupt that blessed energetic state. But just as quickly this comes to an end, a bitter taste in your mouth falls over you from the apples and gooseberries, and the cold water again is felt, and cramps grab your legs, and it become dangerous, and you again have to return to measured and boring tastes and sensations, as though you're sharply waking up from a pleasant dream about green meadows and fairytale palaces, and around yourself you see just tattered old wallpaper, and through the window the autumn gloom and mud, endless Galician mud.

Little was known about Aunt Amalia. More precisely, nearly everything was known, but only what concerned her external side and life — what she wore, what she did, where and with whom she spent her life.

However, the most interesting thing from her unusual biography was — her thoughts, the formation of her outlook and her beliefs, the changes that happened in her views, dreams, her life aspirations and random reflections, as well as the strange ups and downs of her mood, moments when she stood stock still and for several minutes stopped listening and seeing anything around her. All this remained outside the frame, fixed in a strange, not overly detailed way, just in her diaries.

Orest found those diaries, most probably, not all of them, but just several in the attic of their house in childhood. Then his mother told him that her aunt Amalia was the stepsister of his mother. Still in childhood she was different from other girls, strange and a bit of an outcast. Then, when she had grown up, she became really beautiful, with a tight black braid and penetratingly blue eyes under dark, thick lashes. In the winter her eyes grew darker, acquiring the shade of black walnut, and in the summer they again became penetratingly blue. Father didn't love Amalia much, but, as strange as it was, her stepmother did love the half-orphan. Some even thought that it seemed her stepmother loved Amalia more than her own daughter. For some reason everyone was convinced that despite her extraordinary beauty, Amalia would never get married. They began calling her aunt long before Orest's mother was born, for whom she became an aunt. And it's true, Amalia didn't get married. The look of her penetrating eyes, capable of changing their color from brown to blue, frightened away potential fiancés. And in the case of someone not frightened and bold enough to court her, she rejected them herself. Their family was prosperous, her father had a small paper factory, famed for its special, elegant kinds of paper for letter writing and painting, the unique shape of their envelopes, seals to order, expensive greeting cards to order, and other aristocratic accessories, without which in that epistolary era not a single literate city dweller could get by. This small paper factory, which was passed along to Amalia's father as an inheritance from his own father, was really well renowned not just in the area, but far beyond its borders.

Amalia could make a living just from the tourists who bought office supplies from her factory as souvenirs of Galicia and travelled specially there, to look at how they made the famous office accessories up close. The fact of the need for a several-hour trip through the usual for those areas lack of roads failed to stop them, nor the fact that there were no tours of the factory, and, if they happened to get inside, they had to ask personal permission from Amalia's father as well as hers. And far from everyone received that permission. Maybe, it was just that selectiveness, the exclusivity that accompanied the possibility of getting into the grounds of the factory that attracted the majority of the visitors, who hardly would have ridden there if showings of the factory had been generally accessible.

Amalia received a decent home education, and then spent several years abroad, attending lectures at various European universities. On returning home, she became the lover of one of the neighboring landowners. More accurately, she made him her lover, choosing him from among many others, who, in the opinion of Orest's mother, were considerably more worthy. With her lover she started to publish a literary magazine. That kind of thing was in vogue among the landowning intelligentsia of the time. For the magazine aunt Amalia translated poems and prose from books imported from abroad. She translated from French, English and German, of which she had a perfect command. The magazine was called The Galician Woman and became popular in the circles of the reading public. They say, it was as if Olha Kobylianska, with whom Aunt Amalia sometimes corresponded, wrote the articles for it herself.

Aunt Amalia's circle of interest was considerably wider than just literature, music and painting. She was actively interested in politics and boldly expressed her Ukrainophile views, which were dangerous at the time of Polish control over the area.

At the moment when Galicia was beginning to form the first cells of the Sich Riflemen, in the village where Aunt Amalia lived, a cell was formed. Its members called it a "sports club," not overtly publicizing the true aim of their meetings. In the years of World War I Aunt

Amalia gathered her "sports club" and announced that all its mindful members should sign up as volunteers for the army, because this war was the opportunity for Galicia and for all of Ukraine to finally acquire its independence. Her speech turned out to be sufficiently convincing for many. Aunt Amalia signed up for the infantry herself. The Vienna newspapers often would write enthusiastic reports about a courageous Galician woman who was famed for her feats. In time word of Aunt Amalia's military feats spread throughout all of Europe. After being captured by the Russians, she returned home through Finland, Sweden, Norway, and everywhere at the train stations through which the train with former prisoners of war rode, lines of young junior nurses and ordinary women queued up there, who dreamt of getting an autograph or at least of taking a look at the famous Ukrainian woman from close up. Mother told Orest that Aunt Amalia's fame was even greater than that of Olena Stepanivna. But, returning from the war, Aunt Amalia declined any further political or even scholarly activity, so she was quickly forgotten. After the taking of Galicia by the Soviets, Amalia emigrated to France, where she lived to the end of her days.

Mother related to Orest how one time at the beginning of Aunt Amalia's military activity, once Marshal Pilsudsky came to a meeting of the sports club. Back then he wasn't a marshal yet, or the leader of the country, and tried to agitate the Ukrainians to rise up against Russia with the Poles. His brilliant oratorical facts enthralled those present, and his arguments and aim seemed to be correct and transparent, until Aunt Amalia entered the discussion. With several convincing phrases she brought to naught all of Pilsudsky's efforts, demonstrating that the joint aim of the Ukrainians and Poles no less convincingly led to the fact that despite a common enemy — Russia, the Ukrainians and Poles can't be collaborators in the battle because the goal of Ukrainians was independence, and for the Poles — it was about the Ukrainians becoming a part of the Polish state. So there was nothing to speak about any common interests. And although Pilsudsky tried to convince those present that he, as a representative of Polish socialists, didn't support conservative parties, who in truth dream about the inclusion of Ukrainian lands as part of Poland, Aunt Amalia didn't believe in the veracity of those assurances. And, as the future showed, she was correct. After several years, when Pilsudsky began the pacification of the Galician lands, many people recalled Aunt Amalia's foresight.

After her return from being a prisoner, Aunt Amalia to everyone's surprise got interested in fashion.

"I can't calmly sit and see those hideous tortures that women subject themselves to in their awful clothing," she wrote in her diary, "corsets, that are worse than a torturer's wrack, giant monstrous hats, that you need at least two heads to carry, ribbons, lace and countless underskirts and underwear. In all this it's not just impossible to move, it's impossible to even think for a minute about anything else, because you have to not lose your guard and keep after whether all the details of your dress are in order; in that kind of outfit it seems you can barely breathe. Pure adventure!

Aunt Amalia's fashion style was just as fundamental as all her other views and tastes. First and foremost, she threw away and distributed all her corsets, then dresses, and from then on, at all the parties and gatherings she appeared just in comfortable clothing in a man's cut, which she designed independently and under which she demonstratively didn't wear a corset. In that kind of dress she loved to go to the famous Lviv coffee shop the European Cafe, where mostly men used to go. This double challenge so shocked the customers as well as the staff of the coffee shop, that it evoked just numbness and stupor. No one was emboldened to react, to openly attack Aunt Amalia, just at times someone from among the important male customers would abruptly stand up and boisterously exit the coffee shop, in this way demonstrating their protest against the impudent breaking of the precepts of fashion. In the coffee shops for women, especially in the one called Shtuka (Thing), that was in the Andriolli Arcade, where Aunt Amalia also loved to go in her provocative dress, it was even more stormy. Women began to whisper to each other excitedly, cast horrified and at the same time curious glances at Aunt Amalia, and for a long time afterward discussed every detail of her outfit. Persistence is most important in such affairs, slowly the stormy reaction and shock grew into habit, and they stopped reacting to Aunt Amalia so boisterously, and the inevitable happened — after a certain amount of time her manner of dress became popular and gradually more and more the fashionable women of Lviv started to wear outfits cut in the style of men's suits, and later — for the theater and for everyday strolling through the city. One Lviv newspaper of the time wrote:

THE PROBLEM OF UNDERGARMENTS

At women's meetings, in private conversations, in articles in the press and in the expressions of individual persons, for the umpteenth time the problem of lacing and corsets emerges. Truly a revolutionary spirit in recent times has seized the thinking of certain ladies, and not just in Vienna, but in Galicia. Our correspondent just recently met an attractive young Rusyn woman in the European Café in men's clothing and without a corset. Even recently this would have given rise to a scandal, but our correspondent hadn't noticed any stormy reaction from among the customers, and it's well known that mostly men go to this coffee shop.

In time Aunt Amalia cut off her thick braid, exchanging it for a comfortable short haircut. This time people surrounding her were upset with her fundamentality for quite a long time. At first the priest tried to speak with her and convince her not to ruin her soul with such willfulness in her dress, later her friends and acquaintances tried to carefully talk to her, then more friends and acquaintances, but Amalia didn't listen to anyone. Little by little everyone got used to her appearance, and some particularly bold ones even tried to copy her other innovations and also chose a comfortable men's and not a woman's pose for riding horses.

from DANCES WITH MASKS

by Larysa Denysenko
Translated by Yuri Tkacz

AND OFF SHE WENT. TO THAT RATTY CENTER WHERE THE language classes were held. Everyone here forever keeps bowing before you. My God, if you lived here long enough, you'd begin to feel like a Russian tsar who has arrived in Persia on a visit that is vitally important to the interests of the Persian empire. If you have low self-esteem, just come to Korea, or if you are drop-dead gorgeous, or cross-eyed, or just a complete idiot — everyone will continue to bow to you. Because this is part of their culture. Culture is something more sacred than a gambling debt! Koreans are people who are very knowledgeable about cultural traditions, and not only that.

They assembled quite a class. We have two teachers who keep sub-stituting for each another. One teaches pronunciation and the drawing of hieroglyphs, or, to put it more aptly, sketching, or maybe writing. The other one, an old grandpa with a face like a peach stone, teaches the same thing, but according to his own methodology. The grandpa continually raves about himself, but in an interesting sort of way; he leaves the talk shows behind. Maybe he rattles on because, according to his own words, he was a mute up until the age of fifty. He's a legend. He tells one hell of a story. Mei is the other teacher. She constantly scrutinizes me, like Kozetta eyeing a doll in a shop window. She tells me that the old man has made up the story. But it's a lyrical, epic and heroic tale. This is the way it goes.

Up until he was fifty, the old man was blind and a mute. Both simultaneously. That's one thing. Secondly, the old man says that he is an extraordinary person, and is convinced that the Earth has yet to give birth to a person like him and never will. Who would have thought I would come across something like this in South Korea. The old man teaches Korean just because he likes to mix with foreigners, but otherwise he is a millionaire and could easily live an idle existence, just spitting at the ceiling from time to time, although I guess this pastime would probably seem rather boring to him. He is more than eighty years old. Thirdly, when he was fourteen, he found himself in the midst of the Great Patriotic War — that is World War II, where he became commander-in-chief of who knows what (none of us managed to get out of him of what he was commander-in-chief), and then the British captured him, and he spent over three years as a prisoner-of-war in the suburbs of London. A mute and blind underage commander-in-chief held as a prisoner-of-war in the suburbs of London — not bad, eh? I'm just generalizing here, so that I don't lose it completely, because there's more.

One day the Queen herself takes pity on him. Because she's a very compassionate woman, and he's a handsome young man with smooth skin and all that. Besides, at that time it was fashionable among the English aristocracy to help cripples and prisoners-of-war. Of all the cripples being held prisoner, the Queen happens to select the most handsome and the youngest among them, that is, the Old Man. The Queen took it upon herself to take him away to Windsor and sets about educating him. And it appears there's quite a lot of work to be done in that area. She teaches him good manners and courtesy: how to walk, sit down and get up. She teaches him everything that she knows. Thanks to her royal preoccupation with him, he immediately begins to speak English, and frightens the hell out of all the royal horses, which he's been tending, for they had grown used to munching on their prime quality oats without a single voice distracting them.

The queen really fell for her handsome little servant. Especially since he had extraordinary abilities. For example, when there was no electricity, he could iron the royal dresses, tablecloths and suits with his hands (his palms had strong energy powers), so that even the most critical eye could not find a single tiny crinkle. The Old Man's abilities greatly facilitated the day-to-day life of the royal family. But the Queen was exceptional — she had an innate magnanimity and therefore understood that, although a human iron was very useful to have in a household, he was all the same a person and probably yearned to return home. Therefore, having probably wept all night on the shoulders of some major-domo, the queen decided to act humanely and to allow the Old Man to return home with honors and presents. In her farewell speech to the Old Man, the Queen declared that he would always be a welcome guest in their household, for he was almost as dear as a relative.

Having returned to South Korea, the Old Man swore an oath that he would achieve success and return to the Queen on a white stallion. Soon after, he became a millionaire, an expert at raising small domestic fowl (he preferred chickens) and travelled the length and breadth of Western Europe and North America, explaining to the narrow-minded European and American farmers how to achieve phenomenal results in fattening up bird carcasses, and eventually how to squeeze everything out of the corpses of the unfortunate birds for the benefit of an insatiable mankind. Obviously, he itched to drop by the Royal Palace, but he kept putting this off, until one day Princess Diana appeared in his dreams and in a firm tone of voice, coupled with her unguarded snow-white smile, ordered the Old Man to come to the royal household.

After the dream, the Old Man realized his new calling: he had been born to become the guardian angel of the entire British royal family, and especially needed to stand guard over the vital interests of that tender creature — Princess Diana, who, in his view, was created by the Lord God as the ideal woman. He was received with pleasure in the palace (and why not, the Queen's pet had returned, and not as some beggar, but as a real-life millionaire, that is, not the kind of person who constantly tries to sponge off the royal household, consuming innumerable quantities of royal cakes, jars of jam and glasses of milk served at breakfast, but someone who can himself put on a spread, which was very heartening for the modern-day monarchs, who were constantly trying to curtail their expenditures and who were being disenfranchised of their real estate holdings. He was a revered guest and sat for hours with the Princess, who complained about her life and moaned about the actions of Prince Charles, who had dared to betray her with "that terrible red-haired woman."

After that first visit, the chicken millionaire, the former mute and blind commander-in-chief, a diminutive disabled human iron in the court of her monarchic highness the Queen of Britain, attempted to make his way to the capital of the United British Kingdom once a year, so as not to leave Princess Di alone with her sad thoughts, and to entertain her a little, and bring some joy to her heart. He placated the princess with his love, so that when he dreamt about her impending death, he immediately telephoned her and implored her not go anywhere and not to meet anyone, but to wait obediently for his arrival.

However, the special services turned out to be far more fleet-footed than the Old Man, for no sooner had he got on board his private jet, than he learned that the princess had already died in an accident with the man she had fallen in love with, and in one of the most romantic cities in the world; and the paparazzi were accused of causing her death. Obviously, the special services had nothing to do with this. "And I expect she died a happy woman. That is, I know that for a fact. Because she told me so herself, when she visited me in a dream." At this point, the Old Man let slip such a sincere and filigree tear, that it would have made the eminent Russian theater director Stanislavsky bite his tongue.

The Old Man felt he had to do something for the princess. He felt a pressing need to do something. And so that very first night he visited the English composer Elton John and said to him: "Elton, dear, you have to dedicate the song 'Goodbye, English Rose' to Princess Di." Elton couldn't refuse the instructions of the majestic Old Man, for he was a mystical person himself, and he perceived the appearance of the cheeky old Korean in his dreams as a sign of fate. "It's just as well, the old man didn't order Elton John to screw the notorious Prince Charles to avenge Di's messed-up life," chuckled David, one of our students, while the Old Man sang us Elton's uplifting and sad song.

That's the kind of teacher he was. Obviously, compared to him, Mei looked like a sheet of white paper alongside a painting by the famous Russian artist Ilya Glazunov,* who condensed heaps of faces on a single canvas. Besides, Mei was a classic bore, people like her wanted everything to be prim and proper. A proper family, a proper life. In their proper understanding of it.

---

* Russian artist born in 1930. He is best known for his painting to mark the millennium of Christianity in Russia in 1988 "Eternal Russia." *http://orvarvara.files. wordpress.com/2008/11/ilya-glazunov-eternal-russia-1988.jpg*

from THE SARABANDE OF SARA'S BAND

by Larysa Denysenko

*Translated by Michael M. Naydan
and Svitlana Bednazh*

CHAPTER I

*At the Very Least about a Perfect Morning, Imperfect Marriages,
Former Classmates, and a Family Crypt*

WHEN I LOOK AT MY COFFEE MAKER IN THE MORNING, IT SEEMS like I'm an oil tycoon. There it is — my black gold, at first slowly, and then very quickly, it fills the glass pot. It would be interesting to know if the freshly baked tycoons taste their oil? Or whether it tastes good for them if you weigh its value? It tastes good to me.

Every morning I do things precisely this way. At first I breathe in the coffee aroma, then I take my first sip and place the cup on the table. I open up the immense window that goes from the floor to the ceiling a little bit, I light up a cigarette, and then I return to the coffee. It's not as hot. Only after that can I make myself a few bite-size sandwiches. When my morning starts in a different way that means just one thing: I have serious life changes going on or problems.

I spend about an hour in my kitchen every morning, sometimes even more. At that time I manage to drink up several cups of coffee, read the newspaper or a chapter of a book, drink a glass of juice, if I haven't forgotten to buy it, eat several bite-size cheese sandwiches, and if I have inspiration — make and eat an omelet.

I often turn on the television with the intention of hearing something interesting or useful, but something like that happens quite rarely. That is, I turn on the TV nearly every morning, but I heard something interesting or useful just three months ago — that was marked on a sticky on my refrigerator. I note everything that strikes me. That day on the morning news they were talking about people feeding a small whale. I like whales. I like them so much that I'm sure I wouldn't be opposed to keeping a small whale at home, but in as much as that's impossible, I don't have any pets at home. It's likely I like them so much because they're like fountains, and I really like fountains. Once I even used to collect pictures of them, but then something happened and I stopped collecting them.

My kitchen isn't a kitchen — that's what my mother thinks, taking into consideration the kitchen of that apartment, in which my childhood flashed past and in which right now the old age of my parents live. In my kitchen you can easily have a party for ten people, it's a large dining area. Besides the usual kitchen furniture, there's a couch here, two comfortable wide armchairs, a table, and even an old German upright "R. Yors & Kallmann" piano. It's black, shiny, and adorned with two candelabras.

It reminds me of a family crypt. You get the impression that his honor Judge R. Yors and the well-known author of the operetta Kallmann found their eternal repose right here.

On this crypt there is even a family coat of arms, which looks like: an elephant, an Indian Raja gazing at the sky, a UFO, or a Soviet satellite. The upright piano is an inheritance of my former wife. Neither I nor she knows how to play it. Usually, one of our mutual friends played it (most often a canine waltz). But nearly everyone still argued over why this upright piano had a third pedal. I never took part in these arguments, in as much as I didn't know why the piano had a first or second pedal, not to speak already about the third one.

My wife's father, in fact, handed down this piano to me personally. He used to treat my wife less carefully, perhaps because she was younger than the piano and not as expensive. When we got divorced, my wife asked if I wouldn't object to the piano for the time being staying at my place. I categorically objected, but it remained here anyway. My wife was a lawyer, and as it's well known, it's impossible to frighten lawyers with objections.

I just had turned twenty-one when we got married. My wife and I were the same age and former classmates. Between the time that you're sitting at the same desk, and the time you fall asleep in the same bed, it's not a big difference. That's how it seemed to me. I think I simply just didn't really think about it, but gave preference to a person, whose hand I felt warmly all ten years of school. Physical warmth is closer for a child than the spiritual. The need for the spiritual is formed later.

In school I was a cleverer student than she. I can't name a subject I couldn't handle. She was a satisfactory student, but she was very active. Already in the seventh grade they entrusted her to be in charge of the lessons on peaceful Soviet society,* to participate in all the school and extracurricular representative activities, and to be the taskmaster for the others. I see her on stage — purposeful, sure of herself, a blonde with smoothly coiffed hair, not a kilo of excess weight, and without any hesitation. A straight, gray skirt, a cream-colored blouse, skin-colored tights, black pumps, fresh water pearls on her neck.

It's interesting that even back in school I understood that Inna, that's her name, could completely be the helmsman of my life. The question of choice for me has always been the most complicated. I couldn't calmly decide even simple things — I wavered, exhausted myself with doubts. I often fell asleep and woke up with one and the same brain signal, from which my stomach, hands and eyes became moist: "And if suddenly nothing turns out?" Inna knew what needed to be done and in which order. To every one of my questions "And if suddenly nothing turns out?", she answered so sincerely, "Why shouldn't it?" that I calmed down instantly. With her knack, she even charmed my parents, who are quite solitary and childish people.

---

* These were propaganda lessons conducted on September 1 on the first day of the school term about the "peace-loving democratic peoples of the USSR" vs. the bourgeois decadent warmongering west.

Of course, after completing school, my life without Inna began. Not because I wished for that. It's just that she was no longer sitting next to me. She went to study law, and I — geography — at the university. It turned out that we ended up waking up in the same bed — she wanted that. But this differed little from the process of copying homework. The same kind of help at school. I — would give, and she — accepted, as was fitting. Later one of my friends would say, that in this way "your typical women's psychology was formed." However, then it seemed to me that my post-school life was without Inna. In truth, all my important life situations were not resolved without consultations with her. But somehow she asked, why don't we get married, since we understand one another so well and have been with each other for so long? I accepted this question of hers as an inevitable decision.

Our marriage was childless. Inna wanted one, but just couldn't get pregnant. Before we received the results of tests, she blamed me for everything. "Active spermatozoa rush to meet ovules, like joyous dogs that flap their tails! But your spermatozoa are somnambulist dogs, who don't flap their tails, they're ill."

After this observation of hers, for a long time I couldn't come. I couldn't externally release an insatiable flock of feeble dogs. Then it turned out it was not me who was at fault for us being childless. This certainly became the beginning of the extinction of our marriage. She wasn't able to forgive me for my joyous dogs that flap their tails.

"You would have gotten divorced anyway, because you finally began to long for independence," one of my friends said. He was right. I became a successful correspondent and analyst. Then I was working for a well-known travel agency. I prepared materials for their site, pamphlets, analytical notes regarding places for vacations and active tourism. All the leading publications that needed articles on travel trips, the customs of faraway lands, and the behavior of animals, began to publish me. I was able to write about all of that brilliantly.

Despite my school and university successes, which did not augment any of my confidence, my career and creative victories added a certain unknown ingredient to my dough. A different person began to be kneaded out of me. Unaware of this myself, I learned to make decisions. I sold my one-room apartment in the center of town that I had received from my grandmother, took out credit, and acquired a contemporary three-room apartment. With this, certainly, I really surprised Inna's father. He looked at me as though I were Achilles, who had made a shield and a sword from his heel, or stepped on the throat of my enemy with it. This irritated Inna. Probably, this is the way a person feels, who, her entire life, has driven a horse, until later a lord jumps out of the carriage, who has been pampering himself on pillows, and takes the reins in his hands. Such treachery! I understood everything, but I couldn't do anything — her persistent activity and excessive pressure also began to irritate me. "Weigh the fact that the double letters of a name add a sense of purpose from birth to a person. This is like the pecking of a beak — until it nails the unfortunate bug, it will keep pecking. You had very few chances for success with her." That's what my friend Tymofiy said about Inna. He wasn't a psychologist, but always expressed himself with a knowledge of the matter.

Seven years of marriage. I can't believe we lived so many years together. How many times I said "hello" to her, how many times she wished me good night, and how many times there was "thank you, please, I don't understand you, sorry, I also had that in mind, stop that, wait, that's disgusting, don't get worked up over such little things, where's my charger, what should I do with this, that's not my fault, and who's supposed to take care of this, for the third day we don't have freshener in the bathroom, shut your beak, where are we going on vacation, who's going to finish the borsht, did you invite Tanya, it's your fault for everything, and I warned you, you should have listened to your parents, why did you need that, you'll never understand this, you're at home, tea or coffee, an omelet or salad" — thousands, tens of thousands, or maybe hundreds? And how many kisses there were, spermatozoa — those that flapped their tails and those that didn't? How many vowels and consonants of our married interactions? Thousands! But we weren't there. Maybe, because, we had never lived together. It's painful to part at the time when "she" and "you" have managed to turn into "we," at least in part. That was not our case. It seemed to me that our marriage — was "she." When "I" was born, just like for any child growing up, I wanted independence. And I got it. Right now I'm thirty-two. I got used to living like "me," and I really liked that — living like "me!" Despite that, from time to time in my life a "she" appeared, but my life hasn't turned into a "we."

I went to the wardrobe, opened it, and for a long time looked at a sundress. I grabbed the hem of it and put it next to my face. A piece of tiny-petaled azure silk. This was Sara. Sara was in the kitchen. In the kitchen she was a teacup with the image of a rainbow on it, and also with four brown coffee cups, an orange plate with claret red chrysanthemums, and an open bottle of Martini & Rossi. There she was a ceramic tray with dry fruits. There she was a carton of milk and a box of "Start" oat and fruit cereal. Sara smiled while I was champing on the "Start," like pastry, washing it down with coffee. She never did it that way.

Sara was in the bathroom. There she was a means for caring for curly hair. A toothbrush. Almond oil. A comb and a hair dryer. I opened up the almond oil, sullied my nose with it, began to smile. That is the scent of my happiness now. In my bedroom Sara was a silk nightshirt, left on a chair by the bed; a silver frame with a family picture on the windowsill in the accompaniment of azaleas, similar to a medley of southern American girls in multi-colored hats; a straw basket, where from now on, my and her clean socks lived, our running shorts, her stockings, her nylon underwear; a thin hair band with small gold stones, which turned Sara into an Eastern princess, and which today like a golden-toothed smile lay on a bedside table. Sara's heart lived in my stomach, I sensed it every moment.

When I caught sight of Sara (and this happened during a group tour of travel agency managers and travel writers to Prague), I didn't recognize her. It's true, I haven't at all managed to think anything about a slender woman with beautiful hair and a splendid bust, but here Sara Polonska recognized me. "Hi, Underbutt," she greeted me. And she laughed her awful laugh. "I never thought I'd be meeting you at nearly all the geo-tour sites. You spoiled, delicate butt, you've somehow managed to sit down on several chairs! Hi, old man, how long since we've seen each other!?"

Just the word "Underbutt" helped me figure out who this stranger was. Because only one insidious being ever called me "Underbutt" — Sara Polonska, my former classmate. Fat, curly-haired Sara, who looked like a dirty, disheveled ewe. And she called me that because during our studies at the university I used to swim and often tucked a towel under my rear end during class. I was thin, and it was more comfortable for me that way: it's painful to have bones leaning propped against the wood, if, of course they're living bones. Sara, who sat next to me on the left across from the aisle, was the first to notice my habit. She took an interest, what I was stuffing in there? I don't know why I told the truth back then. After that I became several nicknames richer: "spoiled butt, "Underbutt," and "not-on-that-towel."

I couldn't stand Sara Polonska. Even in the pre-Underbutt period she used to annoy me. That happened to me from time to time. For example, I hated my mother's curling iron. Two times I even tried to get rid of it. Even though I didn't use it and should have been indifferent to it or at least more tolerant. But — no. I wanted it to disappear, my mood was ruined each time I saw it in the bathroom where it hung on a common wire hook. One time I said to the curling iron: "I'll fix you, you devil's plague." I remember that till this day.

I didn't use Sara Polonska either, but I wanted her to disappear. Those eternal wide velvet slacks of hers. Always brightly colored, from which her rump seemed even bigger. And those shaggy strands. Her wide face, and on it a small nose, as though she had stolen it from someone. Her eyelashes were so thick, as though someone had cut paper to make a beard for a paper man. Add to that she was extremely stacked. One time in the women's bathroom she tried to put two glasses of water on her breasts and hold them up, but they spilled. Ha-ha-ha! In school I was also interested in knowing if you can hold up a cup on your erect member. But I didn't actually try to check if that were possible, till now I don't know if you can or can't. Let someone else do that. If Polonska had been a guy, maybe she would have checked it out then. It seemed, a grown-up woman, almost a qualified professional, but a dipshit is still a dipshit.

I personally was convinced that this was just an unsuccessful attempt, because Sara Polonska with her huge breasts could hold up two glasses of water on each one, and on her butt she'd be able to balance a two-liter jug. I still remember her black coat-mantle. We called it "the bat." Under that coat you could easily hide about ten or so Chinese from the firm arm of the law. Add to that the fact that she laughed so harshly, that it seemed like she would squash you with that laugh, the way a boot crushes a worm in the rain. And at one party, celebrating the Day of the Department, I saw Sara Polonska puke out bits of pizza and salad at her feet, after which she calmly continued to dance in that puke. Just as I became conscious of what was flying out from under her energetic, powerful feet, I ran to the bathroom to do what she had done, without interrupting the dancing.

And I still remember that she was married, and her husband was a military guy. I recall one time he was waiting for her by the university — a harsh figure in a uniform next to a red-colored Moskvich car. Maybe, because of the color of his car and the uniform, we called him "Fireman." In general I remembered quite a lot about that Sara Polonska.

From that Sara Polonska the Sara of today took just her bust (this time it didn't frighten me with its expressiveness and size, and quite the opposite, drew my gaze) and her manner of laughing, but right now it seemed to me, as though with that harsh laugh, not a boot worm-crusher, but a friend with a gift in her arms was approaching me. In general I've never liked it when someone constantly and harshly laughs, and Sara Polonska was doing it just like that. She was laughing. For me a laugh meant clinical idiocy or derision, but not in any way a nice mood, success, and a friendly attitude. I presume that I lived for so long with Inna because she never laughed behind my back. But I'll return to Sara Polonska — she had slimmed down ten kilograms. She said she didn't want to talk about it. And laughed. She also didn't like to talk about her former husband. She just made the observation that she would definitely introduce us. I can't say I was particularly happy about that prospect. Her hair remained incredibly curly, but it wasn't black, but chestnut-colored now. It glistened, it flowed in the sun and beguiled. She was wearing a simple white sundress and white leather shoes. For reasons unknown to me I fell madly in love with this Sara Polonska.

Sara was also surprised by our feelings. "Underbutt, how the heck could this have happened? Could you even have thought about something like this?" To that I answered, that if she continues to call me "Underbutt," I'll call her "Underboobs," because she was barely visible from under her tits. We laughed loudly, but a wonderful couple was established: Underboobs and Underbutt. The heroes of Czech cartoons: either mushrooms, or birds.

Our colleagues traipsed around Prague, and we with each other. "It seems to me when we were in school, you couldn't stand the sight of me, isn't that so?" She asked. That was a serious question. Sara posed it while she was lying down in bed, playing with her hair, pulling up and kissing her rounded knees toward her head — she loved to kiss her knees — and I looked in the hotel information directory for the number to call to order breakfast. I was naked and happy. I didn't know what I was supposed to answer: the truth, a half-truth, or a half-lie. Or simply lie, to tell her that I found her attractive, but not enough for me to admit it. It was hard for me to tell a woman, with whom it was so good in bed, that I thought she was monstrous. "I was married then," I heard my voice. Fine, like a mosquito's stinger, that's striving to find a hole in a mosquito net. I really was married then. Sara wanted to ask something else, but got distracted by a phone call — it was her mother. She didn't return to that topic later.

About the fact that Sara Polonska will move in to my place, a real sailor told us, who was similar to a fake sailor. Similar to an out of work actor, who for some reason chose the image of a sailor for his life outside the theater. He was wearing a red sweater, an earring hanging from his right ear in the form of a tiny anchor on a golden rope. He was drinking beer. Strange, crumpled wrinkles plowed through his face, which was the color of oak bark. It seemed that each time he crumpled them differently. "I'm a sailor, lovey dovies," he greeted us. "I'm a sailor, and I have to see foam." "If you wish, you can treat him to beer. He's a real sailor," the bartender said. I also thought he didn't notice anything other than that TV series about desperate housewives. We treated the real sailor to beer — at that time our hearts were filled with love for our fellow man. "If you order more for him — he'll also tell your fortune," the bartender informed us. The pair worked in concert. I admired the way the bartender shook out the money from us. We ordered the beer. The old guy slapped a little of the beer foam on our left palms, began to mutter something, and then said: "She's going to move in with you. Soon. Now you have to lick off that foam — then the prophecy will come true." I don't know why we did that. At least I was quite squeamish, but we licked off the beer from each other's palms. Who first started to do that: me or Sara? I don't remember. Sometimes it seems I should remember that without fail.

I made acquaintance with Sara's parents in a movie theater. We were watching *Match Point*, part of that was also about getting acquainted with the parents. I said to Sara that I had seen that flick and, in my view, it wasn't the best movie for meeting parents after watching it. The main character was a mercenary killer son-in-law. Who, additionally, got away with the killing of a woman, with whom he had cheated on his wife. Do I need that? She laughed. She said that her father has a wonderful sense of humor. "He'll like that, you'll see!" I didn't feel very confident. I thought for a long time before that meeting, which tactic to take — to be chatty or reserved? I didn't have any experience in meeting the parents of a girlfriend. Because I met the parents of my former wife in childhood, they for me were just ordinary adults. When I told Sara about this, she just started to laugh: "Well then, just take them for ordinary adults, if that works."

Sara's father reminded me of the joyful characters of an Emir Kusturica movie. From time to time he would sing something (even while watching a movie. People would hiss at him, and he would politely apologize and start singing again), and his fingers either danced in the air or on some surface. A cigarette that he twirled between his pointing and middle fingers looked like the hypertrophically large penis of Indian gods. I imagined the face of Sara's father and face of my own father with two portraits with one and the same signature: "Father." My father looked more convincingly like a father. Under the portrait of Sara's father one would want to write: "vagabond," "honored artist of Moldova, Viorel Nega," or even "Bartok." I would have believed it. On the backdrop of Sara's lively father, Sara's mother looked like a girl on a swing: they were swinging her so fast, that it was impossible to determine what she looked like. This was very strange, because Sara's mother was a large woman. But I managed to perceive her only fragmentarily. A large, puffy mouth. The voice of an opera tenor. In profile her hairdo recalled a black moon. I noticed that her skirt was too short for such shapes and such an age. And her gaze — captivating. She loved dahlias and family holidays. In any case, it was easier for me with Sara's parents than with my own. It seemed, as if they were completely satisfied with me. But, more certainly, they were completely satisfied with one another and with life.

When Sara asked when I would introduce her to my parents, I shriveled: "Listen, do you really feel like doing that?" I asked her then. She said that it's the least interesting for her what they're like, but if it's a problem for me or for my parents, she's not planning on being insistent. I thanked her. I can't say that it was a problem, besides, in our family no one ever introduced anyone to anyone. I understand this can seem strange, but that's the way it was. I didn't know, for example, my father's or mother's friends. It's possible my memory kept their names on long reins, but they were unfilled names. Like movies that didn't interest you: you understand by their title you once saw them, but what they're about or who's playing in them — it's impossible to remember. His parents, of course, were acquainted with Inna and her parents, and also with Tymofiy and his mother — the parent conferences at school helped that — they didn't keep up relations either with Inna, or with Tim, and all the more with their parents.

"If you can imagine a family for yourself, for example, as a dinner service, then our family service consists of accidental objects. Maybe, a similar pattern or color links us, but that's all." "And all that's normal! I realize that everyone has their own traditions. Not all families are like ours. We're quite like a circus dynasty! Each passes along something to another. If we trained lions, then the lions would hang out in our living room! We always show one another something new and interesting." Sara laughed and winked. I was surprised that this didn't anger me, although I realized: her family will take me for entertainment.

It was really easy with Sara generally speaking. First of all, I was constantly waiting: here right now she utters the wrong thing, then I right now insult her, here right now she does something, and we argue. She did and said a lot. For example, she constantly dumped the filters with leftover coffee grinds into the washbasin, which I couldn't tolerate. "Sara, is it hard to toss this out in the garbage can or in the bathroom?" "Take note that I can put this on your azaleas and grow fruit flies, or spread this fabulous mixture on your socks, or even make three piles, and in one of them hide your idiotic little ring. Then you'd start running! Instead I just clog up the washbasin with wet coffee grounds. Big deal — you can always clean it." We didn't argue. When I did something wrong, she just laughed and said "Ehhh, Underbutt." When she did something wrong, I kissed her or feigned that I'd strangle her on the spot. In a week after returning from Prague, we began living together. She moved to my place. The prophecy on the beer foam of the Czech sailor came true.

On the third day of her trip to Mexico, where she went to check out several tours, I got depressed. Rasarasarasara! She was supposed to return in two weeks. A standard tour, I often was on those kinds. I could have gone with her, but because of urgent orders I was forced to stay at home. I immediately finished my usual lengthy breakfast of five cups of coffee and began to get ready — I needed to get going to the city for a meeting. I dialed her number. "The subscriber is temporarily unavailable." "Sara, go away." I said out loud. She was hiding among the dried apricots, prunes and cashews. Sara's sweets, so as not to eat cookies and get fat. I smiled and bit into a nut.

I returned home in an elevated mood, in spite of the fact that the subscriber Sara further was inaccessible. They ordered a big writing project from me on whales. And I adored whales and dolphins, dolphins and whales. Though in truth, dolphins are whales! "What a beautiful day, what a beautiful day," the record spun in my head. I already had pulled out my key when I heard music echoing from my apartment. The key fell. I really heard music, and it wasn't just simply music — music from the TV that had been left on, or a CD. No. Someone in my apartment was playing on the "R. Yors & Kallmann" family crypt. They were making mistakes and playing it over again.

They say when you meet a ghost, you grow cold. I didn't grow cold — I had the kind of impression that someone was beginning to fry my guts. It was stuffy and hot. That's how I felt. I felt just like that when I was given anesthesia. I once laughed at Inna for her account about the ghost of Mayakovsky.* In her girlhood Inna divined fortunes with her friends, summoning the spirit of the dead poet, in order to pose several questions regarding their future. Girls love doing that. However, they summoned the spirit of the poet Vladimir Mayakovsky. And he came, said a lot of crudities, and then for a long time didn't want to fly out of the window vent, as they politely asked him to do. Instead, he grabbed and made the chair under one of Inna's girlfriends break, and her girlfriend fell. In answer to my observation, that that chair had long been broken and haphazardly glued together by Inna's father, Inna directed a wicked look at me. "Don't intrude on this, you don't know anything about this," she said. "After that, at night I heard someone pressing on one or two of the piano keys. And one time someone played a small piece. That was him. Mayakovsky. Our piano reminded him of something. Maybe, it somehow was connected with Lilya Brik."

I didn't believe it. Besides that, when the piano ended up with me, no one from the other side played on it. "Mayakovsky, Inna," I declared,

---

* The great Russian Futurist poet Vladimir Mayakovsky, known for his bombastic writings, who committed suicide in 1930. He was involved in a love triangle with Lilya Brik, the wife of his good friend Osip Brik.

beforehand looking over all the relevant information on the Internet, "didn't know how to play the piano." "He knew how," she stubbornly asserted. "How do you know that he didn't know how to play?" "Because it's not discussed anywhere." "But why talk about this separately? Back then all educated people knew how to play musical instruments," Inna argued confidently. "Almost all his wives knew how to play the piano, and he learned! He played for Lilya Brik." "Nonsense," I responded uncertainly, beginning to doubt myself. I always doubted myself.

"No, this is not nonsense!" Inna the Doubtless insisted.

How do you learn such self-assuredness? If I were a country, then, for sure, my own feuds would tear me to pieces. Inna was an absolute monarchy. One thing was left for her under those kinds of conditions: to be wary of insidious kin, who every minute make efforts to toss poison into your apple juice or into a roasted duck, not to forget about young terrorists, who make explosive charges in cellars. Of herself, of her crown, and of monarchic rules, she was completely sure.

And here now I'm standing outside my door, and he, Vladimir Mayakovsky, the poet and ardent tribune, is playing in my apartment on the "R. Yors & Kallmann" family crypt. Why today of all days? Although, thank God, it's good that it's not at night. I didn't know what to do. I silently stood in front of the door and burned with all my innards. But the door opened. It seemed to me that I began to creak. A sturdy man with curly hair gazed at me lost. I immediately recognized him — it was Sara's uncle, her father's brother. He was among those whose portrait right then was living in a silver frame on my windowsill. What's his name?"

"Oh, is that you? So you've already returned." "Yes. I've returned. Already," I said. "Sorry, I'm in a rush, but Emile is there, he'll explain everything to you. All the best, Pavlo!" "All the best, Gestapo." He looked at me with reproach. "You know, I don't know if using my family nickname will help us build family relations, Pavlo." I also didn't think that way, but I couldn't remember his name, though the fact that he's "Gestapo," I remembered beautifully. "Sorry. I didn't do it on purpose," I said. He academically shook my head. And when I entered the house,

I remembered. Gennadiy Stanislavovych Polonsky. That's his name. Ge. Sta. Po. Sara's favorite uncle. As much as I understood, Sara's cousin Emile was playing on the crypt. Good. But it would be interesting to know, why is this cousin playing in my kitchen, and his father, who's leaving my apartment, saying to me that he's in a rush and disappearing without any explanation?

I went to the kitchen. Like a rat — to the awful sounds that the unknown-to-me Emile was squeezing out of the "R. Yors & Kallmann" family crypt.

LA MEVA FLOR

by Svitlana Povalyaeva
Translated by Vitaly Chernetsky

1. RITA IN LOVE

"THE WORLD AWAKENS," THEY SAY WHEN THE SUN RISES. IN REALity, it is the one who sees it who awakens. The world is never ever asleep. Although... who knows what's up with it, this world, during the time when the one who has seen it is asleep. Still, it cannot be that all the living sentient creatures would suddenly fall asleep all at once.

This is what Rita thinks while peering at only the morning street through the leafy grape vines covering her balcony. Rita awakens with the sunrise. The world and she wake up together — like happy lovers. They kiss — on and on, youthfully, tenderly — before moving on to routine tasks. On occasion they even make love. Sometimes right in bed, amid the sunlit remnants of sleep, despite Rita's attempts to sneak out to the bathroom and at least brush her teeth. At times in the bathroom. Or in the kitchen — granting the coffee the opportunity to overflow.

Rita takes a long time brushing her hair in front of the mirror. The world smiles, it radiates from her eyes toward her own reflection. The dew on the grape leaves like the sweet involuntary tears of the time after sleep. Or the drool on the pillow. "What did you do while I was asleep? Come on, confess, what did you do with me while I was dreaming?" Rita asks, all smiles. The world pushes toward her a large blue-and-orange cup with coffee, then shouts, and launches in her honor, behind the window open into the blue, a street sweeper.

Above the ochre-shingled gables of magic-hat-like houses, a white airplane sails across the bright blue sky like a cruise ship from a postcard. "Airplanes fly, but some of them fall. There are also those that cannot take off," Rita thinks. "However, hidden in the tall grass, from the world's armpit as it were, through butterfly wings and grasshoppers, you can make out passengers in the blind airplane windows. Guess who of them is married, and who isn't; who is carrying contraband; who is stoned on tranquilizers; who was thinking about death early on, but now has forgotten about their fear of flying."

Rita likes to fantasize about the world. For she knows that it loves her, Rita, just the way she is. She has no need for leaving her house. What's out there that she hasn't seen? Rita, thank heaven, is ninety-eight.

2. Foggy-Minded Xenia

The sails of old buildings creak consumptively, fall into the streets, cover people and dogs, strain and take off above the spines of trees from the smallest ray of light. They simply live without faith — they simply know that sunlight exists.

Xenia hides in the doorway. The little pale fire in her chest flickers from the slightest gust of March wind. When the small agile black pits that swarm around Xenia begin to multiply and merge, when darkness obscures the world, Xenia grabs her anchor — two greasy bags. She starts digging through their contents, the sticky foul rotting scraps gathered at nearby dumpsters. With its agile small mouths darkness stretches toward the rot, but then recoils, retreats, and clears.

"Even the darkness is squeamish about me," Xenia thinks with satisfaction. She sees an emaciated gray cat that froze in the midst of a movement, its paw raised. "Like a dog," Xenia thinks.

"Here, kitty kitty!"

The cat tenses up to the point of shivering, but suddenly musters up courage and dashes past Xenia, runs across the street, barely escapes being run over by a car, and looks back only from the other side. Xenia grins with her agile, almost toothless little black mouth.

A couple is walking past the doorway where Xenia is hiding. The woman slips on the icy spittle covering the asphalt, and does a poorer job balancing than she would have if a strong, smiling man weren't next to her. Xenia jumps out in front of them from her hideout like a jack-in-the-box. "Could you please walk me to my apartment, young people?" She mumbles.

The lovers do not feel disgust for any of this world's manifestations. They are very compassionate. Xenia knows this. And they also are brimming with noble-minded shyness. They are afraid of looking worse than they are in the eyes of the others in this world.

"Where is your apartment?" The man asks readily. His female companion leans forward as if she wants to hug Xenia.

"There, around the corner," Xenia waves her wrinkly hand covered in a disintegrating, rot-covered fingerless glove. She checks the sticky contents of her bags, gives them a sullen stare.

The three of them walk down the little side street and turn the corner of an old building, almost fully consumed by aluminum laminate. Having reached her stairwell door, Xenia stops. The small black agile mouths jump on the pale spring day like piranhas. The humid piercing wind pushes them together into packs. Xenia stares at the man, douses him with darkness and foggy madness. The man opens the door for her with a polite, even elegant gesture. She grabs her bags and darts inside.

But the stairs take her an unbearably long time, step by step. One bag. Then the other. One foot. Then the other. Each of Xenia's moves showers the couple with a wave of various odors. At last Xenia stops. Her apartment must be behind one of these three doors. Definitely not behind this steel one, though. Suddenly Xenia sharply turns around to the couple. "Who are you? What do you need from me? Get out! Shoo!" she shouts hoarsely.

"Excuse us!" The stunned man exclaims, and he and his female companion rush down the stairs. Xenia hears the woman's voice, "She could have been a college student now! Did you see? She's actually quite young!"

"I could! If I wanted," Xenia thinks in reply and grins.

She hears the stairwell's door slam downstairs. Paranoia's attack recedes. The small black agile mouths never cross the threshold of Xenia's home. They are afraid of her.

3. THE FIRST DAY OF HOMELESSNESS

She calls him Mistral. He endures it all — the "Mistral," the crimson nails, the blue underpants with nylon frills, the movies about vampire love, the Cardigans, the soft drinks, the discos, the lost passes for all types of public transport, and the drunken girlfriends with their unrequited love — one for all.

He fell for her perfection — a perfect manicure and makeup, perfectly laconic jokes, perfect diction, and perfect restraint. Her temperament, perfect in its fury, could only be guessed from her small perfectly charming gestures. He caught and swallowed, like a fire-eater, every spark of her gaze. With perfect tactfulness, she allowed him to fight for her love and to win.

What he achieved exceeded his wildest fantasies. It even seemed to him that he wouldn't be able to stand it and die instead. From some banal heart attack. For people usually don't live long with this kind of happiness. Either this happiness — or life.

Everything's perfect about her — even her cunning. Her romanticism is also perfect. Once he told her they would wallow in gold if she wrote scripts for TV soaps. And they would buy a yacht with snow-white sails. He said that with the conscious intention of insulting her. She laughed, and her nail polish brush slipped past her fingernail, leaving a large crimson drop.

"Look what you've done!" She said and started crying. And then laughed again.

He recalled that he had run out of cigarettes and darted out of the house. Rushing past the front gate, he saw a repulsive filthy creature with a black agile mouth and cloudy eyes. The creature dug through greasy bags. With two fingers it pulled out a herring spine, sucked on it, then put it back.

He wrapped himself in the coat he had thrown on right over his T-shirt, felt the chill, and thought that any being's home is where that being yearns to return. So began the first day of homelessness.

from BARDO ONLINE *

by Svitlana Povalyaeva
Translated by Vitaly Chernetsky

You Want to Talk About This?

AFTER LIGHTNING KILLED GRANNY, TIME FOR HIM DIVIDED INTO two streams, like a fork in the river in whose delta he settled, right at the water's edge. Time brought along words the way a flood brings with it crashing noises, rotten flowers, and dead fish. This made him feel nauseated, almost on the verge of fainting, and his skin broke into itchy rashes. "This is fear," the words told him. "Fear?" He thought. Thoughts-similes and thoughts-metaphors began visiting him. The first one was: the river spread its legs to give birth to him, but he remained right next to the womb. The second thought was that clouds always resembled something — each of them could be compared to an animal or a plant. After this it was as if a dam burst in his head, thoughts poured like a raging stream, so all his efforts now went into holding on to the river's womb, grabbing at the shrubbery, holding on tight to the rough trunk and knotted roots of an old wild pear, in order not to let the current take him into the unknown.

Granny lived inside the pear tree since time immemorial. She always sat near the place where the trunk divided, on a thick wrinkled

---

* In a prefatory note to the novel, the author explains that "bardo" is a Tibetan word that means "the space between" or "a transitional state." [translator's note]

branch, settling like a dark spot of shade in between smaller branches and leaves, as if she were a dried-up, blackened fruit. Her skin was as dark as the tree's bark, her skin was bark, and the tree's bark was her skin, the crone and the old tree lived in the same skin. Granny's eyes reminded one of wild honey in a honeycomb hidden in the dry-rotting hollow in a tree trunk, suddenly lit by a ray of August sun that jumped in there for a moment. Her gaze, like the dark jasper of a still forest lake, was just the rustling of darkness in the narrow opening of an almost closed door. In this darkness through a keyhole flickered the tongue of a candle's flame or the coals in the openings of an old-time stovetop iron press. Only the accidental glint of the whites of her eyes helped one to make out in the tree's crown granny's figure in a brown dress. The pupils of granny's eyes looked like shards of beer bottle glass that had settled under the weight of cries for help on the river bottom. Granny smiled with her sunken lips and hummed a never-ending tune. This kept him in the state of blissful prostration one feels when pictures from several dreams superimpose in one's sleep like rolls of film. He dozed off and watched his slide shows. He dreamt that he was a giant skull-shaped pot, as big as a mountain, and armed knights stormed the pot's walls, and these knights had insect heads. For the most part, these were the monstrously enlarged heads of flies and wasps. He saw brown algae stuck to the ice yet vibrating from despair. It was impossible to comprehend the scale of these beings' horror. Red dots rushed about, pulsated, divided in half, swallowed one another, merged into colonies... All this made no sense and did not interest him — he simply watched, lulled by granny's humming, as if young pear branches had slowly sprouted through him. And then lightning struck the pear tree. He looked at the old tree engulfed in flames and no longer heard granny's voice through the crackling of the fire. It seemed to him that he had finally comprehended the horror of the algae encased in ice. Then thick black smoke surrounded him. It lasted forever. Then the eternity of the black smoke receded, replaced by the eternity of gray fog. And then he woke up by the burnt pear tree and saw time that divided into two streams, like a fork in the river in whose delta he had settled, right by the water's edge. Crashing noises, rotten flowers, and dead fish carried by the flood came along with time. And in the sky clouds sailed, and each cloud resembled something. He grabbed the pear tree and waited for it to hug him back with granny's wrinkled, twisted arms. But that didn't happen, and the stream only grew stronger. The verbal flood level rose so fast that one had to rush to higher ground in order not to drown. The noise filled him to the brim, and he finally gave up — he stopped fighting and lost the pear tree trunk and the river bottom from which it had grown. Time picked him up and took him away, as if he were a salmon all encrusted in words. And then it threw him out onto the bank. In his throat a giant round pebble, slimy from the silt, had gotten stuck. He swallowed it and said, "I."

He has been coming to this bar for as long as he could remember — at least a week. Outside the pearly darkness pierces him to the bone, handling organic flesh with the agile fingers of a surgeon. The whisper of snow in the blurry light, the rustling of human shadows in the passageways, the sighing of car tires in the runny mud recall the colonies of red dots consumed by their seemingly primitive processes of survival. He stands on the balcony and looks out on the nighttime side street saturated by drizzle, outlined by the spots of equidistant streetlights — this is the last thing retained on his retina before exiting the room. The streetlights lead him astray, like will-o'-the-wisps, they flicker and go out behind his back — darkness swallows them one by one. This rotten December is impossible to hide from in a nighttime bar — even a very cozy one. But he keeps coming here, each time earlier than the last time, and stays longer and longer; he seems to have gotten used to his place in the corner, not far from the bar counter. A place on the stage from which through an opening cut through the reeds and the mists one can see at least something in the orchestra. A slit in the curtain. Ihor the bartender slowly and methodically wipes the beer mugs as if they were the eyeglasses of a gunned down enemy that Ihor had sworn to return to the wife of the deceased. At the counter on a tall bar stool a fragile girl has settled in a bird-like pose. She works as a clown at children's parties. At the table in the center two go-go-girls silently puff smoke; you can say they also work as clowns, just at parties for grownups. This is no laughing matter for them. The slender body of one of them — the one with a bandaged face — is dressed in vintage black leather overalls; the other is wearing doll-like tights and a retro-style doll-like dress, pink, with ruffles and bows — only the cleavage is too deep for a doll. Here they are volunteer cocktail waitresses, bringing drinks to the customers. They say that the real waitress left this place for good, but few people believe it. Most likely, if she ever was here, she must come back at some point, says Woman in a Plastic Bag each time when the conversation turns to this topic. The lights are dim, in its broth the oxygen-starved air simmers like fat; darkness thickens into stains on one's clothes. The air is saturated with the bubbling of muffled voices that condense here and never reach the outside. Sticky sepia of dusk at a train station snack bar, just without the odors.

Soon the Holy Beer Dog will show up, wet, covered in mud, in ripped pants, in boots ready to fall apart, marbled from the street salt, with a jaw harp in a matchbox and a chronic runny nose. He will not order anything until the Bus Diver, brimming with surprise, joins him. Then from a dark corner near the bathrooms, a Bum would emerge sleepily — he used to live under vegetable stands at the farmer's market until the city announced a hunt for dangerous animals. And soon Mad Yura would show up with a crossbow, toss open her long black coat and expose to everyone's gazes her space-themed stripper gear, somewhat goth — as if it had been put together by a sexually obsessed computer game designer. And so on — the bar will fill up gradually, everyone will shiver from inner cold, sip liquid fire from their glasses, and stay silent, tensely awaiting the arrival of someone new. This will go on and on until someone suddenly loses it. Then everyone will sigh, both with relief and with disgust, break into groups, as if they were at a collective psychoanalysis session, stick together in small colonies of sadness and tell each other the same things yet again — each of them is going to share his or her story. Each of the bar patrons have heard the stories of the others countless times. Each one has forgotten how it feels to have others pay attention when you tell your story for the first time; each one has forgotten the sensation of being interested when someone else is telling his or her fresh story.

The clown girl sits down next to him. Her name is Numo. She's thrown a cardigan and a child's jacket over her clown outfit. If he were to try analyzing her outfit and dividing her clothes by color, he would find it impossible. Colors are simply absent, because such a concept doesn't exist. Either it doesn't exist in this bar, or he has missed an entire class on the "Names of Colors." The makeup on Numo's face has disintegrated to such an extent that even knowing the words that create colors, you would not be able to describe this particular color. Around her eyes are dense dark circles, as if she had survived a head injury or recent surgery. A lobotomy, for example. Or failed to survive.

"Hey, Ihor!" he shouts out to the bartender. "Get me another round, with an extra shot!"

Ihor grimaces squeamishly, and he goes on speaking in such a way as if Numo were listening to him, but not for the first time.

"Yes, who knows how much time has passed since I did in that girl, damn it, it was simply a reflex; she found herself in the wrong place at the wrong time! I was sweating bullets, like in a sauna, when I took her in my arms, for I felt how she was getting cold... this was like algae frozen in ice... aaah, no! a living person never feels cold like that, I know this for sure, I've been to the Arctic, I know; if you took a still warm corpse into your arms you would understand. And everything happened so quickly — as if in a dream — a flash — and she's buried, as if nothing had ever happened... one guy even cracked a joke of sorts — this sure is a nice funeral for the mark, extra class, buried with a chick, like a pharaoh, you see... no, not a cop, a real Egyptian pharaoh, you know... Afterwards for several days it even seemed to me that she — and the fact that I shot her — was just a hallucination; her submissive body, she died so unbelievably quickly — without a sound or any convulsions — she just fell down abruptly, and that's it... I kept thinking I hallucinated all this because of nerves; the situation that ended for the stubborn mark in someone else's grave was so freaky that it was better not to recall it, otherwise it's good-bye to your career, get it? For a week I went on a binge. I even started pissing booze, well, you know...."

One of the go-go girls, the one with the bandaged face, brings two glasses and puts them on the table. He throws a casual "thanks" past his story and continues pouring out words.

"And all the same she was there before my eyes — in the mirror, in the bathroom, outside the window, and I tried to convince myself that this was only nerves and alcohol until I noticed that she all the time kept repeating her final gesture from when she was alive, grabbing the silk scarf on her chest... it was that gesture that forced my instinctive movement, because I was on pills, well, you know, shitfaced. And the scariest thing was that she didn't accuse me; she wasn't menacing and spooky like in Japanese horror movies — she was undistinguished, like in the picture I took of her back at the cemetery, yeah, she was like a poor-quality snapshot bleached by the sun, and kept on repeating that gesture... very slowly, you know, perhaps for an entire hour, wherever I looked, I don't know — I came back to my senses getting an IV; next to my hospital bed there was fruit from the guys and flowers from Lesya; she must have thought that when a man was dying he'd sure make peace, well, you know, she's the proverbial blonde, watched too many soap operas, read too much stupid glossy shit from the family porn book club!"

Numo looks as if right through him and barely nods. When he stops, she sighs and says in her quiet hoarse voice,

"You know, among your everyday actions are those that are disgusting to remember, or at the very least unpleasant — well, you know that. But they often emerge out of the various drawers and shelves when you look for something completely different, especially when you pull out, some uplifting memory like a favorite pair of jeans, and then stretch it in your arms against the light to examine how much it has faded and if you can still put it on. And then from the pant leg a dirty rolled up hole-ridden sock of your perhaps trifling but revolting action falls out, spitefully filling the room with the stench of old shame."

"It wasn't an ordinary deed. Some sock — now the only thing I keep doing is sniffing this sock!"

"Wait, let me tell you."

He feigns attention, and Numo goes on,

"One summer I suffered badly from a hunger for books — it was like heartburn preceding a stomach ulcer. I've read all the books in the house several times over and eventually moved on to old newspapers. This is even worse than alcohol-free beer, parliamentary elections, or sex over the Internet. In despair I rummaged through the stuff I already read and finally stumbled on a paperback pocket book by a writer one of whose novels I once really loved. Apparently because of this I had bought one more book by him and then completely forgot about it. But when I started reading the first lines, I felt the way you feel when you suddenly touch someone's snot on a subway escalator's railing, or step into dogshit dusted by the first snow, in other words, I recalled that I had tried reading this book once before. You know, I'm a very conscientious reader, so I forced myself to go on with this text for a fairly long time but still abandoned it all the same. However, when you're hungry, you can swallow even worse stuff. Maybe I was in the wrong mood back then or had something else interesting to read, I thought conciliatorily, and again started torturing myself, forcing down page after page like some bitter medicine. The impression didn't change: I had never encountered a more senseless, sickening downer of a daily routine description. I'd call it *The Book of Corpses*."

"And what was it about?"

"Well, you know, like all 'stories of a little man,' the hopelessness of office plankton. The point is not what it was about... It was how it was written. Worse than an online diary of some complex-ridden office manager who, on a daily basis, notes down his tiniest reflections, and in every word there is — a complaint and a hidden desire for someone to take pity on him. What bad luck he has, what freaks his coworkers are, why some feminist bitch wouldn't sleep with him, how something ruined his vacation. And always it's someone else's fault, and if there's no one next to him, it's the fault of his fate. Well, you must have seen things like that hundreds of times, this is not important."

"Hmm."

"To make the long story short, I couldn't take it any more, made a bonfire on the beach and burned the book — can you imagine? I burned the book — didn't leave it for someone on a park bench, didn't take it to a used bookstore, didn't give it to someone else who might enjoy it. This was like a cleansing ritual from some dreary drag, from an accidental evil eye. But I tore out and kept one page. Not that I agreed with what was written on that page, it was the other way round. Not that this was something out of the ordinary, something that I hadn't read in other people's books or couldn't imagine myself. But for some reason this fragment alone out of that entire book somehow touched me. Perhaps in contrast with the rest of the nonsensical narrative it came across as not that banal. I remember it word for word; it is two standup comedians talking, a man and a woman, and the woman says, "In your dreams, when you're asleep, anything is possible. You can command an army. Or fly with just a wave of your arms. Play poker with the dead. But there is one thing that it seems to me one cannot do in a dream. Do you know what that is?" Well, here we take out the glue that the author splatters to create the illusion of a dialogue, well, it's like this author sniffs glue, you know, and then it goes on like this, "The only thing you cannot do in a dream is dream. If you are dreaming in your sleep you are a healer who treats people through hypnosis, you cannot take a nap in that dream and have a dream that you're a world-famous expert on hummingbirds. You can dream that you are a healer and then become an expert in hummingbirds. But you cannot dream that you are a healer who's dreaming that he's a hummingbird expert. This must mean something. And this is a good way of testing whether you are, in fact, dreaming." At this point that stream of the text ends and goes on to merge with other streams, empties into an ocean of words, letters, one cannot know what it will turn into, foretell its future fate, perhaps someone will find it excruciatingly boring and burn it, and then some fragment will settle like a parasitic epigraph in someone else's text, like hawkweed in a tree. I probably did not have the right to punish someone else's labor with fire, I acted like an inquisitor."

"What hawkweed text are you talking about?" He asks, pushing an empty glass back and forth and listening more to the noise it creates than to Numo's voice. "An ocean of words" — this well-worn phrase meant, like all florid turns of phrase, to cloud the truth with feigned metaphoricity, swims past him like a colorless bubble.

"About a text I once wanted to write," sighs Numo, fidgeting with her earring. "There's an age when almost everyone takes a stab at becoming a writer. Everything appears so simple: every day something happens to you, and you live though it not as a casual observer, but as someone fully immersed in it. I thought no one had written about women clowns and wondered how I could describe all this... for instance, a boy's birthday: a party at the zoo, there are amusement rides there too, everyone's riding bumper cars, the rubber squeaks, the girls squeak, the boys scream and laugh, the bumper cars get stuck together, hissing sparks fly in all directions, the contact poles are still shaking and go on skating on the iron grill of the ride's ceiling, and you rush headlong though sky and water — through the rainbow, the contacts scratch the clouds, causing merry bolts of lightning and holiday fireworks, juggler's balls fly in all directions, past tickertape, past packs of soap bubbles, past glitter and confetti tossed above as if by an upstream current, clouds of varicolored balloons rise up with toys attached to them: bunnies, teddy bears, clowns, ballerinas, baby dolls, balls — and the clouds, like in your childhood, also turn into bunnies, lambs, teddy bears, fish, hedgehogs, turtles, and crocodiles, into masks of magicians, skeletons, and monsters, into winged elephants, into little boxes of dreams, these eternal sleepless clouds, you too scream and laugh from happiness like a child, diving into cotton candy and then reemerging in a rainbow tunnel with cheerful good-natured skeletons on the sides, with glowing monsters, a whole train of seals and sea lions splashing after your small bright car that resembles a flying saucer from the cartoon *Mystery of the Third Planet*, a funny hovercraft from outer space, flocks of parakeets and pigeons follow the contact pole that generates lightning, you rush though rings of fire, and on your sides packs of smiling tigers rush, geese on skates, thoughtful porcupines, everything begins spinning like a merry-go-round, darkness fills your eyes, eventually extinguishing the last rapidly growing distant rainbow dot...."

"Each cloud does resemble something, I've noticed that, " he says. He orders another drink. Numo makes a pyramid out of the objects on the table: a napkin, a matchbox, an empty cigarette pack, pressing it all down with the ashtray. Then she turns to the counter and listlessly waves her hand, "Another round." Ihor follows the order but with visible annoyance, and one of the go-go girls, not the one with a bandaged face, but the other one who looks rather appetizing except for the bluish-grayish color of her skin, gets up to bring over the glasses.

"Everything resembles something else. When bumper cars collide, this also resembles an actual road accident. I even wondered, could one die in such a collision? You know, one can die in a really foolish way. I had an acquaintance whose mother followed his every step — you know, a fanatical mother hen. If he had allowed her, she would have even wiped his ass for him. When he rode a bicycle, he did it very slowly because she ran slightly ahead of him and pushed away branches of shrubbery so they wouldn't hit him in the face. Imagine, he was already close to graduating from high school and his face was covered with volcanic teenage acne. You wouldn't believe it, but he was really in many respects an adult guy, but his mom wouldn't let him ride a bike by himself. And so once he was riding, she jogged next to him to wipe sweat off his brow, and suddenly he went flying. It turned out someone had stretched a rope or a fishing line low above the ground, I don't know, or maybe it wasn't even done on purpose, someone was simply coming home from fishing and the line got stuck in the shrubbery and tore off, you know. And he was going on his bike, ran over it and fell out. Any ordinary person would just get a bruise, or maybe scrape off some skin, or even break an arm or a leg. But he broke his neck and died on the spot."

Suddenly the bar shakes from rumbling and a red roar, the doors open, the glasses above the counter rattle, the cloudy light goes out. One can hear Ihor the bartender swearing as he makes his way to the electric panel. The bar again fills with dim light and everyone continues conversing. Only Mad Yura jumps up and jerkily turns the crossbow in various directions, aiming at invisible targets.

from A GREEN MARGARITA

by Svitlana Pyrkalo
Translated by Michael M. Naydan

Dedicated to partners at all levels of the game plan

All the first and last names and addresses are real.
All the described events are fictional, and the author has no
responsibility for their similarity to life. Information in advertising
announcements has no value in and of itself
and that is why it's included here.

I'm walking along the street and chewing.
What am I chewing, do you want to know?
I'm chewing a cheeseburger. And in a paper box I have one more
cheeseburger.
The paradoxes of our life include this one: two ordinary
cheeseburgers — at least with the current promotion — cost much
less than one double one. After this what point is there to buy double
cheeseburgers? Who can wrap themselves around this in their head?
But everything's in order.

DAY 1

Going Out for Coffee's Like a Walk in the Woods

I'M PLANNING TO TALK ABOUT MYSELF, AND PRACTICALLY ABOUT
nobody else. This story isn't a sharply plotted novel, but just a tale
about a couple dozen days experienced by me — several ordinary days.

You'll come across a lot of boring things, stupid jokes, morsels of my thoughts that are of no interest to anyone. So don't look in my narrative for detailed descriptions of springtime Kyiv — just simply go out onto the street and look for yourself. It's utterly unnecessary for you to know anything about my love — it's enough that I love him and he's my little pumpkin. You don't need to know too much about Nebeliuk, Drum, Roma, and Semén — sooner or later you'll get acquainted with them and see that words here are feeble. You also won't find out whether I slept with Kiril, I'm not exactly sure myself. But here is what's worth remembering: my name is Maryna Pohribna. I'm smart and beautiful, like the raven in the anecdote, and a bit crazy, like that same raven in the very same anecdote. In addition, the only person who can tell you something about me that's not simply interesting, but true, that's me myself. Truth to tell, I don't know why you would need all this.

Last night I had a dream of an underground river of dead people. I saw many of my friends there. They were treating me to mushrooms with red caps. If in the nether world they really subsist on mushrooms, then I want to live a little longer.

That's why I'm walking to the kitchen and taking two multivitamin pills, rich in countless vitamins and lots of extremely useful minerals. I've been told that these minerals remove harmful stuff from one's organism if one drinks, smokes and constantly freaks out. Well, I don't smoke much, if you're talking about tobacco, but all the same: vitamins, people, — that's just super. Vitamins destroy zits. Do you know what zits are? I know. They suck. At the moment there's a self-styled philosopher who walks around Kyiv, who insists that zits are the greatest philosophical problem of humankind. May lightning strike me if it's not true. You begin to start dating a guy — he likes you, everything's going good, but… when he notices that you have zits? (Though the flowering of spots of various colors on your kisser can be seen from a mile away.) I already know that no one gives a damn about someone else's zits, even more so at the tender teenage years, when from a single glance at another teenager of the opposite sex you start drooling and your eyes go dim. Not something I knew just two years ago…

So anyway, since I started to take vitamins my external appearance became much better. And I started to sleep less and miss work less often. But when you sleep less, you dream fewer dreams. And my dreams… oh, a person in their entire life doesn't experience as many adventures as I do sometimes in a single night. Have you ever managed, behind a mountain of empty boxes, to come across a battle between God and the devil for the fate of the world, one that happens just once in ten thousand years? For me that's not a problem. If for several days I don't dream short dreams and at least for a week and a half — a long, great, and colorful dream, everything around me starts to turn pale bit by bit.

I make myself a great big cup of coffee, a quadruple portion. It's very convenient to have eggs, butter, cheese, and coffee in the house. From this I can quickly whip together breakfast, which is, by the way, quite filling. At first look a monotonous menu, nonetheless you need to take into account I have thirty various spices lying around that in the kitchen, six of which are varieties of pepper; that's why over the course of a month I can sprinkle a fried egg every day with a different spice, and it won't taste the same as it did yesterday. And if I happen to add ham to that — I'll get a real English breakfast of bacon and eggs. I can have lunch at work and then scrounge something for dinner. I can also have dinner at work, or in the city with someone, or at home I can prepare something tasty and read part of a book at the table, appetizingly staining and spattering the pages with food. But no one can be present, otherwise it's awkward: they see you act like a pig and ruin a book. For some reason anyone who sees me eat at the table considers it a necessity to lecture me; and, over the last eighteen years, that lecture hasn't changed at all. Those who used to lend me books (which I returned all bespattered) try especially hard. But I know for sure: it's impossible to eat so neatly that you don't bespatter at least a page. Eighteen years of experience have given me the right to be sure about this. That's why I simply have to accept things the way they are. A book is for a person, and not a person for a book. Conversely, some people like to smoke and read in the bathroom. There's even an expression for it: to shit without a ciggy's like water-free tea for a piggy. I personally don't understand that, but if it's good for people — let them be. Though in my "combo" lavatory smoking has been banned since the time Nebeliuk smoked his *Vatras** there; then I had to wash all my clothes again that had been hung up in the bathroom to dry, and wash the walls because Nebeliuk's *Vatras* — I don't know where he gets them — are just like mustard gas. The only thing worse is when he takes off his shoes.

I also love to read at breakfast. In as much as my natural laziness doesn't permit me to run out for the morning newspaper, and I can't afford to order special morning delivery, I read what's unread from Saturday's Mirror Weekly. It takes a full day to read the whole thing. I can't imagine how someone manages to publish it. A year-old Sunday Telegraph is spread out on the couch, and looks like it's not any thicker at all. Truth to tell, I didn't read that one from beginning to end when it was fresh, and right now it's not very interesting.

What is the Sunday Telegraph doing on my couch, you ask? I'm practicing my English. Theoretically, I need that for work: I steal a lot of information from the Internet when I write a column of cultural news, that's why I constantly translate texts from and into English, and also edit stuff stolen by someone else. In reality the reason for this enthusiasm for learning lies in the fact that I want to get a grant to study in the States. In the hated-by-everyone States, that demonstrates its militant maleness, as Zabuzhko might say, slinging phallic-shaped rockets left and right. Not giving a damn. I want to study in the land of cheeseburgers. I think that if I go there, it will turn out that the same kind of people as us live there, just a lot fatter, and some of them are black, to be more precise — dark brown.

True, I have enough common sense not to talk about this aloud, because everyone around me would start scolding me.

All the Americans I know are a little bit loony. True, one of my friends says that's why they're hanging around in Kyiv, because they're

---

* A popular brand of cigarettes from Soviet times. The brand name *Vatra* means campfire or bonfire in the western Ukrainian dialect.

loony. If anybody really needed them back home, what would have forced them to absorb residual Chornobyl radioactivity here? Maybe it's like that. Sometimes it seems to me that my desire to travel to the States is from the very same category of masochism as the desire to peck at a scab on your own body, tearing the skin off it with great interest.

When I say to someone that I want to study in the States, no one believes me. They say that all Americans are dense. I don't think so. At least they've managed to think up the nuclear bomb.

ALSKO
Kindergarten
invites children from ages 2-6

Included in the program: economics, law, computer literacy, mathematics, writing, reading, the English language, logic, chess, origami, mythology, ecology, and other subjects.

SCHOOL HOURS: *from 7AM – 9 PM.*

The possibility of residence on days off, holidays, and at night.

YOUR CHILD WILL BE GRATEFUL TO YOU!

Sometimes I think like this: if they give me a stipend, then finally I'll have the opportunity to at least study normally for a little bit, not to run from my class to work like a madwoman, but go to the library, read my professional literature, go out for meetings with famous people — I know you often meet with famous people there. And not think about money for even a tiny bit, stop thinking like a maniac that you won't have enough money for rent and other things. Am I not deserving of at least a year of normal study, not thinking about how to pilfer some money for a kilo of herring? Is anyone more deserving of that more than me? No way! And then, already after returning to Ukraine, all my problems will resolve themselves on their own. Imagine — I come to hire myself out to you for work, in a beautiful suit, with a white-toothed American smile, learned after a year of study by heart, and I say: "I got my degree at Harvard, or somewhere — let it even be the University of Alabama." Well, you'll say to me then — okay, for the probationary period we can offer you just eight hundred... well, a thousand dollars, but, as a valued employee, we promise you the rapid growth of the amount of compensation for your highly superqualified work. Strictly speaking, I'm not impoverished right this moment. But this is something different, and that is something different.

I finally finish my coffee and cheese that had melted in it. I put on my white blouse and beautiful blue suit — a jacket and slacks that fit me just perfectly. I give the impression of a business lady in that outfit — until I open my mouth. It's hard for me to say something neutral and maintain the impression of an intelligent person. Like in the fairytale when a beauty spoke and roses poured out of her mouth, and pearls from her eyes when she cried, and when she would wash up, golden downpours fell from her cheeks; thus from me from all possible places opinions pour out: some smart, some witty, some cynical, some stupid, but there always remains the impression, as least with me, that it would be better for me to remain silent. The roots of this lie in my childhood. When I didn't have my own thoughts on many important life questions, for example, what kind of coffee is better — instant or brewed, and what is cooler — Imagism or Impressionism, I suffered from an inferiority complex, because all my older friends had solid life convictions. It seemed to me then that they all had the capacity to have opinions, and I didn't. On the other hand, when that capacity developed over the years, it became difficult to shut my mouth in time. Well, of course, I try not to yap out anything unnecessary, and even hung a sign over my work desk: "DON'T MISS A GOOD CHANCE TO SHUT UP." I haven't noticed yet whether it's helped, but, in fact, the sign has been hanging all of two days.

324

My bosses have gone off somewhere on a foreign business trip, that's why I'm planning to peacefully surf the Internet and the press at my work station. (It would seem that a journalist needs to read other publications and learn what's happening in the world, but with us it's accepted just to work on what you're writing. And no one respects the fact that a creative person has to find inspiration from somewhere.) Though I nearly completely just read The Kyiv News tabloid, I don't want other passengers in the microbuses that I take to work to see me with it. No, I like to roll up several newspapers into a tube so that something more or less presentable is on top, and with that look like a serious contemporary person. Sometimes I have to bring myself (after all, I cover celebrity life, if life is the right word here) to buy and read women's magazines. I try to cover them with a newspaper so that none of my friends can see them because they'd make fun of me. In reality at home I read them with interest so I can then yawn and authoritatively say: "They're all more and more awful. They'll all soon go to the dogs." And that will be the honest truth.

But really, who doesn't like women's magazines? Who doesn't like the soul-touching stories about how he you-know-what her…, but still she loved him, and he was such a dick, well, and then she started a new life and out of grief won ten thousand, or better a hundred thousand dollars (nobody would believe she could earn that much, really), and he came back, and she to him — eff you, and then she married a tennis player, and then — eff all of them, there! You got it, you dicks?

Especially, going back to the subject, when I had zits, I loved to read in those kind of magazines that the soul is the most important thing. And then I developed my method of maintaining high self-esteem: I learned to get men to fall in love with me. It's not hard if you know how. Do you remember that one time they loved to write about magical glances, auras and other such things in tabloids? Experience shows that a man takes any kind of direct look into his eyes for magic. In visual terms this looks like this: you narrow your eyes, look into a man's eyes and imagine that you're crawling into his head and turning on an imaginary faucet. I've been convinced of the efficacy of that method since long ago, but confidence in the fact that I can mess with the head of anyone I want has, for my entire life, perfectly co-existed with the feeling that I'm an ugly duckling and no one is in love with me. Strange: I haven't been an ugly duckling since long ago. I'm attractive enough, especially when I've slept well and haven't had too much to drink. Yes, you don't need to doubt this, even if you've never seen me. But my inner self-perception hasn't changed at all.

From the time when I practiced getting men to fall in love with me left and right, there's just one suitor from that series who's left — I managed to get rid of the others already. From time to time he watches me come out of the metro and go in the direction of work, and then he comes up to me, says "hello," and gives me a little bouquet, as they say, of "wild flowers" from the sort "the main thing isn't the bouquet, the main thing is the attention." I make it look like I'm happy to see him, but I'm running late for somewhere (often that's really the case). This dude is always well dressed, wearing fashionable Gucci shoes, but still isn't married. I don't think this is a sign of 100 per cent heterosexuality. On those kind of days I stop by at an inexpensive coffee shop along my way for a cup of coffee; there I put the little bouquet into a vase on the table and read newspapers for a complete nirvana. This takes about fifteen minutes because the news, as a rule, is always the same, and I skip over incidents like "a crazed grannie put a nail through the head of her granddaughter."

It's pleasant when someone "nourishes feelings." Even if he's there with just a bouquet of "wild flowers." Don't let yourself dry up as they say. Well, at least he's neat and dresses well, that doesn't happen too often.

I plow through my emails. One of them simply makes my eyes jump out of their sockets, and right away I run to phone my mother.

"Momma! Guess what just was sent to me! My book is in the Library of Congress in Washington! by email! … one of my Internet friends! Well, he's just a dude; he works there! … I don't know his name, but can you imagine, what a rush! …in the reference department."

Mom expresses her opinion that the library should give me some money.

"Yeah, right, in my dreams," I explain to her. "Libraries don't do those kind of things. Thieves and bloodsuckers do that to cleanse their conscience. Well till later, I'll call you this evening."

We said goodbye, and I returned to my computer. I pondered for a minute whether to add new entries to the reference book we had just discussed (I had gathered the material over a month ago), but I was feeling lazy. All the same there was no one to work on the next edition, and I didn't feel like doing it myself. That's why I got on the Internet, and the next two hours were killed in the aimless exchange of content-free messages: right now is the busiest part of the workday, and there are just idlers online. Convincing myself that enough time had already been sacrificed to laziness, I sighed, regretted the slaughter of time immediately and started to work on my article that I had to turn in a whole week later. But it was already ready in my head, so I had better write it down while there was peace in the office. So, I open up a new file and...

from LIFE. KISS

by Svitlana Pyrkalo
Translated by the author

(This text contains language and descriptions of situations
which some readers might find offensive)

"LIFE IS TOO SHORT TO KISS UGLY PEOPLE," SAYS ZORAN. YOU look at him in disbelief. He's not even trying to pretend that he's first of all interested in the soul, personality or other such like. "You look good in jeans; means you're gonna look good in everything."

Jeans constitute your entire wardrobe. In the last two months since you left your husband, you've lost several sizes, but you've neither the time nor money to buy new clothes. Out of a stubborn Eastern European principle you always shop only during sales, but it's October; there are no sales; discount shops are too far; you're super busy at work, recently during a lunch break you bought this stripy little jumper for full price, and this still causes you pain in some unnamed Ukrainian organ responsible for petty avarice. Somehow spending forty pounds on the jumper feels like the last straw, the insult added to injury, as if life stepped on your foot and then spat at you in the face. You did manage to buy the jeans on sale though, and you really do look good in them, but Zoran's words rub you the wrong way. Maybe you've decided to spend all your life dressed in these jeans and the stripy jumper; and if he doesn't like something, he can go fuck himself right away, because you're not going to spend another five years with some shallow swine.

You know exactly whom you want to see next to you: somebody completely unlike your ex. Somebody very educated (the ex was thrown out of a religious college for sacrilege). Family-oriented (the ex decided five years into the marriage that he doesn't want children). Somebody who would be interested in your world, in your country's traditions, your... your background. What's Ukrainian for "background?" Your... the thing that is in the back of other things and is sort of wide... anyway, you will remember the adequate Ukrainian word later, doesn't matter. (The ex only learned two things in Ukrainian: the word "davaj" with which you end telephone conversations in various Slavic languages incomprehensible to him, and "the beetroot crop is fucked" — the phrase which, in your opinion, would establish a total spiritual harmony between the ex and your mother).

You're looking for a person — like in that Soviet song — grey-eyed, of medium height. You're looking for a person who makes you feel warm. An easygoing person — like that artless song. What's so hard to understand here? Not another two-meter-tall black-eyed lamppost, who can put you, Ukrainian Thumbelina, on one hand, slap you with another, with only a wet spot remaining.

Plus, you know exactly who that person is because you've already met him. His name is Peter, and you met him through the same dating site as Zoran. He's born and bred English. (The ex never got around to adding a UK passport to his American one — this he had to do himself, you couldn't do it for him.) Peter is tall, but not too tall, and together you look like a human couple, not like two humanoids from an anthropological museum demonstrating the extremes in the height of homo sapiens. But the main thing — the most important thing — Peter is super-educated and very, very intelligent. He has three degrees. One from Oxford (philosophy), one from the Metropolitan University (math), and one from you don't remember where (computation of finance).

He works in one of the biggest banks, writes programs for calculating risk in C++ or something along those lines. Peter is fair-haired, has a generous scattering of freckles, and an aristocratic nose.

He's read Spinoza and definitely values not what your arse looks like in jeans, but your generosity of spirit, intellect and warmth.

He wants children and has a house in Camden with a paid off mortgage. How do you say "mortgage" in Ukrainian? (You make a mental note to look up a genuine Ukrainian equivalent for the words "mortgage" and "credit," because you're a patriot of your language. While you're at it, make a mental note to look up a genuine Ukrainian equivalent of the word "patriot".) You want to be with Peter, and that's all there is to it. It's the right, wise, adult decision.

You had known for a while that a breakup with your ex was inevitable. When all a couple does together is eat and watch television, a breakup is just a question of time; provided, of course, that at least one of you has the willpower to give another chance to themselves and to the other. But knowing is one thing; but when you realise that the wound where you tore off your giant American husband, who sucked you dry, is still sore, and phantom pains take away your sleep...

One of the days, when the ex and you still sleep under one roof, but already in different bedrooms, he crawls in home at dawn, pissed, and falls asleep on the sofa. When you wake up, the entire ground floor — living room, dining room and kitchen — is saturated with alcohol vapors; and you, drunk on the flammable cocktail of despair, love and disgust, go on the Internet and sign up to a dating site.

The site — the biggest in Britain — is full of men who look for care, love and loyalty. Almost all of them write the same thing, copying phrases from girls' profiles, who in turn copy theirs from the boys'. The whole site of people, whose friends, according to their inelegant personals, describe them as honest, attractive, loyal, who go to the gym and have a career, who like eating in restaurants and socialise with friends — what's Ukrainian for "socialising"? — and are looking for girls with similar interests. You have a hundred percent identical interests: you go to the gym, sometimes eat in Turkish kebab shops and Vietnamese cafes with friends, and, according to your boss at least, have some sort of a career as a radio presenter in a language nobody here understands.

You never left one man for another — you left when it became apparent that it was better to be alone. Others appeared by themselves, as soon as you started smelling like a free woman Apart from your first year in London, it usually happened pretty fast. But that year passed in solitude. Cool people didn't notice you. Those who were happy with your clumsy English and your looks, rather average for Ukraine but attractive in England, were of no interest to you. Local Ukrainians seemed, like yourself, lost in time and space; you were certain that lots of them still wore the same trousers they had bought in Drohobych in 1993 right before emigrating. You felt terribly lonely and really wanted to shag somebody and talk to somebody, but couldn't find the people. Now for all intents and purposes your English is as fluent as your Ukrainian; you can talk to anybody, but you don't want to talk. Don't want to touch anybody's skin; kiss lips; smell the sweat; let them into your body. Don't want to talk about anything with ripped, career-making London professionals who like socialising in restaurants. You want not to be.

But what choice do you have? All you've kept from your ex are your dreams. What are you looking for, the website asks? You shrug involuntarily, although neither the website, nor the ex, prostrate on the sofa, can see you. What are you looking for: the same only completely different. The same dreams about warmth, a cosy family nest, beautiful children, only with somebody else. With somebody who'll appreciate in you not your lips, or your waist, or you-know-what, but what kind of a wonderful wife and mother you are still going to be in twenty years. These are wonderful dreams, they are proper dreams, and you keep repeating to yourself, like an affirmation from a book that helps lost idiots become even blinder to reality, that they will definitely come true.

You tasked all your friends in London with fixing you up on dates with nice gentlemen. One friend remembered some French guy, a single father whose son went to the same school as hers, but she kept missing him, and, besides, didn't know how to bring the subject up. Another suggested going dancing: that was how she had met her own husband. Another advised you to go to the Ukrainian church on Bond Street and pull out a nice Greek Catholic. Yet another suggested going to the Ukrainian networking event in the City and pick up a nice Ukrainian banker; one more suggested just waiting and trusting in fate that will bring me together with The One, and there would be incredible love.

You had been at the church, and at salsa, and at the networking event. Fate brought you incredible love, but it was all of as much use as a fifth leg on a dog. It looked like the dating website is the most practical and cheapest option.

The most important thing is not to rush. You must get to know him, ask about everything. Meet his friends, his father if possible: that's what he'll be like in old age. Discuss all values. How he wants to bring up children. Children aren't a joke, but a serious responsibility. He must be able to count money and use his energy rationally. He has to be incredibly smart, so you could say "Yes, dear, you're right" and actually believe it. He has to be a serious, adult person, who values an honest, responsible attitude in a relationship. He has to realise what sacrifice you're making as a woman starting a family: with a child you'll lose your chance — already minimal — to have any sort of a serious career in this country.

You find a black-and-white photo with a Yulia Tymoshenko-style braid (somehow this is supposed to show your depth and strength of character), write a thoughtful personal ad, move out of the house in which you had planned to live a long and happy life with the ex, ring up a real estate agent, put it on the market and start looking for the one, for him who will make all your dreams come true.

Several days later, you find Peter. Like you, he just split up with a girl after eight years of living together. He missed her. The girl was a psychiatrist, sang jazz in the evenings, and was the exotic black daughter of immigrants from Guyana. You, a daughter of two psychiatrists from exotic Ukraine, who used to be a singer-songwriter, think you can compete.

On paper — or rather on screen — Peter and you get along famously. He describes in detail how he and his girlfriend had met at a friend's place eight years ago, how it was great during all those eight years, and then how she didn't go hiking with him and eventually moved out. You feel you're helping him with your understanding. Sometime he writes about his day at work, complains about his boss, about being tired, thanks you for reading all this.

Your profile on the dating site attracted several more guys. You ignore most of them because you get turned off by spelling mistakes in their personal descriptions or their idiotic descriptions of themselves that start with the words "Damn, I have no idea what to write here, doesn't everybody hate these things?" But you do answer two emails — from Zoran, a Serb, and Mario, a Sicilian. One of them shows Mario — dark and handsome, in shades — in front of some monument that you took for Bohdan Khmelnytsky, the Ukrainian hetman, in St. Sophia Square in Kyiv. But it isn't. Mario says it's Novodevichy Cemetery in Moscow. He went there, he vaguely explains, to meet friends etc. You have the suspicion that he went in search of a Russian bride, but he's too dashing; plus he says he's head of marketing for one of the biggest global Internet companies. Such a handsome bachelor doesn't need to go all the way to Moscow for a shag.

Zoran was half-naked in all the photos, most of which were taken on the beach. He had good reason for that: while his mug looked like a well-used punching bag, the muscles on the rest of his body were just perfect. One picture — probably taken by himself, because he was so close to the camera that his nose, already giant, took up most of the space in the picture — showed him in some kind of stupid Halloween helmet. Bloody knight. Photoshop some shining armor on him, and Bob's your uncle. The pictures, he explains, are mostly from Croatia where he has a house on an island called something like Hrxszj. His English is great; you assume he just bought a house there. But he demonstrates expert knowledge of Balkan national cuisine, and finally says that he's Serbian. "I'm Serbian; my mother's Croatian; I grew up in Bosnia, in Sarajevo. So I'm really a Yugoslav."

You begin living online. The potential dates, or rather their out of focus pictures and biographies of unknown veracity, grow more and more real and three-dimensional. You start thinking about them on the tube, at work, in the gym. You carry on an internal, thoughtful dialogue with Peter's picture, giggle at some silly stuff said by Zoran's picture, inhale Italian perfume from the picture of fiery Mario. What a wonderful pill from reality! No need for drugs, or expensive travel, which you can't afford anyway, or new clothes you have no time to buy. The Internet is full of willing men, and they are all better than your ex. Or maybe worse, but different, different, different, and that's the main thing.

Peter and you correspond for a week. Finally you agree to meet. He invites you to a French restaurant, to which he always had planned to take his ex, but somehow never did. He is very serious about it, you think. It's a good sign.

You put on a very expensive pair of trousers you had bought for yourself for your birthday in the summer (cross with your ex, because he gave you nothing, but let you buy anything you want, on your own credit card, while he carried on drinking up his paycheck). A leather jacket, an elegant scarf, and high heel shoes: he might not be as the kind of lamppost as the ex, but still tall. And you are, let's say, not. And during the lunch break, you run out of the office and buy the stripy little sweater for full price. Well, sometimes you just have to.

After work you book a course of massages at your gym, because the stress causes your back to spasm; painkillers don't work anymore; and you don't want to look epileptic on a date. After the massage you'll have plenty of time to shower and wash your hair (no matter how much you ask the masseuse not to touch it with her oily hands, she always does), and to have a slow, relaxing walk to the restaurant during this London evening in October.

But the massage is delayed. Somewhere something had blown up, and the previous client had to file a copy urgently, so she was late, and your appointment got shifted too. The masseuse is nervous and hurried; your neck gets irrigated with the oil from her jar. Finally it's over, and you dash for the gym. But instead of water, the showerhead produces just a hissing sound. The second, third and fourth showers don't work either. There's no hot water in the gym.

In the absence of water, you have to wipe the oil off with a towel; the masseuse left tons of it on you. Your skin still feels oily. Ah, screw it, you think; he isn't going to get under your top on the first date. You pull your hair back; luckily there's a hairclip in the locker. You put your trousers and little sweater on and finally look in the mirror for the first time this day. It turns out your expensive designer trousers hang on you like on a scarecrow. Dressing this morning and thinking that you're 33, and who thought you'd need to date at such an age; you forgot how much weight you had lost in the last two months. The trousers hang low and chafe your thighs. You decide to pretend you're sick, wrap yourself in your scarf up to your nose and schlep over to Peter's bank where he suggested you pick him up.

The girl at the reception desk dials Peter's extension one minute before the agreed time. Precisely at 6:30 he comes down. Like adults, you shake hands; you barely manage not to breathe a sigh of relief because he doesn't have any obvious deformities and immediately have to suppress a wince caused by your own spiritual deficiency. What does it matter if he has deformities? Are you not capable of seeing more than that?

Before dinner — there is still time — you pop in to a bar for a drink. Peter asks about your job; you tell him about your crack of dawn radio shows, how tiring it is, but how rewarding when the program works out. How warm you feel when your mother likes them.

"So your mother always listens to you?" Peter smiles. God, what a nice smile he has! Calm, kind, noble.

The restaurant is empty except for several waiters who try to out-French each other despite them all being Moroccan.

"How's your French?" Peter asks while turning pages of the menu.

"Enough to get by," you say with dignity. It's satisfying to know the names of some mushrooms and lamb cuts he doesn't recognise. You don't bother to explain that you only know these words because in the years after moving to the West you just stuffed your face unstoppably with everything you could reach, sometimes going to the sticks in France where nobody speaks a word of English.

He orders lamb, you duck, and a bottle of burgundy. The waiter comes over to open it. Peter tastes it first.

"Now you try," he says.

The wine stings the tongue with its acidity. You expected something completely different, but you've never sent a bottle back. Now the decision depends on you.

"I don't know," you give up. "Maybe it will breathe and get better?"

The wine does get better, but not by much. You regret not sending it back but are happy to have been asked your opinion. The music starts; the other tables begin to fill up. You talk about previous relationships. You ask Peter why he broke up with his ex. He freezes up with a piece of lamb that he was about to put into his mouth.

"I haven't finished analyzing it yet," he finally says and delivers the lamb back into his mouth. "I'm still thinking about it, and so far I can see that our relationship did work very well on many levels. But it didn't on others. For instance, she had a really big bottom, like many black Caribbean women. I wasn't attracted to that."

"But presumably you had enough in common intellectually and spiritually, since you lived together for eight years?" I wager.

"Yes, certainly. But I decided to analyze everything that affected our relationship and the breakup, including such seemingly trivial matters as her bottom. At the end of the day, everything plays a role."

What honesty! We won't have problems with lies and half-truths. Besides, you have a perfect, beautiful bottom. You get up to go to the loo; but luckily, under your baggy clothes, it's absolutely impossible to see your figure, so you two can concentrate on the other, non-physical qualities of one another.

The conversation shifts to his education. He "read" philosophy at Oxford. When one talks about Oxford or Cambridge, one ought to say "read," not "studied." You're pleased to know such details.

You talk about his favourite Australian philosopher you never heard of. Peter is slightly unhappy with his choice of speciality.

"I started by studying math, but three months later I switched to philosophy: didn't like the professors. Now I regret I lost my chance to have a career as a mathematician. You see, the mathematicians' brains get shaped in a certain way when they are young, like... like..."

"Like a ballerina's feet?" I offer.

"Yes, exactly. When I finally started learning math, my brain was already formed; so it's enough for finance, but not enough for science."

They bring the bill; you pay for yourself — the feminist earnestness of the gesture gets somewhat screwed up when your card keeps being rejected. Finally one works. Peters is happy he doesn't have to pay for both. What a good man, doesn't swing his dick around and insist on paying. The money will be needed later, to set up a family nest, for the kids' education, no need to spend it for nothing.

You say good-bye; Peter's look is kind but somewhat distant. Usually guys and girls give a peck on the cheek when they say good-bye; but he doesn't make a move to do it, and you understand: there's no rush. If you decide you're a good match, there will be time for a peck; there will be time for other things.

You shake his hand, wrap even deeper in your scarf — it's October, after all — and go to the tube.

On the platform it dawns on you that such a divine creature as he and such a lame creature as you can have no future together. You only have one degree; and while you did write and publish some silly books in some useless language, it can't be compared with a degree from one of the most prestigious colleges in Oxford. He sees the world differently; he lives in a different world. He goes on hiking trips in Britain, coast to coast, because he doesn't want to harm the environment by flying. Where did you see anyone else like that?

Peter writes that he enjoyed the conversation and wouldn't mind meeting again. Very calmly you reply in kind. The heart beats: "Yes! Yes! Yes!"

The next day, as always in key moments of your life, the poofs arrive. You know it's not a PC word, and you're supposed to say "gays." But what's in a word? A word is a collection of sounds, it means nothing unless people give it meaning. The poofs call each other poofs, queers, sisters, and fairies. Sometimes they do say "gay," but mostly in composite words like gaydar or gay bar or discussing each other's hairstyle. The main poof, your very old friend Dmitrik, hears out your excited talk about Peter and says it wouldn't hurt to have a good look at him.

You invite Peter to have dinner with all of you on Saturday, and, miraculously, he agrees. You ask Dmitrik to behave, not talk shit and not tell things about you, confirm your claim that we all come from a civilised country, not to grab your waist, as usual, while screaming that you're fat. Dmitrik says "umhu." You're not sure he's understood the task.

You go to a decent Italian place. Dmitrik takes a seat next to Peter and starts telling him about Ukraine.

"In Ukraine, we drink bucketloads of vodka, and when the Russians cut off our gas, we catch ones lost in the Carpathian Mountains and break their necks. Like this — hoopla! — the Russian's gone. The Carpathians are mountains populated by a wild Carpathian people. Paulina is from the steppes, it's not Ukraine at all anymore, in fact it's Russia, there are a ton of Russians there. And everybody, everybody drinks vodka. And gays, gays everywhere you look."

In this way, having proven that we come from a civilised country, Dmitrik swiftly moves to the second task — to dig out his secrets.

"Are you gay?" He asks Peter, chewing osso bucco. "No? Are you sure? How do you know? How can you be sure if you've never tried it? Do you like Paulina? Do you realise it means you're almost certainly gay?"

Peter laughs (you breathe a sigh of relief) and says he's not gay, has never been attracted to men, but since we are on the subject, he recently had a dream, in which he was kissing the priest from his church.

"Did the dream have a physical culmination?" Dmitrik demands and refuses to believe it didn't.

The conversation goes on in this vein till the end of the evening. Dmitrik pays for everybody else, including you, while Peter pays for himself. You note that you don't mind at all when Dmitrik pays for you, but for some reason don't really want Peter to do that. Maybe it's because you're very honest and don't want to abuse the kindness of somebody you just met. You like that thought about your own honesty.

Warmed up by the Italian red wine, you hug Peter good-bye, and he holds you close for a second. He probably felt the spiritual connection.

On the tube you expect Dmitrik to speak with a certain trepidation. Of course, you're choosing Peter for yourself, not for him, but you want his approval nonetheless.

"What can I say, Stopudiv," he says looking at you with a certain compassion, which is so unlike him. "It's not for you. I can see why you like him, he's kind…"

"And very smart," you add proudly.

"And probably smart, but it's not for you. Did you see what he was wearing?"

You admit that you never thought to pay attention to that.

"Some stretched sweater, short trousers, hiking boots. Who goes to a restaurant like that? He doesn't care about his appearance at all. You need somebody who has some sense of style. He is…," Dmitrik waves his fingers in the air, looking for words. "He's the kind you want to forgive."

You shrug. Dmitrik is a very smart guy, but what does he understand about men? All right, he understands a lot about men actually, more than you do in fact, but why the hell do you need a man with a sense of style? How is that better than honesty, decency, responsibility? If you want to look at a man with a sense of style, you can always look at Dmitrik.

Your third date again starts with a conversation about philosophy. Peter speaks long and wisely, though it has to be said that at a certain point you switch off a bit, thinking about your ex, the sale of the house, the whole hemorrhoidal pain of separation. When you get back to Peter's monologue, Peter has already finished with the theory of moral relativism and started on the practical rules of online dating. The day before he set aside some time for this, sat down and researched all there was written on the subject.

"We have already broken several major rules," Peter explains monotonously, staring into the table. You feel for him: he clearly is worried, tries not to do anything unethical. "We should not have discussed our exes, and also we should have pretended that we exist in a sort of bubble where there are no other potential partners, and we are only dating each other. And only when two people decide they only want to date each other do they agree to stop dating other people."

"I'm not dating other people anyway," you blag. "There were contenders, but I told them to wait."

Peter raises his stare; his eyes are full of terror.

"Are they people who really interested you, who could potentially be your partners? Do meet them then, absolutely do! We get on very well, but we should prepare as thoroughly as possible for the choice of a potential partner."

from FIFTEEN STORIES ABOUT RAIN

by Dzvinka Matiyash

Translated by Svitlana Bednazh

STORY 3
ISOLDE

For Eva Grokhovska

MY LIPS WHISPER WORDS OF PRAYER, I REMOVE THE BEADS FROM my neck with my disobedient fingers, pull gold bracelets from my hands, take a diamond clip from my hair. The elders step aside from me, uttering in reverence: "May God bless you, Your Majesty," their hands full of gold and pearls. I quietly say: "Pray for me, unworthy one," my words drown in the jangling sounds of the rings slipping off my fingers into the outstretched palms of the old pilgrim. My purple mantle and muslin fall on his shoulders, he crosses himself and cries, I don't know why he's crying, it is I who should be lamenting and pulling my braids off. "Do take my shoes." I bend down to undo the clips, heavily ornate with precious stones. The pilgrim places the shoes under his shirt and there are tears in his eyes, as he says in a trembling voice: "Blessed be the day when you came into the world, queen."

I close my eyes to keep from crying. I don't know whether that day was a blessed one. I believe it was a very bitter day. Maybe you, my Lord, have blessed me with bitterness, because you don't bless everyone with sweetness, although the bitterness you gave me is sweet. Oh, how sweet was the wine that we shouldn't have drunk, and which we had drunk from not knowing, from carelessness, from a lack of understanding. Accidently, because we needed so much to quench our thirst. But then another kind of thirst started tormenting us. But, can love be cautious, Lord? Can love be accidental? Could we have found the jug by accident that we shouldn't have found and from which we shouldn't have drunk? I read joy and pain in Tristan's eyes, suffering and happiness, and I knew that I wanted to go through these scriptures more and more, I knew that I would always be thirsty next to him. For he will be my day and night, my heaven and earth, my sun and rain.

I come close to the holy relics, spread out on fine Nicean silks that quiver like the sea that we travelled to Cornwall. Behind my back barons no longer hide their tears, the elders and pilgrims kneel down and pray on both sides of me. Pray for me, men of God, because I live so unworthily. I also fall to my knees, extending my hands to the holy relics. A white field gives a sigh together with me, and all the trees sigh, and the river, and the birds that circle in the sky.

But my voice does not shake, it rings like a string, like a drawn bow-string, when I take my oath with the preserved bodies of all the saints I see before me. For no man born of a woman has held me in his embrace, except King Mark, my master, and this pitiful pilgrim who took me across the river and fell with me onto the sand. I raise my eyes at my husband asking: "Is this oath acceptable, your highness King Mark?" The King nods with affirmation, his face is pale, his lips pursed together firmly, he clings to his sceptre with both hands as if he is fearful of falling. But, in truth, King Mark will never fall, because, those such as he stand firmly on the ground and know exactly how to act, being unafraid of justice. "Yes, my queen, may the Lord carry out his judgement."

I rise up and turn myself to the fire. The iron is red, the same color as the royal robe. Red is the color of kings, therefore I have nothing to fear. And I know you will be with me, Lord. Not because I deserve justification, but because you have loved sinners and the lost, thirsty and hungry for love. And I ought not to disavow my love, Lord, and you know this. I hear how King Mark clenches his teeth, I know he is afraid of looking at the fire and the red iron. I know that Tristan in his beggarly rags is clawing his fingernails into his palms and biting his lips so as not to scream, not to reveal the truth. And the truth is such that love fears neither fire nor red-hot iron.

I uncover the embers with my hands and take the iron rod in my hands. Lord, help me carry it, as you carried the cross. I take my first step. Have mercy on me, God, according to Thy loving kindness. My second step. By the multitude of Thy bounties cleanse my transgressions. My third. Wash me thoroughly from my transgressions. My fourth. And cleanse me from sin. My fifth. For I know my transgressions. My sixth. I know all about myself, Lord. My seventh. My sin is always before me. My eighth. Against Thee alone, I have sinned. My ninth. But you will not abandon me, because you love me. I throw my iron rod to the ground. And I extend my hands to everyone. They are white and clean, without a single trace of burns. Even my husband King Mark is crying now.

I lift my eyes to heaven and whisper: "Lord, it is good that you have been with me."

It begins to rain and the fire is dying out, the red-hot iron is sizzling and turns black again, just as it should be.

September 9, 2010

STORY 6
RAINING ANTS

For Lyuba Luchkevych-Vozniak

Today mother got off on the wrong foot, as she herself put it, and everything she tried to do came to naught. The cream in a small jar turned sour, and mother is very resentful if she can't drink coffee without cream in the morning. The porridge got burnt, and she had to scrape it off the bottom of the pan. Father took a long time working on the pan, which was a torturous and tedious chore. I would not have put up with it, but would have run away from that pan all the way up to the attic. But father would not give up, scrubbing the dirty pan with a scouring pad while he whistled a waltz. He succeeded in the end, because my father likes to win. He always says that if he did not like winning, he would not have been married by now. "And you, Marta, wouldn't be here either."

I could not imagine I would not have been able to exist, because the world with me in it is so beautiful, and so big. I always believe that when a new person is born, the world becomes wider and richer and gets an extra pair of eyes and can observe itself and all of its wonders more attentively. That is why I had to exist, because the world needs my eyes. My straight fair hair. It's a pity that it doesn't curl at all, not even a little. I would have really liked it, but I have almost accepted that when I grow up, I will have to plait my hair in forty one plaits and use paper curlers. It's good I haven't grown up yet. The world also needs my hands to touch everything around me in order to remember it better.

Mother's dress patterns also came to naught today. She couldn't quite draw sleeves on a very elegant frock, and pieces of paper were flying around the room like white birds, landing on the floor with a quiet rustle. They looked more like huge slabs of snow rather than birds, with mother looking sad and helpless amid the snow. She locked the door on a hook, barricading it with stools so we couldn't disturb her. Father and I wouldn't even attempt to interfere and just peeped through the keyhole, in case mother might need some help. Mother's sighs, like a bit of white smoke, slipped through the keyhole to where we were and tickled father's nostrils as he was desperate to sneeze. I couldn't help but yawn all the time because too much white smoke was hugging the floor and descending the stairs to the ground floor.

Father and I didn't know how to help mother. We even agreed to have rice and seaweed for lunch. Mother believed that eating seaweed was very healthy because it contained a lot of water and amino acids. Father, who could not tolerate seaweed since his childhood, was helping himself to it with enthusiasm, saying that today he had a vital need for iodine. "And, you, Marta, also need amino acid." I looked in horror at a green pile of seaweed rising before my eyes, and I had to eat it. It was a very sad lunch, and father and I could not believe our happiness when it was finally over. "We've defeated the seaweed, Marta," father said, proudly embracing me, "so now we can go for a walk to the forest." Mother sternly ordered us to take an umbrella because it might rain.

Father looked out of the window, then stepped outside and lifted up his head. There was not a single cloud in the sky, and father timidly uttered to mother that the rain was unlikely to come. He really didn't want to carry the umbrella with him because it was very large and awkward, and we always used to lose it under a tree. Mother shook her head in protest, ordered father to make sandwiches for us, and to fetch a thermos of tea and the umbrella.

We had such a good time in the forest. We picked bilberries for mother and a big bouquet of tiny wild carnations in a bright raspberry color. Then we took a rest and sat under our favorite oak tree, and father handed me a buttered piece of bread with cheese that had little holes in it. I was about to take a bite when I saw two ants getting trapped in the butter while three other ants were running across the cheese. Father blew the ants off the cheese, picked them out of the butter with the corner of a napkin, and noticed that there were about ten ants on his own sandwich. As I was helping him to blow them off and remove them from the butter, a whole new bunch of ants dropped on my bread again. It really started to rain ants. We kept blowing them off our arms and shoulders, and finally father decided to open up our big umbrella. The ants drummed onto it like raindrops, except for the fact that raindrops would not crawl here and there on the umbrella, but roll down peacefully instead.

Farther said that we were very lucky, because raining ants were ever so rare. It happened once every fifty years or even more seldom than that. Once, when his grandfather and grandmother happened to encounter raining ants, they didn't have an umbrella and stood there for exactly two hours, covering their heads with grandma's flowery shawl. Granny said that only very lucky people and people with a pure heart and a clear conscience encountered raining ants. I pondered that and thought long and hard about what ants, a pure heart, a clear conscience, and luck had in common. And as I was thinking, it stopped raining ants.

At home mother was waiting for us on the porch. She gave us a big hug and a kiss and uttered with a surprise that we both smelled of ants.

STORY 9
THE DICTATOR

For Vasyl Herasymiuk

The dictator was awakened by the sound of broken glass. A small crystal vase fell on the floor from the bedside table, tiny transparent crystals spilled onto the floor, the water formed a shapeless little pool, and the splendid tea roses looked even more splendid among the broken crystal pieces. The dictator pulled the bell cord, a chamber maid entered quietly, the dictator nodded to her pointing to the floor, she disappeared as quietly and came back at once with a dustpan and brush.

When the maid left, the dictator looked at the clock: it was only nine. His wife was asleep, spreading her tanned arms on a pink coversheet. The dictator wiped away the beads of sweat that were gleaming on her upper lip, her eyelids were quivering, she might be having a dream. The dictator touched her bronze shoulder, it was hot, a little sticky and defenseless. The dictator smiled with the corners of his mouth and wiped away the sweat from his brow with a muslin handkerchief. It was sultry. The dictator pulled on his white linen trousers and stepped into the garden. Hot air warmed his arms and torso, the dictator closed his eyes and turned his pale face toward the sun. He never tanned, his skin didn't even turn red in the summer, it stayed the same pale color, with only a touch of green disappearing from his cheeks.

The summer of 2010 was the hottest summer in the last hundred years. "This is the hottest summer in my 25 years of rule," the dictator thought and rejoiced a bit. He liked the heat and the power that the summer sun has over people. The heat makes them lethargic and lazy, they think slowly, and move about even more slowly, they drink a lot and sleep, they are very easy to control. The dictator dreamed for all his minions to be like this. He approached the swimming pool, neatly folded his trousers, because he didn't like untidiness, and, closing his eyes, jumped into the water.

Lying on his back in the cool water, the dictator is imagining train carriages packed with his rebellious minions at the highest speed moving toward the east. The train arrives in the desert, it slows down, guards push people out of the carriages while they are still moving. The train immediately sets off in the opposite direction, people can barely catch their breath, the desert spreads hundreds of kilometers to the south, north, west and east. There are no oases in this desert where one can hide in the shade of trees from the burning sun and take rest, and with no water at all. There are only gray stones baked red hot under the sun's rays, poisonous snakes, and cactuses.

The dictator can hear babies crying, suckling their mothers' empty breasts with their toothless little mouths, but they've drunk their last drops of milk already on their way to the desert, there's no more food left for them. The same for their mothers and fathers. The men are trying to find water, in twos and threes they flee to the four corners of the earth, not all of them will return, and those who come back will not bring any water.

While the men are absent, the women are also trying to find water, they are digging out a hole under cactuses, digging it with their small combs, because they have nothing else to dig with. The dessert's soil gets stuck between the comb's small teeth, the teeth are crumbling, but women don't pay attention to it. The most beautiful one, Alicia, is digging with her hands, because her comb has already been ruined, she's breaking her nails, cutting her fingers, and the sand feels the taste of her blood. The women let out a sigh, some start to cry, only Alicia neither sighs nor cries as if she doesn't feel the pain and doesn't know what tiredness is. She only breathes heavily and closes her eyes for a moment, wets her fingers and her eyelids with saliva. Then she wets her fingers with saliva again and licks them, so she may want to drink less and not think about water at all.

All the women now have stopped digging. Some have broken down with fatigue, some press their babies to their breasts and console the

347

older children who keep asking when finally they can return back home, because clearly it is nice here and there is lots of sand, but you can't build castles and fortresses from the sand, dig ditches and fill them with water, you can't make sand sculptures, the sand here is such that nothing can be made of it, you can't play with this sand, that's why we want to go back home, have dinner and want to drink, mother, we really want to drink. The children are crying and their mothers are crying.

Only Alicia doesn't cry, she's digging a well. She's digging it all night, by dawn her hands feel water, she's clasping her heart. The water in the well is a little bitter and warm, but you can still quench your thirst. Alicia is waking the women up, whispering "I found water, we must give the children water." The women cup the water in their palms and carry it to the children, but not all of the children wake up, many babies have died, not waiting till morning for the water. The sun rises, women wail in despair over their sons and daughters, the men gnash their teeth, clasp their fists, and curse the dictator.

Alicia is lying on her back, listening to her arms aching and contemplating how he has chosen the best spot for their death. They will die in the sand, the wind will cover their bodies with dust. Alicia frowns because the sand is getting into the small wounds on her palms, and they sting even more. She is licking her parched lips and asking herself whether things would have been different if she had not rejected his love. But she did not want to be the wife of a dictator.

She talked to him about the freedom of the country and he spread his arms in surprise because he didn't understand whose freedom she was talking about. Rather it was important that both of them were free. "Power gives limitless freedom," he said with confidence, swirling a glass of thick black wine. "You will be free with me, Alicia. I can give you everything. You can do anything you wish."

Alicia swayed her gorgeous honey-colored curls, she didn't need anything from him, because she already had everything. The mornings and evenings belonged to her, the days and nights, the heat and cold, because she knew how to enjoy them. Alicia knew that she was beautiful, and was a little ashamed that not everyone was born so beautiful, she greeted everyone she met in the streets because she seemed to pass a little of her beauty to others in this way. She wanted to be generous and, because of her own generosity, she never needed anything, because she could always give away everything she had — she gave a purse full to the brim with large banknotes to victims of fire, took off her gold earrings, diamond rings from her fingers, placing those treasures in the hands of the mother whose daughter was sick with cancer. The dictator got angry with her, but Alicia only shrugged her shoulders because she didn't understand what could be done otherwise. Alicia couldn't get bored, when there was nothing for her to do, she went to archery using a round cardboard target that she hung up on the walnut tree in their garden, or she painted bottles from the wine they drank. The dictator had a whole collection of bottles that Alicia had painted. Fawns danced on the dark green glass, splendid water nymphs swam in waterfalls, hunters in their high leg boots hunted pheasants, and the pheasants ran away from them losing their feathers, and those feathers were scattered on all the bottles.

When Alicia left him, the dictator smashed all the bottles, one by one, and then cried for a long time sitting next to the broken pieces. Then he understood how much he loved her. And he couldn't understand how she could reject his love, because he loved her so much that he would lay down all the world's treasures at her feet. And she simply walked away from him one Sunday morning, she didn't take anything except that dark blue dress and the leather sandals she wore when she appeared at his villa. After that, he hated Sunday, because on Sunday all his dreams were broken, one by one, and their broken pieces were scattered beneath his feet, just like the broken glass of the wine bottles painted by Alicia.

For ten years he tried to kill his love for her inside himself. It was a love that didn't wish to die, but he still made it die. Then, when the dictator knew that his heart was no longer stirring, when at night his lips incessantly whispered "Alicia," but his hands were no longer looking for her next to him, he burst into uproarious laughter while standing in front of the mirror in his bedroom. This laughter could be

349

heard throughout the house, the servants crossed themselves full of fear, and the cook put too much salt in the spinach soup and had to throw it away and start from scratch. The dictator would have preferred not to hear a single word about Alicia, but it was not possible because she was taking part in protests against his regime. He wanted to hate her for that, but he couldn't. He could only imagine a train taking her to the desert, her and the other rebels. Imagine her digging a well, because Alicia would have immediately started looking to escape, she wasn't one of those who would wait to be saved and not one who would cry from her own helplessness while waiting for death from thirst. The dictator couldn't imagine her dying. He could imagine all those thrown out of the train dying in the desert. But not Alicia. Perhaps, she would always lie on her back near the well she dug out herself with bitter water, looking at the cloudless sky, and not a single time would her parched lips whisper the dictator's name.

And his lips are now whispering the name of another woman. The dictator's wife is called Wanda, she is beautiful and she doesn't like to think. The dictator was looking for a woman just like this. Her father was the director of a large industrial corporation that manufactures inflatable rubber boats, they met each other at a party held by Wanda's father in honor of the dictator for lowering the tax on rubber, because the dictator really enjoyed riding inflatable rubber boats. Wanda came up to the dictator, smiling, happily offering him a bowl of cherries. Her ash colored hair covered her bare shoulders, her plump lips were the color of cherries. "What a cute baby" — the dictator thought, and when she touched his hand with her tanned fingers, he was surprised to feel that he liked this pleasant touch. Wanda was thirty-five years younger than he, and, when counting his years of experience, each year of his life would be counted as two, so Wanda was younger than him by seventy whole years. He could be her father, grandfather, husband, teacher, possessor. He taught her everything — how to use the cutlery properly, drive a car, tell good wine from bad, dance a tango. He wasn't only teaching her archery and painting bottles. When they danced, Wanda was suspended in his arms, looking into his eyes with excitement, and the dictator knew that she belonged to him with all her body to almost a millimeter, and she was his property to the tiniest mole, and he thought that power and love have a lot in common.

The dictator stepped out of the swimming pool, pulled trousers on his wet body, and set off to a gazebo where coffee with cream and chocolate croissants were awaiting him. Next to the gazebo stood a huge crystal vase, filled with water, in which roses that the dictator was treating Wanda with every day were swimming. It was so hot that the water had to be changed every hour. But the bees flew in even to drink the warm water. They clinged to the crystal edges of the vase, and those that couldn't endure it fell in the water and crawled onto the roses. The dictator at first ordered the roses to be thrown away and replaced with new ones, but then he thought that the bees would still fall in the water, and changed his mind. "Alicia would have liked it," he thought, and then in a fright brushed the thought away, because for so many nights and days he hadn't mentioned her name.

"How funny the bees are drinking the water!" Wanda took out a purple rose, brushed off a bee, and stuck it into her hair. "Only they mustn't drink the water here, this water is for the roses that you give me as a present. Why are they drinking this water?"

"Because it hasn't rained for a long time. And the bees want to drink. Let them drink," the dictator said and bit off a piece of croissant.

Wanda sat next to him and put her hand on his knee. "When do you think it will rain?"

The dictator looked at her hand, a ruby ring was sparkling on her middle finger, and he said loudly and clearly:

"There will never be any rain."

from MOTHER-OF-PEARL PORN (A SUPERMARKET OF LONELINESS)

by Irena Karpa

Translated by Vitaly Chernetsky

A GIANT PINK MERCEDES TRUCK, SHINY AND POWERFUL, PICKED up trash next to our building every day. The dark green dumpster pandoras belched their content directly into the cargo belly of the handsome Mercedes. So big and pink. Its color should have been the color of Barbie's friend Ken's penis if the designers hadn't castrated him. The fragrant train of trash wafts together with the morning fog from our courtyard to the neighboring one, and then on and on. This scent, like the scent of an old dishwashing sponge, is impossible to misidentify.

Sometimes it seemed that this was the scent exuded by some expensive French cheese. Exceptionally stinky, thus truly exquisite. A hopelessly optimistic view of things. A party in the time of plague. A plague in the time of cholera. Kisses in the time of sinusitis.

Picking through trash is a path of initiation. Any writer of fairy tales would tell you that. As would any homeless guy. Do you know how much he pulls daily from the mysterious chthonic depths of the dumpster into the light of consciousness? The Priest of the Green Garbage Can comes to know the stories of each family: what they live by, what they breathe, what they try to hide, and what they try to get rid of. In this way the Priest comes to know Others. As for knowing himself, he doesn't give a damn.

And then the pink Mercedes arrives and takes it all away into mother-of-pearl oblivion.

To be perfectly honest, we simply went on joyrides. What else can I tell you? We wandered back and forth across Europe and left generous tips everywhere. We hated this rotten Europe. It made us feel nauseated. *Fuck capitalism, fuck imperialism.* We could abandon our shiny car somewhere on an old city street — say, in Krakow — and go sleep on a park bench. Why shouldn't the park in Krakow's Old Town be perfect for a couple of chic punks? "I'm Ukrainian, and he's with me," I liked telling people. The customs officers seemed to shake in their shoes.

When rain or wind created complications, we were forced to seek shelter at expensive hotels. We didn't deal with the cheap ones as a matter of principle, because we considered it a matter of principle to pilfer expensive stuff from expensive hotels and generally damage the hotel property. It would be too perverse even for us to go to cute modest hotels, where the room costs about fifteen dollars and the hostess gladly lends you a pair of warm woolen socks on a cold night, and then smear curtains with shit. Although back in my childhood days my teacher told me that the most virtuoso monster was the one who betrayed a close friend and abandoned someone who saved you from the deepest trouble. I never succeeded in living according to his moral teachings.

We lived as we liked and where we liked. "Only those who have lots of money or have no money at all can be absolutely free," my Dad used to say. We were absolutely free. For a time, we had lots of money.

Highway E65. I think it was this one. The highway leading to Prague at the peak of the tourist season, in late May, when all hotels are packed to capacity. E65. Yes, precisely that number, an unhappy number for neurotic me. It popped up all along our drive then.

"The roads here are better than in Poland," he said.

"But the women worse," I said.

"The roads here are wider" — he.

"Just like the women" — I.

Then he pressed on the accelerator some more, and playing the death game, let go of the steering wheel. A professional speed racer. It is always scarier with these types than even with the *marshrutka* microbus drivers. At that kind of speed one should at least hold the steering wheel lightly. Not grabbing it tightly, like in kart racing, just holding it lightly....

"Why do you drive in such a way that death stares into our eyes?" I screamed into his face when the speed reached 240 km/h. I screamed and didn't recognize my own sentence.

"Don't talk rubbish!" He wanted to grab the steering wheel, but I was already holding it tightly with both hands, having jumped on it from above like tossing netting on an animal. The car continued racing in a straight line. Nothing happened to us that day. Neither that day, nor the next one. Highway E65 ended too quickly.

And this is not important.

His wife got up every morning at seven o'clock. For all four years, seven o'clock sharp. And put on her makeup. He never saw her without makeup. He never knew when she had her period. He never heard her complain of pain during her period. He never even noticed her going to the bathroom.

A heroic woman?

Fat fucking chance! All the same he got tired of her.

She never slept naked, always in pajamas. She never walked around the house in freakish house robes, with curlers in her hair or in stretched-out T-shirts.

All the same he got tired of her.

The wife knew that "the climate at home was the most important thing." As soon as he dirtied something (say, scattered crumbs by the computer, spilled tea on the table, threw a candy wrapper), she immediately picked it up. In a flash. An invisible bio-robot. She listened to the rock singer Zemfira.

And still he got tired of her.

She hated Ukrainian prostitutes from the Moscow beltway. She spoke in a piercing voice. Pierced all the body parts that were good for piercing and subjected her body to tanning and tattoos.

And he got tired of her.

She was thrifty with the money he gave her. She never exceeded two thousand dollars a month, which was difficult. She drove their son to the kindergarten in the morning and picked him up in the evening, and who the hell knows what she did for the rest of the day. (What did she do all day back at home?) An enigmatic woman.

He got tired of her.

She changed moods and faces "in accordance with some incomprehensible, logic-defying rules," was never one and the same; he didn't know who she really was. But why would a man need the truth? The truth is the fate of cattle. The non-cattle go for mysteriousness!

Ha-ha! Got tired of her!

She sat and waited like a faithful Penelope while he was hanging out who-knows-where (in my city) with God knows whom (me). So why

DID HE GET TIRED OF HER?

Istanbul. Constantinople. The Royal City, as the Slavs called it.

Our princes back in the gray-haired (or just highlighted?) days of yore ran here to affix their shields to its gates.

According to a history instructor at the Kyiv Taras Shevchenko University, where my younger sister goes to school, Prince Oleg was the first to drag himself over there:

"So, the guy just sat there in Kyiv. He was bored. There was nothing to do. So, he called his warriors and said, 'Warriors, get in your boats.'

The warriors got into their boats and sailed to the Black Sea. So they sail through the Black Sea and suddenly — bam! — they approach the shore. Wow, can you believe it — it's the Byzantine shore! Then the warriors flipped their boats and attached wheels to them. And now they're not sailing, but driving. And the Byzantines look out from their windows: 'No-o-o-o! What's this! Boats driving on dry land! We've never seen stuff like this!' And out of surprise they surrendered Byzantium. And you say — 'affixed his shield to the gate'...."

Too bad that when we got stuck in an Istanbul traffic jam on Sunday I didn't know this story. Otherwise I would use it to entertain my guy. Then he wouldn't spit, swear, and curse everything in this world. (I get really scared when he does this.) And with Istanbul bridges it is one hell of a job to figure out what leads where.

"Fuck!" He screams.

"Damn!" I say in support.

"So where do we go now? There's no on ramp here. We started from Taksim* and now we're back in this friggin' Taksim!"

His foot hurts. Yesterday, when we wandered through the Martian landscapes of Cappadocia, he climbed a ve-e-e-ry tall rock, and then the cool dude confidently jumped down. And he shouldn't have. He badly bruised his foot. Good thing that he didn't veer some 20 centimeters to the side — then I wouldn't have my guy anymore.

"And what were you thinking?" I asked him lovingly then. "You have all our money, and the tickets, and the car is rented in your name!"

Well, I'm complaining just in case, as he could very well have disappeared into the abyss. Although then at least nothing would hurt him anymore. Not like now. Oh you poor thing.

On Sundays EVERYTHING is closed in Istanbul. With the exception, naturally, of restaurants, cafés, and tourist trinket vendors.

"Tourists, tourists everywhere, and not a pharmacy in sight," out of fear I almost begin speaking in poetry lines.

---

* A neighborhood in Istanbul famous for its cross-dressers, hotels, and pigeons [author's note].

At long last, one pharmacy was indeed located. We got its address from the waiter at the little restaurant where my poor guy wolfed down his kebab. He didn't just tell us, he also drew a map for me with all the details and ran after me all the way to the tram stop (we left the car at a parking lot where they treated us to lemonade and let us charge our cell phones from their outlets, although they couldn't say even one word in English — it's just they are nice Turkish guys!) — he ran to tell me that he made a mistake in one letter of the pharmacy's name. As if I would have been too proud to go to an open pharmacy if one letter in its name didn't correspond to my secret data. He was an excellent waiter, in other words. I even wanted to give him a hug. At the very minimum he changed the balance point of my impressions about the brotherhood of waiters. And at the maximum he imprinted in me the stereotype of the Turks as a hospitable nation. Even though back in the day they took us captive and sent us to harems wholesale, it's now different. You can forgive half of their history just for their baklava. And the other half of their history for the falafels.

I calmly got on the streetcar for three stops (nobody made a pass at me, nobody took me for a "Natasha"*), calmly (nobody ran after me, or tried to bite me, or to kidnap me) walked to the university, showed two older guys with dirty fingernails but clean eyes my piece of paper and they pointed me to the pharmacy: "Here. There you are."

"Hello," I say to the good-looking woman at the pharmacy counter in English, "I need an elastic bandage and something like Fastum Gel.**"

She understood about the elastic bandage, and as for the rest, she smiled. OK, I think, now's the time. I climb a stool, wave my hands happily impersonating a kamikaze on board an IL-86 plane, then noisily fall on the floor. Then I switch to the image of a Lame Duck, limping back and forth across the pharmacy, take my sandal up to my

---

* In Istanbul the prostitutes of European post-Soviet background are called "Natashas" [author's note].

** Brand name for ketoprofen gel, an analgesic used to treat muscle and joint pain, used in many East European countries [translator's note].

mouth and blow at it. The pharmacist looks at me silently. And smiles in a good-natured way. And even more good-naturedly says,

"OK, I got it. Here is an ointment that should help you; its ingredients are helpful in the cases of traumatic injuries, bruises, pulled muscles, etc."

You think I felt ashamed and lowered my gaze? No! I simply paid for my purchase; very-very sincerely, the way Ukrainians can do only when they are abroad, I thanked the good-looking woman at the pharmacy, gave her the money, and pressed the plastic bag with pharmaceutical goods to my heart.

The performance ended well. Both the actors and the audience were deeply moved and, indeed, came.

With a happy expression carved on my face I bring the purchased treasure to my suffering guy. He is also overjoyed and leaves the waiter an unheard-of tip. We walk down a narrow old street (aaaa! blechhh! I too use clichés when describing the details of foreign cities! Ha!) until we find some benches, have a seat there, and apply to the cute size 11 foot the life-giving ointment. Immediately, as in a proper old-fashioned fairytale, it helps, and our three healthy (and one, not very) feet set out in the direction of Hagia Sophia.

On the way my limping companion wants to photograph tall Muslim women fully clad in black, but they adroitly hide behind the backs of their puny husbands. How can six foot six hide behind four foot nine? A miracle.

Everything's so wonderful, everything's so wonderful, damn it, everything. So wonderful....

P.S. Yeah, everything's so wonderful. If only the hyperactive followers of Islam didn't gouge the eyes of Christian saints on the frescos in Cappadocia (as their rules say it's a big no-no to depict humans) — it would have been utterly complete *super gut*.

Tomorrow never dies...
Sheryl Crow

Have you ever had an encounter with death? Did you have an experience like this? I mean, not with your own death. But... somehow with a distant one. I have no right to ask about the death of a person close to you. I know nothing about this person. So far. I only know about a distant relative of this person. But to hell with metaphors. Even such metaphors as letters to Death. Here's a letter like this, half a year old, which I found on my hard drive:

Grant peace to his soul, o Lord. Or perhaps, save him, Allah. I don't know what Muslims say when one of them dies of a brain tumor at the age of twenty-five. Teguh Wicaksono. Yogyakarta. Java. Indonesia.

I rode a moped with you to buy canvas and paint. You were an artist. Not a super talented one, but you painted non-stop. And I painted a self-portrait in your garage, from the nose to the belly button, and you said, "I like it." Back then I restrained myself from returning the compliment out of honesty.

You had long thick dark hair. Someone would say, "luxuriant." But not me. I tried to banish any erotic fantasies that included your tanned back and the long hair cascading on it. I think we hated each other. You hated my tight T-shirts and absence of bras, offensive to your Muslim culture. And I hated your teasing me for my laziness, even though you also did nothing but paint your talentless pictures. You wasted a hellish amount of paint and canvas, because paint and canvas are cheap in your country.

But now you are no more. You know, I have long stopped feeling averse to you. Who knows, maybe your body still lies unburied somewhere in a shady corner of your scorching hot Block C. We lived in neighboring rooms. You showed me each new piercing, each new addition to a tattoo. I occasionally complimented them, but you were afraid I'd touch you. And now you are no more?

You had a Ukrainian-Canadian wife. Jodie was her name, older than you by several years, a plump brown-eyed blond girl. She spoke Indonesian very slowly and always called you, "Mas Teguh?" — invariably with an interrogative intonation. Your English wasn't that great but you were never afraid of tilting your head to the side and asking me about the meaning of this or that word. It's so strange, Teguh.

I now have reggae playing on the stereo, and you can no longer hear any music, nor even the call of the muezzin so common outside your window. I don't understand how you could no longer be living. Remember, you wanted to go to Canada and sell your paintings there for $100 apiece Canadian, and Jodie grumbled at you for giving them away for a pittance. How can this be, Teguh?

You and your wife divorced. It is indeed strange how you could be together. She even almost converted to Islam to marry you. She hated your impracticality. You dragged her to live in an artist commune, together with a bunch of others. You had rats in the attic, geckos on the walls, and a dog on the floor. You had a best friend, a refugee from East Timor. I could never remember his name.

Before leaving you, your wife cried. She told me in India that she had left you. I found out in Delhi that she was gone. And now in Kyiv I learn that you're gone. Does she cry now, Teguh? Tears come easy for women.

It is easy to imagine you dead. Death even becomes you. Perhaps because for a person of color it is harder to go pale. They pale somehow imperceptibly, gradually, their colors dissolve in the world that surrounds them. How much more were you planning to accomplish here? Did you speak about this with someone, Teguh? You had lots of friends with high-pitched voices who screamed and laughed and threw back and forth words spoken with an intonation fit for a carnival. Forgive me my past antipathy. Although you likely do not care anymore. I wonder whether Jodie feels guilty, since even I do. Although, why this "even"? I did feel irritation, anger, antipathy. Even if it was only for a short time, what right did I have to feel like this? And now I feel weak and foolish, and I understand little.

The year of your birth, 1978. The year of your death, 2004. Which one of these two is more important?

Teguh Wicaksono. An artist who liked to cook salted fish wrapped in banana leaves. The guy for whom we brought several patches from Thailand to sow on his motorcycle jacket. I remember your eyes, giant like all of Asia. Farewell.

Amen.

RAINY DAY

by Irena Karpa

from the cycle "Candy, Fruit, and Sausages"

Translated by Vitaly Chernetsky

WHEN WE WERE LITTLE, I ACTED REASONABLY RIGHT FROM THE start, but Halia back then understood little about life. Whether this was because she was six years younger than me or that I was a super-gifted person, I can't tell you for sure. She did take on faith whatever I'd babble about. We did have one taboo: the topic of a rainy day. This topic had been introduced by our art teacher Natalia Petrivna. The rainy day pertained both to ordinary, straightforward things and to not-so-ordinary ones. For instance, during composition class, Natalia Petrivna would talk about a piece of some fabulous colored leather intended for a 3-D appliqué piece, "Don't cut in the middle! Be frugal, cut at the side. Save some material for a rainy day."

Also for a rainy day one would save good glue or high-quality solvent, watercolor paints from Leningrad or squirrel-tail brushes. There was a terrible shortage of the latter — the rainy day was already breathing down our necks.

The rainy day, like nuclear war, while terrifying in and of itself, was also used in ironic educational contexts.

"Sha-ma-la!" Natalia Petrivna would pronounce the name of one of my classmates syllable by syllable. "Why are you painting a black background for the hundredth time? Huh? There's no need to worry — no dirt can ruin a black background. And who did you leave the draperies for? Pushkin? Did you leave them for a rainy day?"

Pushkin, the poor Russian poet, surfaced in the everyday life of average Western Ukrainian consumers much more frequently than the Russian intelligentsia promoters of their "our everything" could hope for. In our world, Pushkin washed dishes, did algebra homework, cultivated vegetable beds, and simply did everything an ordinary kid didn't feel like doing.

So, my sister and I only thought about Pushkin when he appeared from Dad's mouth: "And who's going to put away the shoes? Pushkin?" We imagined his black sideburns doing chores in our hallway. But no matter how much you sigh, the sideburns won't appear on their own — so you pick up a dusting rag, wipe the shelf, and put away the shoes. And the saddest thing is that you get no bonuses for this. It's just that Saturday is Saturday. And on Saturdays, like it or not, you have to clean up the house. And if at school they called on me to set an example, since I was a straight-A student, here it was the complete opposite. Mom would bring up as a model to emulate kids that were somewhat dim but agile and hard-working, like, for instance, Oksana Nakonechna. And of me Mom would say,

"Such a dawdler! You're doing everything to spite me, so that I won't ask you again, right?"

By then I got used to being a dawdler. Even looked at myself calmly in the mirror or in photos where I stood, black-and-white and heavy, holding by the steering wheel a plastic toy car that looked too stupid for my respectable age of eight, with two thin locks of hair stuck to my large sweat-covered forehead. I looked calmly and thought, "Oh. A dawdler."

But as for doing this out of spite, no way. Mom certainly could hold up as a model the hard-working Oksana Nakonechna, who, upon seeing that miracle of technology, a vacuum cleaner (her family still didn't have one), could in twenty minutes vacuum our entire apartment. She was grateful for the miracle of merely touching a stovetop oven..., which I consciously took advantage of. If someone wants to work, who'd be so heartless as to take away this person's right to do it?

"You're like your father!" Mom would continue. "The bosses. Content not to do anything yourselves, just order others around."

In reality, I couldn't even give orders to myself, let alone others. And if Oksana Nakonechna, that saint — according to my Mom — quickly cleaned everything up and ran out to play in the street, I was — what's the right way to put it — of a slightly different constitution. To *run* was an impossible task. I had too much weight and dignity. Consequently, this was also the reason I could not clean the house quickly. For I was an aesthete. I would, say, sit in front of a three-shelf étagère; at the bottom I'd arrange the least pretty and least loved rubber baby dolls, erector sets in boxes and a plastic cup stolen from someone outdoors — that's Hell. Next came our earthly World: dolls and their furniture. They sat there taking tea and showing off their clothes to each other. And at the very top dwelled the ethereal creatures: new toys, plush animals (I hated dolls and loved stuffed animals), and other nice objects that resisted classification. That was my Heaven. And, needless to say, the Universe of the three-shelf étagère could not be arranged quickly and once and for all — it required all the time the designing intrusion of a Higher Reason. Mine, in this case.

So that's where it was. But mom reacted to this mysticism with a jumping rope. That is, she spanked me with it. Someone told her that this would be a catalyst. But it was all like water off a duck's back for me. I sat there arranging the inhabitants of the three worlds, singing mournful folksongs, and dreaming that through the open window some visiting TV reporters would hear me and come up to the fourth floor to do an interview. How, they would ask, do you manage to arrange your toys so logically and to sing in such a special way?

This was the only thing I hoped for, this rescued "specialness." For otherwise I stood no chance — my voice didn't ring like a bell but hummed like a pipe, into which someone stuck the very rag with which I didn't finish dusting the shelves. Thus they would never give me either solo parts in the choir or make me emcee at official events at school, although I did have a good ear and good diction. They would stick me together with those voices where the person "carrying the part" was missing. Or where they desperately needed something low, a baritone, and our boys before their voices broke squealed so high that God help them....

"Karpa. You'll be the third voice."

Or the fourth. Once even the fifth. Although I could howl the first no worse than Lara Protsiuk if I made an effort. Still, the first voice parts were for pretty thin blondes, or at least girls with light auburn hair, with long thin legs and bulging pretty eyes (like Lara Protsiuk). And as for me — just look at the pics with the toy car — few things have changed... Woe is me. But in principle, I always secretly believed that my unique talent was also being saved for a Rainy Day.

Nobody knew when the Rainy Day was supposed to arrive. However, no one doubted its inevitability either: it would come for sure. And for those who didn't prepare — it'll be curtains for you. Check please! So you must be prepared. Not get enough sleep or enough to eat, but be prepared all the same.

Although, on the other hand, my sister and I possibly did not delve into such serious thoughts when we hid the candy and chocolates brought by our parents from Poland or the Czech Republic.

"Children, where are you taking these?" Mom would say in surprise at the unfinished sweets.

"To save for the rainy day," Halia would answer in a businesslike fashion. For her everything I explained looked unquestionably important and understandable a priori to the world of the adults of which I was an ambassador.

"Bite your tongue!" Dad would say fearfully. "God save us from ever getting to this."

We looked our parents straight in the eye and confidently continued our itinerary to the sofa bed. It was there, in the holes in its underside, that we stored all our Rainy Day savings.

Halia liked singing on and on, like a mantra, the nonsensical line "Rubik's cube, Anastasia." And only when Mom and I took turns joining in singing her tune of courtly love (our voices merged with hers and she did not appear to notice our intervention much, continuing instead to play with her long-haired — which was such a rarity for Soviet dolls — Cinderella), and finally Dad, too (it was impossible to ignore his singing, since it came an octave lower): "Ru-bik's cube, A-na-sta-sia!" Halia would fall silent and then start crying.

"So, are you ashamed?" I gloated. "Why sing such stupid stuff?"

Although in reality Dad probably should have been ashamed the most. How could he, so big and with a such a low voice, sing such nonsense?

Among Halia's hits there was another Russian song, "I Met Marusia on a Sandy Beach," from the old musical *Wedding in Malinovka*. To be more precise, the part of the song that began with, "Da-da-da-da-da-da-da, and she wore pink stockings, da-da-da, da-da-da-da ..."

"Her waist in a tight corset!" Halia, that curly-haired angel, finished victoriously.

To be fair, one should admit that my brother Yuri and I also transgressed with Russian pop hits in our innocently foolish age just like Halia. We especially loved Alla Pugachova and the song by a poprock band that went, "And we dream not of the rumble of spaceships launching...." (processing the word *rokot*, "rumble," as *rok ot*, "rock from"). We heard the word "rock" and didn't care where it came from. Generally speaking, the situation wasn't as hopeless as in the case of my friend Artur, who, at the same age, anticipating his future career as an experimental musician, sang in a most businesslike fashion the hook from another Soviet song. The kid imagined it to be about a robot, a silvery "blakinastikum" from outer space. Just like us, when the time came, he was badly shaken when he found out the brutal truth of the song's actual story about *iabloki na snegu*, apples scattered on snow-covered ground.

Apples were one of the fruits that escaped shortages, so Halya and I didn't save them for a Rainy Day. There was no need to buy them still unripe in Moscow and then keep them at home for half a week on top of the radiator so that they would ripen. This way one handled the still tart bananas — if your own lack of patience played a bad trick on you and you bit into a banana like this, it would tie your mouth in knots as if it were knitting a woolen sock there. In fact, bananas also were bad for saving for a Rainy Day because they could rot before it arrived. The story was different with chocolates and candies. As far as our memory could tell, they never went bad but always radiated a fine, exciting chocolaty fragrance. Besides, at night they were protected by my weight, since I slept on that very sofa bed with the secret hideaway. Sometimes I technically slept *inside* the sofa bed, preferring the sturdy particleboard of its frame to the weak deteriorated springs. I don't know why it took us so long to throw away that sofa bed — apparently, it was precious for my father as a repository of memories about his bachelor past.

Sometimes the Rainy Day, not arriving on its own, would send its messengers. This happened on days when it was already some time since Mom and Dad had come back from abroad and all their presents were hopelessly eaten. All save for those that were hidden in the sofa bed. Then Halia and I, weighing all the pros and cons (and in reality led by my appetite, since Halia copied me in everything), reached into the hole and felt up those sweets. We pulled them out and examined them. And then again reached into the hole to get another piece, exactly the same. We hid everything in pairs in order to avoid the panic of division when the Rainy Day finally came.

But for some strange reason it wasn't coming. We got tired of waiting for it, and one fine day devoured all our emergency provisions. Neither our teeth, nor or stomachs, nor our conscience ached at all. We only felt sorry there was nothing left. So for a long time afterward, in expectation of new goodies from abroad, we secretly, hiding it from one another, felt the holes in the sofa bed with our hands. What if there was still something there saved for a Rainy Day?

A VILLAGE
AND ITS WITCHES

by Tanya Malyarchuk

Translated by Michael M. Naydan

I

MY DAD WAS BORN IN A VILLAGE WHERE WITCHES AND WASTED people live. I'm not taking about children and animals. My childhood was left in that village. My children's clothes, especially the bright yellow rubber boots and dubious red checkered coat with bonbon tassels on the chest. Dad's chessboard. Dad's friends from the past, whom I put in the category of wasted people. In this particular village you could also find older men who remember when dad rode through the village on a goat. Dad hides that fact masterfully.

In the village there is also a bread bakery, a plundered Polish Catholic church and a cemetery. The inhabitants of the village are grouped in a mystical way around these three not quite buildings, not quite metaphysical categories, because they all used to work, are working, or will work at the bakery, everyone in one way or another during atheistic times took part in the plundering of the church, and everyone sooner or later will lie shoulder to shoulder in the old Polish-Jewish-Western Ukrainian cemetery.

The majority of the witches worked at the bakery, one of them even happened to be a distant aunt of mine.

Her name was Kateryna. She always smelled of bread. Her root cellar, at which I used to secretly take a peek, was jammed with stale bakery goods. They say she fed the bread to her chickens and pigs, and that her chickens never even looked at feed at all.

Kateryna beat dad several times when he was quite little. She beat two of dad's younger sisters, and even thrashed dad's mother. She hated people for living better off, and particularly for living at all.

Every morning I watched Kateryna carry water from the well to her root cellar. She carried buckets in both hands. With her head stooped over. In a kerchief. I used to gaze from the window through a curtain so Kateryna wouldn't see me. But she would see me. At the last moment, when she was about to disappear in the root cellar, she suddenly would turn her head sharply in my direction and quite intently, with all the hate that could fit in such a small woman, stare right in my eyes, through the curtain through which it was impossible for anyone to see. Out of fear I would suddenly fall to the floor paralyzed for the next half hour.

I felt guilty before Kateryna because I knew about her witchery. Because I was spying on her, because I was constantly suspecting her of something. I liked her. Because in a village such as my dad's, being a witch was the only more or less decent alternative to being wasted. A thinking person had to choose. Either stop thinking, or think in an entirely different way. People will either begin to scorn you, or fear you.

Back then there was nothing more terrifying than that Kateryna. Kaska.

Probably too for my dad, who was already grown-up. When he would come to the village on weekends to see me, it was the same, each morning he would spy on Kateryna through the window. One time I found him paralyzed on the floor. We silently exchanged glances.

"Look, don't tell anyone," my dad said to me later when we were shelling and spitting out pumpkin seeds, "and be careful."

I asked him in surprise: "Not tell anybody what?"

My dad flicked his hand. He loved spitting out pumpkin seeds in the village; that's maybe why he used to come to the village. It wasn't the prettiest of sights. My dad spit out the shells all over himself and everything around him. He sat among the shells like Pantagruel. I tried to spit out the husked seeds the same way he did, but mine came out neater anyway.

"This isn't a village," dad said, "but a witch's spawn."

"I like Kaska."

You might think that you think so. She's put that good will toward her into your head. She needs others to like her, so it's easier to destroy them later. She wants to set you against me even more."

Kaska's granddaughter, who was my age, came to visit her one summer. She was fair-haired and emaciated. There were days when on her white as milk skin you could make out every blood vessel. She talked quietly and slowly. She could have died at any moment. It seemed that way. She was like a small bird. A teeny-tiny bird. I asked the teeny-tiny bird to speak louder so I wouldn't be afraid she might suddenly die, and the teeny-tiny bird, in good turn, with all her strength exerted herself, uttering each word. She followed me like a crystal sleepwalker. I led her along puddles and streams, I took her on purpose to the swamp and to other people's gardens to steal tomatoes, but I never let pale-white girl out of my sight, because she might have disintegrated into tiny crystal bits, or pour out like milk, or dissolve in the air, or fly away. Often pale-white girl would sit on the grass and say that she didn't have the strength to get up, her thin arms and legs reminded me of branches broken off from the trunk of an ash-tree. I dragged pale-white girl onto me, telling her that we can be late for the rails and miss the train. Pale-white girl whined in my ear, and I dragged her, and it was quite easy for me. I took care of pale-white girl as though she were a Barbie doll.

We went to the rail bed every day to wave at the train that passed along the village right at six in the evening. The train was really nice. There aren't any like that now. We hopped on one leg and made faces at the passengers in the windows of the train who were tired from the long road. One time a teenage guy gave us the finger through the window.

The train at six in the evening is almost an event in the village, where there was nothing besides a bakery, with a Polish Catholic church and cemetery with bad words inscribed all over it and a cemetery that smelled of lilac and rotten pears every season of the year.

Promptly at seven in the evening Kateryna stepped out onto the pasture and screamed out with all her strength: "Lyubka! Lyubka! Come get something to eat!"

At that time Lyubka and I were hiding in a bush behind Kateryna. Lyubka didn't want to eat. She ate very little, a single green apple was enough for her the whole day. Though I also fed Lyubka jam from my grandmother's root cellar.

"I have to go," Lyubka whispered bitterly.

"But you don't want to eat?"

"I don't want to."

"Then don't go yet."

"Don't go?"

Pale-white girl always spoke in a questioning intonation. She never was sure of anything, she always needed to ask what to do, what to think, and how to live. It was easy for me to make decisions for her.

"Don't go."

"But my Grammy will get ticked, won't she?"

"She won't."

If Kateryna every showed devotion to anyone, then it was only for Lyubka, who was the only person in the world with whom she could be good. If she could have it her way, she would carry Lyubka for days on end on her shoulders. Every morning, when she had enough strength to run, Lyubka would run away from Kaska to me and would eat a green apple at my place and cherry plum jam — her daily food. A quiet war went on between Kaska and me for the right to be with Lyubka. That's another reason why Kaska hated me, but in silence, not exhibiting her hate in front of Lyubka.

Lyubka was the only one in the village who had no idea her grandmother was a witch.

"Lyubka! Daughter dear! Come get something to eat!"

Then I came from behind the bush and boldly answered instead of Lyubka: "She says she doesn't want to eat."

Kateryna quite intently looked right into my eyes. I trembled out of fear, but stood straight on my legs. Kateryna right at that very second could have turned me into a ball and chucked me all the way to Zelenivka — if not for the fact that her crystal granddaughter had not been monitoring the battle from not far away.

"Where's Lyubka?"

"She's hiding because she's afraid that you'll take her to the house right away."

"But it's already late."

"It's not even dark. Lyubka still wants to play with me a bit."

"She's tired. She can't walk a lot."

"Lyubka says she already can't walk, but she can still sit."

"Kateryna like a mad woman would run into the bushes and carry out Lyubka in her arms. Lyubka whispered quietly:

"I don't want to eat."

"Then you don't have to. But we'll wash your feet, okay?"

"Okay?"

"Okay."

"I was already out of there. Offended, I sat there on a fallen hazelnut tree and watched as Kaska carried out Lyubka to her root cellar.

Lyubka for me was the justification for evil. Proof of its imperfection.

Right about that time for the first time I said to my dad that there is no great evil, just a lot of little ones. My dad answered that I'm stupid.

"But look how good Kaska is with Lyubka, how she cares for her and how she loves her. Is that evil you're talking about capable of love?"

"Kaska is taking care of Lyubka because she feels guilty. Why do you think Lyubka has leukemia? Descendants pay for the actions of an evil person.

2

Lyubka died the way I thought she would. Like a little bird. A teeny-tiny bird. She disintegrated into crystal bits, poured out like milk, dissolved in the air, flew away.

Fairly soon after that when Kaska was carrying water from the well, I stuck my heat out of the window and screamed after her:

"Witch!"

Kaska looked into my eyes quite intently with all the hate that could fit in such a not very big world and said:

"So what?"

from FROM ABOVE LOOKING DOWN

by Tanya Malyarchuk

Translated by Michael M. Naydan

I

LAST NIGHT A WOLF BEGAN HOWLING NEAR MY WINDOW. I WAS lying in bed, covering up my head with a throw, I was afraid to look out, but it was a wolf for sure. He could look inside, or even break the window and jump in, he could do all manner of wolfish things, and that's why I was really afraid.

He left only toward morning.

It's good that I don't have any sheep, which the wolf would have easily killed.

I thought that brown bears live in the Carpathian Mountains, and not wolves.

When I go outside in the morning, I first wash my feet in the dew.

I always get up really early here. That's not the way I usually am.

I do something different every day. Sometimes I sit under the porch on the steps and gaze out at the mountains. They're just right in front of me, in a row, the same in height but different in the way they each look. I've thought up a name and patient's history for each mountain. I've established a gender for each one. From time to time the mountains even converse with me.

Sometimes with a knitting needle I work on knitting a lacy white bed cover. I've done more than half of it. I sit in the yard in a swing chair so that everything looks as idyllic as possible, a light wind blows softly, my legs are covered in a throw, and I, rocking, slowly knit loop after loop, from time to time stopping, I look at the mountains, remember something, even doze off, and then continue. I'm not disturbed by the fact whether the cover will scarcely ever be needed. You could use it for something other than for what it's designed, for example, as a fisherman's net.

I wash up once a week, not more. Here amid the mountains you somehow stop noticing your hair is dirty.

Sometimes I'm terrified there won't be anything to do tomorrow, but I counted up all possible activities, and there have to be enough of them for several years one activity per day. In the worst case you can just wash more often.

Here I've learned to be bored with joy. Boredom — that is also one of the activities. When you give in to it honestly and completely, then you can spend very many needless days quite pleasantly.

Time I really have a lot of it.

Here I've stopped being afraid of it. I'm afraid of wolves. I thought, what if a wolf suddenly comes in the middle of the day, what will happen then? Will he throw himself at me right away, or will he growl for a while at first? Is his growling different than a dog's? Maybe I can tame him and he'll become my dog? He'll sleep with me on my bed. In any case, no one will defend me from a wolf, there will just be me alone. No one will come to my aid, that's well and good.

It's strange that I'm so young and wise.

I don't have a watch or electricity. When evening comes, I lay myself down to sleep.

I very rarely use a candle.

Here I'm also not afraid of thieves, burglars and rapists.

Here I make meals for myself, I sing to myself, I'm my own master.

I truly became peaceful here. And very polite, it's just too bad that there's no one here either to show or verify that politeness.

2

Several times a week I walk six kilometers to my aunt Mytsya's and her daughter Varka's place. Aunt Mytsya is sixty-seven years old. Varka is thirty years younger than her mother — she's thirty-seven, and she's completely blind. The village of Dzembronya ends right past Aunt Mytsya's house.

Aunt Mytsya has two cows, and I get milk, sour cream and cheese from her.

Varka shucks corn — for that she doesn't need her eyes. Aunt Mytsya gives me food, and I give her money.

"How are you gettin' along by yerself?" Aunt Mytsya asks.

"Last night a wolf howled at my window. What do you think, are there wolves around here?"

"I haven't seen one, but my grandmother told me that somehow they even killed one with a stick. What scoundrels! Fer sure they sniffed you've come here and they think you'll be afraid of 'em. Main thing don't be afraid. They sense when someone's afraid of 'em and they can attack."

Aunt Mytsya is the only mother I know who wants her child to die sooner than she. If my aunt dies first, it's unclear what will happen with Varka. Varka was blinded by some disease of the brain and now, with each passing year, becomes more and more helpless. She doesn't even go to the bathroom without her mother. It seems to her that she's on the very peak of a mountain and with one step can sink into the abyss. One time Varka thought that she'll sink right then and there, she fell to the ground and began to scream so that I could hear it six kilometers away. Varka thinks that aunt Mytsya is tricking her, that it's safe for a blind girl to walk around safely.

"What are you eating?" Aunt Mytsya asks.

"I'm cooking what I want. I have a stove. I think when I stay here for the winter, I won't freeze even then, that stove is so good."

"It's hard for you, no?"

"Just when I need to chop firewood, but I gather up brushwood and stoke the stove with it."

"What kind of a fire do you get from brushwood?"

Varka hardly talks to me. She just says "good day." Once she used to work in the neighboring village as a librarian.

"Watch yerself, cause somethin'll happen to you and nobody'll come to help. If somethin' should happen to me, then nobody'll help Varka. It's better for you cause you got eyes. She doesn't. It's hard without eyes."

I feel like aunt Mytsya is happy for me because she stopped being the end of the village. I've now become the end of it. Aunt Mytsya's happy not to be last on the list.

Her cow gives really fatty milk.

"Ya know what to do so's the milk doesn't go sour?"

"What?"

"Put it in a bucket of cold water. And if it doesn't go foul, it's best to throw a frog into the milk."

"I'm turning foul."

"Why'd it turn foul if a frog's the same as milk? It's all the same nature."

"Maybe if you wash the frog well… It doesn't bite?"

"A frog?"

"I heard there's frogs that bite."

"Who told you that? Where could you hear something like that? It's all a lie. Frogs don't bite. Just if some witch puts a spell on one."

I need to go because it's going to get dark soon. In the mountains it gets dark really quickly.

"Good-bye," I say to Aunt Mytsya, "thanks so much for the milk. You're so good to me."

"Sweetie, then who's help you if not for me? Since we're here all alone, we need to help out one another. And we're here alone — just us and God above us. And it's really close to God from here."

LESYA AND HER DENTIST

by Tanya Malyarchuk
Translated by Michael M. Naydan

I

HIS ENTIRE LIFE YURI IVANOVYCH WORKED AS A DENTIST FOR the Communist Party. He lived in a lavish apartment with high ceilings in the center of town. He was extremely wealthy with two cars and a summer home in Koktebel in the Crimea. His first wife dumped him for America, taking their son Orest with her. Yuri Ivanovych didn't hear anything from them for years.

He remarried in the 1990s right at the time he turned ninety. His wife was about thirty. Yuri Ivanovych knew very little about her, just the fact that she had a nice figure, that her name was Lida, that she loved to dress up elegantly and to drink champagne.

An old neighbor, whose name was also Lida, for a while fed Yuri Ivanovych and his cat Marquise. In fact she used to feed Marquise even better than him. Once a month she even washed Yu.I.'s bedding and clothes, and God knows where, she managed to find the phone number of his American son Orest, and in a minute-long conversation informed Orest that no matter what, he is his son and must help his aged father.

From that time on every month Orest began to send the neighbors three hundred dollars, of which fifty dollars was payment for Lesya Zhuravel.

Lesya cared for Yuri Ivanovych for an entire year.

She made $600 in the course of that year.

2

The workday for her began at six AM because Yuri Ivanovych would always wake up at seven.

Lesya got on the first morning trolleybus, and, when she walked into the spacious lavish high-ceilinged apartment, Yuri Ivanovych was already waiting for her.

"Good morning," Lesya said. But Yu.I. didn't answer. He just sat there on his bed, leaning against a cane, with his left leg nervously twitching.

It's good that Yuri Ivanovych doesn't wake up at six, cause then I'd have to walk all the way there," Lesya said to her husband Misha with relief.

Lesya propped up Yuri Ivanovych against herself and led him to the bathroom. There she took off his breeches, stepped out, and waited for him by the door until he finished his business; then she walked in, pulled up his breeches and led Yu.I. back to his room. Then Lesya turned on the TV for Yu.I. to the DISCAVERY channel and went to make herself busy with breakfast. The DISCAVERY channel was on all day, this was Yu.I.'s favorite channel. He never watched the news or entertainment programs. He already was at that age when surrounding reality loses meaning.

Yu. I. didn't speak with Lesya. When she somehow would address him for example, with:

"Yu. I., don't you want to go to the bathroom?"

Or:

"Would it be okay if I bake fritters for you today?"

Or:

"Yu.I., are you sure you want to go to the bathroom or are you faking it?"

…Yu.I. would say to her harshly:

"Don't talk to me."

Yu.I. never went outside. Three years already. One stroke per year. When Lesya said:

"Let's go for a walk."

... Yu.I. grew in a fever and quietly screamed:

"I said don't talk to me! I'll shoot you out of here like a cork!"

On the other hand Yu.I. liked bananas as well as pumpkin pudding, and after several rebukes by Yu.I., she bought a cook book and learned to make it.

Lesya also loved bananas. One time she ate one of his. Yu.I. whacked her with his cane on the back and Lesya began to cry. Then she called him a monster, and Yu.I. also began to cry.

""I don't want to see you here any more," Yu.I. said to her.

Yuri Ivanovych's neighbor hired a different care giver, but she announced from the very first day to her patient that he's an old fart and that she's going to do everything the way she tells him, and worst of all, she turned on channel "1 + 1" instead of DISCAVERY.

Lesya came back. Her working day ended at seven in the evening.

Yu.I. would lay on the bed and shut his eyes.

"Yuri Ivanovych," Lesya whispered, "are you asleep? Turn off the TV?"

He remained silent.

Lesya turned off the TV, turned out all the lights, took off her apron, and was getting ready to go home, but Yu.I. was mumbling something in the darkness:

"I'm so fed up with you. I'll shoot you out of here like a cork. I'm so fed up."

3

"What's he look like?" Her husband Misha once asked her.

"He looks like this. Tall. Really gaunt. Nothing but bones. Almost no hair. His eyes a bit preying. He doesn't go outside. Doesn't talk to me. But he has nice teeth. Super white. Not a single one messed up. His teeth are really really nice."

"He was a dentist, what did you think?"

Once per week Lesya went to the outdoor market to buy groceries for Yuri Ivanovych. She took a long time to pick them out so they wouldn't stink, so they'd be fresh, be the best.

"Why do you fuss over him so much," Misha got ticked off because he had to go with her and carry the bags from the shopping. "He's an old man! What does he need already?"

"He needs to eat well."

"And I don't need to eat well? You never cook anything at home! I live on fried eggs all day long!"

"Listen, Misha! When he dies where will I be able to get a job as good as this?! I won't be able to make fifty bucks a week anywhere else! It's important for me that he lve longer! It's convenient for me to not have him die yet, ain't that so?! That's why he has to eat well!"

"Well, that's true," Misha agreed, "let him eat well."

4

Lesya had two grown-up sons.

She looked like this: short, chubby, hair cropped dyed black. One of her front teeth is a shiny yellow, but not gold.

Misha was her second husband.

She had lived with the first one very little, a year or two. The first one belonged to some kind of secret sect of evangelical zealots and treated Lesya quite cruelly. He didn't allow her to watch TV, constantly talked to her about God, forced her to read weird, incomprehensible literature. When Lesya resisted, her evangelical wouldn't speak to her for entire weeks and months at a time. Lesya turned everything into a joke, hugged her husband and meekly tried to charm him, but it had the opposite effect. For the entire evening he would say just this to Lesya:

"Don't talk to me."

5

Yuri Ivanovych's son Orest sometimes would call his father. Lesya immediately had to run out to the kitchen and not listen in.

With trembling hands Yu.I. placed the receiver to his ear and in a trembling voice asked:

"Is that you, Orest?"

Then an awkward silence fell and Yu.I. continued:

"Thank you, I'm better."

"Yes, the money's coming, everything's good."

"How are things with you? How are things at work?"

"Where do you work?"

"I'm living alone. Along with my cat Marquise. And a cleaning lady comes every day."

"Do you have any children?"

"Grandchildren?"

"What are you saying? Two or three?"

"Maybe you'll visit with my grandsons? Ah… I understand."

"Yes, it costs a lot to call, I understand."

"When can you call again?"

"I understand."

His neighbor Lida came over for a cup of tea and Yu.I. recounted everything to her.

"Orest, maybe, will come in the spring," he said sedately.

Lesya always listened in on Yu.I.'s phone conversations, and he knew it.

6

"Have you stolen my shorts?" Yu.I. shouted quietly at Lesya.

"What shorts?"

"The ones with the dark blue polka dots. They were in the dresser, and now they're gone!"

"You put them somewhere and forgot where. I didn't take your shorts, Yu.I."

"Don't pretend. I know everything. I know that you've been stealing my shorts for your husband!"

"I'm not a thief!"

"Thief! And my socks have also disappeared! You think I'm an old man and can't see?! My blue wool socks! Where are they?"

The things that disappeared didn't reappear. To the contrary. Every day new socks and shorts would disappear.

"You're stealing everything from me! Thief!" Yu.I. repeated incessantly.

"I'm not taking your things."

"So where do you think they are?"

"Yu.I., you know very well where they are!"

"I don't know, tell me an old fool where they are?"

"You've been hiding them under your mattress!"

Lesya lifted up the mattress of his bed and scraped out the socks and shorts."

"It's you who tossed them there," Yu.I. muttered sullenly, and then grew silent for a long time.

While Lesya was on her way home, Yu.I. made his way in the darkness to the drawer with clean underwear, fumbled for a new pair of socks or shorts and hid them again under his mattress.

7

In the spring Yuri Ivanovych said that Orest would be coming in the summer.

In the summer he said that Orest would be coming in the spring.

In the spring Lesya said that Orest wouldn't be coming at all.

"Yuri Ivanovych, Orest isn't coming because he doesn't want to see you. What are you to him? A father?"

"Don't talk to me."

"Thank him that he's been sending you money! You have something to eat. Orest could have not taken any responsibility at all."

"Don't talk to me!"

Then Yuri Ivanovych's cat Marquise croaked. Lesya found him at the entryway door already stiff.

Yuri Ivanovych looked at the dead cat, then at perplexed Lesya, then at his veiny hands and shouted:

"It's you who killed him! You poisoned him!"

8

In the spring Lesya really took ill. In her stomach the doctors found a giant cyst, which for many years had been plaiting a nest in Lesya. They had to operate on her immediately.

"Imagine," Lesya said to Yu.I. while placing some cooked veal and oat kasha on his plate, "I have an entire nest in my stomach! A cyst! The doctor said that it looked very similar to the hairy head of a little child.

"Don't talk to me," Yu.I. said.

"It's as though I'm pregnant with a hairy head," Lesya laughed.

"Don't talk to me!" Yu.I. stood up from his chair and leaned on his walking stick.

"I'm going to talk! What'll you do to me?!"

"Shut up, I said!" Yu.I. began to shake from rage.

"I'm going to talk! I'm going to talk!"

Yuri Ivanovych quivered, leaning on his walking stick like a trembling poplar. Lesya stood opposite him, ready for a blow from the walking stick, for a verbal lashing, and everything in her, even her cyst, radiated courage and fearlessness.

Yu.I. kept quivering, he gasped for air with his mouth and suddenly his shorts began to get wet. More and more. A small puddle had formed on the floor. Yu.I., pale from shame, took a look at the puddle and gave in.

Then Lesya washed him in the bathtub and chirped:

"Forgive me, Yuri Ivanovych, but I really like to talk. That's my nature. When I'm silent it's as though I'm in prison.

"Orest called and said that he'll be coming for Christmas. With the grandsons."

So Yuri Ivanovych allowed Lesya to talk.

9

Yuri Ivanovych became an invisible member of Lesya's family.

Lesya would return from work and the entire evening would tell Misha and her sons what Yuri Ivanovych did that day, what he ate, what he said.

"When I get there, it's as though wings grow on me," Lesya said, "there are such high ceilings, it's so nice everywhere, in the corridor on the wall is a stuffed moose, and you can hang hats on his horns!"

"Hang yourself on those horns!" Misha grew angry.

"If you could see how he eats! There always has to be a fork and knife, and he cuts the meat himself into tiny bits. He cuts up everything, and then eats it."

"If I'd ever eat meat then maybe I'd also cut it up, or maybe I'd gobble it up right away!"

"And sometimes he says to me that I've dressed him so nicely, his pants, his shirt, his leather vest, and then he sits on the balcony and says something. About people for whom he made teeth, about teeth, about his lovers."

"Lesya dear, are you maybe sleeping with him?!

10

Right before Christmas Yuri Ivanovych had his next stroke, and the doctors didn't even take him to the hospital.

"He needs to die now," the doctor diagnosed.

"What are you saying die," Lesya began to sob, "he's a healthy man! Treat him, give him shots, let the man keep living, is that a problem for you?

"Little lady, there's nothing to treat him with. He's so old that he can't hold himself together. We all die sooner or later, and this man will die later.

"Where will I find such a good job?! Let him live a bit more."

"Little lady, he'll die at Christmas, or maybe even sooner.

11

Yuri Ivanovych lay there in his bed not saying anything, just from time to time opening up his eyes and falling into drowsiness again.

Lesya sat next to him and quietly announced:

"Yuri Ivanovych, your son Orest has arrived with your two grandsons."

Yu.I. fluttered. He even raised himself up a bit on his bed. Misha entered the room with Lesya's two sons.

"Dad," Misha said, "good day."

"Orest, you've arrived?" Yuri Ivanovych whispered.

"Yes," Misha answered in English.

12

After Yuri Ivanovych's death Lesya took a job at a private business where she now makes dumplings.

FOREVATOGETHA

by Sofia Andrukhovych
Translated by Mark Andryczyk

IT WAS ONLY THREE P.M, BUT NATASHA ALREADY FELT EXHAUSTED. Routinely counting the coins reserved for change and arranging them in upright little columns on a wooden table covered by a worn and dirty plastic tablecloth, Natasha yawned broadly, letting out a resonant, drawn-out moan. Precise, slim little towers of five, ten, twenty five and fifty kopecks represented, on the table, a frail model of a city of the future with soaring buildings, round in diameter, the top floors of the highest of which were getting lost in clouds and stars; the smaller coins — of one or two kopecks — lay alongside, thrust into an assorted pile; Natasha would stash the metal *hryvnias* in the left pocket of her apron and the wrinkled paper ones, in the right pocket.

Must be some kind of fronts, the girl said to herself while scratching a violet bluebell off of the plastic tablecloth with her broken nail, in which microscopic archipelagos of lustrous, silver nail polish could still be visible. Weather fronts, a change in pressure, or some other trouble, she mumbled, standing up. Weather conditions of a lesser quality.

Slowly planting one leg after another (dressed in wool, grey tights on which, if one were to lift the pleated black skirt, and thanks to one lonely strip on one side and a pair of strips on the opposite side, it is clear what is the front and what is the back), Natasha exited her small room and entered one of the main rooms. In the middle stood a long and narrow mirror that was leaning against the wall and propped up on a little stool. Natasha stopped in front of it, dispassionately drowning into the reflection with her glance. And then, supporting her lower back with her hands, leaned her head back and concertedly and confidently, like a yogi, bent backwards until cartilages cracked in her spine. O-o-o-o-h, Natasha groaned, once again straightening up. Striking light-chestnut hair, tied into a knot on the back of her neck, became a bit frayed from this daft exercise and pretty puffy curls, which she so disliked, slid out from behind her ears and a wavy strand dropped in front of her eyes. The girl moved it behind her ear and then, generously spitting onto the fingers of her right hand, rubbed the saliva with her left hand and then diligently flattened the wayward hairs. She pulled out a lipstick from the breast pocket of her apron; twisting her lips and stretching them out into a strange half-smile, she began to liberally apply the color. Soon her mouth shone in a greasy, plum sheen. Natasha rubbed her upper lip against her lower lip in order to distribute the lipstick evenly and then, smiling broadly and fully, glided her tongue along her upper teeth to erase traces of the lipstick.

Natasha was twenty-eight years old, she ate a lot of cheap, viscid chocolate and smoked Monte Carlo-brand cigarettes — about a pack a day; her back teeth had decayed a long time ago, they had been pulled out and now Natasha could hide the tip of her extraordinarily supple and long tongue there. Besides that, she had four gold teeth — Natasha's greatest treasure, which she inherited from her great-grandmother; oftentimes, in moments of particular grief and despair, Natasha would imagine that she could just go to a dentist and then sell the gold, buy herself an attractive bathing-suit, pointy-toed shoes and a train ticket, and go to Yalta where she would meet a wealthy Armenian man, grey and moustached, with black, coal-like, eyes, who would become so blinded by his love for her that he would ask for her hand in marriage and then would take her far away, to a place where he owned a two-floor building with a bathtub and, for some reason, goats and chickens...

Natasha had a little pug nose with freckles, ample thighs, a large rear-end, big breasts and a nice, prominent gut. She didn't fit in the narrow mirror leaning against the wall, even if she stood sideways; all of her blouses and sweaters were a bit tight on her. Natasha smelled of her cheap lipstick and sweat. And she also enjoyed the buzzing of flies beneath the ceiling in the summer.

In the mirror Natasha saw the reflection of a tall, lanky man, who entered in a whirlwind, unfastening his grey drooping pants as he stormed in.

"I'll just," he said, out of breath, "finish up here at the urinal and then I'll pay! Just a moment, just a moment…just need to…"

Natasha shrugged her shoulders, turned away and, dragging her soft, back-less slippers, lazily trudged over to her booth. This man would burst in here everyday, sometimes more than once. She was used to his nervousness, jagged movements, and panicky hurrying; she had become used to this hunched, skinny individual, to a neck with a particular yellow and emaciated skin dotted with tiny red specks, to the protruding mound that was his Adam's apple. Natasha even knew the jingling of his belt by heart. He would always pay but only after taking care of his business — this didn't bother her. Having calmed down, he would fish out coins from the pockets of those grey drooping pants, and on his forehead and above his thin, thread-like top lip, beads of sweat would glisten. He smiled satisfyingly and apologized. Natasha just shrugged her shoulders once again. Initially, she would continue saying to him, "no problem, don't worry about it" but, in time, she stopped saying this because the man would keep showing up and apologizing.

And this time too, Natasha at first heard a forceful trickling and then a loud sighing — the man was noticeably relieved, and now he, less nervously, zipped up his pants and jingled his buckle. Water dripped from the faucet — he was washing his hands. Natasha remembered that she hadn't supplied any fresh soap — what remained of the little green bar had already been languishing in the soap dish for two days.

"So they haven't fixed the hand dryer yet?" The man asked, having appeared in front of her. It seemed to the girl that he was attempting to smile; she vigilantly looked at his mouth but the latter remained tensely stretched so she just shook her head, not sure if the man wanted to say something pleasant to her or to voice his criticism. He searched in his pocket and pulled out a brand new metal *hryvnia*. Natasha tossed it into the left pocket of her apron and took fifty kopecks from the stack. No-no, keep the change, he recoiled and backed out. Good bye.

Natasha, with surprise, looked on in his tracks and rested her head on her puffy palms. He's probably suffering from some form of illness, she surmised. Must be an overactive bladder, or whatever they call it. Great grandma could have cured him at once.

In a careful movement, she knocked over the precise stacks. The coins, rattling, spilled over onto the table but only a few fell onto the floor. Having yawned sweetly and scratched her armpit, Natasha once again began assembling them.

There was a lot of wet mud on the floor tiles, nasty puddles were forming in the grooves. It was raining outside, and people brought the dirt in with them. Natasha stared at somebody's footprint on the floor, trying to determine what it contained more of: diamonds or circles. Finally she got up, grabbed a mop and exited her little room. She didn't feel like cleaning up, she slowly moved the mop back and forth, left and right, spreading the dirt and, occasionally, glancing at the mirror. Why she placed the mirror in the men's bathroom, she didn't know. But precisely because of that, she seldom entered the ladies' room. She even rarely cleaned up in there.

An old man walked in, behind him — a little boy, wet to the skin. The old man folded his umbrella and placed coins on the table. "Can I leave the umbrella here?" He asked. "Put it on the table," Natasha said, having tossed the mop into the corner and turned on the faucet. Her hands instantly became red from the icy water.

The boy searched his pockets for a while without taking his eyes off of Natasha. She walked up and took the coins. Go ahead, she nudged him with her hand.

On her part, she grabbed a box of matches from the table and went up to the door. It screeched open a bit, Natasha held it with her foot and squeezed herself through the opening. She climbed up the wet stairs. The square was almost empty, people, whom the downpour had caught by surprise, were huddling under store awnings and by the post office. From her breast pocket, Natasha got a pack of Monte Carlos, pulled out a cigarette, rolled it between her fingers and lit it, taking her time. There was a lot of smoke, it flowed from under the roof and immediately dissolved among the thick raindrops.

Natasha's everyday client blew past her. Out of breath, soaked and with bulging eyes, his body twisted, as if from pain. He held the open umbrella beside him and shook it despondently. He didn't notice Natasha. He struggled with the downstairs door for some time, because the umbrella wouldn't fit through it, and then he threw it onto the ground and disappeared through the opening.

"Wow," said the old man, stepping over the obstacle, "that guy really must have had to go."

He smiled at Natasha, straightened his scarf and, accurately avoiding the puddles, wandered away. The wet boy ran off somewhere, in the opposite direction.

The doors squeaked once again, someone stirred down bellow on the stairs. Obviously, the calmed man was now folding his umbrella. He climbed the stairs and stopped by Natasha, stretching out his hand with fifty kopecks for her.

"It's not necessary," she said. "You overpaid last time."

"It doesn't matter," he shook his head.

Natasha turned away.

The man continued standing with his arm outstretched.

"Can I have a cigarette?" He finally asked her.

It seemed to Natasha that his voice was trembling.

She pulled a pack out of her breast pocket with her left hand.

"Thank you."

"Matches?"

The man nodded. He was able to light it on his third attempt. He turned away. His rounded shoulders flinched. Finally, smoke appeared above his undefined head.

He doesn't seem to be inhaling, thought Natasha. This could be his first time smoking a cigarette.

She tossed her cigarette butt into a puddle.

"I really do love snow," the man said unexpectedly.

Natasha nodded her head, somewhat uncertainly.

"Goodbye," she said and went down the stairs.

For a long while, Natasha mused over why she no longer detected the smell. Earlier, during her youth, when she and her great-grandma would enter a public bathroom, she felt like she was going to choke and drop dead from the stench there. Firstly, it was that perpetual smell of diarrhea, from which one gets queasy and one's face becomes distorted. Secondly, chlorine. Tears flow and it gets cold in your nose. Yuck.

Nowadays, Natasha's eyes would only well up a little from the chlorine. She didn't detect anything else. She must have just gotten used to it.

Some loud women were warbling behind the door of the ladies' room. One of them stuck her curly-haired head out and said:

"There's no toilet paper, and there isn't any soap."

"The toilet paper is over here." Natasha pointed to the table, "You have to take it with you when you enter."

She pulled a new bar of soap from the drawer and made her way towards the women. One of them was standing in the middle of the room, and, lifting her skirt up high and holding its hem with her chin, sticking her slip into her long-underwear.

"The hand-drier is not working," the other one said.

"I know," Natasha said.

"And how come you don't have a mirror in here?" the first one asked, without pulling her chin up from her chest.

"I only have two hands," Natasha replied. "I don't have enough time to finish everything."

She returned to her table and heavily sat down on the stool. A pink carnation lay on the table. Natasha pushed it to the edge of the table and folded her arms across her chest.

A forceful trickling could be heard from the men's room.

Natasha moved the carnation back into its original position, stuck her left hand into the pocket of her apron and jingled the coins.

Somebody's buckle clanged in the men's room.

Natasha spun a strand of hair around her finger.

"They'll fix the drier tomorrow," she said to the women, who finally came out.

"Good day," the man with the grey, drooping pants greeted her. "I brought you a flower."

"Uh-huh," Natasha said. "I see it."

The man shifted from foot to foot.

"And I put fifty kopecks over there, on the stack."

Natasha moved her hand, knocking the coins onto the floor. The man turned around and set off for the stairs. The doors creaked.

She yawned once more and pulled a key out of her coat pocket. The morning fog descended along the stairs.

Natasha stuck the key into the lock and unexpectedly found that the door was unlocked. She entered. The light was on. It shed light on a thin, round-shouldered figure in the center of the room. Natasha, in awe, noticed another little table and a stool across from her working station. The man was diligently laying out precisely assembled sheets of toilet paper onto it.

"Can you spare some coins so that I can make change?" He asked. "Can you lend me some coins for a bit?"

Natasha silently took off her coat.

"I'm Petro Dmytrovych," the man said. "I'll be working with you from now on."

Natasha made for the men's room and stopped in front of the mirror.

"Did you catch my name?" The man stood behind her, anxiously rubbing his hands together. "My name's Petro Dmytrovych."

"Uh-huh," Natasha said, braiding her hair. "It will be more convenient this way. The men always had to make a loop in order to come up to your table and, only after that, could they get to the designated spot…," he tried to smile but only unnoticeably grimaced. "Not everyone has time for this."

"Uh-huh," Natasha said, spitting onto her fingers.

"This way will be easier for everyone," he repeated.

Natasha straightened the silly curls that would protrude from behind her ears. They always bothered her.

DEATH IS SEXY

by Sofia Andrukhovych
Translated by Mark Andryczyk

HAVING FINISHED ROLLING IT UP, HE ROCKED FORWARD ON HIS stool and shoved her in the back with the soles of his heavy, laced-up boots. Her head clanged against the huge factory radiator, beside which she had been lying, and she came to.

"Hey babe, let's have a smoke," he offered good-humoredly, wetting the end of the joint.

She clumsily slid along the slippery, cold and wet tiles, finally got up onto her knees and stood like that for a minute, leaning her forehead against the coarse wall, trying to suppress her nausea and dizziness, and then turned around and plopped down hard on her buttocks, compressing the limp hands tied behind her back.

"Fuck" she snarled out in pain and then, somehow, liberated her twisted hands from under her butt. She then leaned her shoulders against the wall and feebly stuck out her head. "Come on. Gimme some of that."

She was thin and long-legged, sort of like a grass-hopper. Her hair was all sticky with blood, and it glistened disturbingly as if it had been smeared with tar in the feeble light of the only working lamp in the whole factory building.

He was surprised to have found her here, in the farthest, darkest corner of this giant workshop filled with rusty fragments of strange machines that looked like prehistoric monsters. Usually, he would take care of his business in tiny, cramped rooms on the top floor of this

half-ruined, forgotten factory located on the outskirts of the city —
but today, stopping his car at a safe distance, he immediately noticed,
through the thick darkness of the depth of night, a blurrily lit wide
window on the first floor and understood this to be a clue. And it
was — the client was indeed there. A female one in this case.

"You ok if we just shotgun this weed?" He asked, looking over her
beat-up face, smashed eyebrow and split lower lip, at the dried up blood
on her forehead, her cheek and above her upper lip and at the dark
swelling below her right eye.

She turned her head silently, shutting her eyes because of a sudden
need to vomit.

"It's more economical this way," he explained before taking a long
drag.

The joint quietly trembled and flashed a small orange bonfire. He
got next to her on his knees, leaned forward toward her chapped gaping
mouth — she jolted, like a fish sensing the touch of a steel blade near its
gills, but then relaxed and obediently drew in the scented cloud of smoke.

He continued to study her face up close.

"So, you must have been a real looker, eh, a model?" He squinted
menacingly, smiling and, either out of shame or confusion, rubbed the
short stubble of hair on his head with his big paw.

"You're not too shabby yourself, sailor boy." She tilted her head
toward her left shoulder, closer to his face, opened her dark damp eyes
half-way and tried to smile, but the pain wouldn't let her.

"Fuck," she cursed, and a stubborn shadow passed over her face,
behind which a gentle conciliation unexpectedly exuded. "It kicked
in. That's good weed, sailor boy. And no need to rush with that 'have
been' — I'm still here, aren't I?"

"Not for long," he promised and then took another drag.

She had already held up her covetous mouth, jealously following
the look of both duty and pleasure on his predatory face. He nestled
close to her — from the side this looked like a kiss.

They smoked in silence for some time. She reeked of sweat and
blood. He reeked only of sweat. A suffocating, thick night air rattled

with cicadas and nasty mosquitoes. At least the smoke was scaring them off a bit.

Suddenly she laughed hoarsely.

"What's the matter?"

"Cotton mouth." He could hear her tongue getting stuck on her palate. "Got anything to drink, sailor boy?"

He found a small bottle of Morshynska mineral water in his backpack, opened it and put it to her lips. She greedily nestled closer, and he watched how long, how slowly and how much she drank, how avariciously she swallowed, how her lower jaw, with its distinct lines, as if carved out of wood, moved during this; he felt the way she satisfyingly moistened and cooled her irritated larynx, how it flowed down her throat into her esophagus; he saw how it dripped into her stomach and knew exactly how great this feels, how pleasant this was for her, regardless of the fear and the pain and of the tickling and burning of the water on her bruised lip and chin, upon which the liquid flows; he knew just that sense of gratification she was feeling at this time.

This continued. Finally, he brought the bottle to his lips and drank the last swig.

"Well, now I wanna eat. How about some herring, a little black bread, some chocolates, maybe some peaches? And some grapefruit juice to wash it all down. You got something to eat, sailor boy?" The girl asked.

He smiled, squinting even more — and now this look, this peaceful, lost and crafty rolling of the eyes seemed to stick to the ray-like wrinkles and scars of his somewhat frayed face — and waved his arms, as if apologizing.

"No, I don't. Listen, how come you're calling me sailor boy?"

"Aah, it's no big deal." She sighed. "I call everyone that. It's a habit I guess. So what is your name?"

He pouted and began searching in his backpack for something.

"No need for that," he mumbled in a muffled voice. "I won't tell you my name and I won't ask you yours. Who, why or what for. That's my rule. To know nothing about the person I am to…"

She winced and moaned. He looked at her almost tenderly.

"Hey, don't get offended. It will be easier this way — for both you and me. Go ahead, you can call me sailor boy." He squinted again, smiled and slapped her on her shoulder.

"Fuck, sailor boy, that hurts," she hissed, sharply jerking. And then she laughed. "I should be howling from fear, but I got stoned and now I'm cracking up."

He gently wiped the tears from her cheeks with his thumb, patiently and good-naturedly, waiting for her to calm down.

"Look, I want to propose something to you. I wanna ask something of you, to be more precise. But it's entirely up to you."

She became quiet, tensed up and looked sullenly at him without blinking.

"I'm in a rather melancholic mood today. Something has happened... In my life... Something that knocked me of my tracks... You understand..." He searched for something in her glance, while choosing his words, worrying, mechanically scratching his head with his bear-like paw. "Well you can see my state right now... I'm nervous. I'm not like this very often. Never, to be more accurate. This may be the first time. Almost no one has seen me like this. You're lucky."

"Fuck yeah, sailor boy, you nailed it — I'm lucky." She blurted out a laugh again, but, this time, an angry and bitter one. And she anxiously shifted on her backside, jerking her legs. "Say it already, would you, 'cause I'm tired of this shit. Damn psycho."

He shut his eyes and made a wry and painful face. He was silent for a few seconds, collecting his thoughts. He then got up and began pacing in front of her, back and forth, cursing to himself. Finally, he hung over her, simultaneously resolute and fated, with knitted eyebrows and with a rigid confidence in the corners of his mouth.

"I need to talk with someone. I can't do this. In theory, you should quickly be... well, you understand. But I feel like I'm losing my mind. And if I've really let this happen, then I'm totally fucked, totally. You can't imagine how strict I usually am, how formal I am. I never, never, stray from the rules. It's just that... whatever — I need to talk with someone. Can we talk? We still have some time before it gets dark. Before they come to gather your body parts."

"You're a fucking asshole, man," she said dryly. And then she started to cry.

He effortlessly sat down on a piece of metal, grabbed his head with his hands and waited for her to calm down.

Ten minutes passed. The sobbing turned into exhausted crying and then into convulsive whimpering.

"Let me go," she said hoarsely. "Please, I beg you, I'm begging you, please let me go. Please."

He stood up onto his feet and hit his fist against the wall.

"Dumb-ass!" He roared. And the whole factory seemed to blow up from his snarl. "Over and over! Enough already! Don't you get it? That's impossible! This is my job. If I don't finish you off, they'll finish me off."

He violently turned away and walked toward the machines, loudly stomping his feet. His steps were fading; something squealed, crackled, moaned, like a giant animal with a spear in its side, and then there was a thud. It became quiet. There, in the corridor, in the total darkness, behind the thick factory wall he could clearly see how she, still wincing from crying, began to stand up. It was difficult. It was almost impossible. She was very queasy, her head was spinning, her whole body ached, her face burned, she was tortured by thirst, hunger, fear and despair, the stuffiness and the obtrusive hum of bugs, her T-shirt was completely soaked and stuck to her body, greasy beads of smelly sweat rolled down her skin, she could barely see, she didn't know where to go, her legs were wobbly and disobedient, the hands tied around her back were making it difficult to move, with every step she kept getting caught on some piece of metal, she fell several times, painfully banging into things, twisted her ankle, planted her elbow into the long handle of the machine tool — right in the funny bone, that nerve ending which, when hit, sends a nasty, disgusting pain throughout the body for some time. But something kept pushing her forward to the dim lamp at the other end of the factory building — the unanticipated and ancient instincts of an animal that has not been fully killed-off smoldered inside her, in a washed out, dim shining, flickering somewhere in the spine, in the spinal cord.

And she ended up in front of a set of massive, metal doors. The doors were open. Beyond the doors — darkness. On her face and neck, the girl feels the cool tongue of a draft and, in a silly way, becomes happy, and even tries to straighten her back with gusto. She stops. She listens. Complete silence. Only the faint scent of cigarette smoke in the air.

In one, motion, he yanked the door toward himself and also stopped, intensely checking her out. They stood like that for about a minute, without moving, without altering their gazes. Not surprised at seeing one another. Like old friends, who had met up this way hundreds of times before and were not surprised to meet up again. Like an old married couple set in their daily routines: she — coming from home, he — heading home. "well there you are," "oh, it's you," "there you are, finally."

"Listen, you'll have to forgive me," he said hoarsely, stepping toward her and lightly taking her shoulder in his hand. "I shouldn't have started all this. This isn't right. This was wrong. We'll take care of this quickly."

They stood very close to one another, almost touching, looking directly into one another's eyes.

"You sure are a skinny one," tenderly, jovially, almost fatherly, he whispered, removing his arm to scratch his head anxiously.

"How about another cigarette?" She asked in a colorless voice.

He shook off his enchantment with her, like a dog shaking off water, dug into his pockets and, having found a pack of cigarettes, started looking for a lighter.

"Of course, of course."

He lit her cigarette and put it to her lips. She inhaled.

"Listen sailor boy," she pleadingly fixed her eyes on him, "this isn't working. Let's go have a seat somewhere and then you can untie my hands. Where am I going to escape to? Let's have a smoke together."

He delicately took her by her elbow and led her away from the workshop into a dark corridor. Without saying anything, he pointed to a concrete pipe across from the door. She sat down. Without saying anything, he approached her from behind, squatted and gently shuffled something in his backpack. Her arms were totally numb, but she could feel how thick and rough the skin on his fingers and palms was when he held her wrists while untying her. He held her this way for a bit longer, without breathing.

"So skinny, it's almost scary — I can wrap two fingers around it." You could hear a smile in the voice.

At first she regretted her request. She couldn't move her arms; they didn't exist, it was as if they had been transformed into those metal fragments lying around her, but, simultaneously, they hurt so bad, filling her whole body with pain. She clenched her teeth and closed her eyes. The pain subsided slowly.

He lit up a smoke for her, and she clumsily grabbed the cigarette and, using all her strength not to drop it, lifted it to her lips.

"Oh, that's better. Much better."

And he too lit up a smoke. A few drags on the cigarette, a few little clouds of smoke into the silent air.

"Ok, let's talk."

"What?"

"You wanted to talk. Let's talk."

"Oh no, that's a bad idea. We can't. We shouldn't."

"…"

"You really want to talk?"

"Yes."

"Ok, but promise me that you won't expect I will then… because it's not going to happen."

"I know."

"Are you sure?"

She quietly put out her cigarette. He became visibly unnerved: with one hand he scratched his forehead while he slapped the pipe several times with the palm of his other hand.

"Ok, then… Ok… Hmm… I want to take you to… To show you a certain place. You're gonna like it."

401

He led her, holding her elbow, into a long and dark corridor, illuminating it with his cell phone. They walked slowly — she became weak and was in great pain and every step was incredibly difficult for her. She carefully looked at her feet, following the pale, faded puddle of light that glided over the beat-up, slippery floor tiles, retrieving from the darkness a horrific web of cracks, chunks of brick, half-living quivering plastic bags, and tattered rags of cloth that looked like they'd been tarred.

Finally they came to a set of stairs at the end of the corridor. It was brighter here. The moon shone through windows, most of which were without windowpanes, some with plywood tacked on. Gray, concrete, crooked, wide steps rose upward, and the man led the girl onto them, taking her narrow and light palm into his large, hot and chapped one.

"It's drafty here," she said quietly and, strangely, the echo multiplied and thinned her words, kicking them up, knocking them into the peeled walls. "It's so drafty, so cold, my teeth are chattering."

"Really?" The man said in wonder, wet and tired from the heat and humidity. But he suddenly realized that her hand was indeed icy. With her other hand she touched the walls — leading the fingers of her wide-open hand like a veil, feeling the embossments on the way.

Then he noticed that he felt very strange today, that the situation was much more serious than he had thought at first, because he began to sense how coldness was just streaming from the girl — a blue coldness, like from an open refrigerator.

He led her upstairs and thought to himself: "Where am I taking her to, and why, I should just finish her off right here, on the steps, gotta do it all very quickly, so that she won't see it coming, so that she won't have time to get scared, I'm so tired, I'm really tired, my head is screwed up, and this is bad, I haven't slept for such a long time, I just couldn't fall asleep, my heart was pounding so hard that it made a big bloody bruise inside me, and now I just can't feel anything, I can't feel it — my heart, it's as if it had turned to stone, it's become numb, become covered by a swollen rot, like a walnut, like a chestnut…" While thinking this, he didn't stop moving, but continued leading her up the stairs, slowly, but without stopping, and she obediently followed him, not questioning, not resisting, touching the walls with her long fingers, hanging her head and looking down at her feet. And he, trying not to be noticed, looked askew at her silhouette, lit up by the bluish glow of the moon as if powdered by hoarfrost, at her defenseless neck, her skinny shoulders, and she seemed incredibly familiar to him, absolutely familiar, like that chick from the kiosk where he bought cigarettes every day, or perhaps someone even dearer to him.

He would catch himself thinking that he would like to taste her — so familiar, she seemed so dear to him. He wanted to touch the nape and curve of her neck with his palm. And smell her ear. And lick her with his tongue — to see whether she was salty and hot, like he assumed at first, or icy, so cold that it would freeze and shock his tongue. He wanted to touch her. To rummage over her with his face. To curl her up on his knees.

But he was scared. And he became consumed from these thoughts with such terror, that his lungs and his whole breathing system would go into a spasm. Lacking oxygen, even his eyes darkened. But he gathered all of the strength of his unyielding will and kept going forward, kept leading her without revealing any sign of weakness.

I gotta stick to the rules, he kept convincing himself.

But he really wanted to ask her what her name was. It was even painful, this need to know her name. Maybe this would clear things up, or maybe not.

"I don't even know where I'm taking her. I don't even know why I'm doing this," he thought despondently.

"Where are you taking me, sailor boy?" The girl asked with a smile in her voice, as if she already knew the answer.

"You'll see," he grumbled. "And stop calling me sailor boy."

"It's just a habit," she rustled.

The curved flights of stairs were like arcs; steel handrails that were corroded became strange banisters that looked like they were chiseled out of marble or some fancy light stone. The man didn't notice how this had happened, but changes rarely affected him. He would detect them, but quite superficially, treating them as unimportant and self-evident.

In the walls, holes gaped in a deaf and mute darkness, through which stars twinkled. "We're in the middle of a sphere with only space around us," the man thought. And this seemed completely logical to him.

Tiny precipices widened under their feet that were suspiciously easy to cross without much effort.

Here and there, they came across stunning antique sculptures, somewhat jagged but dizzyingly beautiful. Little boys with smooth torsos and curly hair, with white unseeing eyes and with contemptuous smiles on their full, arched lips, Dianas with distinguished, bumpy noses embracing virgin-wool goats (all of which had their front legs raised), stern bearded gods with large backsides, satyrs with sharp, shameless beards.

"I'm experiencing de ja vu," the man thought to himself. He stopped. The girl stopped as soon as he did, as if she knew where she was being taken to. She stood, hanging her head, slouching a bit — a bloody T-shirt, bruises on her scrawny shoulders, ribs protruding in mountain ranges. But in the corners of her beat-up lips, the man once again noticed a smile. The captive looked at him for a split second — and her eyes were the eyes of an arctic wolf.

But he decided to ignore this.

"So we've arrived," he said, getting a key from his pocket and opening the leatherette-covered (under the leatherette was some kind of cheap, soft filler, similar to cotton, which created the sense of swelling, puffiness) door, on which, there was a silhouette of a poodle with trimmed ears.

They entered and the man, in a familiar gesture, tugged on the cord of a dusty standing lamp (a white paper sphere on a carved wooden stand, which instantly became circled by fat, hairy moths), removed his backpack from his shoulders and hung it on the hook of a bronze rhinoceros, which stood sullenly by the entrance.

"Who lives here?" The girl asked.

"Lived," the man replied succinctly.

"Well who?" She looked around inquisitively, rubbing down her skinny shoulders with her nervous hands.

"I forget," he said, somewhat lost, studying the room no less inquisitively.

He hadn't been here for so long that almost everything had faded, although, of course, recollections can always be revitalized; they'll surely reemerge, a bit of dusting off is all you need. And the man compellingly wiped a large mirror, which had blackened over time, with his hand.

In that mirror, he saw the faded reflection of her back. She was moving away and seemed to be smoothly swimming forward on a wave of gray fog. The man suddenly noticed bizarre tattoos on her shoulders, two crisscrossed tank-top straps, a few bugs — a dragonfly, a praying mantis, a mole-cricket, and two-or-three beetles, which seemed to be crawling out from under her clothes — such graphics were well suited for her pale, white skin, refined, accurate lines, wing membranes, mustache-strands, sensitive paws. The bugs stirred and rustled. A couple of lazy moths sprawled from under her T-shirt and crawled up the spine to the nape of her neck. "So that's where they're coming from," thought the man, looking over at the lamp, which was now almost entirely covered with bugs. This living sphere moved and crackled, occasionally shooting individual creepy bodies to the side or upward.

"I don't know what's wrong with me," the girl responded in a muffled voice (the man was thinking that maybe he was only imagining she was speaking: that voice rustled in his brain, the moth wings crackled). "I've wandered off, I'm lost. I don't remember, I don't remember anything."

He flinched and abruptly turned toward her. The girl, as if she had not moved, stood next to him, facing him. Frightened eyes opened wide, bluish lips.

"I'll, I'll warm you up," he said in a calming manner, grabbing her by the shoulders with both hands (and with disgust, feeling something living and moss-like under his fingers), turned around and pushed forward.

The moon flooded the room with white light. Somewhere, a clock, or maybe several, ticked loudly — tick-tock, tick-tock, tick-tock, and the longer the man listened to the ticking, the better he was able to distinguish between different clocks, louder ones and quieter ones, speeded-up ones and slowed-down ones, they ticked from all around, sometimes in a calming manner, sometimes menacingly, alarmingly. The man and the girl walked past the rhino, a cane stand, a clothes hanger — out of which felt hats dangled like bunches of grapes. The man and the girl walked along a worn Turkish rug that had a geometric pattern, but it seemed like they were walking against the current and up to their knees in water. In their way there was also old footwear, lying on the floor in piles, gaping solo boots, rubbers, high-heeled shoes, sandals, flip-flops, galoshes, slippers decorated with ridiculous flowers.

A dog, a terrier (perhaps an Airedale Terrier) was sleeping among the pillows on a worn ottoman, snoring and whimpering in his sleep, occasionally jerking his paw.

The room was strewn with furniture: a few hutches sunk from the weight of crystal, a set of porcelain fish (a tea kettle and cups) and porcelain chickens (a carafe and shot glasses), a polka-dotted salad bowl, glasses, plates; in the middle stood a lacquered table covered with an embroidered tablecloth and with a crystal vase in its center. From the vase a blackened willow branch decorated with colored ribbons extruded. Next to it there was a dark red passport covered by an ash tray filled with colorful buttons. A stained couch, obviously once a fancy piece of furniture, but now just simply frightening, with its wide-open mouth jaw and curled springs. Nearby — a coffee table, whose surface was bent from a pile of yellowed newspapers and magazines. A willow tongue stuck out wildly from the vacuum cleaner. The bookshelves were completely woven with wild grape vines, and, in order to look at the volumes there, one had to snap the nimble branches and tear off the leaves. A game of Solitaire was laid out on a desk between a bust of some bald guy and a pile of TV guides. And this room had a TV as well — a reddish-brown box with a bulging eye, covered with lace gauze and tied with a silk bow.

"Have a seat over here." The man swept old, yellowed and twisted leaves from an easy chair and onto the rug (the wide black current bush seemed to be surrounding it with its paws).

The chair covered her with velvet embraces, comfortably swallowing her. The man flung open the crooked closet and, moving a pile of clothes (which created a cloud of dust as well as the rushing escape of a moth nation), pulled out a checkered blanket that was full of holes but unquestionably warm.

"Don't mind the musty odor, no one's been here for a while," the man explained.

The girl made herself as comfortable as she could, tucking her feet in and laying her head back. Simultaneously, her gaze slid from object to object, constantly coming across new things. A wasps' nest. A painting of the Savannah with elephants in the far distance. A chunk of a wall, off of which rubber, lemony-sandy colored wall paper, like pleats, rolled off in a giant lip.

An old radio snuffled from the dark corner. In another corner, a stout old refrigerator hummed. It trembled lightly, seemingly from either fear, excitement or cold and, every couple of minutes, convulsively shook, became still, and before too long, once again repeated its neurotic ritual.

Behind the refrigerator, the room opened up into a kitchen. Cupboards and drawers, dishes, cups, a range with pots and a tea kettle, a kitchen table, and stools. The man quietly and habitually lit the gas burner and placed the scorched kettle, with its protruding nose, onto it. While the water was heating up, he opened the refrigerator and rummaged through it for a while. He moved back and forth with plates and platters, sliced-up something, laid it out, flipped it over, occasionally wiping his hands nervously on the bottom half of his pant legs.

"There's a lot more here than I wanted," faintly, but thankfully, the girl said, looking over everything that appeared before her on the coffee table.

The tea cups swam in crysanthanyms. Drops of juice shone on the divided, plump peaches. Glossy, gray herring fillets, covered with rings of red onion, rudely protruding from pools of oil. The yellow eyes of quail eggs inquiringly gazed through green lettuce leaves. Peppers, tomatoes, and a pheasant, stuffed with wild mushrooms, cheese with cilantro, and salty chocolate with chili pepper, divided into chunky, jagged pieces. And even grapefruit juice, freshly-squeezed by the man.

The girl satisfyingly breathed in, filling her lungs, and stretched out, extending her long, thin limbs. She did this with her legs stretched out under the table and her arms scattering about the plates, grasping scraps of food and sending them off to her mouth. She was hungry and voracious and not ashamed of the fact that oil was dripping off her chin or that egg yolk and chocolate had stained her teeth.

And the man snuggled up next to her legs and gazed off into the distance.

There were no walls where he looked — a shaggy pear tree with heavy fruits unmannerly had invaded the space and, bending over a large bed, hung its tired branches. Through the leaves one could see a pale-lemony full moon with a misty fringe all around. And if you looked attentively, just below that, a view opened up onto a sea port, onto violet and thick water that, somewhere, merged with the sky; onto an unsure, moon trail, that shone on the surface, like a large silver razor; onto the lacy necks of tower cranes; onto commercial vessels and tankers, motionless and silent, that breathed heavily with their sides seemingly rounding out, like the sides of giant whales; onto pipes and masts, onto sails, onto docks, onto yachts, onto the round portholes of the illuminators, onto the yellow light of the lanterns, that shone a drunk, ghostly light on decks and docks. Somewhere, over there, the man knew, sailors slept in their rocking beds, over there fish lazily splash and, a sentient and anxious seagull occasionally screeches, and, bending over the tar-covered cables of the old pier, a skinny prostitute carefully supports the head of a young sailor, who, having thrown up into the foam of the incoming tide, mystifyingly gazes downward, into the whispering waves and sees how a female giraffe, licking the thick, bitter and cold pear leaves with her rough, pumped-up muscle of a dark-purple tongue, straining her neck to a painful extent and turning over her beautiful, sad, apple-eyes, tries to see, through a web of branches, two people stretched out on an old bed, on faded silk sheets, and these sheets feel like a block of ice — so plastic and unbearable, and they don't heat them, they don't heat those two lovers, that girl, tall, crooked, exhausted, who looks like a grasshopper, like a dragonfly with emerald wings, like Gerridae, and that good man with the rugged hands, with dirt under his fingernails, with dried up blood on his palms, this man, with wrinkles on his face that hide both the hunger of a predator and the exhaustion and restlessness of a vegetarian. "And so, they never did get to talk," that is what, for some reason, floats through the young sailor's mind, and the prostitute drapes her faded coat over his shoulders in a motherly fashion and breathes the scent of booze and garlic into his face. "They passed each other by, like we all pass each other by along the streets or through time," the young sailor thinks with the fervor characteristic of his youth. And he becomes so sad, it becomes so unbearable, and he is overcome with such bottomless despair, that he buries his face into the chest of the gentle prostitute with the weathered hands, and she pats him on his back and quietly whispers "It's ok, It's ok." And neither he nor she know that the man will be found tomorrow in the most remote, most cluttered corner of this workshop, on the first floor of an abandoned factory on the outskirts of the city. He will already be cold, with a violet tinge, like after a heart attack, lips (on which the unuttered name of a woman was frozen; he did indeed know it, he had remembered it), and, lying next to him, a just-rolled, not yet lit joint.

And they won't find the girl, no, they'll never find her. If they haven't found her yet — why would they now, all of a sudden.

from DIARY OF A UKRAINIAN MADMAN

By Lina Kostenko

Translated by Yuri Tkacz

[FROM PAGE 5 (OF THE ORIGINAL 2010 UKRAINIAN PUBLISHED VERSION OF THE NOVEL)]

I HAVE ALWAYS BEEN A NORMAL PERSON. MORE MELANCHOLIC, perhaps, than phlegmatic. *Rationalitas* manifestly prevailed in me, until I met my future wife. After that my *passions* had the upper hand for a while; and what's happening now — I have no idea. Ultimately, my wife is smart and beautiful, there were enough suitors chasing after her, and if there had been something not quite right about me, she would have chosen someone else instead of me.

I have good genes too; there were no psychos in our family. I studied at university, rowed, I even have a sports trophy. I finished my doctorate, defended my thesis. My hobbies include music and literature, and as a child I collected stamps. In short, everything was quite adequate, and now suddenly, at the turn of the century I'm feeling uncomfortable, I've lost my marbles; I went to a psychiatrist, but he could find no aberrations. But then this field is so subtle and they have no advanced instruments to properly check you out. I sleep normally, my hands don't shake — I merely sense a kind of unease, like a phantom pain in the soul.

It all began when I had a sudden urge to visit the Canary Islands. Not because they have resorts there, expanses of ocean and exotic landscapes. But because I had read in some magazine that somewhere there, high up in the mountains, in the evergreen jungle lived a tribe that communicated without language, but whistled instead. And a thought occurred to me — what a good idea it would be if we stopped talking and began whistling to one another. Because so much has already been said by people, that the meaning of everything has been lost. And people here use some inhuman language, a surrogate mixture of Ukrainian and Russian, a complete mish-mash, plebeian slang, a legacy of enslaved souls and sick notions, which have left a mark of debility on society's face — and what do I have to do with all this?

If the lumpen class or the homeless had used such language, it would have been understandable, but everyone from the president down is speaking it. He was the guarantor of our Constitution, so what did he guarantee me? It would have been better that they had whistled among themselves in that office of his, then we wouldn't have had the "cassette scandal"*, there would only have been an artistic bunch of whistling.

I understand it's all due to fatigue. Everything needs to be perceived more calmly. I have a contemporary profession, abstracted from this idiotic reality; I can speak solely in the language of computer programs. True, I had dreamed of becoming a research scientist, but our institute had grown destitute, its scientists scooted off all over the world, but I had stayed behind on principle, after all, this is my country, I grew up here, I live here, I don't want to go to Silicon Valley, I don't want to work in the best computer centers in Europe, I want to live and work here. And I want to live well and with dignity, not just any old how. My parents had lived as best they could, and my parents' parents also, and all nice decent people in this part of the world have always had to live as best they could, constantly fooled by whoever was in power, by the regime of the day. I've had enough. I don't want to live hand to mouth any more.

---

* Secret cassette recordings were made of Kuchma purportedly ordering the murder of the journalist Georgiy Gongadze.

I work for a commercially successful company; true, there's lots of work, but they pay a decent wage. I've got a good means of transport from the company, an almost new white "Opel", to dash about on company business, because my own Soviet-era jalopy requires constant repairs. In the evening I park my work car in the yard opposite our windows, it's got an alarm system, so no one can steal it, and we can go somewhere on the weekends. My wife fits nicely into the foreign car's interior, although she's a little annoyed that this "Opel" bears the company's logo, so that we advertise the company when we drive about. But what can one do — there are more advertisements now than street signs; in the past Lenin had stood at every intersection, but now there are advertisements for "Tampax" and "Snickers", "Korona" chocolates and "Durex" condoms. Placards, billboards, flickering LCD advertisements: "Breathe easy, live a mobile life!" — and why not?

We go for picnics, visit the Hydropark,* get away from the city, but I can't go anywhere to get away from myself. I look fearfully at my wife — doesn't she notice anything? Sometimes she sighs, kisses me on the forehead — what would I do, if I didn't have a wife like her? True, my son already swears, he's six years old and goes to kindergarten. He swears because of Borka, I'm sure it'll pass and he'll grow out of it. Borka is their leader, every second word he utters is "dammit" or "cool." Mine does the same. I can't stop him from being friends with Borka, although it would be worth it, for already little girls are complaining that he is spying on them in the toilets, and he even showed one of them his still not very convincing little pistol.

At times my wife loses it and thrashes him, after which she bursts into tears; I comfort both of them, because I'm a man, I'm not supposed to explode, but at times it seems to me that one day I'll leave home by the window and no one will ever see me again. At night she asks me: "Is this sex or love?" I remain silent, I have no idea, for me the two have always been together, now for some reason they are meant to be apart,

___
* A popular amusement park on an island in the middle of the Dnipro River in Kyiv.

I'm afraid things might change, because I love it when my wife's eyes are full of happiness, but she's so annoyed now, and we don't recognize one another.

My mother-in-law looks at me with fear, for she's afraid our family will fall apart, and that I'll find a mistress or become an alcoholic. Neither is likely, 'cause I'm no asshole; my mother-in-law gratefully nods her head and prepares delicious country-style lunches for us with our city ingredients. She's a widow, from the Chornobyl resettlement zone, she has no one left apart from us, and I very much fear that she'll notice that something isn't quite right with me.

By the way, something isn't quite right with her either. Having listened her fill of news items on the official radio channel in the kitchen, she has begun to yell out things, wanting to share her thoughts with someone, unable to digest this cocktail of information and simply screams: "What is happening?!" My wife begs her: "Mum, stop listening to the radio, or I'll throw it out!" She gave her Georges Sand's *Consuelo* to read — that placated her for a few days. Then she heard some more news about the "Tarashcha body" and began to scream again.

I understand her completely. It's enough to make you go mad. For three months now they've been dragging that "Tarashcha body" about, stating that it might be the son of Lesia Gongadze, then that it might not be. That woman has been driven crazy with distress, she's already swaying at the slightest puff of wind, and they keep tormenting her, continually taking blood from her for DNA tests, but they refuse to recognize her son as the victim, because they're not sure that the body died a violent death, and when it comes to that, they're not sure whose corpse it really is, because it doesn't have a head, and no one understands any longer, how it could have come to this, that she is forced to suffer such heart-wrenching things?!

Then it turns out that we don't have a president, merely a factory director, that he can't stop himself from uttering mother oaths, because he's accustomed to it. What can I demand from my young son then — he's used to swearing too. And so is Borka. Only I can't get used to this, being a nerd and a "four eyes." My colleague says: "Man, you're something else, dammit." And I reply: "*Normalno*," but I feel that nothing is normal, and that one of us is crazy, either me or them.

My wife is a philologist, she works in an academic institute. They either have layoffs, or they don't get paid for months at a time, or else they lease out the foyer for some flea market — at first all of this made her indignant and she would explode, now she's uncommunicative and keeps it all bottled up inside her. Her thesis is unfinished, her supervisor has fled to Burkina Faso. But I keep working, I support our family quite well, obviously I could be doing better, but I'm not "progressive" enough, my fantasies don't go beyond appropriate pay for appropriate work. At work they respect me, the people there are okay, though at first they looked askance at me…

[FROM PAGE 47]

New Year's Eve passed without incident. Someone was thrown into the sobering-up cells, another fellow was wounded by a detonator. Persons unknown sawed through the locks of the city's cathedral and stole an icon. In some cafe teenagers trashed the furniture. On trendy Derybasivska Street in Odessa six photographers got into a fight because they couldn't divide up their territory.

Everyone gave everyone a gift. My wife found a present from me under the Christmas tree, which she herself had bought, and said: "Thanks," throwing me a sad ironic look. I received a new tie, my mother-in-law — her usual shawl, which she optimistically approved of on the spot: "Just the thing for my funeral."

I gave our son a globe of the world on a stand. After all, I can't always give him computer games. I gave him a small blue-green globe, just like the one I'd had as a child. So that he could twirl it about, running his fingers over the continents and oceans. But all he said was: "It's crap. I want a gun."

Borka's father got him a cassette player and gave his mother a brand-new silver Honda — successful businessmen know how to spoil their wives, unlike us intellectual loners in out-of-control market conditions.

The first baby to be born after New Year's Eve in Kharkiv received 5000 hryvnias toward its upbringing from the city authorities.

The children who had suffered because of the nuclear fallout from Chornobyl were given free vitamins.

But the war veterans and the war cripples received the best present of all — from now on they would be buried at taxpayer's expense.

To celebrate the Year of the Snake they held an International Beauty Contest for Snakes in Tula: 34 reptilian beauties vied for the title of Miss. The winner was a royal albino snake from California; second place went to a Russian black snake.

In Detroit they opened a "time capsule" — an epistle from the turn of the previous century to present-day descendants. Now the people are considering their epistles to future generations. In Kansas City they also opened a time capsule, and they're thinking hard too. Maybe we too should address the people of the next century? Tell them that we are Ukrainians, that we really did exist.

At the dawn of the new era a fresh squall of rallies has hit the city. There are even more people out in the streets than there were at the gala-concert on New Year's Eve. So the balance between social consciousness and futility has not been conclusively upset yet. People are coming from everywhere. The capital is abuzz with demonstrations. Diplomats watch from the windows of their embassies. Investors are packing their bags.

And so began our Year of Culture, aka the Year of the Snake. Television screens flickered and pulsated with the piebald logo of the new age — the number "XXI." It was supposed to remind us that we had entered a new century. But it reminded us of nothing else. The same tramps were picking through the garbage bins. The same people's deputies were expatiating in their habitual language, which simply made me want to fly off to the Canary Islands. The "Tarashcha body" was still lying in the morgue. It had undergone another forensic examination, this time by the Russians, which again confirmed that the body was that of Gongadze, after which the Prosecutor General's Department issued an announcement that the corpse may be the biological offspring of Lesia Gongadze. When my mother-in-law heard this, she nearly had a heart attack. She's an old woman, but had never heard the notion that a corpse could be a biological offspring. They are ready to hand over the "Tarashcha body" to its biological mother, but the mother is appealing to them to hand over the head as well, because the Orthodox tradition does not allow burial of a body without the head.

Meanwhile an emblem of this head, like a dark undeveloped negative, sails above the heads of columns of demonstrators. And on a placard over there the devil is guffawing, holding the severed head, like an executioner on the scaffold of History.

Rallies and demonstrations are being held every day now. I don't attend any of them. Not because I'm afraid of anything, or because I'm being cautious, but simply because I know that once more everything will come to naught, once more they'll wrap everyone around their little finger. This isn't my cup of tea.

Because when the television workers revolted in Prague, they did so properly. They defended their informational space, driving away the creature that was forced upon them. And they'll succeed in driving it away. But our people won't drive anyone away. They'll make a bit of noise and grow quiet. Our nation is very ill, it tires very easily. Blood doesn't flow to the head of this nation any more; people only break out in a cold sweat.

For the first time this century I visited my father. He lives far away now, on the far side of the Dnipro River. We rarely see each other, for he has a new family now.

My father was one of the 1960s activists, one of the less noticeable quiet passionaries who are not mentioned in any article. He is a fairly well-known translator, well, how well-known? All our people are unknown. Or as one quipster put it: "widely known in a narrow circle." Although that circle may have been narrow, it was a select group of people, who have gradually melted away with time; but I still recall them, those friends of my father's, they were a remarkable lot. The next generation looked back at them, but the one after that kicked up their heels and promptly forgot them.

He now has a new wife, they live well together; I don't know what he saw in her. My mother was tall, well-built, and beautiful, with unruly, jet-black hair which she tamed into a tight knot or into a plait. She sang in a choir; she had a deep velvety mezzo-soprano voice. But most of all I liked her *a capella* singing. After the Chornobyl catastrophe occurred, she was sent there to give concerts. The concerts were held in the open fields, from the backs of tray trucks; the young soldiers simply sat on the grass, sliding the respirators from their faces and she sang them songs such as *The Nightingales Laugh and Weep*. The nightingales both laughed and wept, and the orchards blossomed. The liquidators went into hell, others followed in their footsteps, the yellowed foam rubber of their respirators hung in shreds from their faces, and meanwhile she sang without a respirator, in a light dress, wearing flip-flops. A colonel asked: "What are you doing? Who sent you here?!" She was taken aback. People were being evacuated, forcibly shoved onto buses, women wailed, it was an *a capella* weeping of the people to the Lord Himself. She went there several more times, even when she was no longer directed to go, when those villages were deserted. She sang in the clubrooms of shift camps and in Chornobyl itself. Then she lost her voice, became gravely ill, and her plaits were all that remained of her; although soon she lost even these and became just an armful of bones. She was given evasive diagnoses; back them everything was classified "top secret." She died in agony just one year short of Ukraine's Independence. There are recordings of her songs, occasionally they air them on the radio, but I simply can't fathom the fact that her voice is still alive and she is dead as I look at the photo in the cherry-colored frame, with that unruly hair of hers, her high brows.

This woman, meanwhile, has short hair, she's short and her hair is blonde, and she's all *a la page*. She works as a cardiologist in a clinic, where father spent time after his heart attack; later she visited him at home. Then he unexpectedly moved in with her.

I find this hard to understand. Father loved my mother very much; he cared for her stoically and devotedly. It seemed he simply couldn't get over her death. He had an extensive heart attack and ended up in intensive care. And there he met this woman. She was much younger than him; I thought it would be a temporary thing, but no. She had a son from a previous marriage who was in grade eight, a child prodigy who kept attending various Olympiads and already had some kind of grant; he wouldn't be hanging around here for too long; they would soon entice him away somewhere — young computer geeks were in great demand now. He surfed the Internet for hours on end. Played the Japanese intellectual game of Go. Like it or not, we were now relatives: he was, after all, my stepbrother, but there were no blood ties; he was laid-back, ironical, looked at me as if he was from outer space, and without any call signs.

[FROM PAGE 177]

I feel my destiny is bankrupt.

To be humiliated in the eyes of the woman you love.

I wonder if there is another country where there are so many humiliations per head of population?

Give me back my life! Give me back my Fatherland! If I was born here, then something on this Earth must belong to me.

But the audacious, the insolent and the unconscionable of this world won't give that something back to me! We are homeless in our own homes; we are tramps in our own country. And those dead people, who held lines of defense — they are there in history, but no longer in people's consciousness.

I had a nightmare. A giant, all-encompassing dragon was stirring, hissing, crawling closer. But my dead mother raced up to it and strangled it to death with her bare hands.

I think the trees are alive. They sway from side to side, they grab hold of their heads, and then they let their manes fall like those of horses. They are the only living things to whom I can talk. I look outside the window and talk to them.

And suddenly something flies past outside. At first I don't even comprehend what it is. Then, when I look down, I see the little doggie Alma lying on the asphalt. Later I learn that the professor's widow had tossed it out from the eleventh floor. And so I had to scrape up the dog and bury it. The widow now rarely ventures outside and has stopped exchanging greetings with me.

"Don't judge her. She's had a nervous breakdown," my wife says.

Bit by bit I am receiving replies to my CV: one from Moscow, one from Germany. Even one from Holland. But none from Ukraine. So, I'm not needed here. It's time to look truth in the face: I'm not needed here!

Perhaps I should go off to Germany? Computer programmers have a large entry quota there. But I can't speak any German. To France? I don't know any French either. Over there it's not like here: here pidgin is enough, interspersed with a few Russian swear words. But there you have to know the language.

"Scabby topknots*!" I exclaim suddenly.

My wife is shocked: "Do you understand, what you've just said?!"

"Yeah, I understand. Scabby topknots!" I repeat.

"Stop that!" she screams shrilly.

After this she refuses to talk to me. Every time I try to say something, she winces with indignation. It appears she understands when the professor's widow has a nervous breakdown. But I've had a nervous breakdown too; I wanted to throw my nation out the window. And to jump out after it.

"The day had no date. There was no month either."

I strolled down some street, I don't remember which one.

Someone bumped into me, I excused myself. Someone wanted me to buy something; someone invited me into the "tunnel of horrors" for some "blitz-quest." Someone shoved a yellow advertisement into my hand, with the words: "HE + SHE = 2 PEUGEOTS." For a long

---

* The Russian derogatory term for Ukrainians is *khokhol*, literally a "topknot," harking back to the haircuts of the Cossacks in ages past.

while I pondered what the word PEUGEOTS meant, and why there were two of them. Because if this was the make of a car, then what did "HE + SHE" have to do with it? In any case it should have equaled LOVE, and not some 2 PEUGEOTS. It eventuated that everything was quite simple: one had to visit a certain shopping mall, spend 200 hryvnias or more, fill in the attached form — and you could become the potential owner of two PEUGEOTS. One for yourself, and one for your loving partner.

I didn't head off to the shopping mall. I didn't need a PEUGEOT. I didn't have a loving partner. I struggled on and kept reading the signs. "Eden Café," "Because of Partners Bank." Whose partner am I now? I'm no one's partner.

I was tossed about on the bends.

One sign especially caught my attention: "Bureau for the Registration of Deaths." I thought: "I should step inside and register." But then I changed my mind. "How I can I go in? They'll think I'm alive."

[FROM PAGE 246]

Hurricane Jeanette breathed upon us too. Fallen trees everywhere and a thousand inhabited settlements without power. A billboard fell on a seventy-year-old woman.

"You should lie down and close your eyes, listen to some music," my wife said.

She's right. I imagine myself lying down and listening to music. That would be heaven.

But into that heaven burst the dissonant voices of a universal hell.

A terrorist act in Jerusalem. An explosion in Ecuador.

In Kenya three suicide bombers have driven into a hotel in a vehicle laden with explosives.

That's already a refrain.

In Moscow another victim of a terrorist act has died.

In the Carpathian Mountains there's been a landslide.

This is a counter-point.

The oil tanker *Prestige* has sunk off the shores of Spain and now thousands of tonnes of crude oil is being washed up on the shores.

This is the usual music score of our everyday life.

During an international competition in Japan a hot air balloon caught alight, the people sailed through the air in the burning basket, and jumped out while it was in mid-flight — and where is mankind meant to jump out from its earthen balloon?

Princess Diana's butler sayeth his bit. He is advertising a television show called "What the Butler Saw." * They promise details that will shake the world up.

Nothing will make the world flinch. Except perhaps for the butler's lies.

Raf Vallone has died, he was one of my wife's favorite actors....

---

* In actual fact, **What the Butler Saw** was a *British reality show* that ran in *2004*. It featured the Callaghan extended family. The nine relatives are competing to move from lower class to the best example of nobility. The family knows they are being judged, but do not realize that the judges are the seven servants helping them through their new life.

BIOGRAPHICAL NOTES ON THE AUTHORS

❋ Sofia Andrukhovych

Prose writer and translator **Sofia Andrukhovych** was born in Ivano-Frankivsk, Ukraine in 1982. The daughter of the famous Ukrainian postmodernist author Yuri Andrukhovych, she has authored four books of prose to date: *Milena's Summer* (2002), *Old People* (2003), *Wives of their Husbands* (2005), and *The Salmon* (2007). She received the Smoloskyp Literary Prize from Smoloskyp Publishers in 2001. She translated the novel by Polish author Manuela Gretkovska *The European Woman* and J.K. Rowling's *Harry Potter and the Goblet of Fire* (cotranslated with Viktor Morozov) into Ukrainian. She served as coeditor of the literary journal *Chetver* (*Thursday*) from 2003-2005. Her prose is characterized by a confessional candidness of expression, particularly in her open discussion of sex and sexuality as well as psychological self-analysis.

❋ Emma Andijewska

Surrealist poet, prose writer and artist **Emma Andijewska** was born in 1931 in Stalino, Ukraine, which returned to its original name Donetsk after the death of Stalin. She is associated with the New York Group of Ukrainian poets by her affiliation with the group when she lived in the US with her family (1957-1959) and by the nature of her literary experimentation. Her family was forced to move to Vyshhorod in 1937 and then to Kyiv in 1939, where during the war her father was summarily executed by the Soviets. In 1943 her family moved to Germany where she remained except for her two years in the US and one-month yearly visits to acquire US citizenship. She moved back to Germany in 1959 when she married well-known Ukrainian literary critic Ivan Koshelivets.

She grew up in a Russian speaking environment, but as a child recognized her Ukrainian identity and acquired the Ukrainian language which she first heard in Vyshhorod at the age of six. Since then, she decided to write exclusively in Ukrainian, which she perceived as a language of the oppressed. As a writer she saw her task to "create the Ukrainian state in the word."

Andijewska has authored 27 books of poetry including *Poetry* (1951), *Birth of an Idol* (1958), *The Fish and Size* (1961), *Corners behind the Wall* (1963), *Elements* (1964), *The Bazaar* (1967), *Songs without a Text* (1968), *A Lesson about the Earth* (1975), *The Coffee House* (1983), *The Temptations of St. Anthony* (1985), *Vigils* (1987), *Architectural Ensembles* (1989), *Signs of the Tarot* (1995), *The Land between Rivers* (1998), *Dream segments* (1998), *Villas on the Seashore* (2000), *Attractions with Orbits and Without* (2000), *Waves* (2002), *The Knight's Move* (2004), *The View from a Cliff* (2006), *Hemispheres and Cones* (2006), *Pink Caldrons* (2007), *Fulgurites* (2008), *Idylls* (2009), *Mirages* (2009), *Mutants* (2010), and *Broken Koans* (2011).

She is also author of several books of short stories including *Journey* (1955), *Tigers* (1962), *Djalapita* (1962), *Fairy Tales* (2000), and *The Problem of the Head* (2000). Her novels include *Herostrats* (1971), *A Novel about a Good Person* (1973), and *A Novel about Human Destiny* (1982). In the last several decades she has become extremely well known in the art world as a painter of surrealistic, childlike, playful, monster-like figures. Her concept of "circular time" (*kruhlyi chas*) infuses her creative work, in which she tries to convey other modes of co-existing time, space, being, and consciousness.

❀ Nina Bichuya

Prolific prose writer **Nina Bichuya** was born in 1937 in Kyiv and is considered a major precursor of Ukrainian women's urban prose that emerged in the 1980s and 1990s. In fact, preeminent Ukrainian writer

Valeriy Shevchuk has called her the "queen of Ukrainian women's prose." She received her degree in journalism from the University of Lviv and since then has worked as a journalist and for a lengthy period of time as the literary director of the Lviv Youth Theater. She also has worked for a long time as editor for the *Prosvita* newspaper in Lviv. She is the author of numerous works of short fiction, novellas and novels. Her prose is rich and supple. Her style is characterized by psychological depth, intellectual tension, a meditative quality, and freedom of narrative.

Her extensive publications include the collection of novellas *The Drohobych Astrologer* (1970), a novella and short story *A Usual School Week* (1973), *Chistotel: Novellas and Short Stories* (1974; in Russian), *Tales* (1978), the novella *May in a Boat* (1981); *The Flood: Novellas* (1981; published jointly with Valery Shevchuk), *Genealogy: A Novella and Short Stories* (1984), *Benefice* (1986,1990), *"Ten Words of a Poet": Novellas* (1987), the novel *Rehearsal* (1985), and *Lands of Chamomile: Novellas* (2003). Her young adult and children's books include *Vacation in Svitlohorsk* (1967), *The Sword of Slavko Berkut* (1986, 2010), An *Ordinary School Week* (1973), *Apple Trees and a Seed* (1984), and *The Great King's Hunt* (2011).

She is the laureate of the Bohdan Lepky literary award in 2005. In 2007 she was a recipient of the Order of the Smile literary award given by children. She also translated works by Polish writers Stanislav Lem, Jerzy Grotowski and Olga Tokarczuk.

❈ Liuko Dashvar

Ukrainian screenwriter, journalist and novelist **Liuko Dashvar** (her real name is Iryna Chernova) was born in 1954 in Kherson and is considered one of the most popular writers by the number of books sold in Ukraine. The total print run of her books is more than 300,000 copies. She is the author of four novels and a trilogy: *A Village is not People* (2007), *Milk with Blood* (2008), *Paradise. Downtown* (2009), *To Have Everything* (2010); the trilogy *There are Those Who are Beaten: Makar* (2011), *Maks* (2012) and *Hotsyk* (2012), and *To the Scent of Meat* (2013). Her first novel *A Village is Not People* won the laureate prize in the national Coronation of the Word competition in 2007, *Milk with Blood* the BBC Book of the Year Prize in Ukraine in 2008, and *Paradise. Downtown* won Ukrainian Editor's Choice award in 2009. In 2012 she received the Golden Writer of Ukraine Award given to novel writers whose books exceed a 100,000 print run.

In her previous hypostasis before she started writing in Ukrainian in 2006, Ms. Dashvar was known as Irina Chernova. She was born to a Russian speaking family in the Odessa region. She began taking Ukrainian as a second language in the fourth grade. Her higher education consisted of a degree as a mechanical engineer from the Odessa Institute of Light Industry and a Master's degree from the Academy of Government Administration. She worked as a provincial journalist from 1986 and founded two local newspapers in Kherson. After one of her newspaper's offices had been robbed and ransacked at the end of the year 2000, she moved with her family to a small one-room apartment in the Troyeshchyna neighborhood of Kyiv. She worked for a brief time in 2001 as editor of the Village Party of Ukraine's newspaper *The Village Star*, then for the journal *Stories from Life* and several other women's glossy magazines. At that time she took classes in filmscript writing with Richard Krevolin, who taught for a year in Kyiv, and began to write scripts for Ukrainian film and television. She wrote the scripts *The Moon — Odessa* and *Time — that's Everything*, which were produced by Anatoly Mateshko.

❀ Larysa Denysenko

Of Lithuanian and Greek extraction, the lawyer, novelist, literary and art critic, telejournalist and model **Larysa Denysenko** was born in Kyiv in 1973. Originally Russian speaking, she mastered the Ukrainian language at the age of 23 when she began to work in the Ukrainian Ministry of Justice. She holds a degree in law from the Taras Shevchenko Kyiv National University and has studied at The Central European University in Prague and in the Ministry of Justice in The Netherlands. She currently practices law and is also the host of the culturological television program *Document+* on the *Studio 1+1* channel and well as on the *1+1* International channel.

Her novels include *Games from Flesh and Blood* (2004), *The Coffee Taste of Cinnamon* (2005), *A Corporation of Idiots* (2006), *Dances in Masks* (2006), *24:33:42* (2007), *Mistaken Perceptions or Life according to the Timetable of Murderers* (2007), *The Sarabande of Sara's Band* (2008) and *An Echo* (2012). She also has published three children's books and five other collections on cultural and literary topics. Her first novel won the 2002 Coronation of the Word Grand Prize and *Sarabande* won the 2009 Book of the Year award. Her website is located at: *http://larysa. com.ua/*. *Sarabande* has been published by Glagoslav Publications in the English translation of Michael M. Naydan and Svitlana Bednazh.

❀ Irena Karpa

Punk band singer, telejournalist and prose writer **Irena Karpa** was born in Cherkasy in central Ukraine in 1980 and lived with her family in Ivano-Frankivsk. The family later moved to Yaremche in the Carpathian Mountains where Karpa studied painting in art school. In 1998 she became a student of French philology at Kyiv National Linguistic University. She received her Master's Degree in 2003 in foreign languages, specializing in French, English and foreign literature. In 1999 she became the lead vocalist for the punk rock band "Faktychno Sami" ("In Fact Ourselves"), which in 2007 was renamed "Quarpa." From 2005-2007 she served as a host on the *ICTV* and *Inter* Ukrainian television channels, and from 2007 as a host on *MTV Ukraine*. She has also done photo shoots for *Playboy*, *Penthouse*, and *FHM* magazines.

Her books of prose include *The Descent of a Burned Man* (2000), *50 Minutes of Grass* (2004), *Freud Would Have Cried* (2004), *Pearl Porno (The Supermarket of Loneliness)* (2005), *Bitches Get Everything* (2007), *Glood and Evil (Doblo i zlo*, 2008), *Candies, Fruits and Sausages* (2010), *Pizza Himalaya* (2011), and *From Dew, Water and a Puddle* (2012). In her prose Karpa irritates many because of her provocative stances, but she always quite adeptly reveals hidden depravity in individuals and

426

society, masked by moralizing and an outward show of benevolence. Her prose is sprinkled with over the top breaking of taboos including scenes of sex, masturbation, group sex, and drug use. Her website is located at: irenakarpa.com.

❀ Eugenia Kononenko

Prose writer, translator, poet, and essayist **Eugenia Kononenko** was born in 1959 in Kyiv. She has translated mostly from the French and English and won the Zerov Prize for her book of translations *A Small Anthology of the French Sonnet* in 1992. She completed her degree in the sciences in the mechanics-mathematics department of Taras Shevchenko Kyiv National University in 1981 and shifted her interests to philology, completing a course in French at the Kyiv Linguistics University in 1994. She released a collection of poetry *Waltz of the First Snow* in 1997, a book of short stories *A Colossal Plot* (1998), the novel *Imitation* (2001), the novel *BETRAYAL made in Ukraine* (2002), the children's book *Infantasy: To the Motifs of Claude Rua* (2001), a collection of autobiographical prose works *Without a Man* (2005), the collection *Novellas for Unkissed Girls* (2006), a collection of short stories *Whores Get Married Too* (2006), a novel about the Lviv sculptor Pinzel *The Sacrifice of a Forgotten Master* (2007), a collection of novellas *The Bookstore SHOCK* (2009), a novella *A Russian Plot* (2012); two books of essays, *Heroes and Heroines* (2010) and *In Line for Holy Water* (2013); and several more children's books including *Nelya Who Walks on the Ceiling* (2008), *Nelya Who Comes Down from the Ceiling* (2009), *Grandmothers Were Once Girls Too* (2010), and *A Russian Story* (2012). From her very beginnings as a prose writer she has depicted, in an often brutally realistic and candid way, the difficult lot of Ukrainian women, often in crisis situations, in both Soviet and post-Soviet times. Topics range from marriage, love, men, feminism, and others. Her works have been translated into English, French, German, Russian, Finnish, Czech, Belarusian, and Croatian. An English translation by Patrick John Corness of Kononenko's novel *A Russian Story* was published by Glagoslav Publications in 2013.

❀ Lina Kostenko

Born in 1930 in Rzhyshchiv of the Kyiv region, **Lina Kostenko** is widely recognized as the leading Ukrainian woman writer of her generation. Originally a representative of the "writers of the sixties" (*shestydesiatnyky*), Kostenko has been a pathbreaker in her rejection of the literary tenets of Socialist Realism during the period of the post-Stalinist Thaw. She was restricted from publishing in the USSR from 1965 until 1977. She is the author of the following books of poetry, all of which met with great popular success: *Earthly Rays* (1957), *Sails* (1958), *Wanderings of the Heart* (1961), *At the Shores of the Eternal River* (1977), *Uniqueness* (1980), *The Garden of Unmelting Sculptures* (1987), *Selected Works* (1989). She is one of several featured classic Ukrainian poets in the volume *Poetry* (1998), which was published in Kyiv. She also has published a popular children's book called *The Lilac King* (1987), which was translated into English by Jars Balan (1990). She released the long poem *Berestechko: An Historical Novel* in 1999 (second edition in 2010). Her most successful poems comprise intimate lyrics on nature, love, and art. She also has excelled in the genres of the long poem and the novel in verse. She received the Shevchenko Prize (1987) for her historical novel in verse *Marusia Churai* (1979), the Antonovych Prize in Literature in 1990 for her collection *The Garden of Unmelting Sculptures* (1987), the Olena Teliha Prize in 2000 for her poetry, and the Order of Prince Yaroslav Mudry in the Fifth Degree in 2000 for her lifetime achievements. She refused the honor of being named a Hero of Ukraine by the Ukrainian government to remain aloof from politics. In 2012 she was named a Golden Writer of Ukraine. She published her first novel in prose in 2010 under the title *Notes of a Madaloneman*. She most recently published a selected works edition including new poem in 2011 under the title *The River of Heraclitus*, as well as a volume of new and previously unpublished poems in 2011 entitled *Madonna of the Crossroads*. Two books of her poetry are available in the English translations of Michael Naydan: *Selected Poetry of Lina Kostenko: Wanderings of the Heart* (Garland Publishers, 1990) and *Landscapes of Memory* (Litopys Publishers, 2001).

❋ Sofia Maidanska

Exiled with her repressed family of Ukrainian intellectuals, **Sofia Maidanska** was born in 1948 in the city of Azanka of the Sverdlovsk region of Russia. She is the author of seven books of poetry, three novellas, four books for children, four plays, several novellas and short stories, numerous articles on art, literature and culture, filmscripts, librettos, numerous translations, and the novels *Earthquake* (1994), *Children of Niobe* (1998) and *I'm Relying on You* (2007). She received her high school and college education in Chernivtsi, Ukraine and completed the Lviv Conservatory in 1973, specializing in the violin, which she taught in the Kamianets-Podilsk Pedagogical Institute and later in the Kyiv Institute of Culture. Her first book of poetry, *My Good World*, appeared in 1977. Her other books of poetry include *The Palms of the Continents* (1979), *Praise to the Earth* (1981), *The Scales* (1986), *A Ripe Age of Hopes* (1988), *Declaration of Love* (1990), *Enter this Cathedral* (1993), and *The Sun of Sorrow has Set for Me* (2007). Her children's books include *A Little Mouse Rides the Car* (1989), *Earth, Rejoice* (1990), *The Adventures of Halka Dymarivna* (1991), *Christ is Risen* (1993); and the plays *Magical Sabre*, *Chalynka*, *Bloody Treasure*, and *Betrayal*.

In 2004 she received the Honored Artistic Worker Award of Ukraine, an honorary state title awarded by the President of Ukraine. She is the laureate of the Blahovist (1997) and Oles Honchar (1998) literary awards.

❋ Tanya Malyarchuk

Prose writer and journalist **Tanya Malyarchuk** was born in 1983 in the western Ukrainian city of Ivano-Frankivsk at the foothills of the Carpathian Mountains. She received her degree in philology at the Vasyl Stefanyk National Precarpathian University, which is located in Ivano-Frankivsk. After completing her education, she moved to the capital of Kyiv where she worked as a writer-journalist mostly in the television industry. She is currently residing in Vienna, Austria where she has published a book of her prose in German translation.

She published her first novel in 2004, *Adolpho's Endspiel, or a Rose for Liza*, as well as five more collections of shorter prose works since then: *From Above Looking Down. A Book of Fears* (2006), *How I Became a Saint* (2006), *To Speak* (2007), *Word Bestiary* (2009), and *A Divine Comedy* (2009). Her latest novel *Biography of an Accidental Miracle* (2012) was short-listed for a Ukrainian BBC Book of the Year award. Her prose style can be characterized as minimalistic but to the point in a Chekhovian manner. She also employs motifs of magical realism and surrealism in her works. Her stories and essays have been translated into the Polish, Romanian, German, English, Russian, and Belarusian languages.

❈ Maria Matios

Maria Matios was born in the village of Roztoky in the Bukovyna region of Ukraine in 1959 and is one of the major prose writers writing in Ukraine today. She is from the post-independence post-colonial generation of exciting new Ukrainian women writers who, instead of shunning their rural roots in postmodernistic urbanized culture, like a Toni Morrison or Alice Walker in American culture, embraces those roots to give a voice to the past and to discover higher truths about themselves, their culture, and in the process, the human condition in general. Matios received her degree in philology at the University of Chernivtsi, and the first major publication of her prose was in the journal *Kyiv* in 1992. She has authored fifteen volumes of prose and six books of poetry to date, focusing on prose the past decade of her career.

Her prose works include: *A Nation* (2001), *Life is Short* (2001), *A Dime Store Novel* (2003), *A Smorgasbord from Maria Matios* (2003), *Sweet Darusya* (2004), *Diary of a Fallen Woman* (2005), *Mr. and Mrs. U in Country UA* (2006), *A Nation: Revelations* (2006), *Almost Never Otherwise* (2007), *The Russky Girl. Momma Maritsa, the Wife of Christopher Columbus* (2008), *Culinary Tricks* (2009), *Four Seasons of Life* (2009), *Torn Pages from My Autobiography* (2010), *Armageddon Already Happened* (2011), and *The Shoes of the Mother of God* (2013).

Her books of poetry include: *From Grass and Leaves* (1982), *The Fire of Turpentine* (1986), *The Garden of Impatience* (1994), *Ten Thresher Concaves of Ice Water* (1995), *A Woman's Lasso Dance* (2001), and *A Woman's Lasso Dance in the Garden of Impatience* (2007). She received the 2004 Book of the Year Award and the national Taras Shevchenko Prize in 2005 for her novel *Sweet Darusya*, and the grand Prize in the Coronation of the Word Competition for her novel *Almost Never Otherwise* (2007), which completes a trilogy of works based on her family chronicles and her life growing up in her Bukovyna Hutsul homeland in the Carpathians. And her *The Russky Lady* earned the book of the year award in 2008. Her works are written in a savory writing style that captures the colorful indigenous dialectal elements of the people from her native Bukovyna highlands. Her books have been translated into Serbian, Romanian, Croatian, Russian, Belarusian, Polish, Azeri, Japanese, Chinese, and Hebrew. She currently resides in the capital city of Kyiv in Ukraine where she has become a member of the current Ukrainian parliament. *Almost Never Otherwise* has been published by Glagoslav Publishers in Yuri Tkacz's English translation. Mr. Tkacz has also published translations of Matios's novels *The Apocalypse Already Happened* and *The Russky Girl* under the Bayda Books imprint. Michael Naydan and Olha Tytarenko are in the process of completing a translation of the novel *Sweet Darusya* for publication. Ms. Matios became a deputy of the Ukrainian parliament in Vitaly Klitschko's Udar Party and has been extremely active in the demonstrations at the Euromaidan for a just and democratic government.

❧ Dzvinka Matiyash

Poet, translator and prose writer **Dzvinka Matiyash** was born in Kyiv in 1978. Her sister Bohdanna Matiyash is a poet, literary critic and editor, and her older sister Sofia is a nun in the Lviv Monastery. In 1995-2002 she attended the National University of Kyiv-Mohyla Academy. She did her postgraduate studies at the European Collegium of Polish and Ukrainian Universities in Lublin, Poland in 2003-2006. She has published four books of prose to date: *A Requiem for November* (2005),

A Novel about My Homeland (2006), the children's book *The Fairytales of Pyatynka* (2010), and *Stories About Roses, Rain and Salt* (2012). Her books of translations include those of Belarusian poet Andrei Khadanovych and Polish poet Jan Tvardovsky. Her prose is clear, accessible, and often highly philosophical. Her stories focus on fundamental human values, God's presence in the world, beauty and goodness.

❈ Svitlana Povalyaeva

Telejournalist, poet, translator, and prose writer **Svitlana Povalyaeva** was born in 1974 in Kyiv. Prior to entering university she specialized in biology, chemistry and geography and additionally completed music school, where her primary instruments were the guitar and piano. She completed a course in English in 1993 and worked as a DJ for nighttime radio programs. She received her degree in journalism in 1996 from Taras Shevchenko National University in Kyiv, specializing in telejournalism. She has worked in Ukrainian television for the *New Channel*, for the print journal *Pik*, and for the online newspaper *Forum*.

She is the author of nine novels: *Exhumation of the City* (2003), *Instead of Blood* (2003), *Origami-Blues* (2005), *The Simurgh* (2006),), *Camouflage in Lipstick* (2006), children's book *Wruum-Magician* (2007), *Larvae. The Sky. The Kitchen of the Dead* (2007), *BARDO Online* (2009), and was included in the anthology *The Decameron. Ten Ukrainian Prose Writers of the Last Ten Years* (2010). *The Simurgh* has been made into a film. She often employs magical realism in her prose, which is stylistically full and rich.

❈ Svitlana Pyrkalo

London-based Ukrainian writer journalist and translator **Svitlana Pyrkalo** was born in 1976 in Poltava. She received her degree in philology from Taras Shevchenko Kyiv National University and worked at first as a teacher of Ukrainian language and literature in 1998. In 2000 she became editor-in-chief of the TV talk show *Without*

Taboo at the Ukrainian *1+1* TV channel, dedicated to unusual human stories, with elements of dramatization. She worked as a journalist for the women's magazine *Eva* and eventually for BBC Ukrainian service and presented the Friday evening program in Ukrainian from London. She wrote a weekly column for the Ukrainian newspaper *Gazeta po-ukrainsky* in 2006-2010 and in 2007-2009 penned a weekly column in the Ukrainian magazine *Glavred*.

She compiled and published the first dictionary of Ukrainian slang in 1998. Her books include: *Green Margarita* (2000, 2003); a book about the Channel 1+1 television program *Without Taboo about "Without Taboo"* (2002; coauthored with Mykola Veresen and Tetyana Vorozhko); the novel *Don't Think about Red* (2005, 2006); compiled a collection of essays on food, travel and Ukrainian identity *The Egoist's Kitchen* (2007); and most recently published the novella *Life. To Kiss*, which appeared in the anthology *The Decameron. Ten Ukrainian Prose Writers of the Last Ten Years* (2010). Her literary prose largely deals with the new freedoms for emancipated twenty-something Ukrainian women and the breaking of taboos, particularly sexual and linguistic ones. In 2007 she translated the novel *Two Caravans* by Marina Lewycka into Ukrainian.

She currently works as a press officer for the European Bank for Reconstruction and Development (EBRD) in London. She is also the originator of the BBC Ukrainian annual book prize. Her website is located at: *http://pyrkalo.com.*

❋ Iren Rozdobudko

Poet, translator, journalist, and novelist **Iren Rozdobudko** was born in 1962 in Donetsk in the Eastern mostly Russian-speaking part of Ukraine. She completed her education as a journalist at Taras Shevchenko Kyiv National University. She worked as a journalist in Donetsk and moved to Kyiv in 1988 where she worked at the newspaper *Rodoslav*, as a copy editor of the scholarly and literary journal *Suchasnist*, as a reviewer for channels 1 and 3 of the National Ukrainian Radio Company, as a reviewer for the newspaper *The Ukrainian News*, as Deputy Editor of the glossy magazine *Natalie*, as the editor-in-chief of the journal *Caravan of History: Ukraine*, and as a journalist for the magazine The Academy. She began writing fiction in her late thirties.

Her first book, a detective novel, *A Trap for the Firebird* (2000), was initially published under the title *The Dead* and republished under its original title in 2007. It received second place in the Coronation of the Word competition and was an immediate popular success. This launched her highly productive career as a fiction writer. That was followed by a flurry of publishing activity over the next twelve years, including the novels *He: The Morning Cleaning Man* (2005), *The Button* (2005), *Twelve, or the Upbringing of a Woman in Conditions Not Suitable for Life* (2006), *Withered Flowers Get Tossed Out* (2006), *The Last Diamond of Milady* (2006), *Pascal's Amulet* (2007, 2009), *The Lives of Prominent Children* (2007), *When Dolls Come to Life* (2007), *Olenium* (2007), *Escort to Death* (2007), *Reformulation* (2007), *Two Minutes of Truth* (2008), *Everything I Wanted Today* (2008), *Playing with Beads* (2009), *Crossing the Darkness* (2010), *I Know That You Know that I Know* (2011), *If* (2012), *Twelve...* (2012), *Do that Tenderly* (2012), and *LSD: The Lyceum of Dutiful Spouses* (2013). The book *Travels without Sense and Morals* (2011) is a hybrid work in the style of New Journalism. Rozdobudko is master of the detective novel and psychological thriller. She is one of the most popular writers in Ukraine today and writes in a lively, engaging style that makes her accessible to a wide reading audience. She has also published two books of poetry in Russian, and several of her novels have been translated into Russian. The novel *The Lost Button* has appeared in Michael Naydan's and Olha Tytarenko's English translation with Glagoslav Publishers in 2012. She received the Golden Writer of Ukraine award in 2012 for writers who have sold more than 100,000 copies of their works.

❋ Natalka Sniadanko

Journalist, translator and prose writer **Natalka Sniadanko** was born in the city of Lviv in 1973. She earned her degree in philology at Ivan Franko Lviv National University and also studied at the University of

Freiburg. She has translated numerous authors from German, Polish and Russian into Ukrainian including Gunter Grass, Stefan Zweig, Czeslaw Milosz, Zbigniew Herbert, and Andrei Kurkov. Her prose publications include: *A Collection of Passions, or the Adventures of a Young Ukrainian Woman* (2001, 2004, 2006), *The Seasonal Sale of Blondes* (2005), *Sterility Syndrome* (2006), *Thyme in Milk* (2007), *The Land of Broken Toys and Other Journeys* (2008), *A Bug's Rope Swing* (2009), *A Herbarium of Lovers* (2011), and *Frau Muller isn't Prepared to Pay More* (2013). Her works have been published in German, Russian and Polish translation. In 2011 she received the Jozef Konrad Korzeniowski literary award.

❀ Liudmyla Taran

Liudmyla Taran was born 1954 in the town of Hrebinka in the Kyiv region. She is a poet, literary critic and essayist who currently resides in Kyiv, where she works as a journalist, essayist and editor. She completed her degree in philology and Ukrainian studies at Kyiv State University and has published extensively in the Ukrainian periodical press. Besides her work as a journalist, she has worked as a teacher, as a museum curator at the Maksym Rylsky Museum in Kyiv, and as press secretary of the Kyiv-Mohyla Academy University. She currently works as an editor of the prominent Kyiv journal *Ukrainian Culture.*

Her poetry collections include *Deep Leaves* (1982), *Watermarks*, (1985), *Rafters* (1990), *Defense of the Soul* (1994), and *The Book of Embodiments* (2004). She has also released several limited edition chapbooks of poems including *The Orchestra Pit, Nostalgia*, and *A Collection of Lovers*--all published in 1995. She also has a chapbook of poems entitled *India Ink* (1998) with translations by Virlana Tkacz, Wanda Phipps, and Michael Naydan. She has published a book of literary critical articles *The Energy of Searching: Literary Critical Articles* (1988), issued a book of interviews with leading native and émigré Ukrainian cultural figures entitled *A Horoscope: For Yesterday and Tomorrow* (1995), and published books of essays *Woman and Man: Overcoming Stereotypes* (2002), *A Woman as Text: Emma Andijewska,*

Solomiya Pavlychko, Oksana Zabuzhko. Fragments of Creative Works and Contexts (2002), *The Body or Individual?* (2007), and *Woman's Role* (2007). Her books of creative prose include: a collection of short stories *The Tender Skeleton in the Closet* (2006), *Love Journeys* (2007), *"Anna-Maria" and Other Short Stories* (2007), the novel *The Unicorn's Mirror* (2009), and *"Artemis with a Stag" and Other Short Stories* (2010).

❀ Oksana Zabuzhko

Oksana Zabuzhko was born in 1960 in Western Ukraine. She is a poet, prose writer, translator, and philosophy scholar, who has become one of the most prominent literary personages in Ukraine. Born in the Western Ukrainian city of Lutsk, Zabuzhko's family later moved to the capital of Kyiv. She completed her Candidate of Arts and Sciences degree (the Ukrainian equivalent of the Ph.D.) in 1987, writing on the topic of "The Aesthetic Essence of Lyricism."

Her books of poetry include *May Hoarfrost* (1985), *The Conductor of the Last Candle* (1990), *Hitchhiking* (1994), *Kingdom of Fallen Statues* (1996), *The New Law of Archimedes: Selected Poems 1980-1998* (2000), and *A Second Try: Collected Poems* (2005). She is, perhaps, best known in Ukraine for her novel *Field Work in Ukrainian Sex* (1996) that became extremely popular and opened up discourse on previously taboo subjects in Ukrainian culture, particularly sex and feminism. Her other prose works include: *The Extraterrestrial Woman* (1992) *The Tale of a Guelder Rose Flute* (2000), *Selected Prose* (2004), a collection of selected novellas *Oh Sister, My Sister* (2006), selected novellas in *The Book of Genesis: Chapter Four* (2008), and most recently, her novel *The Museum of Abandoned Secrets* (2009). Her scholarship in the cultural, philosophical and political vein includes: *Two Cultures* (Kyiv, 1990), *The Philosophy of the Ukrainian Idea in the European Context: The Franko Period* (1992), *Shevchenko's Myth of Ukraine: An Attempt at Philosophical Analysis* (Kyiv, 1997), *News Reports from the Year 2000* (2001), *Let My People Go: Fifteen Texts on the Ukrainian Revolution* (2005), *The Chronicles of Fortinbras. Selected Essays*, 3rd ed. (2006), and *Notre Dame d'Ukraine: Ukrainka in the Clash of Mythologies* (2007). She also published her correspondence with noted Ukrainian literary critic and linguist Yuri Shevelov in 2011 as a separate volume. Her novel *Field Work in Ukrainian Sex* has been published by Amazon Crossing in Halyna Hryn's translation, and her *Museum of Abandoned Secrets* has appeared with Amazon Crossing in Nina Shevchuk Murray's translation. Zabuzhko is a Senior Research Associate at the Institute of Philosophy of the Ukrainian Academy of Arts and Sciences. In 2009 Ukrainian President Yushchenko awarded Zabuzhko the Order of Princess Olga award and in 2012 she received the Golden Writer of Ukraine award. And she received the prestigious Angelus Award in 2013 for the best work of Central European prose for her novel *Museum of Abandoned Secrets*. The author's website can be found here: *http://zabuzhko.com/en/index.html.*

A NOTE
ON THE TRANSLATORS

Mark Andryczyk received his Ph.D. from the U. of Toronto and is currently administrator of the Ukrainian Program at the Harriman Institute at Columbia University as well as lecture in Ukrainian literature. He has published translations of several contemporary Ukrainian authors into English and is currently working on a translation of a book of essays by prominent Ukrainian writer Yuri Andrukhovych. His book *The Intellectual as Hero in 1990s Ukrainian Fiction* was published by the University of Toronto Press in 2012.

·

Originally from the Carpathian region of Ukraine, **Svitlana Bednazh** earned an MA in International Relations from the University of Kent at Canterbury, UK. She has co-translated Larysa Denysenko's *The Sarabande of Sara's Band* that has been published by Glagoslav Publications in early 2013. She is Director of S Barnes Media in Cambridge, England and publisher of *Ukraine Business Insight* magazine. She has worked as a professional interpreter and translator for nearly two decades.

·

Nataliya Bilyuk graduated from the Kyiv Institute for Translators and Interpreters with a Bachelor's Degree in translation (English and German); has a Master's Degree from Taras Shevchenko National University of Kyiv; and studied Portuguese and English at Goethe University in Frankfurt-am-Main. She has translated literary works; economics, ecological, and scientific texts; and journalistic articles into

438

Ukrainian, English and German. She teaches English and German at the Language School in Kyiv.

●

Vitaly Chernetsky is an Associate Professor at the University of Kansas and a well-known translator from Ukrainian and Russian. Among a number of other publications, he has published a translation of Yuri Andrukhovych's novel *The Moscoviad* for Spuyten Duyvil Publishers in 2008 and authored the book, *Mapping Postcommunist Cultures: Russia and Ukraine in the Context of Globalization*, with McGill-Queen's University Press in 2007.

●

Jennifer Croft is a Ph.D. student in Comparative Literature at Northwestern University. She is currently residing in Argentina on a grant where she is studying and translating contemporary Argentine literature and writing her dissertation, focusing on Polish-Argentine writing Witold Gobrowicz and Argentine writer Jorge Luis Borges. Her translations of essays on Nietzsche are forthcoming with Fordham University Press.

●

Natalia Ferens is a translator of literary texts, trade press, and other materials from Ukrainian and Russian into English and vice versa. She is an Assistant Lecturer and Postgraduate Student in the Department of Theory and Practice of Translation from English at Taras Shevchenko National University of Kyiv. She has a Master's degree in philology and translation from Taras Shevchenko National University of Kyiv as well as a Specialist degree in philology and translation from the Faculty of Linguistics at KPI National University in Kyiv.

●

Halyna Hryn received her Ph.D. from the University of Toronto and has published book-length translations of Ukrainian writer Volodymyr

Dibrova, *Peltse and Pentameron* (Northwestern University Press, 1996) and Oksana Zabuzhko, *Fieldwork in Ukrainian Sex* (Amazon Crossings, 2011). She is currently working as an Editor of the scholarly journal Harvard Ukrainian Studies at the Harvard Ukrainian Research Institute.

●

Originally from Lviv, Ukraine, **Roman Ivashkiv** received his Bachelor's Degree from Ivan Franko Lviv National University and his MA degree from The Pennsylvania State University. He is currently completing his Ph.D. at the University of Alberta. His primary research interests are translation studies and post-modernism in the Ukrainian and Russian contexts.

●

Askold Melnyczuk is a prominent novelist, author, editor, educator, and translator. He has published three novels, the latest of which is entitled *The House of Widows*, which was an Editor's Choice selection of the American Library Association's *Booklist*. He is the founding editor of AGNI literary magazine at Boston University and teaches creative writing at the University of Massachusetts at Boston.

●

Michael M. Naydan is Woskob Family Professor of Ukrainian Studies at The Pennsylvania State University. He is a prominent translator from Ukrainian and Russian with more than twenty five books translated or edited by him. He is currently completing a translation of Maria Matios's novel *Sweet Darusya* with co-translator Olha Tytarenko.

●

Uliana Pasicznyk Uliana Pasicznyk works as an editor at the University of Toronto. She has published translations of works by Volodymyr Dibrova, Emma Andijewska, and Valerii Shevchuk in the online journal *Ukrainian Literature*.

Originally from Chernivtsi, Ukraine, **Alla Perminova** is a translation studies specialist at Taras Shevchenko National University in Kyiv, Ukraine and a Fulbright scholar at The Pennsylvania State University for 2012-2013. She focuses on poetry translation both from theoretical perspectives and in practice. She is currently working on a book of translations of 20th-century and contemporary American poets into Ukrainian.

Originally born and educated in Ukraine, **Svitlana Pyrkalo** currently works as a press officer for the European Bank for Reconstruction and Development (EBRD) in London. She is a prominent writer, translator, and journalist, whose works have been included in this anthology. See the biographical section on the authors in this volume for more information about her.

Originally from Lviv, Ukraine, **Olha Tytarenko** received her MA from The Pennsylvania State University and is currently completing her Ph.D. in Slavic literature at the University of Toronto, writing her dissertation on the Antichrist in the Russian literary imagination. She has co-translated Iren Rozdobudko's *The Lost Button* that was published by Glagoslav Publications in 2012, and is currently completing a translation of Maria Matios's novel *Sweet Darusya* with Michael Naydan.

Born in Melbourne, Australia in 1954 and educated as an engineer, **Yuri Tkacz** is a prolific translator, who has translated a number of 20th century Ukrainian prose writers, including Anatolii Dimarov, Ostap Vyshnia, Vasyl Shevchuk, Maria Matios, Oles Honchar, and the anthology *Before the Storm: Soviet Ukrainian Fiction of the 1920s* (Ardis Publishers, 1986). His translation of Matios' *Hardly Ever Otherwise* was published by Glagoslav Publications in 2012.

Currently residing in her native Lviv, Ukraine, **Liliya Valihun** received her MA degree from The Pennsylvania State University. Her main interests include translation studies and assisting families with adoptions of Ukrainian orphans.

Olesia Wallo, originally from Lviv, Ukraine, has an MA degree from The Pennsylvania State University and completed her Ph.D. at the University of Illinois in Slavic literature. She has published translations in English and Ukrainian. Her dissertation focuses on contemporary Ukrainian and Russian women writers.

Dear Reader,

thank you for purchasing this book.

We at Glagoslav Publications are glad to welcome you, and hope that you find our books to be a source of knowledge and inspiration.

We want to show the beauty and depth of the Slavic region to everyone looking to expand their horizon and learn something new about different cultures, different people, and we believe that with this book we have managed to do just that.

Now that you've got to know us, we want to get to know you. We value communication with our readers and want to hear from you! We offer several options:

- Join our Book Club on Goodreads, Library Thing and Shelfari, and receive special offers and information about our giveaways;

- Share your opinion about our books on Amazon, Barnes & Noble, Waterstones and other bookstores;

- Join us on Facebook and Twitter for updates on our publications and news about our authors;

- Visit our site www.glagoslav.com to check out our Catalogue and subscribe to our Newsletter.

Glagoslav Publications is getting ready to release a new collection and planning some interesting surprises — stay with us to find out!

Glagoslav Publications
Office 36, 88-90 Hatton Garden
EC1N 8PN London, UK
Tel: + 44 (0) 20 32 86 99 82
Email: contact@glagoslav.com
www.glagoslav.com

Glagoslav Publications Catalogue

- *The Time of Women* by Elena Chizhova
- *Sin* by Zakhar Prilepin
- *Hardly Ever Otherwise* by Maria Matios
- *The Lost Button* by Irene Rozdobudko
- *Khatyn* by Ales Adamovich
- *Christened with Crosses* by Eduard Kochergin
- *The Vital Needs of the Dead* by Igor Sakhnovsky
- *METRO 2033* (Dutch Edition) by Dmitry Glukhovsky
- *METRO 2034* (Dutch Edition) by Dmitry Glukhovsky
- *A Poet and Bin Laden* by Hamid Ismailov
- *Asystole* by Oleg Pavlov
- *Kobzar* by Taras Shevchenko
- *White Shanghai* by Elvira Baryakina
- *The Stone Bridge* by Alexander Terekhov
- *King Stakh's Wild Hunt* by Uladzimir Karatkevich
- *Depeche Mode* by Serhii Zhadan
- *Saraband Sarah's Band* by Larysa Denysenko
- *Watching The Russians* (Dutch Edition) by Maria Konyukova
- *The Hawks of Peace* by Dmitry Rogozin
- *The Grand Slam and Other Stories* (Dutch Edition) by Leonid Andreev

More coming soon…